Her life is in danger.
And so is his heart.

DON'T MISS THE NEXT MAIDEN LANE NOVEL!

Sweetest Scoundrel

Available in Winter 2015

Please turn to the back of this book for a preview.

AND LOOK FOR THE REST OF THE SERIES

Available at a special low price!

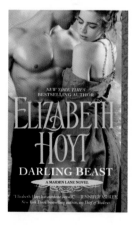

"My lady." He was suddenly closer.

"You may own dogs and horses and pretty dresses but you don't own me. I'm a free man who does as he wills. And right now my will is to leave this place."

She reached out, her hand smashing against his coat, her face only inches from his. "I need you, James."

"You can't," he whispered. "I failed you this morning. I can't—"

"You didn't," she said fiercely. "You've never failed me, not once."

"*I have.*" His words were so vehement, so agonized that she was struck dumb. "Don't you understand? They would've carried you away to God knows where, done whatever—"

She couldn't let him go. She lunged forward, pulling her hands desperately out of his hold, grabbing his coat, his ear, anything that was him. She knew how clumsy and awkward and *blind* she must be, but she couldn't care right now.

"Phe—"

She smashed her mouth to his. It wasn't a sweet kiss by any means—she'd never kissed a man. But she felt a bloom within her chest, a wild, pounding well of hope and joy, feeling his lips beneath hers. Breathing in sandalwood and gunpowder and James.

James. James. *James.*

~~~

"4½ stars! Top Pick! There is enchantment in the Maiden Lane series, not just the fairy tales Hoyt infuses into the memorable romances, but the wonder of love combined with passion, unique plotlines, and unforgettable characters."

—*RT Book Reviews*

"I *loved* it. I loved Artemis. I loved Max, and I loved their story. I have enjoyed every Elizabeth Hoyt book I have read (and I have read most of them)."

—**All About Romance (LikesBooks.com)**

Lord of Darkness

"*Lord of Darkness* illuminates Hoyt's boundless imagination...readers will adore this story."

—*RT Book Reviews*

"Hoyt's writing is imbued with great depth of emotion... heartbreaking...an edgy tension-filled plot."

—*Publishers Weekly*

"*Lord of Darkness* is classic Elizabeth Hoyt, meaning it's unique, engaging, and leaves readers on the edge of their seats...an incredible addition to the fantastic Maiden Lane series. I Joyfully Recommend Godric and Megs's tale, for it's an amazing, well-crafted story with an intriguing plot and a lovely, touching romance...simply enchanting!"

—**JoyfullyReviewed.com**

"I adore the Maiden Lane series, and this fifth book is a very welcome addition to the series…[It's] sexy and sweet all at the same time…This can be read as a standalone, but I adore each book in this series and encourage you to start from the beginning."

—USA Today's Happy Ever After blog

"Beautifully written…a truly fine piece of storytelling and a novel that deserves to be read and enjoyed."

—TheBookBinge.com

Thief of Shadows

"An expert blend of scintillating romance and mystery… The romance between the beautiful and quick-witted Isabel and the masked champion of the downtrodden propels this novel to the top of its genre."

—Publishers Weekly (starred review)

"Amazing sex scenes…a very intriguing hero…This one did not disappoint."

—USA Today

"Innovative, emotional, sensual…Hoyt's beautiful blending of the essential elements of a fairy tale into a stunning love story enhances this delicious 'keeper.'"

—RT Book Reviews

"All of Hoyt's signature literary ingredients—wickedly clever dialogue, superbly nuanced characters, danger, and scorching sexual chemistry—click neatly into place to create a breathtakingly romantic love story."

—Booklist

"When [they] finally come together, desire and long-denied sensuality explode upon the page."
—*Library Journal*

"With heart and heat rolled into one, *Thief of Shadows* is a definite must-read for historical romance fans! Hoyt really has outdone herself...yet again."
—**UndertheCoversBookblog.blogspot.com**

"A balanced mixture of action, adventure, and mystery and a beautifully crafted romance...The perfect historical romance."
—**HeroesandHeartbreakers.com**

Scandalous Desires

"Historical romance at its best...Series fans will be enthralled, while new readers will find this emotionally charged installment stands very well alone."
—*Publishers Weekly* (starred review)

"4½ stars! This is the Maiden Lane story readers have been waiting for. Hoyt delivers her hallmark fairy tale within a romance and takes readers into the depths of the heart and soul of her characters. Pure magic flows from her pen, lifting readers' spirits with joy."
—*RT Book Reviews*

"With its lush sensuality, lusciously wrought prose, and luxuriously dark plot, *Scandalous Desires*, the latest exquisitely crafted addition to Hoyt's Georgian-set Maiden Lane series, is a romance to treasure."
—*Booklist* (starred review)

"Ms. Hoyt writes some of the best love scenes out there. They are passionate, sexy, and blazing hot…I simply adore Ms. Hoyt's books for her sensuous prose, multifaceted characters, and intense, well-developed story lines. And she delivers every single time. It's no wonder all of her books are on my keeper shelves. Do yourself a favor and pick up *Scandalous Desires*."

—TheRomanceDish.com

"*Scandalous Desires* is the best book Elizabeth Hoyt has written so far, with endearing characters and an all-encompassing romance you'll want to hold close and never let go. If there's one must-read book, especially for historical romance fans, it's *Scandalous Desires*."

—FallenAngelReviews.com

Notorious Pleasures

"Emotionally stunning…The sinfully sensual chemistry Hoyt creates between her shrewd, acid-tongued heroine and her scandalous, sexy hero is pure romance."

—*Booklist*

Wicked Intentions

"4½ stars! Top Pick! A magnificently rendered story that not only enchants but enthralls."

—*RT Book Reviews*

DEAREST ROGUE

OTHER TITLES BY ELIZABETH HOYT

ELIZABETH HOYT

DEAREST ROGUE

VISION

NEW YORK   BOSTON

Vision
Hachette Book Group
1290 Avenue of the Americas
New York, NY 10104

HachetteBookGroup.com

Printed in the United States of America

OPM

First Edition: May 2015
10 9 8 7 6 5 4 3 2 1

Vision is an imprint of Grand Central Publishing.
The Vision name and logo are trademarks of Hachette Book Group, Inc.

The Hachette Speakers Bureau provides a wide range of authors for speaking events. To find out more, go to www.hachettespeakersbureau.com or call (866) 376-6591.

The publisher is not responsible for websites (or their content) that are not owned by the publisher.

For my favorite uncle, Frank Kerr—the real storyteller in the family.

Acknowledgments

I might write the books, but it takes an entire team to get them ready to read.

Thank you to my fabulous editor, Amy Pierpont; my wondrous agent, Robin Rue; my fantastic beta reader, Susannah Taylor; the ever-on-the-ball Jodi Rosoff, director of marketing and publicity at my publisher; and last, but certainly not least, S. B. Kleinman, my long-suffering copy editor, who persevered despite the egregious overuse of em dashes.

Thank you all!

And special thanks to my Facebook friend, Judith Sandrel Voss, for naming Toby the dog!

Chapter One

Now once there was a king who lived by the sea. He had had three sons and the youngest was named Corineus....
—From *The Kelpie*

JUNE 1741
LONDON, ENGLAND

Captain James Trevillion, formerly of the 4th Dragoons, was used to dangerous places. He'd hunted highwaymen in the stews of St Giles, apprehended smugglers along the cliffs of Dover, and guarded Tyburn gallows in the midst of a riot. Until now, though, he would not have counted Bond Street among their number.

It was a sunny Wednesday afternoon and fashionable London was gathered en masse, determined to spend its wealth on fripperies and blithely unaware of any impending violence.

As was, for that matter, Trevillion's charge.

"Do you have the package from Furtleby's?" inquired Lady Phoebe Batten.

The sister of the Duke of Wakefield, Lady Phoebe was plump, distractingly pretty, and quite pleasant to nearly everyone, excepting himself. She was also blind, which was both why she had her hand on Trevillion's left forearm and why Trevillion was here at all: he was her bodyguard.

"No, my lady," he answered absently as he watched one—no, three—big brutes coming toward them, moving against the brightly dressed crowd. One had a nasty scar on his cheek, another was a hulking redhead, and the third appeared to have no forehead. They looked ominously out of place in workmen's clothes, their expressions intent and fixed on his charge.

Interesting. Until now his duties as bodyguard had mostly been about making sure Lady Phoebe didn't become lost in a crowd. There'd never been a specific threat to her person.

Trevillion leaned heavily on the cane in his right hand and pivoted to look behind them. Lovely. A fourth man.

He felt something in his chest tighten with grim determination.

"Because the lace was especially fine," Lady Phoebe continued, "and also at a special price, which I'm quite sure I won't be able to find again for quite some time, and if I've left it at one of the shops we've already visited I'll be quite put out."

"Will you?"

The nearest brute—the one without a forehead—was holding something down by his side—a knife? A pistol? Trevillion transferred the cane to his left hand and gripped his own pistol, one of two holstered in black leather belts crisscrossing his chest. His right leg protested the sudden loss of support.

Two shots, four men. The odds were not particularly good.

"Yes," Lady Phoebe replied. "And Mr. Furtleby made

sure to tell me that the lace was made by grasshoppers weaving butterfly wings on the Isle of Man. Very exclusive."

"I *am* listening to you, my lady," Trevillion murmured as the first brute shoved aside an elderly dandy in a full-bottomed white wig. The dandy swore and shook a withered fist.

The brute didn't even turn his head.

"Are you?" she asked sweetly. "Because—"

The brute's hand came up with a pistol and Trevillion shot him in the chest.

Lady Phoebe clutched his arm. "What—?"

Two women—and the dandy—screamed.

The other three men started running. *Toward* them.

"Don't let go of me," Trevillion ordered, glancing quickly around. He couldn't fight three men with only one shot remaining.

"Whyever would I let go of you?" Lady Phoebe asked rather crossly.

He saw out of the corner of his eye that her bottom lip was pushed out like a small child's. It almost made him smile. Almost. "*Left*. Now."

He shoved her in that direction, his right leg giving him hell. The bloody thing had better not collapse on him—not now. He holstered the first pistol and drew the second.

"Did you shoot someone back there?" Lady Phoebe asked as a shrieking matron brushed roughly past her. Lady Phoebe stumbled against him and he wrapped his left arm over her small shoulders, pulling her close to his side. The panicked crowd was surging around them, making their progress harder.

"Yes, my lady."

There. A couple of paces away a small boy was holding

the reins of a rangy bay gelding in the street. The horse's eyes showed white at the commotion, its nostrils flared wide, but it hadn't bolted at the shot, which was a good sign.

"Why?" Her face was turned to him, her warm breath brushing his chin.

"It seemed a good idea," Trevillion said grimly.

He looked back. Two of their attackers, the scarred one and another, had been detained behind a gaggle of screeching society ladies. The redhead, though, was determinedly elbowing through the crowd—straight in their direction.

Damn their hides. He wouldn't let them get to her.

Not on his watch.

Not this time.

"Did you kill him?" Lady Phoebe asked with interest.

"Maybe." They made the horse and boy. The horse turned its head as Trevillion grasped the stirrup, but remained calm. Good lad. "Up now."

"Up *where*?"

"Horse," Trevillion grunted, slapping her hand on the horse's saddle.

"Oi!" shouted the boy.

Lady Phoebe was a clever girl. She felt down to the stirrup and placed her foot in it. Trevillion put his hand squarely on her lush arse and pushed her hard up onto the beast.

"Oof." She clutched at the horse's neck, but didn't look frightened at all.

"Thanks," Trevillion muttered to the boy, who was now wide-eyed, having caught sight of the pistol in his other hand.

He dropped his cane and scrambled inelegantly into the saddle behind Lady Phoebe. He yanked the reins from the boy's hand. With the pistol in his right hand, he wrapped his left arm around her waist, still holding the reins, and pulled her firmly against his chest.

The redheaded brute made the horse and grabbed for the bridle, his lips twisted in an ugly grimace.

Trevillion shot him full in the face.

A scream from the crowd.

The horse half-reared, throwing Lady Phoebe into the V of Trevillion's thighs, but he sternly kneed the beast into a canter, even as he holstered the spent pistol.

He might be a cripple on land but by God, in the saddle he was a demon.

"Did you kill *that* one?" Lady Phoebe shouted as they swerved around a cart. Her hat had fallen off. Light-brown locks blew across his lips.

He had her. He had her safe and that was all that mattered.

"Yes, my lady," he murmured into her ear. Flat, almost uncaring, for it would never do to let her hear the emotion that holding her in his arms provoked.

"Oh, good."

He leaned forward, inhaling the sweet scent of roses in her hair—innocent and forbidden—and kicked the horse into a full gallop through the heart of London.

And as he did so, Lady Phoebe threw back her head and laughed into the wind.

PHOEBE LET HER head fall to Captain Trevillion's shoulder—quite improperly—and felt the wind against her face as the horse surged beneath them. She didn't even realize she was laughing until the sound rushed back to her ears, joyous and free.

"You laugh at death, my lady?" Her guard's dour words were enough to put a damper on the lightest of spirits, but Phoebe had grown used to Captain Trevillion's gloomy voice in the past six months. She'd learned to ignore it and him.

Well, more or less.

"I laugh because I haven't ridden a horse in years," she said with just a *small* amount of reproach. She was only human, after all. "And I'll not let you spoil it for me with false guilt—you were the one who killed that poor man, after all, not I."

He grunted as the horse cantered around a corner, their bodies leaning as one. His chest was broad and strong behind her, the holstered pistols against her back hard reminders of his potential for violence. She heard an indignant cry as they whipped past and fought the urge to giggle. Strange. She might find the man irksome, but she'd never had any doubt at all that Captain Trevillion would keep her safe.

Even if he didn't particularly like her.

"He was trying to do you harm, my lady," Trevillion replied, his tone dry as dust as his arm tightened around her waist and the horse leaped some sort of obstacle.

Oh, that feeling! The swoop of her stomach, the momentary weightlessness, the *thump* as the horse landed, the movement of powerful equine muscles beneath her. She hadn't exaggerated to him: it had been *years* since she'd felt this. Phoebe hadn't been born blind. In fact, until the age of twelve her eyesight had been quite normal—she hadn't even needed spectacles. She couldn't recall now when it had started, but at some point her vision had begun to blur. Bright light made her eyes smart. It wasn't anything to be worried about at the time.

At least not at first.

Now…*now*, at the ripe age of one and twenty, she had been effectively blind for a year or more. Oh, she could make out vague shapes in very bright sunlight, but on an overcast day like today?

Nothing.

Not the birds in the sky, not the individual petals on a rose, not the fingernails on her own hand, no matter how closely she held it to her face.

All those sights were lost to her now, and with them many of the other simple pleasures in life.

Such as riding a horse.

She tangled her hands in the horse's coarse mane, enjoying Captain Trevillion's confident horsemanship. She wasn't at all surprised at the easy grace with which he guided the animal. He'd been a dragoon—a mounted soldier—and he often accompanied her on her early-morning trips to the Wakefield stables.

Around them the cacophony of London continued, eternally unabated: the rumble of carriage and cart wheels, the tramping of thousands of feet, the babble of voices raised in song and argument, people buying and selling and stealing, callers of wares, and the shriek of small children. Horses clip-clopped by and church bells tolled the hour, the half hour, and sometimes even the quarter hour.

As they rode, people shouted at them angrily. A canter was quite fast for London, and judging by the bunching of muscles beneath them and the sudden changes of direction, Trevillion was having to weave in and out of the traffic.

She turned her head toward him, inhaling. Captain James Trevillion wore no scent. Sometimes she could discern coffee or the faint smell of horses on him, but beyond that, nothing.

It was quite irksome. "Where are we now?"

Her lips must have been scandalously close to his cheek, yet she couldn't *see* him to be sure. She knew the captain had a lame right leg, knew the top of her head came to his chin, knew he had calluses between the middle finger and ring finger on his left hand, but she had no idea at all what he *looked* like.

"Can't you smell, my lady?" he replied.

She raised her head a bit, sniffing, then immediately wrinkled her nose at the distinctive stink—fish, sewage, and rot. "The Thames? Why bring us this way?"

"I'm making sure they aren't behind us, my lady," he said, calm as ever.

Sometimes Phoebe wondered what Captain Trevillion would do if she reached up and slapped his face. Or kissed him. Surely he'd not maintain his maddening reserve then?

Not, of course, that she actually wanted to kiss the man. Horrors! His lips were probably as cold as a mackerel's.

"Would they follow us this far?" she asked doubtfully. The whole thing seemed quite unlikely, now that she thought of it—being attacked in Bond Street of all places! Rather belatedly she remembered her lace and mourned the loss of a really good bargain.

"I don't know, my lady," Captain Trevillion replied, somehow managing to sound condescending *and* emotionless at the same time. "That's why I'm taking an unexpected route."

She tightened her grip on the horse's mane. "Well, what did they look like, my attackers?"

"Like common footpads."

"Perhaps they were?" she ventured. "Common footpads, I mean. Perhaps they weren't after me in particular."

"In Bond Street. In broad daylight." His voice was completely without inflection.

It would serve him right if she *did* turn and kiss him, really it would.

She huffed a breath. They'd slowed to a walk now and she patted the horse's neck, its hair smooth and slightly oily beneath her fingers. It snorted as if agreeing with her opinion of Captain Trevillion. "I can't think what they wanted with me in any case."

"Kidnapping for ransom, forced marriage, or mere robbery come to mind immediately, my lady," he drawled. "You are, after all, the sister of one of the richest and most powerful men in England."

Phoebe wrinkled her nose. "Has anyone ever told you that you're excessively blunt, Captain Trevillion?"

"Only you, my lady." He seemed to have turned his head, for she could feel the brush of his breath against her temple. It smelled very faintly of coffee. "On numerous occasions."

"Well, let me take this opportunity to add to them," she said. "Where are we now?"

"Nearing Wakefield House, my lady."

And with his words, Phoebe suddenly realized the full ghastliness of the situation. *Maximus.*

She immediately started babbling. "Oh! You know my

brother is terribly busy today, what with gathering support for the new act—"

"Parliament isn't in session."

"It takes *months* sometimes," she said earnestly. "Very important! And...*and* that estate in Yorkshire is flooding. I'm sure it kept him up half the night. Was it Yorkshire?" she asked with disingenuous desperation. "Or Northumberland? I never can remember, they're both so very far *north*. In any case, I really don't think we ought to bother him."

"My lady," Captain Trevillion said with stubborn male finality, "I shall be escorting you to your room, where you might recover—"

"I'm not a little child," Lady Phoebe interrupted mutinously.

"Perhaps have some tea—"

"Or *pap*. It's what my nanny always used to give us in the nursery and I *loathed* it."

"And then I shall report today's events to His Grace," Trevillion finished, not at all perturbed by her interruptions.

And *that* was exactly what she was trying to forestall. When Maximus learned of this morning's debacle he'd use it to hobble her even further.

She wasn't entirely sure she'd not go insane if that happened. "Sometimes I rather dislike you, Captain Trevillion."

"I am most gratified that it's only sometimes, my lady," he replied, and he brought the horse to a halt with a murmur of approval for the animal.

Drat. They must already be at Wakefield House.

She caught one of his hands in a last-ditch effort, holding it between her far smaller palms. "*Must* you tell him?

I'd really rather you not. Please? For me?" Silly to make a personal appeal—the man didn't seem to care for anyone, let alone her—but there it was: she was *desperate*.

"I'm sorry, my lady," he said, not sounding sorry at all, "but I work for your brother. I'll not shirk my duty by keeping something so important from him."

He disentangled his hand from hers, leaving her fingers holding empty air.

"Oh, if it's your *duty*, then," she said, not bothering to keep the disappointment from her voice, "far be it for me to stand in your way."

It'd been a rather wild hope anyway. She should've known that Captain Trevillion was too bloodless to be moved by entreaties aimed at his nonexistent compassion.

He ignored her surliness.

"Stay," he said, rather as if she were a particularly silly canine, and then belatedly added, "my lady." And she felt the sudden absence of his heat as he dismounted behind her.

She huffed, but obeyed because she wasn't nearly such a ninny as he seemed to think her sometimes.

"Cap'n!" That was the voice of their newest footman, Reed, who had a tendency to lapse into a Cockney accent when he was hurried.

"Get Hathaway and Green," Captain Trevillion ordered.

Phoebe heard the footman running—presumably back into Wakefield House—then several raised male voices and more footsteps, traveling here and there. It was all so confusing. She still sat atop the horse, stranded, unable to dismount alone, and suddenly she realized she hadn't heard Trevillion's voice in quite a while. Had he already gone in?

"Captain?"

The horse shifted beneath her, stepping back.

She grabbed for its mane, feeling off-balance, feeling *afraid.* "*Captain.*"

"I'm right here," he said, his deep voice quite close at her knee. "I haven't left you, my lady. I'd never leave you."

Relief flooded her even as she snapped, "Well, I can't tell if you don't move and I can't *smell* you."

"Smell me like you do the Thames?" She felt Trevillion's big hands about her waist, competent and gentle as he lifted her from the saddle. "On the whole, I'd prefer not to stink of fish in order for you to identify me."

"*Obviously* perfume would be more the thing."

"I find the thought of being drenched in patchouli equally distasteful, my lady."

"*Not* patchouli. It'd have to be something more masculine," she replied, her thoughts diverted to scents and the possibilities as he set her on the ground. "Perhaps quite *dark.*"

"If you say so, my lady." His voice held polite doubt.

Trevillion wrapped his left arm about her shoulders. Probably he had one of his awful big guns in his right hand. She felt him lurch just a little as he stepped forward and realized suddenly that he must've lost his cane. Dash it! He shouldn't be walking without it. She knew his leg pained him awfully.

"Phoebe!" Oh, dear, that was Cousin Bathilda Pickle-wood's voice. "Whatever's happened?"

There was a shrill bark and then the patter of paws before Phoebe felt Mignon, Cousin Bathilda's darling little spaniel, jump at her skirts.

Cousin Bathilda's "Mignon, down!" clashed with Trevillion's deeper tone saying, "If you'll just let me bring her inside, ma'am."

And then they were climbing the front steps to Wakefield House.

"I'm quite all right," Phoebe said, because she didn't want Cousin Bathilda worrying unnecessarily. "But Captain Trevillion's lost his stick and I really think he ought to have another."

"What—?"

"Sir." That was Reed again.

"Reed," Trevillion snapped, completely ignoring both Phoebe and Cousin Bathilda. *Men.* "I want you and Hathaway to accompany Lady Phoebe to her rooms and stay with her there until I order otherwise."

"Yes, sir."

"Oh, for goodness' sake," Phoebe said as they made the threshold and for some reason Mignon began yapping excitedly, "I hardly need *two*—"

"My lady—" Trevillion started ponderously. Oh, she knew *that* tone of voice.

"I don't understand," Cousin Bathilda began.

And then a baritone voice cut across the commotion, sending an absolute thrill of dread down her spine.

"What the hell is going on?" asked her brother, Maximus Batten, the Duke of Wakefield.

TALL AND LEAN with a long, lined face, the Duke of Wakefield carried his rank as another man might carry a sword—no matter how ceremonial it looked, the blade was sharp and deadly when put to use.

Trevillion bowed to his employer. "Lady Phoebe is unhurt, Your Grace, but I have matters to report."

Wakefield arched a dark eyebrow beneath his white wig.

Trevillion held the other man's gaze. Wakefield might have been a duke but Trevillion was more than used to staring down irate superior officers. Meanwhile his lower right leg shot daggers of pain up to his hip and he prayed that it wouldn't choose now of all occasions to give out on him.

The front hallway had grown quiet the moment the duke had entered. Even Miss Picklewood's lapdog had stopped barking.

Lady Phoebe shifted under his arm, her petite body warm beside his, before sighing heavily into the silence. "Nothing happened, Maximus. Really, there's no need—"

"Phoebe." Wakefield's voice halted her attempted deflection.

Trevillion's arm tightened about her small shoulders for just a moment before he let it drop. "Go with Miss Picklewood, my lady."

If his voice had been capable of being gentle he might've made it so now. Her light-brown hair was coming down around her slender shoulders, her round cheeks pink from the wind of their ride, her mouth a reddened rosebud. She looked young and a little lost, though she stood in her own ancestral home. He wanted rather badly to go to her and take her into his arms again. To offer comfort where it was neither needed nor wanted. Something in his chest ached—just once, briefly—before he shoved it down and covered it with all the reasons his instinctive reactions were impossible—and foolish to boot.

Instead he turned to the footmen. "Reed."

Reed had formerly been a soldier under his command. He was tall and on the thin side, his narrow chest not quite filling out his livery. His hands and feet were too large for his frame, his knees and elbows knobby and awkward. But his eyes were sharp in his unhandsome face. Reed nodded, having received and understood the command without needing further instruction. He jerked his chin at Hathaway, a young stripling of only nineteen summers, and both men fell into step behind the ladies as Miss Picklewood guided Lady Phoebe away.

Lady Phoebe was muttering about overbearing gentlemen as she left, and Trevillion had to bite back a smile.

"Captain." The duke's voice chased any desire to smile from Trevillion's mind. Wakefield tilted his head toward the back of the house, where his study lay, before pivoting in that direction.

Trevillion followed.

Wakefield House was one of the largest private residences in London and the corridor they now traversed was long. Trevillion's leg grew progressively worse as they passed elegant statuary, the door to the Little Library, and a sitting room before arriving at the duke's study. The room wasn't big, but it was well appointed in dark wood and had a plush, jewel-colored carpet.

Wakefield closed the door before rounding the enormous carved desk and seating himself.

Normally Trevillion would stand before His Grace, but it was simply impossible today, rank be damned. He dropped rather clumsily into one of the chairs before the desk just as the study door opened again to reveal Craven.

The manservant was built a bit like a walking scarecrow: tall, thin, and of ambiguous age—he could have been anywhere from his thirtieth year to his sixtieth. He was nominally the duke's valet, but very shortly after entering

Wakefield's employ Trevillion had realized the man was much more than that.

"Your Grace," Craven said.

Wakefield nodded at the man. "Lady Phoebe."

"I see." The manservant closed the door behind him and came to stand at the side of the desk.

Both men looked at Trevillion.

"Four men on Bond Street," Trevillion reported.

Craven's eyebrows arched nearly to his hairline.

Wakefield swore under his breath. "*Bond* Street?"

"Yes, Your Grace. I shot two of them, procured a horse, and spirited Lady Phoebe away from the danger."

"Did they say anything?" The duke frowned.

"No, Your Grace."

"Anything to identify them?"

Trevillion thought a moment, replaying the events of the afternoon in his mind to make sure he hadn't missed any detail. "No, Your Grace."

"Damnation."

Craven cleared his throat very quietly. "Maywood?"

Wakefield scowled. "Surely not. The man would have to be mad."

The valet coughed. "His lordship *has* been uncommonly persistent in wanting to buy your land in Lancashire, Your Grace. We received another letter with quite uncivil language just yesterday."

"The fool thinks I don't know that it has coal seams." Wakefield looked disgusted. "Why the man is so barmy over coal, I haven't the foggiest."

"I understand that he thinks it can be used to fuel large mechanical machines." Craven studied the ceiling.

For a moment Wakefield looked distracted. "Truly?"

"Who is Maywood?" Trevillion asked.

Wakefield turned to him. "Viscount Maywood. A neighbor of mine in Lancashire and a bit of a crackpot. A few years ago he was going on about turnips, of all things."

"Crackpot or no, he was heard to make threats against your person, Your Grace," Craven gently reminded.

"*Me*. Threats against me, not my sister," Wakefield replied.

Trevillion kneaded his right thigh, trying to think. "How would hurting your sister help him with his coal scheme?"

Wakefield waved an impatient hand. "It wouldn't."

"*Hurting* Lady Phoebe wouldn't, Your Grace," Craven said softly, "but if he were to kidnap her and hold her until you agreed to sell the land...or worse, force her to marry his son..."

"Maywood's heir is married already," Wakefield growled.

Craven shook his head. "The boy's marriage was to a lady of the Catholic persuasion and, as I understand it, not recognized by the Church of England. Thus Maywood has declared his son's nuptials invalid."

Trevillion's lips tightened at the idea of *anyone's* forcing Phoebe into a loveless marriage—let alone a *bigamous* loveless marriage. "Is Maywood mad enough to try such a thing, Your Grace?"

Wakefield leaned back in his chair and stared fixedly at the papers on his desk, deep in thought.

Abruptly he brought his fist down on the tabletop with a bang, making everything rattle. "Yes. Yes, Maywood might be that insane—and stupid. Damn it, Craven, I won't have Phoebe's life put in danger because of me."

"No, Your Grace," the valet agreed. "Shall I look into the matter?"

"Do. I want definite answers before I move on the man," Wakefield said.

Trevillion shifted uneasily. "We should investigate other suspects in the meantime. The man behind the kidnapping attempt might not be Maywood at all."

"You're right. Craven, we'll want a general investigation as well."

"Very good, Your Grace."

Wakefield's gaze suddenly lifted, pinning Trevillion. "Thank you, Trevillion, for saving my sister today."

Trevillion inclined his head. "It's my job, Your Grace."

"Yes." The duke's gaze was pointed. "Can you continue to protect her with that leg?"

Trevillion stiffened. He had his own doubts, but he wasn't going to air them here. Simply put, no one else was good enough to guard Lady Phoebe. "Yes, Your Grace."

"You're sure."

Trevillion looked the other man in the eye. He'd commanded men for nearly twelve years in His Majesty's dragoons. Trevillion didn't back down from anyone. "If ever I feel that I cannot do my duty, I'll resign before you need ask me to, Your Grace. You have my word on it."

Wakefield inclined his head. "Very well."

"With your permission, I should like to assign Reed and Hathaway permanently to guard her ladyship until such time as we have eliminated the present danger."

"A sound plan." Wakefield rose just as a knock came at the door. "Come."

The door opened to reveal Powers, Lady Phoebe's lady's maid. The petite maidservant styled her black hair in an intricate coiffure and wore an embroidered yellow gown a royal princess wouldn't be ashamed to be seen in.

The woman curtsied at once and spoke in a carefully cultured voice with just a trace of what had once been an Irish accent. "I beg your pardon, Your Grace, but her ladyship wished for Captain Trevillion to have this."

She held out a walking stick.

Trevillion felt heat climb his neck, but stood carefully, his hand on the back of his chair. It cost him—by God, it cost him—but he asked in a level voice, "If you might bring it to me, Miss Powers."

She hurried over and gave him the stick.

He thanked her and made himself look at his employer. "If that is all, Your Grace?"

"It is." Thank God Wakefield wasn't a man inclined to pity. There was no trace of sympathy in his eyes. "Guard my sister, Captain."

Trevillion raised his chin and spoke from his heart. "With my life."

And then he turned and limped from the room.

Chapter Two

*One day the king sent for his sons and said, "It is time I
give you your inheritances."*
*To his eldest son he gave a gleaming chain of gold. To his
second son he gave a thick chain of silver. But when the
king turned to Corineus all he had was a thin chain of iron.
He placed this about his youngest son's neck and said,
"Though it be but of iron, I give this to you as a token of my
faith in you. Go forth and make your fortune."* …
—From *The Kelpie*

"Darling, I simply can't believe it," Lady Hero Reading
exclaimed early the next afternoon. "An attempted kidnapping in broad daylight and in Bond Street of all places.
Who would do such a thing?"

Phoebe smiled a little wanly at her elder sister's words.
"I don't know, but Maximus wouldn't even let me go out
today—to *your* house. You'd think he'd consider his own
sister's home safe."

"He's worried about you, dear," came the slightly huskier voice of their sister-in-law, Artemis. All three of
them had been forced to take their weekly tea at Wakefield House since Phoebe had been effectively confined to
the town house.

Phoebe snorted. "He's using the attempted attack to do what he's always wanted to: imprison me utterly."

"Oh, Phoebe," Hero said quietly, her voice soft. "That's not Maximus's true intent."

She and Hero shared a velvet settee in the Achilles Salon, so called because the ceiling was painted with a depiction of the centaurs educating a youthful Achilles. As a little girl Phoebe had been rather frightened of the mythical creatures. Their expressions had been so stern. Now…well, now she wasn't entirely certain she could remember their expressions.

How depressing.

Phoebe turned her face toward her sister and caught the comforting scent of violets. "You know Maximus has been growing ever more overbearing since I broke my arm."

That had happened four years earlier, when Phoebe could still see somewhat. She'd missed a step in a shop and fallen headlong, breaking her arm badly enough that it had needed setting.

"He wishes to protect you," Cousin Bathilda said bracingly.

She sat across from Phoebe and Hero, next to Artemis. Phoebe could hear the asthmatic breathing of Mignon on her lap. Cousin Bathilda had been like a mother to both Phoebe and Hero since the death of both their parents. They'd died many years ago at the hands of a footpad in St Giles when Phoebe had been only a baby. At the same time, though, Cousin Bathilda generally sided with Maximus as the patriarch—fratriarch?—of the family. She'd gone against his rule once or twice, but it was rare.

And Cousin Bathilda had never stopped Maximus imposing his overheavy brand of protection on Phoebe.

Phoebe absently stroked the velvet of the settee, feeling the soft nap one way, the slightly rougher texture the other. "I know he cares for me. I know he worries for me. But in doing so, he's constrained me utterly. Even before this attack Maximus didn't let me go to parties or fairs or *anywhere* he deemed dangerous. I'm afraid after this that he'll pack me in cotton wool and set me at the back of a cupboard for safekeeping. I...I just don't know if I can *live* like this."

Her words weren't adequate for the rising panic at the thought of being *constrained* even more.

Warm fingers covered her own, stilling them. "I know, darling," Hero said. "You've been very good following his direction."

"Let me speak to him," Artemis said. "In the past he's been quite adamant about your safety, but perhaps if I can impress upon him how restricted you feel, he'll let up a bit."

"If nothing else, he could remove my constant shadow," Phoebe muttered.

"That is entirely unlikely," Cousin Bathilda said. "And besides, Captain Trevillion isn't here now, is he?"

"Only because I'm within Wakefield House." Phoebe blew out a breath. "I wouldn't be at all surprised if he lurks behind the door when I'm at tea. And you see Hathaway and Reed?"

"Yes—?" The confused question came from Hero.

"They're still standing by the back window, aren't they?" She didn't wait for an answer. She might not have heard the footmen move in several minutes, but she just knew they were staring at her. "Maximus added them to my guard."

There was a silence that felt rather uncomfortable to her before Artemis said, "Phoebe…" and then almost immediately interrupted herself. "No, darling, not the tea-cup. 'Tisn't for babies, I'm afraid."

This last was directed at Hero's eldest child, William, an adorable two-and-a-half-year-old who, by the sound of the sudden ear-splitting shriek, had really wanted that teacup.

"Oh, William," Hero muttered, exasperated, as a whimper heralded the awakening of her second son on her lap. "Now he's woken Sebastian."

"I'm so sorry, my lady." Smart, William's nursemaid, must've come over to collect her charge.

"Not your fault, Smart," Hero said. "The tea things are terribly tempting."

"May I?" Phoebe held out her hands to Hero.

"Thank you, dear," Hero said. "Careful now, he's a bit drooly, I'm afraid."

"All the best babies are," Phoebe assured her as she felt the wriggly weight of her nephew on her lap. Immediately she closed her arms over the baby protectively. Sebastian was only three months old and couldn't quite sit up. She grasped him by his pudgy middle and held him upright, smelling the sweet scent of milk on his skin. "Never mind your mama, Seb, sweetie. I simply adore drooling males."

She was rewarded for her nonsense by a burbling coo and the sudden introduction of tiny fingers into her mouth.

"You *did* ask for him," her sister reminded her.

"Shall I take Master William out, my lady?" the soft voice of William's nursemaid murmured.

"Now, William, would you like to go with Smart and explore the garden?" Hero asked briskly. "Here, take a sugar biscuit with you. Thank you, Smart."

The door opened and closed.

"I like that gel," Cousin Bathilda observed as Phoebe gently mouthed Sebastian's little fingers. "Seems competent, but kind with our Sweet William. Where did you find her?"

"Mm," Hero agreed. "I like Smart as well. So much better than the first nursemaid we had. She was a rather silly girl. Would you believe that Smart was recommended by Lady Margaret's former housekeeper? Such a terrifyingly competent young woman—the housekeeper, that is, not Megs—but she gave notice and left Megs quite suddenly. Found a better place, I expect."

"What would be better than the daughter of a marquess?" Artemis asked.

"A duke," Cousin Bathilda said bluntly. "I've heard the gel went to Montgomery to keep his town house."

"However do you learn of these things?" Hero asked with not a small amount of exasperation. Phoebe could sympathize. Cousin Bathilda always knew the best gossip before anyone else.

"What else do you think I discuss when I take tea with my circle of white-haired ladies?" Cousin Bathilda said. "Why, only yesterday I learned that Lord Featherstone was found admiring the duck pond in Hyde Park with Lady Oppertyne."

"That doesn't seem terribly scandalous," Hero said, sounding puzzled.

"Lord Featherstone wasn't wearing his breeches at the time," Cousin Bathilda said triumphantly. "*Or* his smallclothes."

Phoebe felt her eyebrows arch.

"But he *was* wearing *Lady Oppertyne's* garter on his—"

"Would you like some more tea?" Hero hastily offered, apparently to the room at large.

"*Please*," Artemis replied.

China clinked.

Phoebe made a very rude noise with her lips, which caused her nephew to giggle. She squinted, peering as hard as she could, but the light must've been too dim in the sitting room. She couldn't even make out the shape of Sebastian's head. "Hero?"

"Yes, dear?"

"What color is his hair?"

There was a short silence. Phoebe might not have been able to see, but she knew the other women had looked at her. For a moment she wished—wished with all her heart—that she were normal. That she weren't a worry, maybe even a *burden*, to her family. That she could simply look and *see*, damn it, what her precious nephew looked like.

She couldn't, though.

Something clattered on the tea table. "Oh, Phoebe, I'm sorry," Hero gasped. "I can't believe I've never told you—"

"No, no." Phoebe shook her head, tamping down her frustration. She hadn't mentioned it to make everyone else feel guilty. "It's not . . . you don't need to apologize, truly. It's just . . . I just want to *know*."

Hero drew in her breath and it sounded almost like a sob.

Phoebe tightened her lips.

Artemis cleared her throat, her voice low and soothing as always. "His hair is black. Sebastian's a little baby, of course, but I really think he'll look nothing like Sweet William. His eyes are a darker brown, his complexion seems to be quite tawny—unlike William's naturally fair skin—and I do think he'll have the Batten nose."

"Oh no." Phoebe felt a grin split her lips, her shoulders relaxing. Maximus had a mild version of the Batten nose, but if their ancestors' portraits were anything to go by, the affliction could be quite prominent.

"I think a largish nose gives a man a certain air of gravitas," Cousin Bathilda broke in with just a touch of disapproval in her voice. "Even your captain has a bit of a nose and I think it makes him quite dashing."

"He's not exactly *my* captain," Phoebe said, and then, as much as she knew she shouldn't, she couldn't help adding, "Dashing?"

"Rather *handsome*," Cousin Bathilda began.

At the same time Artemis said, "I don't know if *dashing* is *quite*—"

"Too severe." Hero's voice ended the verbal melee.

Everyone paused to take a breath.

In the ensuing silence, baby Sebastian whimpered.

"He's probably hungry," Hero murmured, taking her son.

Phoebe listened to the rustle of clothing as her sister put the baby to her breast. Hero was unfashionable in her desire to nurse her sons herself, but Phoebe rather envied her.

It would be so nice to hold a little warm body to her breast. To know she could nourish and cherish her own child.

Phoebe bowed her head, hoping her longing didn't show on her face. The fact was, she had pitifully few chances to meet eligible gentlemen—assuming she could even find a man willing to take a blind woman as wife.

"So what exactly *does* Captain Trevillion look like?" she asked, eager to avoid her morose contemplations.

"We-ell," Hero began thoughtfully. "He has a long face."

Phoebe laughed. "That doesn't tell me anything."

"Lined." Artemis spoke up. "His face is lined. He has these sort of indents about his mouth, which is a bit thin."

"His eyes are blue," Cousin Bathilda cut in. "Rather nice-looking, really."

"But *piercing*," Hero said. "Oh, and he has dark hair. I understand he wore a white wig as a dragoon, but since retiring he's let it grow and braided it into a very tight queue."

"And of course he wears nothing but black," Artemis said.

"Truly?" Phoebe wrinkled her nose. She'd had no idea she'd been escorted about all this time by an embodiment of Death.

"The Ladies' Syndicate," Cousin Bathilda suddenly exclaimed.

"What about it?" Artemis asked.

"Why, we meet tomorrow," Cousin Bathilda said.

"Of course," Hero said. "But will Maximus allow Phoebe to go?"

The Ladies' Syndicate for the Benefit of the Home for Unfortunate Infants and Foundling Children was Hero's pet project. A club made up exclusively of ladies—no gentlemen were allowed to join—it had been formed to help an orphanage in the slums of St Giles. The Ladies' Syndicate met irregularly, but Phoebe quite looked forward to the meetings, as they were among the few social events Maximus let her attend.

Or at least he had up until now.

"He won't let her go," Artemis said quietly. "Not after yesterday's events."

"Oh, but we were to review a possible new member." Hero's voice held dismay. "Shall we postpone the meeting, do you think?"

"No." Phoebe said very firmly. "I'm tired of hiding and being told when and where I can go."

"But, darling, if it's *dangerous*—" Artemis began.

"A meeting of the Ladies' Syndicate?" Phoebe asked incredulously. "We all know the meetings are safe as can be."

"They *are* in St Giles," Cousin Bathilda pointed out.

"And all the noble ladies of the Syndicate bring their strongest footmen. I shall be surrounded by protectors, including my own captain and his two soldiers. I'm not sure Reed even knows anymore that he's employed by Maximus and *not* Captain Trevillion."

"At least you'll acknowledge he is *your* captain." Hero's voice was teasing before she sobered. Somewhere across the sitting room the door opened. "I don't see how you'll get around Maximus, though."

"I don't know either, but I shall," Phoebe declared. "I'm a woman, not a caged singing finch."

She felt his presence before she heard the boot falls behind her. *Dash* it. If he would wear a scent she'd at least have *some* idea when he was about.

"My lady," Captain Trevillion rasped. "I've received word from His Grace that the man behind your kidnapping attempt is no longer a threat to you. May I say, however, that while you may not be a caged bird, neither are you merely a woman. You're a precious artifact. As long as there are men who wish to steal you, I'll be right by your side."

Phoebe felt the heat invade her cheeks. As soon as she could get her captain alone she would tell him exactly how this "artifact" felt about his words.

TREVILLION WATCHED AS Lady Hero took leave of the other women. They had formed a protective circle around his charge and he thought that had they not been well-bred ladies he would be receiving an earful right now.

From the delicate pink in Lady Phoebe's cheeks, he still might. She wore a sky-blue dress today. Instead of the usual fichu, her bodice was trimmed with fine lace, framing and cupping her round breasts distractingly. He couldn't help thinking the cool color of the gown made her mouth look like a ripe berry. Soft. Sweet. Luscious. A mouth he could bite into.

He glanced away, reining in his thoughts.

"I'm so glad that you'll be able to attend the Ladies' Syndicate meeting," Lady Hero murmured as she bussed her sister on the cheek. She sent a dark look at Trevillion before sweeping from the room, head held high.

Trevillion sighed silently.

Miss Picklewood's lapdog wriggled in her arms and the lady bent stiffly to let the dog down. "I believe Mignon is ready for her daily perambulation."

"Lovely," said Her Grace, smiling at the tiny dog dancing against the ladies' skirts. "I'll have my maid fetch Bon Bon and we'll join you, shall we?"

"Excellent," pronounced Miss Picklewood. "Phoebe, will you be coming as well?"

"I think I'll take a turn in my garden," Lady Phoebe replied. She had a polite smile on her face, but Trevillion caught the edge in her voice.

His suspicion was verified when she turned without a word to him and stomped from the sitting room.

He caught a sympathetic glance from Her Grace as he followed after his charge, but he really wasn't interested in her sympathy.

The sitting room was at the top of the grand staircase leading down to the main floor of Wakefield House. Trevillion watched closely as Lady Phoebe descended the gleaming marble steps. She never even faltered—she never had—but he hated those stairs nonetheless.

On the lower level, Lady Phoebe turned and headed to the back of the house, trailing her fingertips along the hallway wall as she did so. He stalked less gracefully after, watching the sway of her bright-blue skirts as he did so.

She was nearly to the high doors that let out into the garden before he caught up with her. "Childish, my lady, trying to outrun a crippled man."

She didn't turn, but her back did stiffen. "We artifacts tend to be a childish lot, I'm afraid, Captain."

With that she opened the doors and swept out onto the wide granite steps leading down into the garden. The blue of her dress against the gray of the granite and the deep green of the grass brought out the auburn of her light-brown hair. She looked like the embodiment of spring, near angelic in her loveliness.

Well. If she hadn't been determinedly marching away from him.

He strode forward and caught her arm. "If you'll *permit*, my lady."

He rather thought she growled at that, but he didn't wait for her answer, simply placing her hand on his left arm. The grass was uneven and she must have realized that she'd look foolish if she fell on her proud little nose.

"You're hardly a cripple," she said abruptly.

His mouth twisted as he led her down the steps. "I'm not sure what else one should call a man unable to stand without the help of a cane, my lady."

She merely snorted in reply. "Well, you may consider yourself a cripple—even though you're clearly *not*—but I wish to inform you that whatever else I may be, I'm most certainly not an artifact."

"I'm sorry if I've offended, my lady."

"Are you?"

He stifled a sigh. "Perhaps if you explained why my perfectly reasonable observations *should* offend you, my lady."

"Really, Captain, it's no wonder at all that you're not married."

"Isn't it?"

"No one wants to be called an *artifact*, especially no woman."

A calculated retreat might be in order. "Perhaps my assessment was overly blunt, but you must allow that you are indeed precious to your entire family, my lady."

"Must I?" She halted, making him stop as well if he didn't want to leave her. "Why? I'm loved by my family— and I love them in return—but I have to tell you that being called a precious *thing* makes my stomach turn."

He glanced at her, surprised at so visceral a reaction. "Many men will see you as such. You're the sister of a duke, an heiress who—"

"Do *you*?"

He stared at her, this lovely, vehement, *maddening*

woman. *Of course* he didn't see her as a mere artifact. Were she not blind, surely she'd know already.

He'd taken too long. She folded her arms across her bosom, scowling ferociously. "Well, do you, Captain Trevillion?"

"It's my duty to keep you safe, my lady."

"Not the question I asked, Captain," she shot back. "Am I merely a valuable object to you? A jeweled box to protect from thieves?"

"*No,*" he said, hard.

"Good." She laid her hand on his arm once more, her touch like a brand upon his flesh even through the layers of fabric that separated them.

One of these days he would break, and when he did she'd see he wasn't made of stone.

Not at all.

But that day wouldn't be today.

The steps ended on a square of grass. Beyond that was Lady Phoebe's garden, a tangle of neatly graveled paths that meandered here and there among extravagant mounds of flowering plants. The garden was like none Trevillion had ever seen before. First of all, the flowers were all white. Roses, lilies, daisies of all sorts, and dozens of other blooms that Trevillion was unable to name, for he'd never been that interested in plants.

The second difference in this garden was one only discovered when a person neared it: the perfume that lay heavy in the air. Trevillion had never asked, but as far as he could tell, every single flower in the garden bore a scent. Entering the garden was like stepping into a fairy's boudoir. Bees buzzed lazily over the blooms while the scent-laden breeze enchanted the senses.

Trevillion turned and watched as Lady Phoebe visibly relaxed. Her shoulders dropped, her hands loosened from half-clenched fists, and a smile played about her plush mouth. She lifted her face to the wind and he caught his breath. Out here, alone with her, he could look his fill. Let his eyes caress the tender curve of her cheek, the stubborn arch of her brow, her mouth, half-parted and moist.

He glanced away again, his lips curling sardonically at his own weakness. She was everything he was not: young, innocent, filled with the joy of life. She had the blue blood of centuries of aristocrats running in her veins.

He was a cynical, older ex-soldier and his blood ran common red.

"Who was he?" she asked, her voice breaking into his thoughts.

He had to clear his throat before he spoke. "To whom do you refer, my lady?"

"My kidnapper, silly." Her expressive face crinkled. "Oh, I don't like the sound of that. '*My* kidnapper' sounds much too intimate. Rather, the scoundrel who attempted to kidnap me. Who was he?"

"Ah." The gravel crunched beneath their feet as they stepped onto the garden path. "He was, apparently, a neighbor of your brother's in Lancashire. A man by the name of Maywood."

She stopped at that, turning to face him, her eyes wide. "Lord Maywood? Really? But he must be sixty at the very least. What did he want with me?"

"His Grace isn't sure," Trevillion replied slowly. His meeting with the duke this afternoon had left many of Trevillion's questions unsatisfied. It made him uneasy. "Possibly Lord Maywood wished to force you to marry his son."

She frowned at that, her eyebrows gathered above eyes that seemed to stare at the pistols strapped over his heart. "But Lord Maywood confessed to the crime?"

"Not exactly." Trevillion's lips flattened. "Lord Maywood sent a threat to your brother last week and one of the men I shot was found to be originally from Lancashire."

Her dark brows knit. "What did Lord Maywood say when confronted?"

"Nothing, my lady," he admitted reluctantly. "Maywood died this morning from a sudden attack of apoplexy."

"Oh." She blinked, her hand gently stroking the petals of a nearby rose as if for comfort. "I'm sorry to hear that."

"I am not," he replied. "Not if it means your safety."

She said nothing to that, merely turned to continue on their perambulation. "So Maximus feels the affair is over."

"Yes, my lady."

The duke seemed content that the matter had ended so neatly, but Trevillion would've been much happier had Lord Maywood confessed to the kidnapping. He'd argued that they should still be investigating to see if there was any other possible identity for the kidnapper. Wakefield, however, was convinced that the affair was over.

But without a confession there still remained doubt in Trevillion's mind.

He didn't share that thought with Lady Phoebe. No need to worry her without specific cause. Besides, he would remain as vigilant as always.

"Oh, this one's gone to seed," Lady Phoebe muttered, fingering a bloom that had lost most of its petals. "Have you a basket?"

He raised his eyebrows. Where and why would he have procured a basket? "No, my lady."

"Shortsighted of you, really, Captain," she muttered, and produced a small scissors from a chatelaine at her waist. She snipped off the bloom and held it out to him. "Here."

Trevillion took the bloom and, with nowhere else to put it, shoved it in his pocket.

"Do you see any others in need of cutting?" she asked, her hands dancing over the plant.

"One." He caught her fingers, cool and delicate in his larger hand, and brought them to the wasted rose bloom.

"Oh, thank you."

He flexed his hand. "Don't you have gardeners to do this?"

"Yes." She snipped the bloom and again gave it to him. He was forced to place it with its sister. "But why would I wait for them?" Her hands were busily seeking again.

"Because it's a chore, my lady?"

She laughed, the sound trailing uncomfortably down his spine. "You truly are no gardener, Captain Trevillion."

She offered no further explanation, but bent to her task. Trevillion was struck by how comfortable she was here, among her flowers, her face bright and open.

"Pity it's overcast today," she murmured absently.

He stilled.

He made no sound, yet she must've sensed something. She straightened slowly, her too-young face turned toward him, the scissors clutched in her hand. "Captain?"

He'd never before understood what people meant when they talked of breaking hearts.

Now he did.

Still. He'd not ever lied to her before and he wasn't going to start now. "The sun is shining."

*   *   *

EVERYTHING WAS BLACK, though Captain Trevillion had told her it was broad daylight.

Phoebe had expected this to happen one day.

Of course she had. Her vision had been getting steadily worse for years. Only a mental incompetent wouldn't realize where it was leading.

Except…it was one thing for her *mind* to understand, but it was entirely different for her *heart* to comprehend. Foolish, feckless thing. Apparently it had held out hope for a miracle.

She laughed at the realization, though it came out more a gasp.

He was there at once, her faithful captain, stern and without humor, but always there. "My lady?" He took her hand in his large, warm one, wrapping an arm about her shoulders as if she might fall.

And really she might.

"It's silly," she said, and swiped at her face with a shaking hand, for it seemed she was weeping. "*I'm* silly."

"Come. Sit."

He led her two steps and pulled her down gently to a stone seat, letting her lean into his solid strength.

She shook her head. "I'm sorry."

"*Don't*," he rasped, and if she hadn't known better she'd have thought he was nearly as shaken as she. "Don't apologize."

She inhaled unsteadily. "Do you know why all my flowers are white?"

She half expected him to point out the non sequitur, but he merely replied, "No."

"The white blooms stood out best for my fading eyesight when I first planted the garden three years ago," she said. "And of course white flowers are usually the most fragrant. But it was mostly because I thought I might see them better."

He said nothing, merely tightened his arm about her shoulders, and she was a little grateful that it was he with her now. Had it been Hero or Maximus or Cousin Bathilda she'd have had to worry about their own pain— pain for her loss. But with Captain Trevillion she had simply a sturdy presence. He wouldn't break down weeping for her. He wouldn't try to think of comforting words.

That at least was nice.

"It's so stupid," she said softly, "to mourn the inevitable. I knew there was no cure. I was the one who insisted Maximus send away all the doctors and miracle workers. I *knew*..." She couldn't quite suppress the sob that rose in her chest.

She covered her open mouth with her hands and gulped quite awfully, shuddering.

His hand was in her hair, bending her head to his chest, letting her rest there as the tears soaked his shirt. One of his pistols pressed quite uncomfortably into her cheek, but she really didn't care at the moment. She wept until her face was hot and wet, until her nose was stuffy, until her eyes felt as if they had been sprinkled with sand. When she at last subsided, she could hear the thump of Captain Trevillion's heart, steady and strong, beneath his chest.

"It's a little like death," she whispered, half to herself. "We all know that we'll die someday, but *believing* it is another thing entirely."

For a moment the hand still in her hair tightened painfully. Then it was gone, smoothing over her shoulder instead. "You're far from death, my lady."

"Am I?" She twisted her face upward, toward his. "Isn't this like a small death? I cannot see light. I cannot see *anything*."

"I'm sorry," he said, his voice like gravel, grating and rasping and yet, somehow, comforting as well. "I'm sorry."

It sounded . . . as if he truly cared.

She frowned, opening her mouth to ask, and heard the door to the town house open. "Oh, goodness. Who is it?"

"Powers, coming to fetch you," he replied.

She straightened at once, touching her hand to her hair, attempting to put it to rights. She must look ghastly. "How do I look?"

"As if you've been weeping."

His stolid answer surprised a laugh from her. "I know I look a fright, but you might at least *lie*."

"Do you really require lies from me?" His voice sounded . . . tired.

She frowned, opening her mouth to reply.

"My lady, the dressmaker is here." That was Powers's voice, and quite close.

"Drat," Phoebe muttered, distracted. "We'll have to go in."

"Indeed, my lady." He was as unemotional as ever.

Still she pressed her fingers into his arm as he led her back to the house. "Thank you, Captain."

"For what, my lady?"

"For letting me soak your shirt with salt water." She smiled, though it was harder than usual. "For not giving me platitudes. You're quite right. I don't need lies from you."

"Then I shall endeavor to give you nothing but honesty," he replied.

Which was a perfectly respectable answer, and yet still it made her shiver. She thought suddenly of her family's description of him. *Handsome. Dashing.* Strange, she'd never considered Trevillion as a man who might be attractive. He was simply *there*. A massive shape at her right side keeping her from balls and outings, always on the alert to stop any fun.

Except that wasn't quite true, she chided herself guiltily as they made the stone steps. Trevillion had been quite comforting as she'd fallen apart.

He'd been a friend. She'd never considered him a friend before . . . and if she had *that* wrong . . .

Well.

Perhaps that wasn't the only thing she had wrong about her guard.

Chapter Three

*Prince Corineus vowed to have his own kingdom one day,
so he gathered a dozen brave men and boarded a ship to
sail the sea. They sailed for seven days and seven nights
and on the eighth day land was sighted: jagged cliffs
with only one small safe inlet. But as Corineus saw the
shoreline he heard an eerie song, a seductress promising
love and lust and everlasting bliss....*
—From *The Kelpie*

Late the next morning Phoebe stood in the front hallway of Wakefield House and pressed a note and a small purse into Powers's hand. "Now mind you give this to Mr. Hainsworth himself, not one of the shop boys."

"Yes, my lady," Powers said. Her voice was light and pleasing, though she did have a tendency to apply far too much of the patchouli scent she favored.

"Thank you, Powers," Phoebe said as she detected the approach of Captain Trevillion's uneven tread on the stairs.

"My lady, do you still wish to attend the Ladies' meeting?" he asked in a raspy voice with skeptical undertones.

"Ladies' *Syndicate* meeting," Phoebe replied. "And yes, of course I still wish to attend. Don't try to weasel out of taking me—I have Maximus's blessing." Her brother's blessing to go out, at least. She hadn't actually informed Maximus *where* she was going, but she wasn't about to tell the captain that.

Was that a masculine sigh? "Very well, my lady."

Strong, warm fingers took her hand and placed it on his sleeve. Funny. Had she not been blind, such a touch—bare skin to bare skin—would have been scandalous. Come to that, having a man in his prime follow her about, sometimes without any other escort, would have been the height of impropriety. And yet no one seemed to think anything of Captain Trevillion's lurking always at her side.

Blindness had neutered her in the eyes of the world.

Phoebe huffed to herself as she stepped out into the warm air. The sun must be out today—she could feel it on her skin.

"My lady?" Trevillion's voice rumbled next to her.

"Oh, nothing, Captain," she said only a little grumpily. No doubt he too thought of her as a sort of mobile doll rather than a woman with blood running in her veins.

"If there is anything troubling you—"

"Sometimes I wonder if you should just put me on wheels," she muttered as they descended the front steps.

"Good mornin', sir, m'lady," called Reed the footman.

"Reed," Trevillion intoned. "You and Hathaway can stand on the back of the carriage, if you will."

"Yes, sir."

"Is it really necessary to bring *both* footmen?" Phoebe asked softly.

"I think so, yes, my lady. Here are the steps."

She edged her toe forward until she felt the first step and then climbed into the carriage. She sat and smoothed her skirts. "It's only the Ladies' Syndicate."

There was a rustle as Trevillion sat across from her. Despite his cane, he made far less noise than most men as he moved about his day.

It was quite irritating.

"The Ladies' Syndicate meets in St Giles, my lady, arguably the worst part of London."

"It's the middle of the day."

"It was the middle of the day when the attempt was made against you on Bond Street." His voice was deep and even and Phoebe wondered if *anything* would make Trevillion lose his air of calm disinterest. "Sometimes I think you enjoy arguing, my lady."

She pursed her lips. "Well, not with *everyone*, Captain Trevillion. You're a very special case, you comprehend."

She thought she heard a huff that might've been quiet laughter, but it was drowned in the rumble of wheels as the carriage set off.

"Truly I'm honored, my lady."

"As you *should* be." She fought to suppress a smile. She always felt a sense of accomplishment whenever she got her stern captain to play. "Tell me something. I've noticed that you favor Reed above the other footmen. Why is that?"

"It's a simple enough matter, my lady. Reed used to be a dragoon under my command. When he left His Majesty's service, I recommended Reed to your brother as a good man, loyal and not afraid of a hard day's work. His Grace was kind enough to take my recommendation, my lady."

"Ah! How easily a mystery is solved." The carriage rocked as they turned a corner, and Phoebe caught a fragment of song from without as they passed—probably the singer had a hat out, hoping to make a few pennies with her voice. "Was he with you in the dragoons for long?"

"Since he first took the King's shilling, my lady," Trevillion replied. "Some five years, if I recollect correctly."

"And how many years were you in the dragoons?"

There was a pause and she thought, not for the first time, how awful it was not to see the face of the person she spoke with. Was he surprised at her question? Offended that she asked such a personal query? Or saddened by the thought of a career he no longer had? Such a simple matter, easily answered with but a glance.

"Almost twelve years, my lady," he said at last. His voice was entirely emotionless and she could get nothing from it—save that its very lack of emotion meant he felt *something* strongly.

She cocked her head, considering. "Did you like it?"

"My lady?" Oh, now his voice was ever so faintly censoring. *That* was interesting. *Why* had she never asked him these questions before?

"Being in the dragoons? Commanding men—you did command many men as a captain, didn't you? Doing… whatever it was you did?"

"I commanded twenty to fifty men, depending on our assignment," he replied.

And now he commanded only her. She realized suddenly what a comedown in life this work must be for him.

But he continued, "I did whatever my King ordered me to," and for a moment she thought that was all she was going to hear about his time in the dragoons. Then he unbent a little. "We chased smugglers along the coast for many years, but in the last several my regiment was assigned to London, specifically to find and catch gin makers and other miscreants in St Giles."

"Really?" She frowned as she realized she knew very little about this man. Good Lord! She'd spent six months, day after day, with Captain Trevillion and yet she'd never asked him the simplest questions about his background. Phoebe felt a stab of shame before she leaned a little forward, determined to right her past lapse. "That seems a very specific area to patrol."

"Yes." His voice was dry. "But then we had a very specific order—from an important member of Parliament."

"From... you don't mean my brother?"

"I do mean your brother, my lady."

"He has always hated gin making to a quite unhealthy degree," Phoebe muttered to herself. "So you've actually known Maximus for years?"

"His Grace and I have been acquainted for over four years."

"I had no idea you were such friends."

The pause was small but marked. "I would not describe our... association as such, my lady."

"What? As friendly?" Phoebe asked. "I assure you, I'll not think the less of you, Captain, for succumbing to the weakness of friendship."

"Your brother is a duke, my lady—"

"And yet he still blows his nose."

"—and I am only a former dragoon from—" He stopped abruptly.

She leaned forward, her curiosity piqued. "From where, Captain?"

"Cornwall, my lady. I see we've arrived at the orphanage."

And the carriage shuddered to a stop.

"Don't think this conversation over," Phoebe said pleasantly as she gathered herself in preparation for exiting the carriage. "I have many more questions to ask you, Captain Trevillion."

As the carriage door opened she heard a resigned sigh from her protector.

Phoebe bit back a smile. She enjoyed riling the stoic dragoon captain, but she couldn't help wondering: why that slight hesitation over his origins?

THE HOME FOR Unfortunate Infants and Foundling Children was, at first glance, an unprepossessing place for an introduction into fashionable society. Eve Dinwoody descended the carriage with the help of her manservant, Jean-Marie Pépin, and glanced up the street.

The home sat square in the middle of St Giles, on a lane too narrow to allow for the passage of a carriage— they'd had to stop at the end of the lane. Even in daylight the extreme poverty of St Giles hung like a dark cloud over the place. A beggar in rags so tattered it was impossible to tell his or her sex sat slumped against the corner of a house. Across the street from the carriage, a woman shuffled by, her head and back bent under an enormous covered basket, while a lone child, bare from the waist down, stood and frankly gawped at the fine carriage.

They must have seemed like gods descended from Olympus to the poor boy, Eve thought with pity. Hastily she fumbled in her pocket for the purse hanging inside her skirts and withdrew a penny. She held it out to the naked child and he darted forward, snatched the coin, and scuttled away.

The home itself was a large, new brick building with wide front steps. Nonetheless it was obviously a working institution, with few of the architectural flourishes common to charity buildings. Yet this was where the Ladies' Syndicate for the Benefit of the Home for Unfortunate Infants and Foundling Children met—and the Syndicate was composed of some of the most influential women in society.

Among them her sponsor.

Eve turned to watch Amelia Huntington, Baroness Caire, step from the carriage. The elder lady was just entering her seventh decade, but her beautiful face was hardly lined. The only possible sign of her age was her snow-white hair—though Eve had heard that Lady Caire's hair, like her son's, had turned white in her youth and therefore wasn't the result of age at all. She wore an elegant deep-blue frock—the exact shade of her eyes—trimmed with black lace on the sleeves, on the square neckline, and in a tiny row down the bodice.

"They live like rats here," Lady Caire murmured, not without sympathy, as she glanced about. "That's why I always bring a brace of sturdy footmen with me." She nodded to the footmen accompanying them, one in front, one in back. "You were wise to bring your own man." She glanced thoughtfully at Jean-Marie. "He's quite exotic, isn't he?"

Jean-Marie's skin was a glossy black, he stood over six feet, and with his white wig and silver-and-white livery, he was striking.

"I no longer find him so." Eve didn't bother correcting Lady Caire's assumption that Jean-Marie was her footman. She fell into step with the older woman as they made their way down Maiden Lane to the home. "I must thank you again for the kindness of an introduction to the Ladies' Syndicate."

"My pleasure, naturally," Lady Caire drawled without

smiling, her eyes cold—a reminder that she'd been pres-
sured to bring Eve to the meeting today.

Eve mustn't forget that fact. She had no friends here,
not truly. Carefully, she drew her lips into a small, polite
smile as they both started up the wide steps. More carriages had stood at the end of the lane, suggesting that the
other members of the Syndicate had already arrived.

Eve took a deep breath as the door to the home was
opened, smoothing down her dove-gray skirts. Black and
cherry-pink flowers were discreetly embroidered at her
shoulders, on the elbows of her sleeves, down the front
of her bodice, and the on edges of her wide overskirt.
Underneath she wore cream skirts—simple and elegant.
She was fashionably dressed, at least, though she'd never
been—nor would ever be—fashionably pretty. A very
correct butler stood in the doorway, which was a bit odd
for a foundling home, but Isabel Makepeace, the wife of
the home's manager, had been a wealthy widow before
her second marriage.

"Good afternoon, my lady, miss," the butler said,
standing aside. A black tomcat sat by his feet, for all the
world as if welcoming visitors as well.

Suddenly a barking whirlwind erupted from the back
of the house. A small white dog, snapping teeth bared, ran
at them. Eve couldn't still her involuntary step backward,
jostling into the butler.

Then Jean-Marie was in front of her, scooping up the
nasty thing and holding it against his chest. It immediately quieted, licking at his chin.

"I do apologize!" the butler exclaimed. "Dodo does
bark quite loudly, but she never bites, I assure you."

"Think nothing of it," Eve said, trying desperately to

steady her voice. "The animal merely startled me." She smoothed down her skirts and nodded discreetly to Jean-Marie, who was firmly holding the awful creature.

Lady Caire had been watching the entire scene without comment. Now she spoke. "Butterman, I expect we're in the downstairs sitting room?"

"Indeed, my lady," Butterman replied, taking her gloves and hat. "Your footmen may make themselves at home in our kitchens."

Jean-Marie glanced at Eve and, at her nod, followed the footmen back into the house, still holding the wriggling dog.

The entryway opened into a hall, painted a soothing cream color. At the far end, the hall widened and a huge staircase could be seen, but she and Lady Caire walked only to the first door on the right. This was the sitting room, and it was already crowded with the members of the Ladies' Syndicate. A fireplace was at one end, empty now, with several settees and cushioned chairs gathered around. A low table sat in the middle of everything, crowded with tea things, while a half dozen or more little girls solemnly offered the seated ladies refreshments under the watchful eye of a blond maidservant.

"My lady, how lovely to see you." A slim woman with gorgeous red hair stood and exchanged polite cheek kisses with Lady Caire.

The older woman turned back and Eve was relieved to see that Lady Caire now smiled. "Hero, may I introduce Miss Eve Dinwoody? Miss Dinwoody, this is Lady Hero Reading."

"An honor, my lady." Eve sank into a deep curtsy as Lady Hero murmured a greeting.

She mentally went through her files and found Reading, Lady Hero: eldest sister of the Duke of Wakefield; wife of Lord Griffin Reading. Lady Hero had, along with Lady Caire, founded the Ladies' Syndicate. An important woman to know.

But then so were all the other members.

Eve braced herself as Lady Caire led her deeper into the room, intent on introducing her to everyone. That was why she was here, after all, to mingle with these ladies and meet one very specific person. That Eve rather disliked large gatherings and found herself a bit awkward when meeting strangers was beside the point.

She would do her duty.

So she smiled as Lady Caire ushered her over to a woman standing by the fireplace and introduced Eve to her daughter-in-law, Temperance Huntington, Baroness Caire. The younger Lady Caire was a lovely dark-haired lady with brown eyes so light they were nearly golden. It was hard to tell—and Eve would never ask, naturally—but Lady Caire appeared to be expecting.

Next to her was Isabel Makepeace who, along with her husband, Winter Makepeace, managed the home. Eve knew from her mental files that Mrs. Makepeace, unlike her husband, had come from the upper tiers of society. Despite her lowly status overseeing an orphanage, Mrs. Makepeace was in an exquisitely cut yellow-and-scarlet-striped robe à la française. Both ladies nodded courteously at Eve, though she noted the spark of curiosity in their eyes—the elder Lady Caire had given no explanation for her acquaintance with Eve.

The Duchess of Wakefield stood to be introduced and said, "A pleasure to meet you, Miss Dinwoody."

Eve rose from her curtsy. At first glance the duchess

was a plain woman, but her gray eyes were very fine—not to mention quite perceptive. Eve made sure to hold her gaze as she murmured her greeting.

"I'm afraid you'll be unable to meet Her Grace, the Duchess of Scarborough, as I believe she's traveling the Continent with her husband," Lady Caire said as she led Eve over to the last settee. "Italy, you know."

Eve didn't know—she'd never been to Italy or traveled merely for pleasure—but she nodded as if she did. Then she was being introduced to a dark, exotic beauty: Miss Hippolyta Royle, rumored to be the wealthiest heiress in England now that the former Lady Penelope Chadwicke had wed the Duke of Scarborough. Miss Royle stood and curtsied, though her companion on the settee did not.

"And this is Lady Phoebe Batten, sister to Lady Hero, whom you've already met, and, of course, the Duke of Wakefield," Lady Caire murmured.

Eve felt her heart jolt.

"So lovely to meet you," Lady Phoebe said, turning toward Eve. She was a pretty, petite woman, her face glowing with good humor. "I hope you don't mind if I don't rise. I'm liable to trip in a room I'm not familiar with, I'm afraid."

"Please, my lady," Eve replied. "Don't bother on my account. If—"

But her words were drowned by a commotion at the door. A lady breezed in wearing a lovely peach-colored frock, her curling hair coming down quite becomingly from her coiffure, and holding a baby in her arms.

The newcomer exclaimed rather breathlessly, "Oh, dear. I'm sorry I'm late."

The Duchess of Wakefield made a sound very close to a squeal. "Is that baby Sophia, Megs?"

Megs—Lady Margaret St. John, Eve's mental file informed her—blushed a becoming pink. "Yes. I hope no one minds that I brought her?"

Judging by the rush to surround Lady Margaret and her daughter, no one minded at all. In fact, everyone crowded round the duo save Eve and Lady Phoebe.

Eve turned back to the younger woman and said quietly, "Would you mind if I sat next to you? I'm afraid I really oughtn't have worn these heels today."

"Oh no, please." Lady Phoebe patted the place beside her, vacated by Miss Royle.

From across the room Lady Caire glanced over quickly, her eyes narrowed.

Eve ignored the look. "Thank you," she murmured as she sat. "Vanity shall be my downfall. I bought these shoes to wear to the theater last week."

Lady Phoebe turned fully toward her. "Which one?"

"*Hamlet* at the Royal." Eve shook her head. "Played by a *much*-too-old actor—he had a bit of a paunch—although he did have a lovely booming voice."

"The voice is all I care about," Lady Phoebe said on a sigh. "Though I prefer a nuanced voice rather than a simply loud one."

"Naturally," Eve replied. "Have you heard Mr. Horatio Pimsley perform?"

"Oh yes!" Lady Phoebe said, beaming. "He was a *lovely* Macbeth—or at least his voice was. I don't much like tragedies usually, but I could sit and listen to his voice all night."

Eve bit her lip, truly enjoying the discussion, but she was here with a purpose. "I wonder if you might be interested, my lady—"

Several of the ladies around the new mother laughed, interrupting her.

Lady Phoebe tilted her head toward Eve. "You can tell me: what does baby Sophia look like?"

"It's hard to tell from here," Eve replied, looking over at the baby. "She's quite crowded around. But I do see a bit of fuzz peeking out of the swaddling. She seems to have light-brown hair." She glanced at her companion. "Rather like yours, my lady."

"Does she?" Lady Phoebe's hand rose to her hair as if she could feel the color. "I'd almost forgotten."

The new mother approached with the other ladies. "Would you like to hold her, Phoebe?"

Lady Phoebe's face lit up. "Oh, might I? But do sit on the other side of me, Megs. I should hate to drop her."

"You won't," Lady Margaret said firmly. She sat on the other side of Phoebe and carefully laid the sleeping infant in Lady Phoebe's arms.

"She looks so solemn," Lady Hero whispered.

"Doesn't she?" Lady Margaret examined her offspring as if she were a strange insect found under a leaf. "She frowns just like Godric, I'm afraid. In another couple of years I'll be facing two disapproving looks across the breakfast table."

"How is he?" the younger Lady Caire asked.

"Utterly besotted by his offspring," Lady Margaret replied. "I caught him pacing the corridor the other night, Sophia in one arm, a book in his other hand. He was reading to her. In Greek. The worst part is that she seemed quite enthralled."

"I can see why." Phoebe brought the baby close to her face, closing her eyes and laying her nose gently against Sophia's cheek. "She's perfect."

Eve swallowed as she watched the other woman.

"I don't think we've met," Lady Margaret said suddenly. "No, don't get up"—this as Eve hastily began to rise—"I'm Margaret St. John."

"My fault," Lady Caire said, her smile fading. "This is Eve Dinwoody. She'd like to join the Syndicate."

"In that case I suppose we'd best get started," Lady Margaret murmured. "Come to me, baby." And she picked up Sophia and cradled her in her arms.

One of the little girls, a redhead with a quite amazing smattering of freckles across her nose, brought around a plate of what looked like rather lopsided buttered bread as the other ladies began to settle.

"Thank you . . . ?" Lady Phoebe said to the girl as she took a piece of bread.

"Hannah, ma'am." The girl tried to curtsy while still balancing the plate and Eve hastily put out a hand to steady it.

Lady Phoebe looked startled. "Not Mary Something?"

"I already had a name, ma'am, when I comed here."

"And a lovely one, too," Lady Phoebe said stoutly. "This bread is delicious, Hannah."

The little girl blushed and grinned at Lady Phoebe, and Eve felt a pang. The younger woman was so nice. Perhaps it wasn't too late to—

Lady Phoebe turned to her, still smiling from her interaction with the little girl. "You see, all of the girls at the home have the first name Mary, and all of the boys Joseph, unless of course they're old enough to *already* have a name, like Hannah. Quite confusing, even adding a different last name. I don't know who came up with the idea—"

"*Winter*," the younger Lady Caire and Mrs. Makepeace said in unison.

"He thought it was more tidy," Lady Caire continued on her own.

Mrs. Makepeace merely snorted.

Lady Phoebe smiled and turned back to Eve. "You began to say something, Miss Dinwoody, just before Sophia was brought over?"

"Yes, my lady." Eve took a deep breath. "It's just that I'm having a sort of gathering of those interested in the theater tomorrow afternoon. Just a few people to discuss the latest plays and actors. I'd be most honored if you would attend."

"I'd be delighted." Lady Phoebe smiled and popped the last bite of bread and butter in her mouth.

"My friends," Lady Caire said, standing. "We have several orders of business to attend to…"

Eve kept her eyes on her sponsor, but she listened with only half an ear.

For better or worse, she'd already gotten what she'd come for.

THE NEXT AFTERNOON Trevillion scanned a letter once more, a corner of his mouth curving up at the childish hand, before folding it carefully. He stood from the one armchair in his rooms at Wakefield House and walked to the chest of drawers on the far wall. In the top drawer was a fat bundle of letters and he slipped the new one in with the rest before closing the drawer.

He glanced at his clock. Almost time to escort Lady Phoebe to her afternoon event.

He checked his pistols, picked up his stick, and made his way downstairs. This time last year he'd commanded dozens of men—men who'd followed him without complaint or second thought. All of them might not have liked him, but they all respected him—that he'd made certain of. It'd been a good life. A life he'd been more than content with.

Now he commanded two footmen and a society lady.

Trevillion snorted softly to himself as he stepped onto the ground floor. His current position might not be terribly glorious, but he intended to carry it out to the best of his ability.

And that meant keeping Lady Phoebe safe.

Five minutes later Trevillion stood on the front step of Wakefield House and surveyed the street. The sky was spitting drops of rain, which made it easier: few people lingered outside. Two chairmen trotted by, their buckled shoes splashing through the puddles, their burden bouncing on the poles between them. The gentleman inside the convenience was quite dry, but scowled nonetheless as he went by. Wakefield House sat on a quiet square. Across the way Trevillion could see a peddler of some kind slouching in a doorway. But as he watched, the man was rousted from his shelter by a footman belonging to the house.

Trevillion grunted and pivoted carefully back to the doorway to find the Duchess of Wakefield watching him. Beside her was the elderly white lapdog she'd brought with her on her marriage. The animal's name was Bon Bon, if he recollected correctly.

"Ma'am." He bowed.

"Whatever are you doing standing in the rain, Captain Trevillion?" Her Grace inquired as her pet ventured out onto the steps. Bon Bon eyed the dripping sky, sneezed, and hastily trotted back inside.

"Simply watching, Your Grace."

"Watching?" She glanced over his shoulder and her brows knit as she looked back at him. "You're looking for kidnappers, aren't you?"

He shrugged. "It's my job to be alert to any danger to Lady Phoebe."

"The duke told me that the kidnapper was dead," she said bluntly. "Do you have reason to think otherwise?"

He hesitated, choosing his words carefully. "I am... cautious in regard to her ladyship's safety."

The duchess was a perceptive woman. "Have you told him that you still think there may be danger to Phoebe?"

"I meet with His Grace nearly every night to discuss my job."

"And?"

He met her gaze squarely. "His Grace is aware of my concern, but does not share it in this particular instance."

She looked away, biting her lip. "She hates it, you know. Phoebe, I mean, and this"—she waved a hand at the pistols strapped to his chest—"well, of course you know. You're not an insensitive man."

Trevillion waited, a little startled that she thought him sensitive. Of course he knew of Lady Phoebe's unhappiness with being guarded—with *him*. She'd made it more than plain right from the start of his employ that she hated the constraints her brother had laid upon her life. But he wouldn't let her displeasure deter him from his duty to protect her.

Let her hate him if she must, as long as she was safe.

She sighed. "If I push the point with Maximus, he might constrict her movements even more, and I don't know—I truly don't know—what she'd do then. She hides it well, but she's unhappy. I don't want to make her more so."

"Your Grace," Trevillion said quietly. "While I am with her I will make sure nothing happens to her ladyship."

Something cleared in the duchess's face. "Of course you will, Captain Trevillion."

"Artemis?" Lady Phoebe was descending the stairs inside the house.

"Yes." The duchess quickly crossed to her. "I was just speaking with Captain Trevillion."

Lady Phoebe took Her Grace's hand as she made the hallway. "Already here, Captain?"

He nodded, though she could not see. "You said you wanted to leave at two of the clock."

She wrinkled her nose. "You're always so punctual. I'm not entirely sure it's a virtue."

"I assure you, my lady, it is in a guard," Trevillion replied.

"Humph." Lady Phoebe turned to her sister-in-law and spread her arms. "What do you think of my new gown?"

The gown in question was green-blue with a yellow underskirt, and brought out the red tones in Lady Phoebe's brown hair. If the question had been aimed at him, Trevillion would've replied that she was beautiful. She was always beautiful—no matter her attire.

But the question hadn't been asked of him.

He glanced away as the carriage drew up before the steps.

Behind him Her Grace was murmuring appreciatively over the dress.

"Your carriage is here, my lady," Trevillion said, stepping forward to take Lady Phoebe's hand and place it on his arm.

"Where are you off to?" the duchess asked.

"Miss Dinwoody invited me to discuss theater with a select few of her friends," Lady Phoebe replied.

Her Grace's eyebrows winged up her forehead. "Miss Dinwoody from the Ladies' Syndicate yesterday?"

"Yes." Lady Phoebe smiled at her sister-in-law, her gaze off by several inches. "She seems a little reserved, but I quite liked her."

"As did I," the duchess said slowly.

"Artemis?"

Her Grace shook her head. "It's just... I thought it a bit odd that Lady Caire never mentioned who Miss Dinwoody's people are."

"I noticed that as well," Lady Phoebe said. "But then I realized how much we judge another person by their antecedents." She shrugged. "Perhaps it's better not to know from whence she came?"

Trevillion felt a stirring of unease. "How else to judge a person, then, my lady?"

She turned her face toward him, her lovely hazel eyes unfocused. "Perhaps simply on the person themselves? Who they are? What they do?"

She was so very young and sheltered. "Who a person is and what they do is often a product of their background and family, my lady."

"Indeed," she murmured. "Which is why I'm so interested in your own mysterious background and family, Captain Trevillion." He frowned, but before he could reply she nodded in the direction of the duchess. "If you'll excuse us, Artemis, I don't want to be late."

"Of course," that lady said. "Have a good time, dear."

Trevillion half bowed to the duchess before guiding Lady Phoebe down the front steps. "I had not thought to ask, but as the duchess seemed surprised at your outing, perhaps I should," he growled. "You *did* seek permission from your brother for this afternoon, did you not, my lady?"

Lady Phoebe entered the carriage and settled herself. She waited for him to climb in and knock on the top of the carriage to signal their readiness to the coachman before answering. "I told Maximus that I intended to visit a friend this afternoon."

The carriage lurched forward. "You didn't tell him the name of your friend?"

She pursed her lips. "He didn't ask—he was rather busy with some legal documents at the time."

"My lady—"

"Do you know how old I am, Captain?"

He frowned, then bit out, "One and twenty."

She nodded. "And *quite* out of the nursery."

"If you—"

"Do you know, I've never inquired how old *you* are, Captain."

"You're trying to change the subject," he clipped out, frustrated. "*My lady.*"

"Why, yes, I am." She smiled devastatingly and he had to look away. She was always too near, let her feelings show too easily. Did she think he was a damned eunuch? "I'm rather surprised you realized it, Captain."

There was a short silence.

Then he sighed. "I'm three and thirty."

She leaned a little forward. "So young!"

He couldn't stop a wince. How old, exactly, had she thought him?

"I'm a dozen years older than you, my lady," he said, sounding ponderous even to himself. "The same age as your brother, in fact."

The thought made him unaccountably grim.

"And yet you seem *much* older." She wrinkled her nose. "Maximus is very stern, but at least he laughs. Well, now and again. Once or twice a year, anyway. Now you, Captain, you never laugh and I doubt very much that you smile. I thought you at least fifty—"

He scowled. "My lady—"

"—or even five and fifty—"

"Phoebe."

He stopped, shocked by his use of her given name. She'd made him lose control.

She smiled very slowly, a little cat licking the cream from her chin, and he felt himself tighten. "Tell me about your family and background, *James*."

He narrowed his eyes. "You never thought me five and fifty."

She shook her head, the damnable smile still playing around those luscious lips. "No."

He looked away. For his own sanity. For his own *honor*. She was twelve years younger than he and a hundred years more innocent, the daughter and sister of a duke, fresh, gay, *beautiful*.

He had two loaded pistols, a lame leg, and a hard cock to his name. If she knew, she'd run screaming from him.

"I'm from Cornwall, my lady," he said. Calm. Controlled. Without even a hint of discomfort. "My father breeds horses. I have a sister and a niece. My mother is dead."

"I'm sorry," she said quietly, her lovely face grave, and he had the feeling she truly meant it.

"Thank you." He glanced out the window with relief, not caring if it made him a coward. She was the very *Devil*. "I believe we've arrived, my lady."

She sighed exaggeratedly. "And you've been saved once again."

He gave her a quelling look—not that it was much use on a blind woman—and preceded her out of the carriage. Trevillion glanced to the back and nodded to Reed and Hathaway, standing on the footboard. Then he turned and helped Lady Phoebe from the carriage.

They stood in front of a small town house. It wasn't in the most fashionable part of London, but the neighborhood was quite respectable. He mounted the steps with Lady Phoebe and knocked, leaning on his cane.

After a moment an enormous blackamoor answered the door, his skin gleaming ebony beneath a white wig.

"Lady Phoebe to see Miss Dinwoody," Trevillion said to the man.

The butler gave only one long glance to Trevillion's pistols before standing aside to let them in.

He led them up a polished rosewood staircase and in to the upper floor. Trevillion could hear the sound of voices and laughter as they approached an open door.

"Lady Phoebe," the butler intoned in a deep, rich voice.

There were three ladies in the room—a beautiful woman in her mid-thirties, an older woman, and a plain woman with blond hair and an overlong nose—but it was the sole gentleman who rose at once. "Miss Dinwoody, what a lovely surprise—I had no idea that Lady Phoebe was attending."

Trevillion eyed Malcolm MacLeish with dislike. He was young, handsome, and jovial.

In short, everything Trevillion was not.

Chapter Four

*The dozen brave men were transfixed by the song.
Other voices joined in, raised in sweet, dangerous
harmony. Corineus saw that maidens swam the cold
sea waves, their bodies pale, their white hair trailing
like sea-foam in the dark water. One of the sea maidens
had eyes the color of emeralds. She raised slender
arms toward him, and the prince was overcome with
the desire to touch her.
The ship began drifting toward the cliffs....*
—From *The Kelpie*

Phoebe turned in the direction of the tenor voice and
held out her hand. The gentleman took it, leaning close to
brush his lips over her knuckles. She could smell...ink,
and was it...yes! Rosewater.

She smiled. "Mr. MacLeish, I vow I never thought I'd
see you again after our meeting at Harte's Folly."

Bright, deep laughter.

Captain Trevillion's arm tensed under her fingers.

"My lady," Mr. MacLeish said, "I vow you are a sor-
ceress to've discovered my identity. Did the butler tell
you it?"

"No indeed," she replied.

"Then how——?"

She shook her head gently, enjoying herself. "Oh no, leave me a few meager secrets."

"Not meager at all," he said gallantly. "Come, let me take you from your fierce guard and introduce you to the others of Miss Dinwoody's gathering."

For a moment Captain Trevillion didn't move and she wondered if he would refuse to leave. Then he stepped back, slipping his arm out from under her hand.

She felt bereft.

"If you'll excuse me, my lady," he said in his deep voice. She couldn't help but think how grave it sounded next to Mr. MacLeish's lively words. "I'll be waiting for you downstairs. Please send a maid when you are ready to depart."

And with that his footsteps retreated.

Phoebe half turned, almost as if she meant to follow, which was simply ridiculous.

"Come. Come!" Mr. MacLeish said. "I say, do you mind if I lead you?"

"Not at all." She faced him again.

He caught her hand gently. His hand was big, the fingers long, the only callus on the first knuckle of his ring finger: a scribe's callus from holding a pen.

"Miss Dinwoody, our hostess, you already know," he was saying as he led her forward. "She sits here, to your right, facing the seat I will give you."

"I'm so glad you could attend," that lady's cool contralto sounded.

"Here, my lady. Sit here," Mr. MacLeish continued, guiding her hand to a wooden back. "Veritably the best seat in this lovely sitting room—and I should know, since I was lounging here before you entered."

She sank into what felt like an overstuffed settee. "I thank you for warming the seat, then, sir."

"I endeavor to please in all things, my lady," he replied, a ripple of laughter in his voice. "Even if it means using my least gentlemanly parts."

"Oh, Mr. MacLeish!" a second feminine voice cried to Phoebe's right. "So risqué!"

"And have you met the bewitching Mrs. Pamela Jellett?" Mr. MacLeish continued. "She shares the settee with you."

"Naughty, sir," Mrs. Jellett responded. "Such flattery to a woman of my years."

"I have indeed met Mrs. Jellett," Phoebe said. "We both attended a house party at my brother's country estate last autumn, did we not, Mrs. Jellett?"

"Yes, my lady," Mrs. Jellett said eagerly. "I believe that's where His Grace met his duchess."

"Quite so," Phoebe replied with amusement. The beginnings of Maximus and Artemis's courtship had been a bit scandalous—which Phoebe was not supposed to know, but which she most certainly did know because she was blind, not deaf. In any case she was long used to riposting little digs from such society gossips as Mrs. Jellett.

"And," Mr. MacLeish cut in hastily, "The fourth member of our party, Ann, Lady Herrick, sitting directly opposite you."

"So very pleased to meet you," Lady Herrick said, her voice high and a bit nasal.

"Now I," Mr. MacLeish said, "shall be very presumptuous and take the seat to your left so that I can gaze upon your profile and fall helplessly in love with it and you."

Phoebe laughed at that. "If a profile is all you need for love, sir, then you must go about quite drunk on that emotion."

"Hear! Hear!" Mrs. Jellett clapped her hands. "A fine comeback from the feminine front. What have you to say for yourself now, Mr. MacLeish?"

"Only that I'm outflanked, outranked, and outgunned by the company here," Mr. MacLeish replied, laughing. "Perhaps I should at once fashion a white flag from my cravat?"

"Hmm, and whilst you're busy with that," Miss Dinwoody murmured, "perhaps I can offer Lady Phoebe some refreshment. Would you care for tea, my lady?"

"Yes, please," Phoebe replied. "Sugar, no milk."

She heard the silver and china clink. "I also have here some seedcake and an almond tart. What would you like?"

"A bit of the seedcake, please."

"It's very good," Lady Herrick said. "You must give me the recipe so I can show it to my cook."

"It would be my pleasure," Miss Dinwoody said. "Now here's your cake"—Phoebe felt a small plate laid gently in her hands—"and your tea is just in front of you, slightly on your right."

"Thank you." Phoebe felt with her fingertips, first the table edge and then the teacup. She picked it up and took a sip. Just right.

"Mr. MacLeish was telling us about the repairs to Harte's Folly before you arrived," Miss Dinwoody said.

Harte's Folly had been the preeminent pleasure garden in London before it burned to the ground the year before. The garden had been known not only for its winding paths where lovers might meet but also for its theater and opera house—all gone now, much to Phoebe's disappointment.

"Do you think it can be fully restored?" she asked.

"Oh, most definitely," Mr. MacLeish said at once. "The garden is coming along nicely under the supervision of Lord Kilbourne. He's actually managed to plant full-grown trees, can you imagine?"

There were murmurs of wonder from the ladies.

"And I've finished drawing up my plans for the new buildings," Mr. MacLeish continued. Of course! He was the architect for Harte's Folly, which explained both the scribe's callus on his finger and the scent of ink he always carried about him. "Mr. Harte has contracted me to build a grand theater house, an outdoor musician's gallery with boxes for the summer months, and several amusing follies to be set here and there throughout the grounds."

"It sounds lovely," Phoebe said, a little wistfully, for however nice the plans were, if they hadn't started building it would be at least another couple of months before the gardens would be fit to reopen.

Mr. MacLeish's voice was grave for the first time since she'd entered the room. "It'll be more than lovely, I assure you, my lady. Mr. Harte plans to make Harte's Folly the grandest amusement in all the world. He's brought in tilers from Italy, stone carvers from France, and wood carvers from strange little princedoms in the far wilds of the Continent. I can't understand a word they say, but the things they make are wondrous. And now he says he'll hire dozens, nay hundreds, of workmen, all so that my buildings will be finished by the autumn season."

"So soon?" Mrs. Jellett gasped. "I don't believe it, sir. It simply cannot be done."

"And yet he plans to," Mr. MacLeish assured that lady. "By Christmas all of you will have seen and been amazed by a theatrical production at Harte's Folly. My word upon it."

"Then I shall be very happy indeed, Mr. MacLeish," Phoebe said. "I fear that I've missed Harte's Folly most grievously. I've enjoyed the other theaters in town, naturally, but they haven't the air of a fairyland that Harte's Folly has."

"Oh, I do agree," Lady Herrick said. "I like the Royal, but it's so dark inside and quite a cramped space, don't you think?"

"It was built for Lilliputians, I vow," Mrs. Jellett sniffed.

"The actors' voices seem to be dampened by the building," Phoebe said. She turned to Mr. MacLeish. "I hope your new buildings will let the music and the actors' voices expand, sir. The best buildings do this, I find."

"I promise they will, my lady," Mr. MacLeish said. "In fact... if you won't think me presumptuous, would you be interested in visiting the gardens?"

"Oho!" Mrs. Jellett chortled. "Do beware, my lady. Mr. MacLeish may sound the innocent, but he's just as much the devil as any gentleman."

"He's not so wicked as all that," Lady Herrick said. She sounded amused. "I've met much worse, I assure you."

"Never fear, ladies," Phoebe replied. "I always have my guard with me, by decree of my brother."

"It sounds like your brother cares very much for you," Miss Dinwoody murmured.

"Yes, it does sound that way, doesn't it?" Phoebe replied lightly. She turned her face toward where she thought Mr. MacLeish sat. She knew very well what Maximus would think about a trip to an abandoned pleasure garden so soon after the kidnapping attempt. She also knew that if she didn't have a chance to be free—just a little bit—she might very well explode. "I would very much like to visit Harte's Folly again."

TREVILLION SET HIS empty teacup down on the kitchen table and nodded to the cook, a buxom woman with pink cheeks and a cloud of red-blond hair. "Thank you."

She bobbed a shy curtsy. "M' pleasure, sir." The poor woman hadn't known what to make of his invading her kitchen domain.

Trevillion grimaced wryly to himself as he got laboriously to his feet with the aid of his cane. The little maid who'd come to fetch him gave him an uncertain glance before turning to lead him down the back hallway.

Neither fish nor fowl, was he? His position was paid, but he wasn't quite a servant and therein lay the problem: servants didn't know how to treat him. Which had made the last couple of hours in the kitchen rather awkward— not to mention boring. He should've brought a book.

The maid mounted the stairs and Trevillion suppressed a sigh. Upstairs the ladies had come out onto the landing as they said their good-byes to their hostess. Miss Dinwoody was the blond woman he'd noticed when he'd escorted Lady Phoebe in to the tea. Miss Dinwoody looked to be somewhere in her twenties—generally much too young to have her own establishment. Curious, but Trevillion saw no sign of an older female relative to keep her company. She was fair, but not beautiful—her features, especially her long nose, too prominent for loveliness.

Lady Phoebe was flushed a becoming pink with excitement and she was smiling in amusement as Malcolm MacLeish bent over her hand.

Trevillion had a sudden rather violent urge to strike the man across the back of the head with his stick.

"Tomorrow, then?" MacLeish said.

"I look forward to it," Lady Phoebe replied.

"My lady," Trevillion interrupted.

She turned to him and her smile dimmed just a little.

His withered old heart didn't crack at all. "If you're quite ready, my lady."

"Of course, Captain Trevillion," she said to him. She turned her face back to the sitting room doorway where the other ladies were congregated. "Thank you so much for inviting me, Miss Dinwoody. I enjoyed myself enormously."

For a second a strange emotion crossed Miss Dinwoody's face—one that Trevillion couldn't quite decipher.

Then it was gone. "Thank you for attending my little party, my lady."

They turned and Trevillion guided Lady Phoebe to the stairs. "The first step is just here," he murmured as they neared.

She nodded, saying nothing, and they descended in silence, Trevillion alert. Stairs were always a challenge—not just because of his leg but because the consequences should his charge miss a step would be catastrophic. He lived in fear of her falling to her death down a staircase, though to date she'd never even stumbled while in his presence.

When they made the lower level Trevillion nodded to the butler and then they were at the outer door. The weather had turned worse, the rain coming down steadily now.

"A moment, my lady. It's raining." He motioned to Reed, out by the carriage.

"Mmm. I can hear and smell it." She tilted up her face

as if she could drink in the sound of the rain and he smiled, tempted to linger and simply watch her.

The footman came running from the carriage.

"Your coat, if you please, Reed," Trevillion ordered.

"Oh no," Lady Phoebe began, but Reed had already stripped off the coat to hold it over her head.

"This is his job, my lady," Trevillion said. He gave an approving nod to Reed and then they were carefully making their way down the front steps.

The carriages for the other guests were lined up farther along the street. There was a flurry of movement as footmen ran out to shield their mistresses and the ladies picked up their skirts, exclaiming at the rain.

A bright-pink coat brushed by as they hastened to the carriage. Trevillion looked up sharply and felt a small jolt at meeting a pair of familiar blue eyes.

"Captain." The other man nodded, his mouth twisting in sardonic amusement.

"Your Grace," Trevillion replied.

The man flashed a grin and turned to run to Miss Dinwoody's town house.

Lady Phoebe tilted her head back and sniffed. "Amber and...jasmine, if I'm not mistaken. Who was that?"

Trevillion's eyes narrowed in speculation as he watched the pink-silk-clad back nimbly leap the front steps. "The Duke of Montgomery, my lady."

"Really?" she asked innocently. "I wonder what he's doing in this part of town?"

What indeed? "Come," he said. "The carriage step is just here."

Reed was holding open the door of the carriage. Trevillion held her elbow firmly as she mounted the step.

He glanced over his shoulder.

The door to Miss Dinwoody's house had opened, but it was Malcolm MacLeish who stood there, not the blackamoor butler.

MacLeish frowned at Montgomery. "What are you doing here?"

"Checking on my investment," the duke drawled. "It's raining, MacLeish. Let me in and put a civil tongue in your head while you're at it."

Both men disappeared inside.

"Are you coming?" Lady Phoebe called from inside the carriage. "You're letting the rain in."

"I apologize, my lady," he murmured as he settled himself then knocked his cane against the carriage roof.

The conveyance rocked forward.

"You're the most exasperating man, you know," Lady Phoebe said conversationally.

"Hmm," Trevillion replied distractedly.

He rubbed the calf of his lame leg. The damp, cold weather was making it ache. He could think of several reasons Valentine Napier, the Duke of Montgomery, might be visiting Miss Dinwoody.

Sadly, not one of them was good.

"I think you're doing it apurpose," Lady Phoebe muttered darkly.

Trevillion pulled himself from his musings to attend to matters closer at hand. "I beg your pardon, my lady. I couldn't help but notice that you had made plans with Mr. MacLeish. Might I hear what they are?"

She wrinkled her nose so adorably that he found himself catching his breath. "I'm meeting him at Harte's Folly tomorrow afternoon."

He straightened at the information. "I don't think—"

"If you remember, that's where I met Mr. MacLeish in the first place—when *you* brought me to Harte's Folly several months ago."

"I was there about business," he said stiffly. "And if you recall, it wasn't entirely my idea that you accompany me. My lady."

She waved an airy hand. "Pishposh. Mr. MacLeish said he'd show me the new plantings and where he plans to build his theater. I'm going and that's final."

"Not," he growled, "if I make your brother aware of your intentions."

"Sometimes I simply loathe you, you know," she breathed, her color high.

His heart stumbled. "Yes, I am aware, my lady."

"I don't..." She shook her head. "I don't mean it like that. You know that, James."

Why was she calling him by his Christian name? The last time, in the carriage earlier, had been to goad him, he knew. This time...he had no idea what she could mean by it. Perhaps nothing at all. Perhaps it was just another of her many whims, something he should just ignore. If it weren't for the fact that every time she used his Christian name he felt a jolt somewhere in his chest. No one had called him by his first name in *years*.

Which was probably why his next words came out sounding especially cold. "It hardly matters what you think of me, my lady—"

"Doesn't it?"

"No. Because however you feel about me, I shall continue to protect you. No matter what, my lady."

"Well," she said, and oddly enough his nearly cruel

words had made her perk up. "We'll just have to see about that, won't we?"

THAT EVENING PHOEBE descended the stairs to dinner accompanied by two dogs. One of Maximus's greyhounds pressed against her left side and Bon Bon, Artemis's fluffy little lapdog, pranced about her feet.

"Careful, my lady," came the voice of her guardian from behind her on the stairs.

Phoebe felt her heart leap a little, as if she'd missed a step, though she most definitely hadn't.

She clutched the marble railing. "I'm always careful."

"Not always, I'm afraid, my lady." His voice was closer and she heard the thump of his cane on the marble of the steps.

"Perhaps you ought to be careful yourself, Captain," she said as she continued her descent. "These stairs can't be good for your leg."

In a rare instance of thinking before she spoke, she didn't tell him she could hear that his limp was heavier after he'd been on the stairs.

Naturally he didn't reply to that. Instead he said, "Shoo."

She stopped. "I beg your pardon?"

"Shoo," he repeated, even more sternly.

She heard the scamper of dog claws on marble as both animals went on ahead of her. "Why did you do that? I like Bon Bon and Belle."

"Actually, I think that was Starling, my lady," Trevillion replied. "And though they like you as well, it wouldn't stop them from accidentally tripping you."

She sighed heavily in lieu of an answer and stepped down onto the ground floor. "Will you be dining with us tonight,

Captain?" She held out her hand and his left arm immediately slipped beneath her fingers, solid and warm. "I believe that Maximus has deigned to drag himself away from whatever business he's preoccupied with at the moment and will be with us tonight. He'll need your masculine support."

"Very well, then, my lady," Trevillion replied. "I shall attend dinner."

"Lovely." She grinned, feeling giddy for no reason at all, really. Trevillion might not dine with them all that often, but she did spend time with him every day.

And since when had dining with her *guard* made her lighthearted?

He ushered her into the dining room and Phoebe immediately heard Artemis's and Cousin Bathilda's voices. "Is Maximus here yet?"

"Yes, Phoebe, I am," her brother's deep voice came from the head of the table.

"And a good thing, too," Artemis said serenely. "I was contemplating setting fire to your study."

"You'd have help from me if you did," Cousin Bathilda announced.

"Pax, ladies," Maximus said. He sounded in good cheer this evening, Phoebe thought as Trevillion helped her to sit to the left of her brother. Trevillion himself was on her own left. "We have both pheasant and salmon to feast on tonight. Let us enjoy."

Phoebe felt for the table's edge and then her plate. There was a shallow bowl on the plate and she realized she'd already been served the soup.

"And what did you do today, my wife?" Maximus began in what Phoebe privately thought of as his Member of Parliament Voice.

"I did some shopping and then visited Lily in the afternoon." Lily was Artemis's new sister-in-law, recently married to her twin brother, Apollo.

"And how is she?"

"She's started writing a new play."

"Oh, has she?" Phoebe cut in. "How marvelous! What's it about?"

"She wouldn't tell me." Artemis sounded a bit peeved. Few people turned down a duchess. "But she's been writing furiously. There was a smudge of ink on her forehead when I went to see her, and their dog—you remember Daffodil?"

"I do indeed." Daffodil had attacked her knees when she'd gone to Harte's Folly last. Phoebe took a sip of the soup and found it to be a lovely oxtail.

"Daffodil had ink all down her tail for some reason."

Phoebe smiled at the thought. "I shall have to tell Miss Dinwoody that Lily is writing again. We were just discussing her today. Mr. MacLeish was quite disappointed that Lily had decided to retire from the stage in favor of her writing."

She took another sip of soup and was savoring it so much that it was a moment before she realized the table had gone silent.

"Who," her brother said, sounding as if he were at least five and eighty and near apoplexy to boot, "are Mr. MacLeish and Miss Dinwoody?"

She put down her soup spoon carefully. "He's the architect designing the new buildings for Harte's Folly. He was at Miss Dinwoody's tea. Or rather salon, I think. It was such an interesting discussion! All about the latest plays and the actors and who was arguing with whom and the soprano who is under the protection of a royal duke but might be in love with her theater manager."

She stopped suddenly to take a deep breath.

"Phoebe," Maximus said slowly, and her heart absolutely sank. "You haven't told me who Miss Dinwoody is."

"We met her at the Ladies' Syndicate," Artemis hastily cut in. "You remember I told you about the new prospect Lady Caire brought to the meeting?"

"I remember you told me she had no background, no people," Maximus said.

Phoebe could feel the pressure, just under her breastbone, bubbling up. "What does that matter? Why do you have to know the background of everyone I meet?"

"It matters," he snapped back, "because you are my sister and for all we know she's a kept woman herself."

"Oh, now Maximus," Cousin Bathilda objected. "Surely not if she's a protégée of Lady Caire's."

"I blame you, Trevillion—"

"Oh no you don't!" Phoebe was shaking now. "I'll not have you shoving my actions onto him as if I'm an idiot."

"Then perhaps you shouldn't act like an idiot—"

"By going to *tea* with a *friend*?"

"A friend we don't know—"

"You mean *you* don't know," Phoebe said, her heart beating faster and faster.

"What difference—"

"Because I don't care, Maximus. I don't bloody *care* where Miss Dinwoody came from!" She heard a sharp inhalation from someone, but she couldn't stop. She loved her brother—he was years older than she and had always cared for and protected her, but she simply couldn't stand this anymore. The frustration, the fear, and the anger were all frothing up, steaming over, burning everything in their path. She stood, knocking something off the table. China smashed on the floor. "She's my friend, not yours, Maximus, and I deserve friends. I deserve to run and trip and fall without having my every move plotted and planned and...and *tied down* so that I never, ever risk *living*. I've never—"

"Phoebe, you know that—"

"*Don't interrupt me!*" Her screamed words were loud and terrible and hurt her throat. "I never even had a damned *season*. No new gowns, no new friends, no new *beaux*. You wouldn't let me. You keep me hidden and swathed like an elderly aunt with dementia. It's a wonder I *haven't* gone insane in the last several years." She laughed, wild and unseemly, bile pouring from her mouth. "I can't breathe, do you understand me? You can't do this to me anymore, Maximus, you simply can't! I loathe what you've made me into and, Maximus, soon—very soon— I'll loathe *you*, too."

Her chest was heaving, her face hot and wet with tears, her breath rasping in her throat. She stood for a moment, no doubt looking like a deranged woman, but it didn't matter, did it? She couldn't *see* what she looked like.

She sobbed a laugh at the thought, the sound loud in the sudden silence.

"Phoebe," Artemis whispered.

She thought she felt masculine fingers on her wrist— from her left, not her right. Trevillion.

But it was too late now. Much too late.

She turned and ran from the room.

Chapter Five

*Near the shore were sharp rocks and the ship
broke upon them, casting the enthralled men into
the merciless sea. Each one of the dozen brave
men was caught and dragged deep, deep below by
the sea maidens. But as the emerald-eyed maiden
reached for Corineus, pity flickered across her pale
face. As Corineus watched, she turned into a great
white horse with cloven hooves, sharp fangs, and
eyes of deepest green....*
—From *The Kelpie*

Trevillion watched Lady Phoebe rush from the room and
tamped down an urge to punch her brother.

"I'll go after her," the duchess said, rising.

"No." Everyone in the room looked at him. Trevillion
inclined his head. "Please, Your Grace. I'll go."

She stared at him a moment, her gray eyes unnerv-
ingly perceptive, before she reseated herself. "Very well,
Captain."

The duke's fists were clenched on top of the table, his
knuckles white. "Trevillion—"

His wife placed her hand on one of his fists and simply looked at him. Apparently they shared some sort of

marital communication that was purely mental, for after a moment the duke grunted, his grip relaxing, and nodded.

Trevillion rose at once, his stick thumping against the floor as he tracked his charge.

There was no sign of her in the hallway. She might've fled upstairs to her rooms, but he rather thought not.

He turned to the back of the house, toward the garden.

Outside, the sun had long set. Trevillion made his way down the wide granite steps, still damp from this afternoon's shower, and into the grass before her flower garden. He could see, just dimly, a pale shape standing very still in front of the garden.

Lady Phoebe had worn a white dress to dinner.

"My lady," he called low, careful not to startle her.

The shape turned.

"Have they sent you after me, Captain?" Her voice was thick from weeping.

The thought made his chest tighten. She saw him as the enemy, he knew—her brother's creature, her keeper—but he couldn't help but want—*need*—to try to make it better.

She shouldn't feel like a caged bird, not his Phoebe.

"I came of my own volition." He had caught up to her now and could see the pale moon of her face, upturned toward his.

"Truly?" She wiped at her cheek like a little girl.

The problem was, she wasn't a little girl anymore. And no matter how he'd tried, he'd never thought of her as one. "Truly."

She sighed forlornly. "Will you walk with me?"

"Yes, my lady."

She laid her hand on his arm. "I suppose I ought to go in and apologize to Maximus."

He didn't reply, but privately he thought that there was no pressing need for her to do so.

The gravel grated under his boots.

"Careful," she warned. "There's a turn just here."

And he realized with a sense of amusement that in this place at this time she was the one who led, not he. "Thank you, my lady."

"Not at all, Captain."

The scent of roses, heady and nearly overwhelming, washed over his senses, and he knew at once where they were. At the back of the garden was a bower overgrown with white roses, the blooms full and heavy, hanging luxuriously. It was a sweet place in the day.

At night it was a wonderland.

"Let's sit." Lady Phoebe's voice was still hoarse from shouting.

He lowered himself to the stone bench that sat beneath the bower, stretching out his lame leg to give it ease. Lady Phoebe settled next to him, a discreet couple of inches between them.

He saw the movement in the dark as she tipped back her head, her face raised to the roses. "Do you ever feel constrained?"

"Of course, my lady."

"Really?" She turned to him. "How strange. I've always thought a man like you—capable, intelligent, and with a strong will—would simply do as he liked."

"Everyone has times or situations when they are not allowed to do something, my lady," he said gently. "Those who are not born into ducal families most especially, perhaps."

She snorted. "You must think me naïve."

"No, my lady. Merely young."

"And you are an ancient Methuselah, so wise and worn from all your labors."

"I fear you mock my gray hairs, my lady," he said.

"You don't have gray hairs!" She sounded quite indignant.

"I vow I do, my lady."

"I'll ask Artemis tomorrow, you know, and she'll tell me if you do or not."

"And yet I do not fear Her Grace's information."

"No, of course you don't." She huffed a laugh. "I'm beginning to think you don't fear anything at all."

"In that you would be wrong, my lady," he said, remembering the shame he'd felt when last he'd seen his childhood home.

There was a pause and he wondered where her quicksilver mind had darted.

Her voice whispered in the darkness, "When were you not allowed to do something, James?"

His name on her lips made the hairs stand up on the back of his neck. He inhaled...and found himself telling her honestly. "Years ago. I wanted to stay in Cornwall, but...circumstances made that impossible. So I was forced to join the dragoons."

She shifted closer, her shoulder brushing his. "What circumstances?"

He shook his head. That old tragedy was too personal and brought nothing but painful memories.

She couldn't see the movement, but she must've realized that he wasn't going to answer that. "But you didn't want to join the dragoons?"

"No."

"How strange," she breathed. "I always had the notion that you loved being a soldier."

"I did, but not at first." He remembered that wild despair. His firm resolve to take the only action left to him. "I never wanted to be a soldier. It was a cruel blow, but in the end I did learn to like my service."

She leaned back against the bench. "There were the horses. I would think that would help."

He peered at her, but the darkness thwarted his attempt to see her face. How had she known that he loved horses? "They did," he said slowly. "That and the men. They came from all over England, but we found a common ground in fighting the iniquities of St Giles."

"Do you miss it?"

"Yes." He closed his eyes and inhaled the scent of roses and things lost. But that was maudlin. He wasn't a man to spend his life looking backward. "I can still ride, though. Despite the leg. Despite the pain. For that I am grateful."

She exhaled. "And I can still garden. Despite the loss of my sight. Should I be grateful for that?"

He knew he should step carefully, but perhaps that was part of the problem: others treated her with kid gloves. Didn't give her the respect of adulthood. "Yes, I think you should be grateful for whatever you can still do. For whatever new things you might find you can do."

"I am grateful," she admitted. "But I want more. So much more."

"Your sight."

"No." Her voice was loud with her vehemence. "I know I will never regain my sight. There's no use endlessly pining for it—I already spent years doing that. Maximus brought in doctors from all over Europe and beyond. I was dosed with the most hideous potions, had stinging drops placed in my eyes, took baths in freezing water and hot concoctions, and each time I thought: maybe this time. Maybe my sight will return. Maybe just a little—a little, *please God*, I would be content with a little. Only it never did. Not even a little."

He swallowed, his muscles tensing as if he could rescue her from torture long past. "And now?"

"Now," she said, her voice sweet, seductive, mingling with the scent of the roses. "Now I want to *live*, James. I want to ride a horse again. I want to go where I will. I want to meet a gentleman and be courted and marry and have children—lots of children. Shouldn't I be allowed that at least?"

He remembered MacLeish from that afternoon. Handsome, the white of his teeth flashing as he'd grinned, so bright with his red hair clubbed back. Lady Phoebe had been smiling when Trevillion had come to fetch her.

MacLeish was perfect for her.

"Yes," he said, his voice hoarse, his chest aching as if he'd taken a shot to the heart. "Yes, you deserve that and more."

PHOEBE INHALED THE scent of roses, listening to Captain Trevillion's deep rasp. He sounded wrong somehow. Perhaps angry? She shook her head. She simply couldn't tell without seeing his face. Maybe he didn't really approve her desires, despite his words.

"Don't you want that as well?" she appealed to him. "A wife? A home? A family?"

She felt the movement as he stiffened next to her. "I hadn't thought the matter over, my lady."

His tone was dismissive, which lit something within her—a spark of…of…*outrage* perhaps, at such a blatant lie.

"Never?" she asked incredulously. "You're a man in your prime, Captain, and yet you'd have me believe that you've never thought of the comforts of a warm home, a warm *wife*?"

"My lady, I've spent the last several years of my life in hard work. I haven't had the time—"

A thought struck her and she bit her lip. "Unless you're one of those gentlemen who prefer the company of other gentlemen."

There was a short, tense silence.

Really, come to think of it, she'd never heard Captain Trevillion pay attention to any lady—other than herself, of course.

"No, my lady," he bit out, sounding exasperated. "I am not such a gentleman."

Wondrous the relief she felt, quite out of all proportion to the information. Well, anyone would, surely? The life of a gentleman who preferred other gentlemen was not always an easy one. Obviously *that* was her main concern. As a *friend*—

"We *are* friends, aren't we, Captain?"

"I am your guard against danger, hired by your brother, therefore—"

He was so terribly pompous when he wanted to be! "*Friends?*"

A very heavy sigh. "If you wish to consider us so, then yes, we are friends, my lady."

"I *am* glad," she said, giving a little bounce on the bench. "Then as a friend tell me: you have courted ladies before, haven't you?"

Perhaps he was simply socially awkward, poor man.

"Though it isn't any of your concern, my lady," he said, his voice so low it sounded like a growl, "and it's quite improper to be having this discussion at all, yes, I have . . . *courted* females before."

She pursed her lips. His emphasis on the word *courted* made it sound almost as if he meant something else entirely. Perhaps the females he'd been in association with hadn't been ladies at all and he was too circumspect to tell her about it. He probably thought she had no idea about such things.

Being younger than nearly everyone else could be very trying sometimes.

"You know I *have* heard of ladies of easy virtue before," she informed him kindly.

He made a choking sound. "My lady—"

"Call me Phoebe," she said impulsively.

"I will not."

"You did so once before."

"And that was a mistake, my lady."

"Very well. Are you interested in anyone right now?"

"I think this particular line of inquiry is over, my lady."

She shook her head, sighing, and as she did so, her hand brushed against her skirts and the lump in her pocket. "Oh, I forgot."

"Forgot what?" He sounded very suspicious.

She slipped her fingers through the slit at the side of her skirts and into the pocket hanging from her waist. Inside was a small stoppered bottle.

She held it up triumphantly. "This might help in your search."

"I'm not actually searching, my lady."

She ignored him and gingerly pried the cork stopper loose from the bottle. Immediately the scent of bergamot and sandalwood filled the bower.

"What is that?" he asked flatly, though any simpleton could've told him and whatever else he was, Captain Trevillion certainly wasn't a *simpleton*.

"Perfume," she said. "For you."

"I don't wear perfume."

"I know, and it makes it terribly hard to find you in a room sometimes, particularly if you're not moving," she said. "Besides, ladies *like* perfume."

He was silent for a moment as if digesting this information.

"I had it especially made," she said enticingly, "by Mr. Hainsworth on Bond Street. He's ever so clever with perfumes, and this one is very nice, I think. Not sweet. Not really floral at all. Quite manly. I think you'll like it, but if you don't we can try another. Perfumes do rather change after you've worn them awhile."

"Very well," he said abruptly.

"Lovely," she said. "Now hold still."

"You intend to put it on me now?"

Her lips twitched. She would've sworn that was alarm she heard in Captain James Trevillion's voice—and she'd never heard it there before. Not even when armed men had come after her.

"Yes," she said, placing her fingertips at the bottle's opening and tipping it so that the perfume wet her skin. She reached up, sandalwood and roses filling her senses, and touched him.

Touched the bare skin of his face.

Her breath stuttered.

She'd touched very few men in her life. Her brother...

she couldn't think of any others, really. Her mind seemed to be slowing.

She felt stubble under her fingertips, almost tickling, as she stroked down. There was a chin, the edge of his jaw.

She inhaled, drawing her hand back to wet her fingertips again with the perfume, now heady in the air.

His breathing was very quiet.

She reached out again... and touched something soft. Oh, his lips!

"I'm sorry," she whispered, moving her fingertips down under his chin where the stubble was heavier.

A third time she wet her fingers and this time when she touched him, she knew she'd found his throat, warm and living. She stroked slowly down, her fingers trailing over his Adam's apple.

It flexed as he swallowed.

Lower, to the smooth skin at the base of his neck.

Her fingertips met his cravat, a maddening barrier, and she stroked along it, dipping her fingertip just a little beneath the cloth.

She realized suddenly that she'd quite passed the bounds of propriety.

Shaking, she drew her hand away and stoppered the little bottle. "Well. That's done."

He didn't reply and she wished very much that he would.

She held out the bottle, waiting for a long second for him to take it.

His warm, big hand closed around hers and she felt it suddenly, his moist breath across her lips. He was close, so very close, and she could smell bergamot and sandalwood and roses and wine, everything mingling together to make a heady elixir.

She froze, waiting, *wanting*.

But he drew back, taking the bottle of perfume with him, and stood in a rustle of clothing. "Come, my lady, it's time to go in."

And really, there wasn't any reason at all to feel disappointment. He was her bodyguard, nothing more.

Even if she no longer saw him in that light at all.

THE SUN SHONE brightly on the putrid waters of the Thames the next morning as Trevillion, Lady Phoebe, Reed, and Hathaway crossed to the south bank in a long flat boat.

"Your brother won't like this, my lady," Trevillion muttered. He'd voiced the sentiment twice already and yet here he was. He ought to question his sanity.

"It's only Harte's Folly." Lady Phoebe's face was turned to the wind and the far shore as if she could see it. She wore a bright-pink dress trimmed in white lace, which made her look particularly young and innocent—and made him feel particularly old and cynical. "There won't be anyone about save the workmen. And you've brought both Reed and Hathaway with their pistols and yours. Really, Captain, there's no reason to fret so."

And yet he did. "Bond Street seemed perfectly safe, too."

"Thank you for allowing me to come." She placed her soft palm atop his hand. "I do so want to see the gardens."

"And Mr. MacLeish, my lady?" He couldn't help asking. Damn him for a jealous old man.

She turned her bright smile on him. "Yes, of course. He says the most amusing things. I quite like him."

He withdrew his hand from hers. "I hope, then, that his amusing conversation is worth the trip, my lady." What a pompous ass he sounded.

"You're very kind to indulge me, Captain," she said, trailing her fingertips in the water. "I think I would've gone mad if you hadn't."

And that was the problem. He'd let her talk him into this trip. Let his sympathy for her overturn his own best judgment on the matter. Trevillion glanced sideways at Reed, wondering if the man had lost all respect for him, but the footman was watching the shore stoically. Next to him Hathaway fiddled nervously with his pistol. The footman had said he could shoot a pistol, but Trevillion wondered if he could do so with any accuracy.

The wherry bumped against the Harte's Folly dock. Last time they'd been here the dock had been barely standing. Now a sturdy new dock had been erected, with several places for passengers to disembark.

"We're here, my lady," Trevillion said, though she probably had guessed when the boat jolted. "Reed, please get out first so that you can assist her ladyship."

The footman nimbly scrambled up the steps attached to the dock and then helped Lady Phoebe out of the wherry. Hathaway came next and Trevillion last, hindered by his lame leg. Just beyond the dock was a clearing and beyond that what appeared to be a tangle of half-burnt trees and shrubs.

"Mr. MacLeish said he'd meet me at the site of the old theater," Lady Phoebe said. "Apparently they've already torn it down."

Trevillion nodded, offering his arm as they made their way along a path deeper into the destroyed garden. The two footmen trailed close behind.

"Can you tell me how it looks now?" Phoebe asked.

Trevillion cleared his throat, glancing around. In truth

the garden was still a very long way from being restored. Green now covered the trees and shrubs that remained, but underneath were fire-blackened limbs, and the smell of soot still lingered in the air.

"The path has been cleared of debris from the fire," he said carefully, "and properly leveled and graveled, my lady. Perhaps you feel it beneath your feet?"

"Yes, it's much more even now."

Trevillion had never attended the pleasure garden before the fire that had destroyed it, but there were signs of what it might've been. What it might be in the future.

"There are plantings along the path," he said. "Some type of bush, I think, in a row."

"Hedges," Lady Phoebe supplied. "They used to line the paths, directing the visitors."

"Quite." He looked up. "A few rather large trees have been planted since we last came. Deciduous, I believe."

She cocked her head in interest. "How large?"

"Twenty feet at least," he said with some curiosity. "However were they planted?"

"Lord Kilbourne has been experimenting with transplanting young trees," she replied. "At least that's what Artemis says."

"As far as I can see he's been successful, my lady."

"Are there any flowers?"

"Yes, daisies and something tall and thinnish with blue flowers."

She gave him a look, which proved quite effective though she was blind. "Let me feel."

He stopped and guided her hand to the flowers.

"Bellflowers?" she murmured to herself, touching the blooms and stem gently. "No, larkspur, I think. How nice, though it doesn't have much of a scent." She straightened and smiled up at him. "I'm so glad you've worn the perfume I gave you last night."

"Of course, my lady." He glanced at the footmen, who were studiously looking the other way. "Perhaps you ought to scent-mark Reed and Hathaway as well?"

Reed shot him a wide-eyed look, but Lady Phoebe waved the suggestion away. "No need. It's only you I need to keep track of."

Her words warmed something in his chest, made him blink and look away. *I'm no longer a fit guard*, he thought, *I can't keep my objectivity around her anymore. God help me. God help her.*

He'd have to tell the duke. Soon. He was no longer able—

"Goddamn it, MacLeish!" The irate shout interrupted his near-desperate thoughts. "I don't care what that conniving fop said, it's *my* garden and I'll have the final say on the bloody theater plans!"

Their party rounded one of the newly planted trees and the source of the shouting was immediately apparent.

Mr. Harte, the owner of Harte's Folly, stood, legs spread, fists on hips, and face reddened from anger, confronting Malcolm MacLeish. He wore a gaudy scarlet coat trimmed in gold, the seams straining across his massive shoulders. His head was bare, the sun glinting on shoulder-length tawny-brown hair.

MacLeish had his arms crossed defensively as he faced the other man, but he dropped his arms and straightened when he saw Phoebe.

Harte turned at MacLeish's movement. His scowl immediately transformed into a slightly over-genial smile at the sight of Lady Phoebe, but when he glanced at Trevillion the smile dimmed. "Captain Trevillion! What brings you to my gardens—and with such a lovely companion?"

"Harte." Trevillion nodded. He'd met the man only once or twice, and then not under the best of circumstances. "This is Lady Phoebe Batten, the sister of the Duke of Wakefield."

"My lady," Harte said, bowing low. "I'm honored by your presence in my gardens, though I fear it's not yet in the best of shape for a lady to see."

"Well then, it's just as well that I'm blind," Lady Phoebe replied easily.

Astonishment was clear on Harte's face for a moment. To his credit, though, it was short-lived. "Would you like me to guide you about my garden, my lady? I'd be honored to do so."

At Harte's offer, MacLeish cleared his throat. "Actually, *I* invited Lady Phoebe to come see our progress. Besides, did you not say that you meant to meet with a new actress?"

Harte looked alarmed at the reminder. "Damn me, I'd nearly forgotten. I must go, my lady, but you're in capable hands with Mr. MacLeish. And Malcolm"—Harte gave the younger man an unsmiling glance—"we'll continue this discussion tomorrow, yes?"

"Yes, sir," MacLeish replied, looking nervous.

Harte nodded and strode off down the path toward the river.

MacLeish seemed to breathe a sigh of relief as soon as the other man was gone.

He turned to Phoebe. "Welcome, my lady. I'd begun to fear you would not come." The man's red hair shone in the sun, bright and youthful, not a gray hair in sight.

Damn him.

"Did you think I'd forget your invitation?" Lady Phoebe smiled, a dimple flashing beside her lush mouth.

She took her hand from Trevillion's arm, holding it out to the architect.

MacLeish bent over her hand, his lips brushing her knuckles. Trevillion wished he could knock the other man's touch away from her. MacLeish's grass-green suit complemented the deep-pink gown Lady Phoebe wore.

Trevillion stepped back.

They looked a perfect couple.

"I'm so glad you're here, my lady," MacLeish said, glancing up at her from his bow. "Come. Let me show you what I plan."

She linked her arm with his.

As they turned, Trevillion fell into step a discreet distance behind them.

MacLeish bent his head to hers, but his voice still carried. "Is it necessary that your guards follow you so close?"

"Well…"

"Yes," Trevillion growled. It mattered not that she might wish him elsewhere. His job was to guard her.

"Then I welcome your three chaperones, my lady," MacLeish replied in an amused tone. "Now, we're presently strolling along the path that will lead to the grand theater. On your right is the ornamental pond that Lord Kilbourne has taken such pains over. He hopes to erect a bridge to a small island in the middle of the pond and when it is ready, I may invite you once again so that you may traverse it."

He spoke to her as an equal, Trevillion mused with

grudging respect. That is, MacLeish didn't talk to Lady Phoebe as if being blind had made her soft in the head. Sadly, this wasn't always the case.

"Oh, how lovely," Lady Phoebe replied. "Tell me, does Lord Kilbourne plan to plant scented shrubs and flowers in the garden?"

"I'm afraid I don't know," MacLeish replied regretfully. "I'll ask him the next time I see him, depend upon it."

"Is he not here today?"

"No, I believe he's taken his family to visit a fair outside London."

"That sounds a lovely outing." Her voice was wistful.

MacLeish had drawn her near the ornamental pond and Trevillion watched Lady Phoebe closely as she leaned down. One slip on that bank and she'd go in.

Which was perhaps why he didn't see the six men advancing on them until it was too late.

Chapter Six

*Corineus grasped the long, flowing mane of the
white horse. He held fast as she surged toward the
shore, bearing him with her until they both touched
the sand beneath the waves. But when the enchanted
horse would've returned to the sea, Corineus took
the iron chain from his neck and flung it over the
horse's neck, bridling her. . . .*
—From *The Kelpie*

Phoebe was bending down, listening carefully because
she thought she might've heard the deep croaking of
frogs, when several footsteps approached at a run.

A very gruff voice bellowed, "Hand over the woman!"

Phoebe straightened, fear shimmering down her spine
like ice water.

Mr. MacLeish shouted something next to her, but when
she reached for him, he wasn't there.

No one was there.

She was alone, confused, unable to tell where the danger was now. Everyone was yelling, and she could hear
scuffling and what sounded like blows landing on flesh.

BANG!

She flinched horribly, stumbling, hands outstretched, the stink of gunpowder in the air.

Trevillion? Had he fired? Where was he? She couldn't smell his scent, couldn't tell where he was.

"James!"

Someone rushed by her, catching her arm and squeezing quite painfully.

Another shout from Mr. MacLeish.

The hand was ripped from her arm.

"James!"

BANG!

Dear God, she was going mad. She wanted to run, but was too afraid to move.

"James!"

The scent of bergamot and sandalwood, familiar, comforting, surrounded her and then Captain Trevillion bore her to the ground.

She sobbed in relief. Blessed relief. The sounds of struggle still went on around them, but she was enveloped by his body, by his smell. She could feel him against her back, the hard edges of the belts he wore across his chest to holster his pistols, but not the pistols themselves. He must've drawn them. His cheek was warm against hers, a bit rough with stubble.

The ground was hard and cold under her and her palms were scraped where she'd caught her fall.

Trevillion's breath was measured, not in any hurry, and she wondered wildly what would make him breathe faster. Wondered if she could make him breathe faster.

"My lady," he said in her ear, his voice a caress, deep and sure and protective. "My lady."

The sound of running feet—moving *away* from their position.

"Lady Phoebe," Mr. MacLeish called, quite close, "are you all right?"

"Are they gone?" she asked Trevillion.

"Yes," he said, and she knew suddenly that everything was wrong. His voice was dead. "Mr. MacLeish has saved you."

"What? How?"

His warmth left her back and she felt suddenly cold even as he pulled her to her feet.

"Are you at all hurt, Lady Phoebe?" MacLeish asked anxiously. "Damn those scoundrels! To attempt kidnap of a gentle lady in broad daylight. Thank God I was here to help."

"I . . . no, I'm fine," she said. "Captain, what—?"

She heard running footsteps drawing closer and tensed, but then Reed said breathlessly, "I'm sorry, Cap'n, we lost the buggers. I think you got one with your pistol, though—'e was bleeding bad. They 'ad 'orses waiting just around them trees."

"You did your best," Trevillion replied, still in that flat tone. "How are you, Hathaway?"

"I've a graze on my arm, sir." The young footman's voice shook. "There . . . there's an awful lot of blood."

"Steady on, lad," Trevillion said. "Take his other arm, Reed." He sighed. "What a fucking mess this is."

Phoebe's mouth opened in shock at the vulgarity. Trevillion had never used such language in front of her before. Something truly must be the matter.

She held out a trembling hand to Trevillion, but it was Mr. MacLeish who took it instead. She caught the scent of ink and it wasn't right. Ink didn't make her feel better.

Didn't make her feel safe.

"Come, my lady," Mr. MacLeish said. "This must have

been a terrible shock to you. I have a temporary shelter nearby, not much more than a lean-to, I'm afraid, but I can make you a hot cup of tea there."

"No," Trevillion said, short and clipped. She wanted to touch him again, smell the spiciness of bergamot and sandalwood. *Why was he so upset?* She was safe now, the kidnappers routed. "We'll take Lady Phoebe home, out of the way of danger."

"I'm coming with you." Mr. MacLeish sounded defiant.

But Trevillion didn't argue the point. "Very well."

She heard his distinctive footfall with his cane and realized—*awfully*—that he wasn't going to guide her to the boat.

"This way, my lady," MacLeish said with tender consideration, but all she really wanted was Trevillion.

Trevillion, who was moving ever farther away.

Something in her heart seemed to clench in fear—more fear than she'd been in when they'd been under attack.

Then she'd been safe in Trevillion's arms.

"I'll protect you, never fear," Mr. MacLeish said to her.

"I have Captain Trevillion for that," she replied a bit tartly, but she *did*. Mr. MacLeish was being presumptuous.

"And yet it was Mr. MacLeish who saved you, my lady," Trevillion said from in front of them, his voice cold.

"What?" she asked peevishly. Had the world gone mad? "You covered my body with your own, Captain. I think I wasn't imagining it."

"I did cover you, my lady." His voice wasn't completely dead anymore. Instead there was some faint emotion in it—one she couldn't quite identify. "But it was Mr. MacLeish who led the charge against the attackers. Mr. MacLeish who drove them back armed only with a knife against their pistols. It is he who deserves your thanks... and mine."

"Oh, I say," Mr. MacLeish said, sounding embarrassed. "I only did what any gentleman would."

"Perhaps," Trevillion replied, "but I thank you even so for saving my lady's life."

Grief. The emotion in his voice was *grief.*

Phoebe's heart sank to her toes.

HE FELT LIKE vomiting. The carriage rocked rhythmically as Trevillion looked out the window, trying desperately to school his features.

He'd failed—*failed again.* He should never have allowed Phoebe to go to Harte's Folly. He'd let himself become too close to her. Let his affection for her sway him into permitting the outing. He'd wanted to make her happy, he realized, and *that* had been a near-fatal mistake.

Trevillion closed his eyes, helplessly reliving that horrible moment. He'd lain atop Phoebe, protecting her small form with his own body. He'd already fired both his pistols and somehow failed to fell any of the attackers. Reed and Hathaway fought on, but two men were advancing on him and his charge and he simply couldn't fight them both. Worse, he recognized one of the men from the attack in Bond Street. Then MacLeish had dashed forward, striking with his knife, and somehow driven both men away.

If MacLeish hadn't been there, they would've taken Phoebe, and then—

No. He simply couldn't think of what might have happened to her—what might've been *done* to her—without going mad.

Lady Phoebe and MacLeish were on the opposite seat,

and out of the corner of his eye he could see that MacLeish still held her hand. The lad seemed truly smitten, he thought with a small, dispassionate part of his mind.

Too bad MacLeish was not of the aristocracy. Without a pedigree of the highest sort, it was doubtful that the duke would let the architect anywhere near his sister.

Especially after this afternoon's debacle.

Trevillion suppressed a wince. His leg was giving him the very devil. He'd landed on it hard when he'd leaped to cover Lady Phoebe. He'd pay for it in the next several days and though he had an urge to rub the affected calf, he refrained.

It seemed he still had a bit of pride left.

The carriage drew to a halt and he was jolted from his bitter thoughts. They'd arrived. It was his duty to see Lady Phoebe safely into the house.

"Keep by her side," he told MacLeish.

Fortunately the man wasn't perturbed at taking orders. He merely nodded and waited as Trevillion climbed out of the carriage.

Trevillion took a moment to look up and down the street. They must've been followed to Harte's Folly—how else could the kidnappers have guessed they would be there? Yet he hadn't noticed any followers, and too, the attackers had been waiting with horses. Obviously they hadn't been followed on horseback across the Thames. No, the would-be kidnappers had *known* Lady Phoebe would be at Harte's Folly and at precisely what time.

Had one of the guests at Miss Dinwoody's tea party gossiped?

Trevillion grimaced. Gossip, he found, was inevitable.

However the attackers had learned of their trip to

Harte's Folly, he didn't see any lurkers now—no suspicious carriage, no group of men hanging around. He turned back to the carriage.

Reed and Hathaway had already dismounted from the back, Hathaway looking faintly green about the edges. The blood from his arm had soaked through his livery, despite the hasty bandage they'd put on the wound at Harte's Folly.

Trevillion nodded to Hathaway. "Report to the kitchens at once and see that wound is taken care of. Reed, stand by the front door."

Reed hurried to assume his position as Hathaway disappeared inside. Trevillion drew one of his pistols though it was no longer loaded—at least he gave the appearance to any onlookers of being armed.

"MacLeish." He watched as the architect carefully helped Lady Phoebe from the carriage. "Go straight in the house. Don't stop."

Lady Phoebe turned her face toward him. "I'm right here, you know."

"My lady, we'll talk inside."

MacLeish followed his orders to the letter, hurrying her inside without another word.

Trevillion took the rear and shut the door to Wakefield House behind them. "Reed, show Mr. MacLeish and Lady Phoebe to the sitting room and send for some tea."

Lady Phoebe frowned. "Where are you going?"

"I need to report to your brother."

She grabbed his arm with remarkable accuracy. "You said we'd talk."

"And so we shall, my lady." Gently—regretfully—he removed her hand from his arm. "After I've reported to the duke."

"James—"

He turned before she could make further protest and made his way down the hall to His Grace's study. The door was shut, but he entered without knocking.

The duke was leaning on his desk, examining some sort of map laid out over the entire surface. Beside him was his valet, Craven.

Both looked up on his arrival.

Wakefield's eyes narrowed. "What is it?"

"Lady Phoebe was attacked again," Trevillion said. He refused to sit this time, no matter how his leg protested. "She is unhurt."

"Thank God," Craven said softly.

"When did this happen?" Wakefield growled.

"At Harte's Folly, Your Grace, just an hour ago. I brought her straight home."

"What," the duke said dangerously, "was my sister doing at Harte's Folly?"

Trevillion bowed his head. This was on him, he knew. He'd made the decision to let her go.

In hindsight, that had been sheer idiocy. "She was invited there by the architect designing the buildings, one Malcolm MacLeish."

Wakefield glanced at Craven. "Find out who he is."

"Yes, Your Grace." Craven took a notebook from his pocket and wrote something in it.

"What do you know of this man?"

Trevillion shook his head. "Not nearly enough, beyond the fact that your sister likes him. He's the architect for Harte's Folly. He has some sort of connection to the Duke of Montgomery, which bears further looking into, but he seems a good man."

Wakefield stared at him balefully.

Trevillion held his gaze. "She could do worse, Your Grace."

The duke waved aside that thought. "Phoebe should never have been at Harte's Folly."

"Yes, Your Grace," Trevillion said. "I bear full responsibility."

"As you should," snapped the duke. "Whatever possessed you to let my sister visit an abandoned garden? Anyone might've been lurking about."

Trevillion closed his mouth. What could he say in his defense? That he'd endangered Phoebe because he'd been thinking with his heart rather than his head?

Wakefield frowned irritably. "How is this possible? Maywood is dead. It beggars the imagination that she should be attacked twice in one week by different men."

"She wasn't."

Wakefield stilled. "Explain."

"This isn't Maywood," Trevillion said. "It was never Maywood. I recognized one of the attackers—a man with a scar on his face—from the first attempt on Bond Street. Whoever was behind this was behind Bond Street."

Wakefield swore. "You were right all along, Trevillion. I owe you an apology."

"Thank you, Your Grace, but that hardly matters now." Trevillion clenched his fist. "You need to look for this man with the scar, but you also need to broaden your investigation. Look closely at your enemies and business associates. Find out who holds a grudge against you, who might want to sway you in Parliament by holding Lady Phoebe's safety hostage, what fortune seekers would want her dowry, and any man that showed special interest in her in the past."

Wakefield nodded, looking weary and grim. "Of course." He glanced at Craven.

The valet had been busily scribbling on a piece of paper as Trevillion listed the investigation points. Now he folded the paper and stood. "I'll see to it immediately, Your Grace."

He bowed and left the room.

"There's one more thing I must tell you, Your Grace." Trevillion fisted his hands, feeling his fingernails dig into his palms. "If it weren't for Mr. Malcolm MacLeish she would've been taken."

"What do you mean?" Wakefield asked slowly.

Trevillion met the other man's gaze directly. "Exactly what I say. There were six men this time. I had Reed and Hathaway, with a pistol each. A shot each, but all went wide, even mine, though Reed thought later that I might've winged one. I was knocked down and one of the men actually had hold of Lady Phoebe's arm when I got to her. There were two charging at us as I lay covering her, unarmed. MacLeish drove them both away. Simply put, if MacLeish hadn't had a knife in his boot, if he'd not been brave enough to take on two men, they would have had the day and your sister."

"Why do you tell me this?" Wakefield said slowly.

"Because I can no longer protect Lady Phoebe," Trevillion said. Head up, gaze steady. "Because I am resigning my position as her guard."

TREVILLION HAD GONE to talk to Maximus an hour ago and Phoebe still hadn't heard from him.

"Will you have more tea?" Mr. MacLeish asked solicitously.

They were in the Achilles Salon, drinking tea while poor Reed stood somewhere in a corner keeping guard.

Thank goodness both Cousin Bathilda and Artemis had been out when they'd come home, otherwise she'd probably be in bed right now with a cloth dipped in lavender water on her forehead.

"And there's some tiny, rather oddly colored cakes here," Mr. MacLeish continued, apparently unaware of her impatience, "that probably taste much better than they look."

"I'm sure they do," she said absently. "I wonder what's taking Maximus so *long*?"

"Oh…er…well, I assume he's discussing how best to protect you, my lady," Mr. MacLeish said. He must not've seen her wince, for he continued. "I confess I'm rather worried on that very point myself. I would hate to see anything happen to you, my lady. In…in fact, you've become very dear to my heart. When I saw those men threatening you this afternoon, why I was simply overwhelmed with rage."

"You were very brave to come to my defense," Phoebe said absently.

Footsteps sounded outside the sitting room and Phoebe straightened, turning her head in that direction.

The footsteps passed and her shoulders slumped.

"It was my pleasure to keep you safe, my lady," Mr. MacLeish said. "In fact I hope that you'll count me as a… friend? Perhaps even a good friend?"

"Of course." Phoebe smiled briefly.

She was having trouble concentrating on their conversation. Maximus would be wild when he heard the news from Trevillion, and when he had his temper up, he was apt to do rather drastic things. What if he decided to send her to the country? What if he decided that Trevillion should no longer guard her?

Surely he wouldn't do something that stupid?

Phoebe bit her lip. Mr. MacLeish had been very nice to sit with her and try to take her mind from things, but really, however kind he was, he'd begun to get on her nerves.

And she was *dying* to know what Trevillion and Maximus were talking about.

"I'm sorry, Mr. MacLeish," she said, standing rather abruptly. "But I think I will rest now."

"Oh, of course, my lady," he said, ever the gentleman. "The distress of this morning's events must be quite overwhelming for a delicate constitution."

"Erm…quite." Trevillion would have been laughing himself silly over the idea of her having a delicate constitution…well, if Trevillion laughed himself silly over anything. "I hope you understand?"

"Indeed, my lady. I'm only sorry that I did not realize sooner," he said, sounding terribly kind and sweet.

Which gave her an awful twinge of guilt, but Phoebe forced herself to continue smiling…weakly.

Mr. MacLeish bowed over her hand, said his goodbyes—several times—and finally exited the room.

The door shut behind him.

Phoebe sat down on her hands and began silently counting, aware that poor Reed was probably staring at her and wondering if she'd gone mad.

At one hundred and fifty—she'd never been so patient in her entire life—Panders, the butler, entered.

"Mr. MacLeish has left, my lady. Would you care for—"

"Nothing for me at the moment, Panders," she said as she leaped to her feet. "Is my brother still in his study?"

"Indeed, my lady," Panders replied, an ever-so-faint hint of bewilderment in his voice as she scooted past him and out the door. "Might I—"

She waved a hand in the air. "No need, thank you!"

She was down the grand staircase in a trice, and then she was hurrying through the hall, her fingers trailing along the wall as her guide.

Maximus's door was closed, which meant he didn't want to be disturbed, but *hang* that. Phoebe burst in. "Captain Trevillion, I really don't think—"

"He's not here, Phoebe."

She frowned, feeling quite put out. She hadn't talked with Maximus since her grand tantrum the night before and she really should be mending fences—or at least not tearing more down—but *now* was not the time. "Well, where is he, then?"

"I suspect in his rooms."

"Why—?"

"Phoebe."

He rarely used the ducal voice on her, but when he did, she had a tendency to shut her mouth.

Not today. "It's my fault, you know. I badgered and badgered him until he took me to Harte's Folly, and I still don't think it was that bad an idea. I mean, who would've thought? Not me in any case. But that's beside the point. Maximus, you can't censure Captain Trevillion. He's my guard, not my jailer. It's quite unfair to give him a job he simply can't do because I won't let him."

She paused to take a breath and her brother spoke very rapidly—a skill he'd no doubt honed in Parliament. "Captain Trevillion's ability to do his job is no longer a matter of concern."

And she nearly strangled on the breath she was taking. "Maximus! You *didn't.* Hire him back this instant or I'll go to Artemis and I really don't think you'd like that."

Which was rather an ambitious threat, as Artemis, as a rule, either took her husband's side or remained neutral, but in this case Phoebe felt she had a cause her sister-in-law would back.

"It's out of my hands," Maximus said. "I didn't let Captain Trevillion go. He resigned without any prompting from me."

Resigned.

She felt her heart plummet to her very toes. No, it couldn't be. He couldn't be so noble and *stupid*. Not because of her insistence that she visit a destroyed pleasure garden, of all things.

Phoebe whirled to the door, stepping out and closing it behind her while her brother was still saying something to her.

She hadn't the time to argue with Maximus. Not now.

"Panders!" she called as she hurried to the front of the house. "Panders, I rather need your help after all."

"My lady?" Panders, as always, popped up just when someone in the household wanted him.

"I'm afraid I've changed my mind." Phoebe inhaled, steadying her voice. "I need a footman to show me to Captain Trevillion's room."

And this was where Panders showed himself to be the best butler in London. He made no comment or demur to her wanting to go to the room of a bachelor—*quite* improper; he simply snapped his fingers and called, "Green."

Five minutes later Phoebe was knocking on Captain Trevillion's door, which as it happened was almost at the back of the house, near, but not quite in, the servants' quarters.

"Come," he called.

"You may go, Green," Phoebe said, and opened the door.

"My lady. Of course," Trevillion said, and while before he would've been exasperated, now he seemed merely... tense.

"You don't sound entirely pleased to see me, Captain," she said lightly, trying to hide the twinge of hurt. Damn it, this was all her fault.

"Perhaps I'm not," he responded. "Where's MacLeish?"

"MacLeish?" She shook her head in confusion. "Home, I would think by now, although I certainly didn't inquire about his further plans for the day. For all I know he's taking a trip to Inverness."

"My lady," he said in that chiding tone that oddly she'd come to rather enjoy.

"It's common courtesy to offer a lady a seat," she informed him.

He sighed and she heard something being moved. "Here. All I have is a straight-backed chair."

"That will do," she said as she sat, arranging her skirts and taking the time it provided her to marshal her argument. "Now then, you simply cannot leave my brother's service."

"My decision is already made, my lady," he said. "I'm packing now."

She'd been afraid of that. She straightened, licking her lips. "James, I won't have it. You must go down to Maximus and explain that this morning's events caused a fever in your brain making you do quite unwise things."

"No."

Panic was beginning to beat against her chest. "Yes, James! I won't let you go just because I was stubborn and spoiled and made you take me to Harte's Folly. I'm *sorry*, don't you see? I'm truly sorry and I shan't do it again."

"This wasn't your fault. You have every right to wish

to go places," he said gently—which only made her more worried. He was being much too kind and his next words confirmed her fears. "It's mine for not telling you *no*."

"That's absolutely ridiculous," she burst out. "Just tell Maximus you've changed your mind and that you intend to stay. *Please*."

"My lady." He was suddenly closer, the scent of bergamot and sandalwood drifting over her. "You may own dogs and horses and pretty dresses but you don't own me. I'm a free man who does as he wills. And right now my will is to leave this place."

She stood and reached out, her hand smashing against his coat. She felt up with her fingers, over the empty straps of his holsters, over buttons and the linen of his cravat.

He captured her hands before she could reach skin.

She leaned close nevertheless, her face only inches from his. "I need you, James."

"You can't," he whispered. "I'm old and scarred and lame. I failed you this morning. I can't—"

"You didn't," she said fiercely. "You've never failed me, not once."

"*I have*. I have failed you." His words were so vehement, so agonized, that she was struck dumb. "Don't you understand? *They would've had you* had not MacLeish been there. They would've carried you away to God knows where, done whatever—" He seemed to choke for a moment, his hands squeezing hers so hard they hurt and she could only hang on, listening to the terrible sound of his voice. "God, Phoebe. They could've *raped* you, could've killed you, and I would not have been able to stop them."

"Yes, you could've," she said, desperate. "You would have stopped them had Mr. MacLeish not been there."

"*No, I wouldn't have,*" he replied, his words more terrible because of the very softness with which he said them. "If my pride hadn't kept me by your side for so long I would've left long ago. I talked your brother into letting me stay as your bodyguard and my hubris nearly made me lose you. This is all my fault. I've destroyed lives before with my failure. I *will not* do it to you. I don't belong here. I have to go."

No. *Nononono.*

She didn't know whose *destroyed lives* he was talking about, but it didn't matter now. She couldn't let him go. She lunged forward, her nose hitting his cravat, pulling her hands desperately out of his hold, grabbing his coat, his ear, anything that was *him.* She knew how clumsy and awkward and *blind* she must be, but she didn't care right now. Somehow her mouth found his jaw and she inhaled sandalwood.

"Phe—"

She smashed her mouth to his, cutting off her name. It wasn't a sweet kiss by any means—she'd never kissed a man. But it was strange and wonderful anyway. She felt a bloom within her chest, a wild, pounding well of hope and joy, feeling his lips against hers. Breathing in sandalwood and bergamot, gunpowder and James.

James. James. *James.*

He groaned and for a second she felt triumph.

And then he took her hands in his and detached them from his person. He pushed her back, bundled her up, and half-carried, half-frog-marched her to the door and out into the hallway.

The door slammed behind her.

She heard the lock click into place quite distinctly.

Chapter Seven

*Now 'tis well known that all things iron are as poison
to the faery folk. Once bridled by iron, the sea horse
could neither change back into a maiden nor escape.
Corineus scrambled onto the creature's back and,
taking hold of the iron chain, rode her into that
unknown land....*
—From *The Kelpie*

That evening Trevillion let his bag fall to the floor and
looked around his tiny rented room. There was a narrow
bed, a washstand, a crooked chair, and the fireplace. Over
the fireplace someone had hung a small round mirror,
flyspecked and dim. Not luxurious accommodations by
any means, but clean at least. He had a small sum saved
up—more than enough to live on for several weeks before
seeking another job.

In that time he intended to find and eliminate Phoebe's
kidnappers.

Wakefield had put five armed footmen to guard her, but
while the kidnapper was still out there, she wasn't safe.
And he wouldn't leave London until she was.

He stood for a moment, remembering those fleeting
seconds in his rooms at Wakefield House. She'd been so

urgent—so innocently passionate—that he'd had to put a door between them to forestall his own urges.

Which hadn't been innocent at all.

A knock sounded at his door.

He flung it open to reveal a slim youth. Trevillion glanced up and down the hall and motioned the boy—or rather the girl disguised as a boy—in. He locked the door and then turned to examine his visitor.

He hadn't seen Alf in over a year, but in that time she hadn't changed much at all. Too short for a boy her age, Alf was all elbows and knees in a dingy brown too-large coat and rusted black waistcoat. Her brown hair was halfheartedly tied back with a bit of string, but most fell around her oval face. The disguise was quite good, actually. It wasn't until Trevillion's third sight of Alf, deep in the stews of St Giles, that he'd guessed her sex. He'd never mentioned the discovery to her. There was no need—Alf obviously felt more comfortable with the world thinking her a boy, and most would never see past her outer appearance.

A good thing, too. A young girl on her own in St Giles was prey to many. She was better off in her male clothes. Trevillion just hoped she could keep up the disguise as she aged and came into a more womanly figure.

At the moment Alf was busy exploring Trevillion's room, delicate fingers tracing over the empty mantelpiece. "Got word you was wantin' to talk to me, Cap'n." She glanced up at him through her fringe of limp hair.

"Yes." Trevillion sat on the bed and motioned to the lone chair. "I want you to look into a matter for me."

Alf didn't bother to sit down. "That'll cost you, it will."

Trevillion arched a brow. "I didn't think your services would be free."

"An' they ain't." Alf crossed her arms over her skinny chest and rocked back on her heels. "Best information gatherer in London, I am."

Trevillion pursed his lips at this bit of bravado, but made no comment. "I want to know who's trying to kidnap Lady Phoebe."

"Arr," Alf said meditatively, looking at the ceiling. "That'll be a bit of work, that." And she named a quite outrageous sum of money.

Trevillion shook his head and countered by plucking his purse from his coat pocket and shaking out six silver coins. "I'll give you as much again when you've brought back my information."

"Done." Quick as a wink Alf had snatched the coins from his hand and pocketed them. "You'll 'ear from me when I gots news."

With that Alf slipped out the door and was gone.

Trevillion sat a moment longer, then shook himself. First things first. He loaded his pistols and holstered them across his chest. Then he went out.

London was a different city after dark. Lanterns hung from the better houses, reflecting off wet cobblestones and lighting his way. Fiddle and pipe music sounded from a nearby tavern and as he passed, a trio of drunkards staggered out, nearly falling into the street in their merriment.

Trevillion kept to the shadows as much as possible. He didn't doubt he could defend himself—he was armed, after all—but an altercation would be an inconvenience.

Fifteen minutes later he came upon a rather better type of boardinghouse than the one he'd taken a room in. MacLeish might not be an aristocrat, but he was patently in more favorable financial circumstances than Trevillion. But then an architect—a man who'd had a university education—was a large step up from a former soldier.

Trevillion was about to approach the front door when a familiar figure came out.

The Duke of Montgomery wore saffron yellow this evening, his suit shimmering in the pale light of a crescent moon.

He turned on the step and spoke to MacLeish, who was hovering in the doorway. "See that you do, Malcolm darling, or you know what will happen, I think, yes?"

MacLeish's fair face was flooded a deep red, visible even in the uncertain light of a lantern by the door. "Yes, Your Grace."

"Lovely," the duke drawled, placing a silver lace-trimmed tricorne on his head. "I do so like it when we're all in accord."

With that he set off, swinging an ebony stick as he walked.

Trevillion's eyebrows rose. Odd for an aristocrat to be on foot so late at night. But that did make it easier on him. He hurried after the duke, limping rapidly for another block before Montgomery suddenly turned, drawing a sword from his stick. The duke smiled, showing teeth as he held his sword in an indolent hand. A single gold ring glinted on his forefinger, nearly lost in the silver lace falling from his wrist. "You might as well show yourself, whoever you are."

He sounded amused, and even with the foppish manner in which he held that sword, Trevillion had an idea the duke knew how to use it.

"Your Grace." Trevillion stepped from the shadows, letting the light from a nearby lantern reveal his face.

"Ah, Captain Trevillion, I should've realized 'twas you

from the sound of your cane." The duke didn't lower his sword. "Well met on this dark and dreary night, but pray tell: why are you following me?"

Trevillion examined his face. He knew the duke only slightly—but in that slight acquaintance he'd found him mercurial. The Duke of Montgomery was a beautiful man with nearly feminine features—a narrow nose, high cheekbones, and a voluptuous mouth. He stood slightly shorter than Trevillion and wore his curling golden-blond hair unpowdered and clubbed back. He looked like a frivolous dandy, but Trevillion didn't make the mistake of venturing within striking distance of that sword.

Only a few months ago he'd seen the duke shoot a man without remorse.

"I'd like to know what business you have with MacLeish," Trevillion said.

"Indeed?" The duke arched an eyebrow. "And what business is it of yours what business I have with young Malcolm?"

Trevillion didn't bother replying, simply waiting.

"Oh, and I suppose you'll follow me about London like some dire omen until I tell you something. How very tedious." Montgomery sighed impatiently. "He's my protégé, if you must know, although I can't understand why you'd *care*, frankly."

Trevillion ignored the verbal trimmings. "A protégé that you threaten."

Montgomery waved his sword lazily. "Some people work better with threats, I find. Gives them a certain incentive, shall we say."

Trevillion took a step closer. "You have something on the boy."

"He's hardly a *boy*. Must be five and twenty at the very least, *quite* old enough to get himself into a *man's* trouble." Montgomery smiled to himself. "A certain type of man, anyway."

Trevillion drew his pistol and Montgomery stilled, watching him. "You'll not threaten MacLeish anymore, Your Grace. Is that clear?"

"Clear like the murky waters of the Thames." Montgomery tilted his head, his blue eyes sparkling in the lantern's light. "Now why, I wonder, do you take any interest at all in bonny Malcolm MacLeish? Is it his fair skin? That gorgeous head of auburn locks?"

Trevillion's pistol didn't waver. "Is that what you want from him?"

"Not at all." A sly smile still played about Montgomery's lips. "Our association isn't as personal as all *that*, I'm afraid."

"Then why keep him under your thumb, Your Grace?" Trevillion asked, truly curious. "What do you want with him?"

"The world and all its secrets," Montgomery promptly shot back.

"What in hell does that mean?"

The duke shrugged elegant shoulders. "You shouldn't ask if you can't comprehend the answers."

"Perhaps I'd understand better if you stopped talking in riddles." Trevillion took a menacing step closer.

The duke's gaze darted away even as he threw up his hands, a wide grin on his mobile lips. "Stand down, Captain. I say, stand down! Let us part friends this night. You have my word as a gentleman that I'll not bother the Scotsman anymore henceforth."

Trevillion's eyes narrowed. The duke had capitulated too quickly for his surrender to be real. Whatever his reason for using MacLeish, he obviously wasn't about to give up the man.

Interesting.

But if Montgomery was determined not to tell him the truth, there wasn't much Trevillion could do. Despite his threats, it wouldn't be very wise to shoot a duke in the streets.

"Very well." Trevillion lowered his pistol.

"And shall we shake on it?" Montgomery held out his hand, draped in that silver lace.

Trevillion looked at the man's face and a shiver ran down his spine. He didn't trust the duke an inch—the man was far too pleased with himself.

And far too interested in playing games.

"I have your word, Your Grace. That's more than enough for me."

"Very well." Montgomery tipped his ridiculous hat. "Good evening to you, Captain." Dropping into a Scots accent, he continued, "And may ye be delivered from ghosties and ghoulies and long-legged beasties this night."

So saying, the Duke of Montgomery continued down the street.

Trevillion waited until he could no longer hear the duke's retreating footsteps, and then he turned and retraced his steps.

The list of questions he had for Malcolm MacLeish was even longer now.

He used his cane to knock upon the door to MacLeish's boardinghouse, waited a minute, knocked again, and then stood waiting for quite a long time before the door was pulled open by the scowling landlady.

She wore a shawl thrown over her nightdress and an enormous mobcap. "Knocking at all hours! This ain't a bawdy 'ouse, I'll 'ave you know. Now what can you want at this time o' the night?"

"I'd like to see Mr. MacLeish," Trevillion said.

"An' so would 'alf o' London, so it seems," said the landlady, turning about without bothering to ask him in. "First that gentleman, all fancy-like, and now you. Told 'im I run a nice quiet 'ouse. Won't 'ave riffraff about, no I won't!"

"Perhaps this'll make your labors sweeter," Trevillion said drily, pressing a coin into the harridan's hand.

She narrowed her eyes, palmed the coin, and jerked her head to the stairs behind her. "'E's up this way."

She mounted the stairs, one hand gripping a candle, and Trevillion followed.

On the upper floor, she rapped sharply on the first door to the right. "Mr. MacLeish! You've a visitor—another one."

The Scotsman opened the door, looking wary. When he saw Trevillion, though, relief seemed to flicker in his eyes. "Captain, please come in."

"I don't run to tea this time o' night," the landlady warned.

"That's quite all right, Mrs. Chester," MacLeish assured her drily. "I'm sure we'll manage on our own."

Trevillion stepped into the room and, as MacLeish closed the door behind him, took a look around. As in his own rooms, there was a narrow bed, a chair, a washstand, and the fireplace, but here the similarities stopped. MacLeish had a large rectangular table before his fire, huge sheets of paper spread upon it. In addition he also had a rather nice chest of drawers, an overstuffed chair, and several small paintings hung on the walls.

"My inheritance, such as it is."

Trevillion turned to find MacLeish gesturing at the paintings.

The other man smiled. "My grandfather was the younger son of a baron. At his death he had but few worldly goods, but as he knew I had an eye for art, he left me what paintings he had collected." His smile turned rueful. "I'm afraid I was forced to sell the better pieces to pay for my education, but I'm still rather fond of the remainder." He shrugged. "Will you have something to drink? I've a half bottle of wine."

"No, thank you," Trevillion replied, sinking into one of the chairs. "I hope not to stay overlong."

MacLeish nodded, watching him warily.

"I wanted to ask you some questions about this afternoon," Trevillion began. "It would've been near impossible to trail us to Harte's Folly across the Thames—not and have horses waiting on the other side."

"You think they knew Lady Phoebe would be there," MacLeish said.

"I do."

"And do you think I informed her kidnappers?"

"Did you?"

MacLeish's eyes widened at his blunt question. "No. No, I…" He turned away, running his hand through his red hair. "I've been giving the matter some thought myself, and the problem is that it could've been anyone at the tea party." He swung back around, looking pleading. "Not to mention someone within Wakefield House itself."

Trevillion's eyes narrowed. "You think there's a spy in Wakefield House?"

"It mightn't be anything so formal." MacLeish shrugged. "A servant gossiping would do the trick."

Trevillion thought about that a moment, absently rubbing his leg. Then he glanced up at his host. "I don't think I ever properly thanked you for saving Lady Phoebe this morning."

"Oh." MacLeish looked embarrassed. "It was nothing, truly."

"And yet if you hadn't, she might now be God knows where instead of safely in the bosom of her family," Trevillion said, the words like acid on his tongue. "I thank you most sincerely."

MacLeish blushed and ducked his head.

"Tell me," Trevillion murmured. "Do you always carry a knife about with you?"

MacLeish's head snapped up. "I...erm...yes, I do. Got in the habit while traveling the Continent viewing the classical ruins. Some places are rather uncivilized and a foreigner is seen as fair game."

Trevillion nodded. It seemed a likely enough explanation. "I saw the Duke of Montgomery coming from this house earlier."

MacLeish paled. "Are you watching me, Captain?"

"Should I?"

The other man snorted. "A lot of good it'll do you. The duke is my patron."

"He seemed to be threatening you."

"Did he?" MacLeish's upper lip curled and he suddenly looked quite a bit older than his years. "He has a curious way about him sometimes, I'll grant you, but his bark is worse than his bite."

"Odd." Trevillion narrowed his eyes. "I would've said it was the other way round."

"He's an aristocrat," MacLeish said. "They're used to ruling the world, aren't they?"

Trevillion couldn't argue with that. He stood. He was weary and he didn't seem to be getting any information here. "If you do have cause to regret your...association with the duke, you might come to me."

"You?" MacLeish looked at him, puzzled. "Not that I do have a problem with Montgomery, but what can you do against a duke?"

Trevillion smiled grimly as he opened the door. "Anything I want."

He closed the door gently.

PHOEBE TRAILED HER fingers over a rose the next afternoon, letting the scent drift up to her face. She usually enjoyed walking her garden, but today she was sunk in a kind of cloudy melancholy. Trevillion had left Wakefield House the previous evening without another word to her. Rather as if her kiss had been so repelling he couldn't stand the sight of her.

She hadn't thought the kiss *that* bad.

Strange. Six months ago she would've felt nothing but relief to be free from her bodyguard's constant presence. Now he was no longer just a bodyguard to her. Trevillion was companion, verbal sparring partner...friend.

More than friend, she realized, now that it was too late.

Phoebe crushed the blossom beneath her fingers, the sharp scent of the rose perfuming the air. The scent reminded her of the last time she'd been in the garden— with Trevillion. Regret was a bitter taste on her tongue. If only she'd not insisted on going to Harte's Folly.

If only she could be content to be caged.

She tore the bloom from the bush and scattered the petals beneath her feet.

The problem was she wanted both things: to be free and to have Trevillion back in her life—a blatant contradiction. He was a *guard*. She couldn't be free with him there. And yet she couldn't be entirely happy with him gone.

Phoebe sighed and continued down the path, the gravel crunching beneath her heeled shoes.

Maximus had, of course, assigned a group of strong young footmen to guard her, including both Reed and Hathaway, whose wound hadn't been that dire after all. Her brother had refused to even discuss the guards with her. The scene in the dining room the other night might never have happened at all. Maximus treated her with polite courtesy... and turned away when she attempted to make her case.

She might as well have been mute as well as blind for all the notice her words got her.

Phoebe could hear her guards, even now, shuffling about the outskirts of the garden, no doubt armed to the teeth and giving her little to no privacy. It was incredibly awkward when she had to use the necessary.

"My lady."

She turned around at the call—one of the footmen, obviously, but she wasn't sure which one. Definitely not Reed with his Cockney accent, but other than that... bother. Trevillion would've found a discreet way to alert her to the speaker, but he wasn't there, was he? No, she'd driven him away with her stubborn desire to be free.

Or maybe it was her kiss that had driven him away. Awful thought. She'd liked that kiss, as brief as it had been. It'd seemed to hold a world of discoveries, just beyond a closed door.

If she could kiss Trevillion again, perhaps she could open that door.

The footman cleared his throat, reminding her he was still there.

She sighed. "Yes?"

"Mr. Malcolm MacLeish is here to see you, my lady. Will you receive him in the sitting room?"

"Yes," she said, then immediately changed her mind. It was a lovely day after all. "No, show him out here, will you...?"

"It's Green, my lady."

"Of course. Green. Perhaps you can ask Cook to put together some refreshments to serve in the garden?"

"Right away, my lady."

She assumed he went back into the house, but as the grass rather muffled Green's footsteps it was hard to tell.

A moment later, though, she heard Mr. MacLeish call. "Lady Phoebe! Good afternoon. Have I told you how like your roses you are—both beautiful and delightful?"

"I don't believe so, Mr. MacLeish," she replied, her lips twitching. "At least not today at any rate."

"A terrible oversight on my part, I'm sure." And then to someone else, presumably one of her guards, "I say, good fellow, I'm merely here to chat with your mistress. I've no nefarious plans against her, I assure you."

Phoebe smiled for the first time today—it was impossible not to in the face of Mr. MacLeish's good humor. She held out her hand to him. "I fear in the excitement yesterday that I was rather brusque in my thanks to you for saving my life. Let me try again: thank you so very much for standing between me and those kidnappers."

She felt his hand as he took her fingers in his. The slight

brush of his lips over her knuckles and his warm breath against the back of her hand. "It was my honor, my lady."

His voice had lowered and he sounded strangely serious.

She cocked her head, wondering about the reason for his mood.

He still held her hand when he said, "Where is Captain Trevillion this afternoon? Is it perchance his afternoon off?"

"He's resigned and left my brother's service," Phoebe replied, her lips turning down.

"He has?" Mr. MacLeish sounded startled. "But..."

"Yes?"

"Oh, nothing, my lady," he replied. "I'm just surprised at his action. I would've thought your safety would be at the forefront of Captain Trevillion's desires."

She stiffened, the casual observation unaccountably hurting her, though she was sure that was the last thing Mr. MacLeish intended. "I think it is. He has this odd notion in his rather thick head that he can't protect me just because he's lame."

"Ah."

"Ah?" She frowned suspiciously. "Why, ah?"

"It's just that perhaps he's the best judge of what he's capable of," Mr. MacLeish said far too reasonably. "In a way it's quite brave of him to admit a fault and gracefully stand aside because of it."

"Brave." She snorted. "Brave if you think being soft in the head is brave."

He laughed lightly at that. "I see I'm not winning any arguments on this front with you, my lady, so I concede: Captain Trevillion was indeed a softheaded cad to abandon you just because he worried for your safety."

She smiled weakly and turned to stroll along the garden path, aware that he kept step with her at her side. "I have to make you aware of a terrible fault you have, Mr. MacLeish."

"Your words strike terror in my heart, my lady," he said, a quiver of laughter in his voice. "What is this fault?"

"You make it very hard to remain at odds with you, sir," she replied. "In fact, I find I cannot."

"I shall endeavor to try and be more unlikable, my lady," he said. "Perhaps if I practice every day, in time I can become quite loathsome."

"Do," she said. "I expect a report at the end of every week regarding your progress."

They'd come now to the bench where she and James had sat just a few nights before. She paused, her heart squeezing at the memory.

"Lady Phoebe." Mr. MacLeish suddenly caught her hands in his, drawing her down to the bench. "Forgive me, my lady. I'd hoped to take more time. To write a speech fully worthy of you, but I fear I simply cannot. Your bravery, your wit, above all your charm..."

He pressed his mouth to the backs of her fingers—not a polite greeting, but a passionate kiss, and Phoebe had a sudden horrible idea where all this was going, followed immediately by bewilderment. Had she missed something? Had her blindness caused her to misread Mr. MacLeish's intentions all along?

"Mr. MacLeish," she said, and then stopped, because she *liked* him. If it weren't for...

Dear God. If it weren't for James Trevillion, she might even consider him.

Well, if he weren't acting so very rashly.

But Mr. MacLeish had disregarded her interruption. "I'm not rich by any means, Phoebe, but if you'll permit me—if you'll do me the great honor of consenting to be my wife—please know that I'll work every day joyfully, with all my heart, to make sure you never want. I swear upon all I hold holy that I'll protect you with my body from daily irritants and the bigger dangers of life. You need never go out without a guard and a husband. I'll keep away anything that might possibly bother you. I'll make it my life's work from this day hence, I swear."

"But," Phoebe said, because sadly she had a tendency to latch on to the wrong thing at moments like this. "I don't *want* a bodyguard for a husband."

"Of course not, my love. I spoke badly. I simply mean—"

"No, actually," she said thoughtfully, "you were quite eloquent. You mean to keep me from any little bump or misstep in life. Any irritant. Any bothersome thing. But you see, the thing is, I don't quite think one can live like that, all rolled up in a blanket of care. One rather has to be bumped now and again to know one is alive, don't you think?"

"You're a lady of refinement," Mr. MacLeish began in a puzzled tone that, sadly, gave her answer enough. "You need to be protected from the rougher things in life."

"Actually, I don't," she said as gently as possible. "And I'm afraid, though you do me great honor, I can't accept your suit."

"My lady," said the very correct voice of one of the footmen. It must be Green, surely? "Your tea."

"Oh, lovely," Phoebe said with a great deal of relief. She felt the tray carefully and found the teapot and a mound of some sort of iced cakes. "Would you like a cup, Mr. MacLeish?"

"I fear I have another appointment," Mr. MacLeish said rather stiffly. "If you'll excuse me, my lady?"

And he left precipitously, making Phoebe feel guilty that she didn't, in fact, care more.

She did like Mr. MacLeish, she really did, but his proposal had come quite out of the blue—very puzzling, surely? And didn't he know enough to ask Maximus first for permission to court her?

Phoebe shook her head, trying to work through what had happened. Not that it mattered much, in the end. Even if Mr. MacLeish had followed the correct steps she wouldn't have accepted him.

He wasn't James Trevillion and he never would be.

Was Trevillion now the pattern to which she held all other men? How odd. She hadn't even known that was how she felt until now. The realization—that she needed him in her life, that something was missing without his steady presence by her side—had crept up on her.

And now he was gone.

On that thought she called Reed over.

"My lady?"

"Reed, do you know where Captain Trevillion has taken himself off to?"

"No, my lady."

"Well, find out, please, for me."

"Yes, my lady."

She listened to the retreat of the footman's shoes, and then she was alone again—or as alone as she ever was these days.

Strange that one could be surrounded by guards and still feel isolated. That hadn't been the way she'd felt with Trevillion. He'd often made her cross or irritated, sometimes amused with his quiet wit, rarely incandescent with rage, and, more recently, warm with a sort of longing.

But she'd never been lonely with Trevillion.

Phoebe straightened. Reed would find where James had gone to ground and then she would visit him—guards and all—and convince him somehow that life simply wasn't the same without him here.

Really, it was his *duty* to guard her.

And with her mind made up she bit into a lemon cake.

EVE DINWOODY BENT over her desk later that same day and peered through a large brass magnifying glass on a stand. She took a breath and very carefully touched a thin sable-hair brush to the pink cheek on the miniature portrait of a man she was working on.

"Ma'am?" Jean-Marie called from the doorway. "His Grace is here to see you."

"Show him in, please, Jean-Marie."

A moment later His Grace Valentine Napier, the Duke of Montgomery, breezed into her private study, carrying a rectangular package with a cloth draped over it. He wore a yellow-green suit today, embroidered in black and gold. On anyone else it would've looked excruciating.

On him, it merely highlighted the guinea-gold of his hair.

"Darling Eve, you must stop your labors at once. Not only will you give yourself a squint if you insist on painting every day, but I've brought you a present."

"Have you?" She sat back and dabbed her brush in the pink watercolor before bending once more over her task. "It's not another box of marzipans, is it? Because I *did* tell you that I don't like them."

"Nonsense," the duke said briskly. "Everyone likes marzipans."

"You don't."

"*I'm* not everyone." A heavy breath at her shoulder. "That's not me, is it?"

"Why," she asked, "would I paint you?"

"Well"—Val set the package next to her—nearly in her paints—and whirled across the study, no doubt to rearrange her books—"I am acquitted quite a beauty."

"Can gentlemen be beauties?" she asked, eyeing the package suspiciously.

"In my case, yes," he said with a conceit so complete it was actually rather endearing.

"Then perhaps I ought to paint you." Eve sat back and examined her art. Very nice and at a good point at which to halt. Val was too volatile for her peace of mind while painting. She wiped her brush clean. "Of course, you'd have to sit still for me."

Val made a rude noise. "Sitting for a portrait is so tiresome. Do you know I had my portrait painted this last winter and I swear the man gave me a double chin."

"That's because you didn't sit *still*," she said tartly. She uncovered the package to find a white dove blinking back at her from inside a wooden cage. "What is this?"

"A dove," came his voice from the far side of the room. It sounded muffled. "Have you already impaired your eyesight squinting? I found it at the market on the way over and made my chairmen stop just so I could buy it for you."

Eve frowned at the dove and then at him. "What am I going to do with a dove?"

Val straightened across the room. Several of her books

were scattered haphazardly about his feet. "Coo at it? Feed it? Sing to it? I don't know. What does one usually do with a caged dove?"

"I haven't the faintest."

He shrugged and began stacking her books into an unsteady tower. "If you don't like it, you could always give it to your cook to make into pie."

Eve shook her head wearily. "I can't eat a tame dove."

"Why not?" Val looked honestly confused. "I'm sure it tastes just like pigeon and I do like a pigeon pie."

"Because..." Fortunately Eve was saved from having to try to explain to Val the wrongness of killing a bird meant as a pet by the maid's coming into the room. She bore a huge tray of tea and what looked like orange-iced fairy cakes.

Tess, her cook, knew Val's favorites.

She nodded for the maid to set the tea on the low table in front of her blue-gray settee, then rose and crossed to the settee. "Come sit and have some tea."

He alighted on the armchair opposite her and then frowned. "That settee is fading. Let me buy you another."

"No," Eve said composedly, but quite firmly. One did have to be firm with Val or one found oneself aswamp in unwanted—and often bizarre—gifts.

He flung out his arms petulantly. "Fine. Keep that ugly thing."

She eyed him as she passed his teacup to him. "You're in a mood."

He suddenly gave her one of his real smiles—wide and boyish, dimples on both cheeks, and enough to make any heart, particularly hers, squeeze. "Have I blanketed you in my ill humor, my darling Eve? Forgive me, please."

She took a sip of her tea. "I will if you tell me what's bothering you."

He twirled his sword stick at the side of the chair. "All my mechanisms and workings ought to be bearing lovely ripe fruit right now, and yet they aren't."

"Sometimes I think it's best for you when not everything goes your way," she said lightly.

"Do you?" His look was dark. "But sweetling, that merely makes me cross. And you know how I am when I'm cross."

She looked away, repressing a shiver though the room was warm. The fact was that Val played a dandy and a fool when the mood took him, but the people who dismissed him because of his manners did so at their own peril.

And to their regret.

"Is this about the favor I did for you?" she asked carefully.

"It might be." He sat up suddenly and helped himself to a fairy cake. "There are workings within workings, cog upon cog, wheel within wheel. Someday, dear Eve, I shall rule this city, nay, this very isle, and mark me, no one will ever be the wiser."

So saying, he popped the cake in his mouth and smiled.

And while it might be easy to look at Val with orange icing smeared at the corner of his lips and think he was merely painting castles in the air, Eve knew better. She'd seen the full will of the Duke of Montgomery.

Seen it and nearly not survived.

Chapter Eight

*The land Corineus and the sea horse traveled was
lovely and fine, but it was near deserted and this
was the reason why: three giants ravaged that
land, stealing cattle, destroying dwellings, and
slaughtering any who resisted them. Their names
were Gog, Mag, and Agog....*
—From *The Kelpie*

Phoebe padded lightly through the hallways of Wakefield House very early the next morning. She could hear a
maid sweeping out the fireplace in the sitting room as she
passed, but other than that she was quite alone.

Which was how she wanted it.

Maximus kept her ringed round with guards during the
day. She couldn't move a step without their constant presence and she just wanted a moment alone.

Alone to be as free as she once had been.

Her longing to be unrestrained had cost her Trevillion.
She paused at the thought. Should she find a way to accept
her restraints—her *cage*—now that she was completely
blind? Perhaps she was being a fool, refusing to accept
that being blind meant she simply couldn't go out as she
used to do.

But she *had* accepted most of the reality of her lack of sight. She knew that she relied upon others to choose the color of her clothes, to help her navigate new rooms and situations, to tell her where her food lay so she wouldn't stick her fingers straight into the gravy. She could no longer read a book by herself. Couldn't see the actors on the stage at the theater or a painting others thought beautiful.

She'd never see Trevillion smile at her.

Did she really have to give up going out as well?

Wasn't freedom a universal desire? Something every human being longed for no matter their circumstances?

Maximus might've kept her caged these past several years, but she found that she chafed against her restraints now more than ever before. Perhaps it was because she'd grown into womanhood during that time.

Perhaps it was simply that she'd had enough.

Phoebe shook her head and continued down the hallway. She bumped into a table—had it been moved?—caught herself, and continued toward the back door. Opening it, she could hear the birds greeting the day loudly. The air was brisk and still cool from the night before, and when she reached the grass, it was quite soaked with the morning dew.

Phoebe inhaled happily. It'd been days since she'd made a pilgrimage to the stables in the mews. She couldn't ride the horses anymore, but something about a stable— the shuffling of hooves on hay, a quiet whicker or stamp, the smell of horse and manure—made her quite content.

Trevillion, of course, hadn't liked the thought of her venturing out alone—even to as mundane a place as the Wakefield stables. He'd insisted on accompanying her, which at the beginning of their relationship she'd resented quite vigorously.

Lately, however...

Phoebe sighed as she drifted through her flower garden, trailing her hand over wet blooms, showering herself
with dewdrops. In the morning air the roses' perfume was
sweet and new. Recently she'd quite welcomed Trevillion's presence. He'd seemed to enjoy the horses as much
as she. Without him it was a little lonely: she missed his
company.

Actually, she missed him, plain and simple. Who
would've thought? When he'd first entered her life, she'd
thought him so stern, so correct, and so very immovable
when it came to her safety. Well, he still was all of those
things, truth be told. But back then she'd thought she
would go mad with him constantly in her presence.

Now she just wished she could have him with her
again.

She shook the thought aside as she came out the other
side of the garden. There was a gravel path here that led to
the far wall and the gate to the mews. The bolt on the back
gate was a trifle rusty and she struggled with it before it
abruptly slid open in her hands. Relieved, she pushed the
gate open and stepped into the mews.

And was immediately grabbed by rough hands.

TREVILLION HAD JUST taken a bite of some rather lumpy
porridge, courtesy of his landlady, when someone started
pounding wildly on his door.

He stood and picked up one of his pistols from the
mantel before opening the door.

Reed stood without, his eyes wide, sweat on his brow.
"Lady Phoebe!"

Trevillion clenched his jaw, tamping down instinctive

rage and worry. He turned back into the room to begin strapping his belts to his chest. "Report, Reed."

"Sir." The commanding tone seemed to calm the footman. He gulped and then said, "Lady Phoebe is missing, Cap'n. The back gate to the mews was standing open early this morning and she was seen being bundled into a carriage."

Trevillion swore, low and vile. "She liked to visit the stables of a morning."

"Yes, sir," Reed replied. "The duke reckons she must've gone out and someone took her."

"Understood." Trevillion shoved both pistols in their holsters and motioned to Reed to accompany him as he left his rooms. "What's being done?"

They clattered down the stairs, Reed talking as they ran. "The duke has called all the staff, stableboys included, to question them."

"Does he know you came for me?" Trevillion asked as they made the street. Two horses waited there, most likely from Wakefield's stables.

"No, sir."

Trevillion looked at the young footman. He could lose his job over this. "Good man."

He gave his cane to Reed and mounted one of the horses, then held out his hand for the cane. Reed was about to mount his own horse when a thought struck Trevillion.

He turned to the footman. "Do you remember Alf from St Giles?"

"Indeed I do, sir," was Reed's reply.

Trevillion nodded. "Can you find her and fetch her back to Wakefield House?"

"I can try," Reed said. "I've an idea where I might inquire after her."

"Good. Tell her it's about the matter I discussed the other night with her. And Reed?"

"Sir?"

"Tell her I need everything she knows *now*."

"Yes, sir." Reed mounted his horse and turned its head toward St Giles.

Trevillion nudged his own horse in the opposite direction.

It was early yet—not quite eight of the clock—but the London streets were crowded. Still he was able to maintain a trot most of the way to Wakefield House and made good time.

Trevillion dismounted, limped up the front steps, and knocked on the front door.

Panders opened it, took one very worried look at Trevillion, and said, "This way, sir."

The butler led him back to the duke's study and a scene of chaos.

Wakefield paced before the fire, looking for all the world like a tiger about to charge the bars of its cage. Craven sat at the desk, writing furiously. The duchess was seated by the fireplace, watching her husband with deep concern in her eyes, and in the middle of the carpet stood three weeping maids.

Her Grace looked up at his entrance and stood. "Captain Trevillion, thank God." She crossed to him and took his hand between her two soft ones. "You must help him. He's nearly out of his mind."

Trevillion's mouth set firmly. It was bad if the duchess was turning to others to calm the duke. "I'll do my best, Your Grace."

She squeezed his hand. "If the kidnappers forced Phoebe into marriage I don't know what he'll do. She's his *sister* and he loves her dearly. They could hold her happiness, her *safety* over his head. Make him change his votes in Parliament." She met his eyes, her own wide and fearful. "Captain Trevillion, you can't comprehend what power these men hold while they have Phoebe."

Trevillion swallowed hard at the thought of Phoebe forced into marriage, forced to—

For a moment he closed his eyes to steady himself. Then he opened them and looked at the duchess. "Let me speak to the duke."

She nodded and drew him farther into the room. "Maximus."

The duke stopped his pacing and whirled. "Trevillion."

"Your Grace." Trevillion made an abbreviated bow. "What happened?"

"Damnable incompetence is what," the duke snarled, low and furious, and the maids sent up a fresh wail as they cowered from his wrath.

Craven looked up and motioned Trevillion forward. He bent lower to hear the valet over the noise.

"At six of the clock His Grace was woken by Bobby, a stable lad of some thirteen years, who said he witnessed Lady Phoebe being shoved into a carriage at the end of the mews. She had a hood over her head and was making no sound."

"Where is Bobby now?" Trevillion asked.

"In the kitchen being revived by Cook, no doubt," Craven said drily. He glanced at his employer. "I believe we extracted all the information possible from the lad."

"What else?" This was too little to go on. A carriage

without any sort of description? "Did he say how many men he saw?"

"Anywhere from three to a dozen, I'm afraid." Craven sighed. "I understand from the stable master that the lad is a genius with the horses but otherwise is somewhat mentally deficient."

"What else has been done?"

"All those employed in the stable were questioned." Craven spread his hands. "No one else saw or heard anything."

"The investigations you started after the last attempt?"

Wakefield slammed his fist down on the desk, making the things on top shake. "*Nothing.* We haven't even been able to locate the man with the scar."

"The investigation has been exceedingly slow." Craven cleared his throat. "It has been most unfortunate."

Damned right it was unfortunate. "And now?"

"His Grace has commenced questioning the indoor staff." Craven nodded at the three weeping maids. "That is where you find us."

Trevillion turned to examine the maids. Two—a gray-haired woman and a tiny little redhead—were obviously housemaids. The third was Powers, Phoebe's lady's maid. All three women held handkerchiefs to their faces as they wept. All three looked both grief-stricken and terrified.

Except Powers's eyes weren't red.

Rage, fire-hot and cleansing, rushed through Trevillion's soul.

"You," he growled, making everyone in the room stop and turn to look at him. "*You.* Come with me."

PHOEBE CAUTIOUSLY LIFTED her head and listened. They'd taken off her hood—and really, why bother hooding a blind woman?—when they'd left her, but her hands were still bound in front of her. She sat on a wooden chair with arms in what she assumed was an empty room.

"Hello?"

Her voice came back to her in a way that she could think of only as *contained*. A small room, then. Without, she could hear the voices of her kidnappers. She'd counted four in the carriage: one very young, one with an Irish accent, and two Londoners, one with a slight lisp. At least one other to drive the carriage. So a minimum of five men.

Why had they kidnapped her? She realized now that this question was rather belated—Trevillion's defection had been a distraction. Three times they'd tried to kidnap her, which seemed very persistent if nothing else. Maximus had told her curtly and without explanation that poor mad Lord Maywood was no longer suspected of the first attempt.

Phoebe raised her hands to scratch her nose as she contemplated her situation. Obviously they knew who she was, so perhaps they hoped to hold her for ransom? The carriage hadn't traveled very far, so she thought they were still in London. By the stench of sewage and rot when she'd been pulled out of the carriage and escorted into the building she now sat in, she thought not a very nice part of London.

She sighed.

Being kidnapped, after the first few minutes of absolute terror, was really rather boring. She tried her teeth against the rope binding her wrists, but after a couple of minutes decided she would wear her teeth down to nubs before either untying the knots or chewing through the rather disgusting rope.

Loud laughter came from the outer room. At least her kidnappers were enjoying themselves.

Gingerly she rose, inching first one foot and then the other forward to test for obstacles on the floor. She reached the wall by the simple expedient of knocking her elbow against it.

"Ow," she whispered to herself, holding her breath in case the small noise had alerted her kidnappers.

They didn't seem to have noticed, however, and she began making her way along the wall, searching for the door.

She reached it in a few seconds more and applied her ear to the wood, listening.

The words were sporadic.

"—comin' 'ere. Don't understand at all," growled one of the Londoners.

"He'll come soon enough now and then we'll be paid the rest," said the Irishman clearly enough.

"But…" The boy's voice was so low it was nearly impossible to make out.

"Because he's bringing th' vicar, that's why," the Irishman replied, and Phoebe's heart plummeted.

If Maximus didn't find and rescue her very soon she might very well be married by the time he got to her.

"TELL ME WHAT you know," Trevillion said, his voice low, flat, and grim, "and you might not be hanged for your crime."

"I…I never did anything," Powers sputtered, cringing back in the chair she sat in.

They were in a little-used sitting room at the back of the house, just the two of them, and though Trevillion had never struck a woman in his life, he was tempted now.

The lady's maid knew something and the thought of her blustering while Phoebe was in danger—while she might even now be enduring the worst sort of assault against a woman—

He slammed his hands down on the chair's arms, leaning into Powers's face. "Mistake me not. If your mistress is in any way harmed, I shall make it my life's mission to destroy yours."

"I'm sorry!" cried Powers. "I didn't know they would do this, truly I didn't. You mustn't tell the duke."

Trevillion shook the chair, making the woman's teeth rattle. "*Who?* Give me a name, damn your eyes."

"He didn't have one!" Her eyes were wide, the whites showing all around the irises, and at any other time Trevillion might've felt remorse for so thoroughly terrorizing a woman, but not now. "I swear! He...he sounded Irish."

Ten minutes later Trevillion entered the duke's study.

Wakefield looked up. He was still on his feet as if the mere thought of relaxing while his sister was in peril was anathema. "What have you learned?"

"She was bribed by an Irishman," Trevillion said, "a quite considerable sum. Powers told the man that Lady Phoebe sometimes liked to visit the stables early in the morning. She says the man was quite average—dark hair, a laborer's accent, wearing clean but old clothing. She met with him twice and the only other thing she had to add was that he mentioned having rooms near Covent Garden."

Wakefield whirled on Craven. "Send out all the men we have to search Covent Garden and the neighborhoods surrounding it."

"Yes, Your Grace," Craven replied, ducking out of the room.

Trevillion stared at Wakefield, knowing there was no point in telling him how impossible a task he'd just sent his men on. "Near Covent Garden" was simply too big an area to search.

The duke continued to pace like a caged animal until Craven returned and gave a small nod of his head, presumably indicating that the Wakefield House manservants had left.

"Who's this?" Her Grace asked suddenly, and Trevillion turned to see Reed and Alf in the doorway.

"The best informant in London," Trevillion replied, not taking his eyes off the girl. "Reed's told you that Lady Phoebe was kidnapped?"

Alf jerked her head in assent.

"What do you have for me?"

Alf was twisting a floppy hat in her grimy hands, looking both defiant and scared out of her wits. She'd probably never been in so grand a place as Wakefield House. "'Eard was a woman taken to Maude's bawdy house. Black hair, though."

Trevillion shook his head. "No."

Alf took a breath. "Body o' a woman taken out o' the Thames just an hour ago."

"Dear God," the duchess said, and the duke crossed to take her hand.

"That's not it, either," Trevillion said, praying he was right. But no. They wouldn't kidnap Phoebe merely to kill her. She was worth much more alive. He kept that thought in his head, refusing to consider any alternative. "What else?"

Alf knit her brows. "Onliest other were a woman taken from a carriage wi' a 'ood over 'er 'ead."

Trevillion straightened, his muscles tensing. "Where?"

"Little lane near th' south side o' Covent Garden," Alf said. "One next to that cobbler."

"You know the place?" Trevillion asked.

Alf nodded.

"Then take me there."

"And me." The duke began to pull away from his wife.

But she held him fast. "Maximus. You must stay here in case there is news."

He looked at her.

Her face was brave and firm. "In case they ask for ransom. Only *you* can make the funds available—and decide what to do."

"Your Grace," Craven said. "The duchess is correct. Your place is here."

"He only has Reed!" The duke flung out his arm at the footman. "Two men against how many numbers?"

"I'll send one of the stableboys after our men," Craven began. "Try to catch up with the others and—"

"*Your Grace*," Trevillion interrupted tightly. There was no time to wait for the others. The duke's wild eyes turned on him. "I'll rescue Lady Phoebe. I swear it."

Wakefield stared at him a second longer as if searching to see the truth. Then he nodded once. "Go!"

Trevillion limped out of the study, followed by Reed and Alf. "Are you armed?" he asked Reed.

"Yes, sir."

Trevillion nodded at Alf. "Do we have something for him?"

"I'll fetch another pistol." Reed jogged ahead.

"You need only show us the place," Trevillion said to Alf as they continued down the hallway. "Anything else is up to you."

"Aye," Alf said with her usual bravado. "Fact is, I've never liked men who prey on women."

"Good lad," Trevillion said.

They made the front entryway and found Reed already waiting, a pistol in his hand. He thrust it at Alf. "Mind that, lad."

"Mind yourself," she shot back cheekily. "I knows well enough 'ow to shoot a gun."

"And to ride a horse?" Reed asked as they walked outside to see the two horses that they'd ridden earlier.

Alf paled a bit.

"He can ride with me," Trevillion said.

He swung himself up on the horse and reached down a hand to Alf. She gave another nervous look at the horse and then set her jaw stubbornly. She took his hand, clambering behind him.

"Hang on," Trevillion said, and kicked his gelding into a canter.

The wind whipped his face as they clattered down the cobblestone street, turning in front of a brewer's wagon. The wagon driver shouted obscenities in their wake, but Trevillion never looked back.

He had a destination. A purpose and a target.

Pedestrians scattered before his gelding's hooves. A dog cart sat in the middle of the street, though.

"Hold fast," he shouted at Alf, and then the gelding was leaping the cart.

Her thin arms were a tight band around his waist and he thought he heard a hastily smothered shriek in his ear.

They were nearing Covent Garden now. "Which way?"

"To the right!" Alf pointed straight-armed to a narrow lane that turned south—toward St Giles. "Down there."

He leaned with the horse as they slowed to a trot. "Where?"

"There's another lane comes off this un. She's in a 'ouse there."

Trevillion nodded, pulling the horse to a halt where the lanes met. This area was very close to St Giles, the houses built one on top of another, the upper stories and eaves hanging over the narrow lanes, nearly blocking out the light. A channel of refuse ran down the middle of the narrow lane, making everything stink.

Trevillion slid from the saddle, helping Alf down.

He looked at Alf and knew despite her bravery that she was but a young girl. "Stay here and guard the horses. We may need to make a hurried escape."

She opened her mouth to protest, but he shoved the reins into her hands.

He turned to Reed, who had dismounted and drawn his pistol. "Keep close. If you can't see what you're aiming at, don't fire. We don't want to hit Lady Phoebe."

"Yes, Cap'n."

Trevillion drew both his pistols and started down the lane with Reed behind. The other end was shadowed, but Trevillion could see two figures coming toward them. One of the figures was cloaked.

He and Reed came abreast of the house Alf had pointed out. It was a decrepit thing, half-leaning into the lane, with empty spaces where bricks had fallen or been pried from the outer wall. The door was set below street level, down several steps. Trevillion glanced at it and then back at Reed. The figures at the end of the lane had disappeared. It was empty now, despite the daylight. But then the type of people who lived in environs like these knew when to lie low.

Trevillion gestured to Reed.

Reed ran down the stairs and kicked the door in.

The footman fired immediately and the guard inside the door fell inward on a cloud of smoke and the smell of gunpowder.

Trevillion stepped inside, squinting. Three men were gathered around a table, apparently playing cards. They began to rise and Trevillion shot the biggest.

The remaining two men stared.

"I've one more bullet for the next man who moves," he said.

"James!" came Phoebe's voice from the inner room.

Trevillion handed his second pistol to Reed. "Don't bother to give warning before you shoot."

He went to the inner door and examined the latch. It was a simple bolt and he unlocked it.

Phoebe nearly fell into his arms. "Oh! Is it you?" She wore an old blue dress—the one she liked to put on to visit the stables. She tucked her nose into his neck and inhaled before beaming. "Yes, it is!"

Something came loose in his chest and he had a nearly overpowering urge to kiss Lady Phoebe's smiling mouth. Instead he cleared his throat and said, "Let me untie you, my lady."

"Oh, thank you," she said as he drew a knife from his boot and began carefully cutting through the rope that bound her wrists together.

"You," he called over his shoulder to one of the kidnappers. "Do you have more rope?"

The man looked between Trevillion and the gun that Reed held on him before answering. "Yes."

"Good. Tie up that other fellow," Trevillion ordered. "And make the knots tight. I'll be checking them."

The rope fell away from Lady Phoebe's wrists and he gently examined the abrasions there.

"But if'n I move—"

Trevillion sighed. "You can move enough to tie up your friend."

He drew out his handkerchief from a pocket and tore it in half. He gently wrapped Lady Phoebe's wrists.

"Thank you," she whispered. "I knew you'd come for me."

"Did you?" he asked. He'd deserted her. Left her to be kidnapped.

"Yes." She smiled winsomely. "Didn't you?"

He looked at her oddly as he finished bandaging her wrists. Didn't she know all of this was his fault? He should never have left. He should've stayed by her side day and night until the kidnappers were found and arrested.

Well. He wouldn't make the same mistake again.

When he turned, Reed had the last kidnapper bound and lying on the floor. The footman looked up and nodded.

"Come on," Trevillion said, urging Lady Phoebe out the door.

"Are you just gonna leave us 'ere?" one of the kidnappers called.

Trevillion turned, frowning. "Better gag them. They'll keep well enough until His Grace arrives to question them."

Reed did and they left, closing the door behind them.

"We have horses down here," he said to Lady Phoebe as he led her down the lane.

"Oh, lovely," she said.

Alf was still standing exactly as they'd left her, the horses' reins gripped in her white-knuckled hand. Trevillion had a fleeting thought that maybe she'd not moved the entire time they'd been gone.

"Good lad," he said to her. "I've one more job for you today. Can you deliver a message for me?"

Alf looked insulted. "O' course."

"Then tell the Duke of Wakefield this." And he bent to whisper in her ear. When he straightened, her eyes were as round as he'd ever seen them. "No one else, mind. And I expect you to continue with the task I set you last night."

"Yes, sir!" Alf grinned and started off at a lope.

"Reed." Trevillion turned to the footman. "I have a job for you, but in order for you to do it, you'll need to leave the duke's employ and enter mine temporarily. I can't guarantee that he'll take you back afterwards."

"I'm your man," Reed said stoutly. "Always 'ave been, always will be."

Trevillion smiled at him. "Thank you." He didn't quite whisper his instructions to the footman, but he made sure no one could overhear them.

When he was done, Reed saluted. "You can count on me, Cap'n."

"I know I can."

Reed swung onto his horse and trotted away.

"You've become quite mysterious since last I saw you, Captain," Lady Phoebe said.

"Have I, my lady?" He touched her hand to guide it to the stirrup.

"Yes, indeed," she said. "Are we riding together again?"

"If you don't mind, my lady," he replied.

"I find myself quite amenable to whatever you suggest now that I've been rescued from kidnappers," Lady Phoebe replied. "The prospect of forced marriage is rather off-putting."

"Is that what they intended?" Trevillion asked calmly

as he mounted the gelding behind her. Inside, rage was boiling in his chest.

"I think so, from what I overheard."

"Then be assured, my lady, that I shan't allow any such thing to happen to you. Not while you're with me."

He'd already made the decision, but this latest information only served to solidify it.

Trevillion was taking no more chances. He trusted no one but himself to make sure Lady Phoebe was entirely safe until the kidnapper was found.

Chapter Nine

Corineus determined that he would slay the giants and become king of this new land. So he rode the sea horse to the desolate moors where Gog, the smallest of the giants, dwelt. Gog stood as tall as two men, one atop another, and had a hideous face, nearly covered in boils and bits of black hair. Corineus set spur to the sea horse and she charged, fangs flashing. In a trice the giant lay dead upon the moor....
—From *The Kelpie*

Phoebe leaned back against Trevillion's broad chest as they rode through London. She cared not at all about the impropriety of such an action. He'd come back to her, saved her when she'd been at her most desperate. His scent—the one she'd given him—surrounded her and she was touched and grateful that he still wore it.

Sandalwood and bergamot meant safety to her now... and maybe something more.

She felt him tighten his thighs around the horse, urging the animal into a canter for several minutes, his arm around her waist holding her securely.

When Trevillion let the horse slow again, he asked her, "What happened? How were you kidnapped?"

She blew out a breath and straightened a bit. "I went out to the stables this morning to visit with the horses. But when I opened the gate into the mews someone grabbed me and put a hood over my head."

She shuddered just at the memory. It'd been close under the hood and even though she'd been able to breathe perfectly well, the awful feeling that the air might be taken away from her lungs had been almost overwhelming.

The arm he had about her waist tightened, his palm flat on her stomach. "Damn them," Trevillion whispered, so close he might've had his lips against her ear.

"They treated me quite well, considering," Phoebe hastened to assure him. "They hardly spoke at all, of course, but there was no hint of, er…impolite touching."

She tilted her head and listened. Something seemed to be vibrating in Captain Trevillion's throat. Good Lord! Was he growling?

"Could you tell how many there were?" he asked gruffly.

"Four. Just the four you found there where they were holding me, though there must've been a carriage driver as well, for that's how they brought me there." She reached for the horse's mane and threaded her fingers through the stiff hairs. "But I overheard a bit of what they were saying just before you and Reed arrived. They were waiting for someone—and he was bringing a vicar."

"To force you into marriage," Trevillion rasped.

She moved one hand to the arm he had around her waist. The muscle beneath her fingers was as hard as steel. "James, do you or Maximus know who the man is? The one who wants to marry me?"

His forearm flexed beneath her fingers. "I'm afraid we have no idea as of yet. I'm sorry. I did recognize one of the attackers at Harte's Folly—he was at Bond Street as well."

She turned her face toward him. "What? Why didn't you tell me earlier?"

"I didn't want to alarm you," he said tightly.

"So instead you left me quite literally in the dark?" she asked sweetly.

"I see now that decision was most likely a mistake," he replied. "In any case, both your brother and I have been investigating the matter. The problem is, we haven't found a clear suspect."

"That's rather disappointing," she said evenly. Would she be living in fear of kidnap at any moment until the villain was found?

"Indeed," Trevillion bit out. "Did the kidnappers say anything else about the man they were waiting for?"

She shook her head. "I'm afraid not."

He swore under his breath. "He could be anyone, then."

"Anyone willing to force a lady into an unwanted marriage," she agreed. "I had no idea I had so many suitors."

"What do you mean?"

"Mr. MacLeish proposed to me only yesterday," she said lightly.

The arm around her waist tightened almost to the point of forcing the air from her body, and then abruptly relaxed.

"Congratulations," Captain Trevillion said in a flat, emotionless voice.

Really, sometimes it would be much easier if one were allowed to simply hit gentlemen over the head.

"I refused," she said rather tartly.

"Why?" he asked, his voice softer.

She twisted to bring her face closer to his even though she couldn't see him. "What do you mean, *why*?"

He cleared his throat. "Malcolm MacLeish is young and handsome—"

"A fat lot of good that does me, since I can't *see* him."

"—a gentleman of high spirits and quick wit and seemingly smitten with you as well."

There was a silence.

"Smitten," Phoebe said at last. "*Smit*-ten. The word sounds like a skin disease if you think about it too much."

"He smiles every time he sees you," he murmured quietly. Was he jealous?

"I smile every time I smell cherry pie."

"You're being ridiculous," Trevillion said disapprovingly. "I don't see why you've rejected him out of hand."

"You sound like a querulous old aunt, scolding children for running through the house."

"I *am* older than you," he replied stiffly, "as I've pointed out on numerous occasions."

A terrible thought struck her. "Are you shoving me at Mr. MacLeish because I kissed you?"

"I—"

"It was my very first kiss, you ought to know," she said very rapidly, because sometimes it was just better to say the embarrassing thing and get it over with. "I'm sure I'll improve with practice. In fact, I'm sure of it. Almost everything improves with practice, don't you think? And really, if I had a just a *bit* of help from your end next time—"

"I am *not* kissing you," he said with the awful finality of a judge pronouncing a death sentence.

"Why not?"

"You know very well why not."

"Nooo," she said slowly, thinking it over. "No, I can't say that I do, really. I mean I know why you *think* we oughtn't kiss again: you're as old as the Thames, you're below me in rank, I'm too young and frivolous, and you much too serious, et cetera, et cetera, and et cetera, but frankly I don't have any reasons not to kiss you." She stopped for breath and to think and amended her statement. "Unless, of course, you're either (a) a murderer running from the law or (b) hiding a secret wife. Are you?"

"I... *what*?"

"Are you," she repeated patiently, "either a murderer running from the law or hiding a secret wife?"

"You know I'm not," he said with impatience. It was a good thing she was so stubborn, because that tone might have put off many another young girl. "Phoebe—"

"So then there's no reason at all not to kiss me again." She folded her hands in her lap and smiled.

He drew the horse to a very abrupt halt. "We're here."

"Oof," she muttered. "This isn't Wakefield House."

"No, it isn't," he replied. "I'm not taking you back to Wakefield House until your brother has found the kidnapper."

She turned her head again, her lips brushing his hair. "Does Maximus know you're doing this?"

"He will when he gets the message I told Alf to give him." His voice was hard, almost foreign in its steeliness.

"You didn't work this out with him beforehand?" she asked with interest, because her brother was after all a *duke* and *Maximus* to boot. He wasn't used to other people's taking charge.

Not at all.

"No," he said quietly.

She shivered suddenly. In his own way, Trevillion was just as stubborn as her brother.

Perhaps even more so.

Hadn't she had enough of autocratic men in her life? Did she really want to become *closer* to Trevillion? What if he was no better than her brother?

What if he was *worse*?

But Trevillion was still speaking. "Your maid, Powers, was the one who sold the information that you liked to visit the stables of a morning."

That diverted her attention. "What? That can't be."

"I'm afraid it is, my lady," he replied, not unkindly.

"But…" Of all the events of the day, this was the one that made her lips tremble. Powers hadn't been with Phoebe long, but she'd *seemed* quite nice. They'd had a lovely discussion about the proper height of heeled shoes just yesterday.

"I'm sorry," Trevillion said as he dismounted. "But if Powers could be bought, there may be others in his house who can be as well. Until the kidnapper is caught you aren't, in my estimation, safe at your brother's house. And since we cannot determine who is to be trusted and who is not, I've decided to trust no one at all except myself."

"What do you mean?" she whispered.

He wrapped his hands about her waist. Strong. Competent. Safe.

His voice was low and not a little dark when he replied. "I'm removing you from London entirely and not even your brother shall know where I take you."

LADY PHOEBE'S WARM waist was caught between Trevillion's palms as he waited for her to do the sensible thing and protest his high-handed declaration.

Instead she beamed at him as if he'd shown her a particularly clever trick. "Really?" she said, sounding ridiculously excited. "Where do you intend to take me, then?"

"I'll tell you once we've started," he replied. "Come, let's get you inside first."

He'd ridden to an inn on the outskirts of London—one that happened to be owned by a former soldier who had been under his command. Reed was supposed to meet him here, but Trevillion saw no sign of him. He wasn't particularly worried, though, given the tasks he'd asked Reed to perform for him.

Trevillion lifted Lady Phoebe carefully down from the horse, reluctant to let her go when he'd set her on her feet.

"Where are we?" she asked, her berry-red lips curved in a smile.

"A posting inn outside London called The Piper." He handed the reins of the horse to a boy and led her inside.

The interior of the inn was dim after the brightness of the courtyard, the ceiling beamed and very low. Round tables were crowded in the common area about a roaring fire, and a dozen or so travelers sat eating. Trevillion wasted no time in renting a private back room. The sooner Lady Phoebe was out of public sight, the less likely that she'd be recognized.

"There's a chair here for you to sit," he said when the lass who'd shown them the room had departed in search of the innkeeper. The private room was small, with a rectangular table, six chairs, and a fireplace. "I've ordered something for you to eat."

"Beer?" Lady Phoebe perked up. "I've never had beer."

"No." He cocked his head. Common women drank beer but ladies didn't. "Some tea, ham, and eggs."

"Oh well," she said, exploring the wooden table before her delicately with her fingertips, "I expect I'll have a chance to try beer later on our trip. We are going on a trip, aren't we?"

"We are."

She frowned suddenly. "But you *did* send word to Maximus that I'm safe?"

"I sent Alf—he's nimble enough to dodge should the duke become overly irate," he replied drily. "He also has the address of our destination so that your brother can send word when it's safe."

She still didn't look easy. "But what if Maximus forces Alf to tell him the direction?"

"Alf is very hard to find when he doesn't want to be found. I gave him instructions to make himself scarce until the kidnapper is discovered and apprehended. He'll also be doing his own investigating—for me."

Trevillion had expanded Alf's directive to find the kidnappers when he'd given the instructions for informing Wakefield. Now Alf was to find out all she could about both the kidnapping and the Duke of Montgomery's relationship with Malcolm MacLeish. The latter didn't seem to bear on the former, but there was MacLeish's proposal to Lady Phoebe now. That, if nothing else, called for MacLeish to be thoroughly examined.

Her eyes widened. "You've thought of everything, haven't you?"

Before Trevillion could answer, the door to the room burst open. Instinctively his hand went to the pistols on his belts, but the newcomer was no threat.

"Captain, sir!" The innkeeper enveloped Trevillion in a bear hug and then, as if recollecting himself, stepped back and, standing at attention, saluted him. "What can I do for you, sir?"

Ben Wooster, formerly Sergeant Wooster of the 4th Dragoons, was a barrel-chested man with flaming orange hair, a massive nose that had once been broken, and a wooden leg he'd received courtesy of a gunshot to the tibia. The injury had put an end to his army career. Fortunately Wooster had had a much older brother who owned The Piper. Wooster had come to work for his brother after his retirement and eventually bought the inn outright when his brother decided to move to the countryside.

"It's good to see you, Wooster," Trevillion said. "I have a favor to ask of you, if you've a mind to help me."

"Anything at all, Captain," replied the innkeeper. "Was your quick thinking that saved me from losing more than this old leg the night I was shot."

"Good man," Trevillion said. "I'm protecting this lady from those who would do her a terrible wrong. I shan't give you her name, for it won't be in either of our interests. Should someone come inquiring about her after we've left, I'd be obliged if you'll forget we were ever here."

Wooster's cheery face turned grave. "O' course, Captain."

"Further, I have need of a carriage and team, and a change of clothes for the lady," Trevillion continued. "I'll pay for both, naturally."

"Won't be a problem for the carriage, though the vehicle I've in mind is a bit old."

"No matter," Trevillion said, relieved. His biggest worry had been finding a carriage on such short notice.

"But I 'aven't such clothes what are fit for a grand lady," Wooster said, scratching his head. "Only some of my wife's things. If you don't mind waiting I can send one of the girls out—"

"No need," Trevillion interrupted. "Your wife's clothes would be just the thing."

Wooster grinned, revealing a missing eyetooth. "In that case, sir, I'll send me wife right away with the articles."

"Thank you, my friend." Trevillion shook the other man's hand.

Wooster left just as a maidservant entered, bearing a tray of food.

"Oh, that smells wonderful," Lady Phoebe remarked as the dishes were laid on the table. "Will you join me, Captain?"

It seemed too intimate to dine alone with her—no matter recent events she was still his charge—but he hadn't been able to finish his own breakfast this morning.

"If you'll permit," he said.

"Of course I permit," Lady Phoebe replied. "Really, Captain, when have I ever *not* permitted you anything?"

He shot her a suspicious glance, but she seemed engrossed in serving herself some of the coddled eggs, carefully feeling with her fingertips as she filled a spoon and transferred it to the plate in front of her.

"Would you like some tea, my lady?" he asked gruffly.

"Oh, please," she replied. "My throat is quite dry after being held so long."

"Did they gag you?" He paused with the teapot half lifted, and found himself staring at his hand. It was trembling. With rage. If he could have, he'd have gone back and cut their fingers off for daring to touch her.

She turned to him as if she sensed his inner fury, her brows knit over vague hazel eyes. "One of them placed his hand over my mouth, but I wasn't gagged. I suppose they handled me quite gently, all things considered. I really oughtn't complain."

He poured her tea without comment, too afraid of what he might say.

He added sugar and pushed the cup toward her across the table. "Your tea, my lady. It's just to the right of your plate."

She found the cup and took a sip. "Lovely. Just the way I like it, with sugar—but then you knew that, didn't you?"

Any answer he gave would just incriminate him, so he dished up some eggs of his own. They were quite good and for a moment they simply ate in silence.

A knock came at the door before it opened a crack, revealing a small, smiling woman in a mobcap and apron and with a bundle of clothes in her arms. "Now I'm Mrs. Wooster come to 'elp the lady dress," she said, "as Wooster said I should."

"Thank you, Mrs. Wooster." Trevillion stood. "I'll wait in the outer room while you do so."

"Why, thank you, sir," Mrs. Wooster said, bustling in. "Wooster is waiting for you with your man, as I understand."

Trevillion nodded and went out. After a bit of searching, he found Reed and Wooster in the courtyard inspecting a carriage that had seen better days.

Wooster turned at his arrival. "I knows it's not much to look at, but she's still in working order an' will carry you where you need to go, sir."

"I don't doubt it," Trevillion returned. He glanced at Reed. "Did you do as I asked?"

"Yes, sir," Reed responded. He lifted Trevillion's own soft bag. "Got your things from the boardinghouse."

"Well done," Trevillion said. He took the bag that Reed handed him and rummaged in it to find his purse. Then he counted out several gold coins. "Will this do?" he asked Wooster.

"Indeed, sir, more'n enough by my estimate," Wooster said. "Now let me show you the nags I have, for I know you like to choose your own horseflesh."

Trevillion nodded. He plucked one thing more from his purse, then pocketed it and stowed his bag in the carriage.

In another fifteen minutes he'd picked four sturdy animals from those in Wooster's stables. He turned to Reed. "Do you think you can drive this carriage? I can if you feel unprepared to do so, but I think it better that I ride inside with the lady."

"I've driven a team before, sir," Reed said.

Trevillion clapped a hand on the man's back. "Then let's ready the carriage and be on our way. I'll fetch our lady while you oversee the hitching of the horses." He looked at Wooster. "I'm in your debt, Sergeant."

"Never say so, Captain," Wooster replied. "I'm that glad to 'elp ye, sir. You were the best officer the dragoons ever 'ad and that's a fact."

Trevillion smiled his thanks and made his way past a new coach and various passengers, dogs, and stableboys to the inn. Inside he quickly slipped back to the private room and knocked.

Mrs. Wooster opened the door. "Well, she's all set, though it's a shame to trade a silk gown for plain fustian."

"It's all for the best, Mrs. Wooster," Trevillion said. "I thank you for your kindness."

"She's already thanked me, she has—and given me her gown." Mrs. Wooster suddenly grinned. "Won't old

Wooster be that surprised to find 'is wife in silk come Sunday morning!"

So saying, the innkeeper's wife bustled away.

Trevillion turned to find Phoebe standing in the private room, waiting for him.

"Well?" she asked, nervously twisting her fingers together. "What do you think?"

She wore an indigo gown with a lighter-blue bodice. A neat white apron was pinned to the front and a white cap and fichu completed the ensemble. Her cheeks were flushed a delicate pink and the blue brought out the green in her hazel eyes.

"You're perfect," Trevillion said, and then found he had to clear his throat. "I have one thing more to add to your costume."

She cocked her head. "What's that?"

He stepped closer and took her left hand, slipping a plain gold band on her finger. "A wedding ring, Mrs. Trevillion."

MANY HOURS LATER Phoebe sat in the carriage and surreptitiously felt the ring on her finger again. It was very smooth with no sharp edges, which really didn't tell her anything at all. Now if she could see the ring . . .

She sighed and let her hands fall to her lap. It was terribly monotonous traveling by carriage, especially when one couldn't even see out the window. She'd spent part of the afternoon sleeping fitfully in between being jostled as the carriage bumped over what felt like furrows in a field. Now, however, she was wide awake and bored beyond belief.

"Whose ring is it?" she asked. Trevillion had spent a good deal of time riding with Reed up in the box, but he'd come inside again at their last stop.

"What?" He sounded distracted. She knew that he was worried about being followed and about keeping her safe, but she really did think they must be well away from London by now.

"The ring." She held up her hand in case he was looking her way. The carriage hit a rut in the road and she bounced on the seat. "Oof! Whom does it belong to?"

"No one, my lady," he said in a voice that meant he'd really rather not discuss the matter. "At least not anymore."

She waited, but apparently he was going to leave it at that.

Well, not she.

"You know," she began as gently as possible, "you can't just pop a ring on a woman, declare her your wife, and not have to answer a few questions."

"I told you, it's only a ruse until we can get to a safe place," he said. "A man and wife are much less likely to cause comment than a man traveling with a woman not related to him."

"Yes, that's certainly true," she said sweetly. "I suppose I should be happy you just happened to have a wedding ring lying about the place."

"It was my mother's," he said abruptly.

The carriage was small, she knew, and he sat across from her. She could smell, faintly, the scent of sandalwood and bergamot. Physically he was very close, but from his tone of voice?

He might as well be on another continent.

"I'm sorry," she said at last, choosing her words carefully. "She's dead, isn't she?"

"Yes," he said, flat and toneless. "Died of fever when I was four. We all caught it, apparently, but only she died of it."

She'd lost her own parents, of course, but she'd been only a baby. She didn't remember them at all. But a four-year-old boy would remember his mama—remember and mourn her.

Not of course that Trevillion was the type of man to tell her that. "That must've been very hard for you. Very hard for your family."

He didn't reply.

She tried again. "What was she like?"

There was a silence and she thought he might not answer her question—it was rather intrusive.

"Soft," he said. "I remember her being very soft. Her arms, her hands, her lap, and her cheeks. I thought her very beautiful—the most beautiful woman in the world—though I've heard from others that she was an ordinary sort of pretty. She used to tell me stories."

He abruptly stopped talking.

"What kind of stories?" she asked quietly, afraid of breaking the spell.

"Oh, of giant slayers and knights fighting dragons," he said. "Sometimes she told me about the mermaids in the sea."

"What about them?"

"Be wary of their song," he answered drily. "Ah, we're stopping."

"Already?" she asked, disappointed now that she'd finally gotten him to talk just a little about his family.

"It's eight of the clock, my lady, and quite dark. I'd continue, but Reed and I agreed earlier that it wasn't prudent to travel far after the sun set. Especially as we're not traveling the main road."

"Then where are we?" she inquired.

"I believe"—she heard a rustling as if Trevillion looked out the window—"we're at a small inn. Very small."

The door to the carriage opened. "They have a room, sir," Reed said. "I'll sleep with the carriage."

"Very good." Phoebe felt Trevillion touch her arm lightly. "Are you ready?"

She took a breath and smiled. "Of course." They'd discussed this earlier: she was to be his wife and let him do the majority of the talking. With any luck most of the people they met wouldn't even notice that she was blind.

Trevillion took her hand, guiding her down from the carriage. She could hear a dog barking quite close and the soft whicker of horses. They walked across a soft earth courtyard and then Trevillion ushered her into the inn.

It was warmer here, the soft chatter of country accents coming from a common room. She could smell the smoke of the fire and meat cooking. Trevillion spoke to someone—presumably the innkeeper—and then he was leading her back through a passage, the voices of the common room fading behind them. He opened a door and led her through it.

"Here we are," he said. "A private room, with a ceiling blackened by the fire smoke. We are in a venerable establishment. Here's a chair by your left hand."

She felt the chair arm under her hand and sat. The chair was in front of a table and she began to trace the wood, deeply grooved in places, the initials H.G. carved at the edge.

The door opened again and a woman with a high voice brought in some savory-smelling dishes, then left again.

She heard the scrape of a chair as Trevillion sat down, presumably across from her. A spoon clinked against a pewter dish. "Ah. It seems we have a sort of stew. Mutton, perhaps? With cabbage and a fair amount of carrots and peas. May I serve you some?"

"Please, dear husband."

For a moment the spoon stilled, and then she heard the sound of stew being ladled into a bowl.

The edge bumped gently against her knuckles.

"There's a spoon at three of the clock and a piece of bread at nine, darling wife."

She nearly giggled.

"And, just for you, I've ordered a mild ale instead of wine," he said.

"Have you?"

"Much against my better judgment. It's a common drink, my la—ahem, *wife*, and I cannot think it'll be pleasing to your palate. Although," he added under his breath, "considering where we are, the beer is probably better here than the wine."

She brightened at the prospect of a new experience. "Then I must taste it at once."

"It's right here." He took her hand and placed it on a pewter tankard.

"To your health, husband," she said solemnly and took a sip.

Or rather tried to, for her nose seemed to be buried in foam. She inhaled in surprise—not the best thing to do—coughed, and then sneezed.

"I do beg your pardon," Captain Trevillion said, and she couldn't help noticing that his voice was oddly muffled.

Phoebe sneezed again—rather violently—dabbed at her eyes and nose with her handkerchief, regained her breath, and immediately demanded, "Are you laughing at me?"

"Never my...wife. *Never*," he assured her, his voice shaking.

He *was*. He was most certainly laughing.

She sat up straight, threw her shoulders back, and brought the tankard to her mouth again. This time she kept her nose out of the way and delicately sipped through the foam. The beer was...well, sour. And oddly prickly on her tongue. She held it in her mouth for a moment, thinking, and then swallowed.

"Well?"

She held up a finger and took another sip. Sour. Yeast. Something earthy. And those funny little prickles. She swallowed and took another sip. Did she like the aroma? She'd smelled it all her life—most of the people of London drank beer—it was the common man's water. That sour tang, so warm and strong.

She plunked down her tankard. "I think...I *think* I shall have to experience it more."

"Why?" he asked. "If you don't like it, then drink wine."

"I didn't say I didn't *like* it."

"Nor did you seem overcome with your enjoyment of it," he pointed out drily.

"It's...different—very different—from anything I've ever tasted before," she said, her finger tracing the cool metal of the tankard. "I'd like to try it again."

"If you wish to do so, then I'll certainly obtain you beer at our meals while we travel, but I don't understand. Why force yourself to drink what you don't like?"

"But I'm not forcing myself," she returned, tracing the edge of the tankard, feeling the bubbles pop against her fingertip. "Don't you see? I want to explore different things—food, places, people. If, after several tastings,

I find I cannot stomach the beer, then I shall give it up. Often something tasted for the first time seems foreign to us—strange and off-putting. It's only after repeated tries that one realizes that this new thing, this once-strange thing, is quite familiar now. Familiar and beloved." Phoebe inhaled, her breath coming too quickly with the force of her argument. "To only try but once and declare a thing lacking...why, that's quite cowardly."

She felt the warmth of Trevillion's hand as his fingers touched hers on the tankard lip. "The one thing you'll never be, my lady, is a coward."

Phoebe smiled as the warmth of his fingers seemed to spread to her hand, up her arm, and to her very heart.

She cleared her throat. "We've been traveling for a day. Can you tell me now where we're bound?"

His hand was immediately gone from hers. "We're bound for the safest place for you that I can think of."

She cocked her head, analyzing his voice. He sounded... *resigned*, as if he didn't like this place very much. She'd even have said that there was a touch of dread in his voice, if such a thing hadn't been completely impossible when it came to Trevillion.

"Is it..." Phoebe licked her lips. "Is it a place you've been to before?"

"Yes." Toneless.

"Do you want to see it again?"

"*No*." A deep breath. "But that doesn't matter. What matters is keeping you safe above all things."

But Phoebe couldn't help thinking: *Even above Trevillion's safety?*

Chapter Ten

*That night Corineus and the sea horse slept upon
the moor under the wide, moonless sky. A breeze
stirred among the stars, and seemed to bring a
faint, melancholy song, as if dozens of maidens
lamented the loss of their sister....*
—From *The Kelpie*

It wasn't until a wheezing innkeeper showed them their
room later that night that Phoebe fully comprehended
what it meant that she and Trevillion were traveling as
man and wife.

Married couples shared a room.

And a bed.

All day riding in the carriage and not once had that fact
occurred to her. Perhaps all the jostling from the poorly
sprung carriage had made her soft in the head.

She heard the faint scrape of a boot as Trevillion
turned at the other side of the room...some ten feet away.

He cleared his voice. "The bed is small, but quite adequate for two adults. We will, of course, place a pillow or
some such thing in the middle."

She cocked her head. "Are there more than two pillows?"

"No."

"Then what will one of us place our heads on?"

"I'll think of something," he said repressively. "Now. Directly to your right is a washstand and basin." He crossed over and she heard the sound of pouring water. "Plenty for you to wash, although I'm afraid it isn't heated. The . . . er, chamber pot is just under the bed, on the side nearest you. I shall go check on Reed and make sure he's comfortable. I'll be about half an hour."

And he went out of the room while she was still blushing over the chamber pot instructions.

Phoebe blew out a breath and took a step to the right, her hand outstretched. Immediately she bumped against the washstand. She traced her fingertips over the top until she came to a small pitcher—pewter—and the washbasin—china with a chip on the lip.

Nodding to herself, she untied her bonnet. There was a chair by the washstand and she laid the bonnet there. Fortunately the clothes provided by Mrs. Wooster were a working woman's apparel—things, unlike her own, that she could take off and put back on without a lady's maid. She had a pang at the thought of Powers. Where was the girl now? Maximus would've let her go without reference at the very least. Phoebe shook her head. She didn't think Powers had hated her—although it was always hard to tell what a good servant truly felt about their master or mistress. But to risk a plum situation as a duke's sister's lady's maid, Powers must've been quite desperate. Phoebe made a vow to herself to inquire after Powers once she returned to London, and find out if she needed help.

That settled, she removed her fichu, apron, skirt, and bodice and placed them neatly on the chair. Then, standing in only her stockings, shoes, stays, and chemise, she washed her face and neck. Brrr! Trevillion had been correct: the water was chilly.

The thought of his perhaps returning while she was in her undergarments spurred her on to untie the laces of her stays, and then the thought struck her: what if Trevillion *did* return while she was undressed?

For a moment she was frozen. Would he like the sight of her body—or merely think her wanton? How would she feel, knowing he looked at her?

Strange. She didn't think often of her body or face anymore. She couldn't see them, so she couldn't pose before a mirror, examining flaws, finding parts she was particularly proud of.

Her body was merely serviceable now—not something to lure a man.

But if she became closer to Trevillion…if someday she let him make love to her…then her body would be more, wouldn't it?

Slowly she continued to unlace her stays, feeling as her breasts dropped free, as her ribs and waist cooled in the night air. She cupped her breasts through her chemise. The chemise was her own, made of linen, light as a feather, slippery under her fingertips. She had plump breasts, overflowing her palms. Well, everything about her was a bit plump: rounded tummy, curving hips. Did Trevillion like plump, petite women? Or was he more drawn to one of those swanlike creatures, tall and slender, with long legs and necks?

Slowly she smoothed her hands down her sides, feeling her own flesh, warm and soft. Goosebumps prickled over her skin, but not from the slight chill.

Something clattered outside the room and she jumped.

Oh! He mustn't catch her daydreaming—*that* wouldn't be attractive at all. Hurriedly Phoebe took off her shoes and stockings, and then began work on her hair.

It had started the morning in a simple knot—redone with the help of Mrs. Wooster. She pulled pins from her hair and carefully laid them on the washstand, for she might not have a chance to replace them anytime soon. But then she ran into a dilemma: she had no hairbrush or comb. Dash it! She should've asked Mrs. Wooster for one to take with her.

At that point someone knocked at the door.

Phoebe squeaked and darted for the bed. She banged her shin on the side—quite painfully!—before leaping in and pulling the covers to her chin.

She cleared her voice before calling, "Come in."

The door opened.

"Everything to your satisfaction?" Trevillion asked.

"Yes." She listened as something thumped to the floor—his bag? "Actually, might you have a comb I can borrow?"

"Of course." A rummaging sound and then he came closer to the bed.

She felt both self-conscious and a tiny bit excited. She wore only her chemise under the blankets. Her hair was down about her shoulders. She'd never been in so intimate a situation with a man before.

With *Trevillion* before.

She took a breath and held out her hand and felt the comb placed in it.

He walked away again as she began to draw the comb through her hair, starting at the ends, working her way up to untangle the strands. The blanket still covered her breasts, but she felt it slipping as she worked. Impossible to hold it and comb her hair at the same time.

She wet her lips. "How was Reed?"

"Quite comfortable. He had some of the mutton stew and is bedded down with the horses in the stable."

She heard a boot thump softly to the floor and realized that he was undressing. Right now. *In front of her.*

She might have squeaked.

He stopped. "I'm sorry?"

"Oh, nothing!" She gathered all her hair over her left shoulder.

The blanket slipped to the tips of her breasts.

"Ah." He cleared his throat again.

"Are you getting a cold, do you think?" she called.

"No."

More rustling. What exactly was he taking off? How many clothes did he have on? Would he come to bed *nude*?

"You're sure? Because I thought it was quite chilly this evening and perhaps after your evening stroll you should have a hot posset. It wouldn't do to come down with a fever."

"I haven't a cold," he said, suddenly quite close. He moved so silently without his boots on. "And I'm not the one sitting in a cold room in only a chemise."

Oh, he'd noticed! Phoebe felt rather gratified.

She smelled sandalwood and bergamot, and then his voice was a purring growl near her ear. "Are you quite done?"

Most likely he was referring to the comb.

Most likely.

"Er, yes." She held it out.

"Thank you." It was plucked from her fingers.

The bed dipped on the other side and Phoebe grabbed

wildly for the mattress so she wouldn't roll toward the center.

"I'm putting out the candle," he informed her. "And I've placed my coat between us."

She gingerly lay down on her side and felt with one hand until she encountered the rough coat fabric. He'd rolled it into a long tube between them. "You know, this really isn't necessary."

"Good night, Phoebe."

She smiled—though he probably couldn't see it, as blind as she in the darkness. "Good night, James."

She lay for a while then, drifting in the warm quiet, nearly asleep until a sudden thought roused her.

Phoebe turned on her other side, facing him. "If my brother doesn't know where we're headed, then how will he pay you?"

"Pay me?" His voice was slow and puzzled.

"Your salary."

"He owes me no salary, my lady," he replied, his voice now alert. "Your brother no longer employs me."

She frowned, confused. "He didn't hire you again to rescue me?"

"No."

"If my brother didn't send you…" She considered his words sleepily. "Then why are you here?"

But he didn't answer and she fell asleep still wondering.

TREVILLION WOKE THE next morning as he often did: all at once, at exactly six of the clock, and with a stiff cock.

What wasn't usual was the soft breath against his neck, the small hand draped over his chest, and the face pressed into his shoulder. Apparently his rolled coat had lost the battle in the night to Lady Phoebe and her unconscious stubbornness.

He lay for a moment, simply listening to her breathe. He could feel her soft breast pressed into his side. He'd somehow draped his arm around her so that she lay within his embrace. To anyone entering the room, they'd have looked like lovers, he and Lady Phoebe. He closed his eyes. If he were truly married to her, this was what every morning might be like: sweet and unhurried, full of potential.

But he wasn't married to Phoebe and they most certainly were not lovers—now or in the future.

The thought was a bitter draught, hard to swallow, harder to keep down: this woman wasn't for him.

Cautiously he began inching his arm out from beneath her neck.

But Lady Phoebe was never as easy as that.

She murmured something intelligible and curled into him, like a hedgehog resisting being disturbed. He craned his neck, looking down, and watched as her nose scrunched adorably. Her light-brown hair was spread upon her pillow and draped over the side of her face, one strand caught between her lush, rose lips.

Blowing out a silent breath, he let his head fall back to the pillow, trapped by a slip of a girl.

God, but his cock was hard—he could feel the pulse of his blood, hot and insistent. Were he in the bed alone he'd slip his hand downward, over the flat, hard planes of his belly, into the coarse hair below. Fondle his balls, drawn up tight below that jutting flesh, and finally take his cock into his hand. Touch the tip, sensitive and wet, take some of that moisture and spread it down the shaft, squeezing just a bit as he—

"Um?" Phoebe sighed the sound into his neck, reaching up one hand to scratch her nose. "Wha—?"

He swallowed before he could speak. Still, his voice came out a deep rasp. "Good morning, my lady."

Somewhere, somehow, a god was laughing at him.

He knew the moment she came completely awake, for she immediately froze.

She inhaled, breathed out, inhaled again, and said, "James?"

"Yes?"

"What are you wearing?" Her nimble fingers were already exploring the broadcloth over his rib cage, sliding, feeling their way.

She was going to drive him insane.

"My shirt, my lady."

Her fingers stilled a moment. "Is that all?" Her voice was rather husky, but that might be from disuse.

He cleared his throat. "No, I have on my breeches as well." *Thank God*.

"James?"

"I think you ought to cease calling me by my given name, my lady," he said, sounding to his own ears like a virginal eighty-year-old—rather ironic since the *actual* virgin in the room was presently slipping her fingers inside the open V of his shirt.

He held his breath as she traced his collarbone.

"Why?" she asked. "I like your name. *James* is so very practical. I always think one can rely on a James—and I can rely on you, can't I?"

He cleared his throat again, trying to remember his argument. "Yes, but—"

"You've got chest hair!" she exclaimed, as if discovering

he had wings. "How very strange that must be. Does it get tangled in your shirts?"

"Ow," he remarked, because her exploring fingers had caught a few. "No. Not unless I were to decide to wear chain mail shirts."

"It's very thick," she said next. "How far does it go down—"

He rolled off the bed. Rather fast in fact, losing a few of those chest hairs to her fingers as he did. And for the first time he was actually glad she was blind, because if she could see she'd have gotten quite the eyeful. His cock had been more than happy with her curiosity.

She sat up, which did *not* help matters at all, because as he'd observed last night her chemise was damnably fine. He could see her nipples if he looked.

Only a base cad would look.

They were bright pink and pointed and sat atop the most gorgeous round breasts he'd ever seen. He just wanted to—

He looked away and began dressing.

"What's the matter?" she asked.

"You know damned well what the matter is," he surprised himself by replying heatedly. This wasn't the way to speak to a lady, to an employer's sister, to—

"No, I don't," she said. "Why don't you come back and we can practice the kissing that—"

"You're too young!" he shouted. "Too highborn, too reckless with your own safety, too sweet, and too damned young. *Stop.* Stop baiting me, stop using me as your own personal plaything. I might be your brother's servant, but I'm a man as well."

"I never thought you weren't," she said quietly. "I know

you're a man, James. I wouldn't have it any other way. I don't want a personal plaything. I want *you*."

"You can't have me, my lady," he said. "I'm sorry."

And he walked out of the room before he could take the words back.

"BUT MY DEAR, surely you've heard?" Lady Herrick leaned ever so slightly forward, the smile playing about her lovely mouth announcing that she had an exquisite point of gossip.

. Eve took a sip of her tea and politely shook her head. "As I've said, I'm not sure to what you refer, my lady."

They both sat in Lady Herrick's front room, which was done in pale blue, pink, and gold. Tiny gilded spoons were stacked on the tea table along with small hard biscuits. They were prettily decorated in pink icing, but they tasted like chalk. Eve had just given Lady Herrick the miniature portrait of a certain gentleman that she'd painted for her.

"Why, Lady Phoebe's kidnapping," Lady Herrick said with just enough relish to confirm Phoebe's opinion that the lady was a rather nasty piece of work under all that gold silk brocade. "She was taken from her very home, darling—the Duke of Wakefield's town house right here in London. Some say she's already been returned to her brother's house, but if so, no one's seen her." Lady Herrick gave a delicate shudder. "Who knows what might've been done to the poor girl—blind and in the clutches of men without scruples?"

Her hostess took a sip of tea, her eyes smiling maliciously over her teacup rim.

Eve decided she'd had quite enough tea. "Are you satisfied with the portrait, my lady?"

Lady Herrick picked up the tiny piece. It was oval, painted on a thin ivory board, suitable for ornamenting a snuffbox or simply framing. "Oh yes. You have his likeness exactly, Miss Dinwoody. Your talent is really quite extraordinary."

"Thank you, my lady." Eve set her teacup down precisely. "I hope you won't mind terribly if I depart? I'm afraid I have an appointment I truly can't miss."

"Indeed?" Eve could see Lady Herrick's mind working, trying to think whom she might be off to meet with. "Well, in that case I won't delay you. Thank you again for the portrait."

"My lady." Eve rose and curtsied, discreetly collecting the small purse of coins Lady Herrick had earlier given her.

A footman escorted her out of the sitting room and down the stairs. Jean-Marie was waiting for her in the front hallway. He turned from inspecting a rather gaudy statuette of a Moorish boy in turban, loincloth, and earrings. The statuette was made of some black marble and the earrings, eyes, and lips were gilded.

"Ma'am." Jean-Marie inclined his head as she made the hallway. He held the front door open for her. "Do you think I should wear gold earrings?"

"I think," Eve said as they walked to her carriage, "that Tess would never speak to me again if I said yes."

"Hm," Jean-Marie murmured as he opened the carriage door and set the step.

Tess was Jean-Marie's wife and Eve's very talented cook. For the sake of her stomach she liked to keep Tess happy.

Eve stepped into the carriage and waited for Jean-Marie to step inside as well.

"Home?" Jean-Marie asked, raising his hand to knock on the roof to signal the driver.

"No," Eve replied. "I should like to visit Val."

Jean-Marie gave her a long look and then shouted to the driver, "To the Duke of Montgomery's town house!" before sitting down again.

"Is zere any partic'lar reason you wish to visit 'Is Grace?" Jean-Marie asked. Sometimes when he was tired, or excited, or felt some strong emotion, the French Creole accent crept into his speech.

"I heard something quite"—Eve paused, carefully selecting her words—"*distressing* at Lady Herrick's house."

"And what was zat?"

"Someone kidnapped Lady Phoebe Batten." She felt her face suddenly crumple for just a moment—a second of panic-inducing loss of control. She dug her fingers into her palms, fists shaking, as she pushed down old memories.

Old fears.

She squeezed her eyes shut and willed the fear away. She was strong. She was Eve Dinwoody, a grown woman with a house and servants of her own.

And most importantly, she had Jean-Marie, patient, strong, and absolutely lethal if he wished it.

She was safe.

Eve inhaled slowly. But Phoebe hadn't been safe. Even in her brother's house in the middle of London, she'd been stolen, a blind girl.

She must've been completely terrified.

"Eve, *mon amie*," Jean-Marie said, his deep bass voice distressed.

She opened her eyes at once and smiled at him. "It's all right. *I'm* all right."

His coffee-brown eyes were worried, but before he could challenge her statement, the carriage pulled to a stop.

At once Jean-Marie jumped out to set the step.

He helped her down.

Eve looked up at him. "Wait here."

Jean-Marie didn't like the order, she could tell, but he nodded grimly.

She turned and faced the huge town house Val lived in. At least six stories high and newly built, with massive columns and a pediment, it screamed outrageous expenditure, which rather fit the man himself. Within the pediment was a bas-relief of a smiling Hermes in traveler's cloak and hat, holding his caduceus. The god of trickery and thieves bore a rather uncanny resemblance to Val himself.

Eve snorted.

She climbed the front steps and let the massive gilt knocker fall.

Almost immediately the door was opened, but instead of a butler a young woman stood in the opening. She was tallish, standing very straight, and dressed all in black, save for her apron, fichu, and an enormous mobcap, tied neatly under her chin. "Yes?"

Eve blinked, momentarily taken aback. "Who are you?"

The woman didn't seem at all put out by Eve's blurted question. "I am Mrs. Crumb, the Duke of Montgomery's housekeeper. How may I help you?"

"I wish to see Val," Eve said, then frowned. "What happened to the butler?"

That question Mrs. Crumb ignored. "Who may I say is calling?"

Eve looked the woman up and down. Mrs. Crumb might be a servant, but she was rather formidable...and didn't seem easily cowed at all. "I'm Eve Dinwoody. Val will see me."

For a second Mrs. Crumb's eyes narrowed. Then she seemed to come to a decision. She nodded once, decisively, and stepped back, allowing Eve into the house. "His Grace is at present in the library."

"Thank you. I know the way."

The door opened into a massive entry hall. Beneath her feet was gray-veined pink marble. Gilded vines, curlicues, and flowers covered the walls, forming arches and medallions. Overhead the domed ceiling was painted a robin's-egg blue and divided into more medallions, and from the very center hung an enormous crystal chandelier.

Eve crossed the hall, the tap of her heels echoing on the pink marble. A curving grand staircase was at the far end and she mounted it, climbing to the first floor. She made her way down another hall and to the first door on the right. Val's library was a long room painted a pale sea green. Gilded pillars lined the walls, with bookcases in polished wood set into niches between them. No doubt they were made from some fabulously expensive wood. Sometimes Eve felt as if she'd walked into an Oriental fairy tale when she entered Val's domain.

Val himself was at the far end, sitting cross-legged on a huge overstuffed cushion in front of a fire.

He wore a purple banyan with a gold-and-green dragon embroidered on the back and he glanced up from a tiny jeweled book as she entered. "Eve!"

"What have you done, Val?" she asked, advancing on him. *"What have you done?"*

Chapter Eleven

*The second giant, Mag, made his home in the cold,
rocky hills of the moor. He stood three times the height
of a man, his hands were the size of cartwheels, and his
breath smelled of rotted meat. When Corineus and the
sea horse charged him, Mag roared his rage, but still
the giant fell before them....*
—From *The Kelpie*

It was raining. Great gusts of rain came down in sheets as
the day steadily fled.

Trevillion huddled on the box with Reed, who no
doubt thought he'd lost his mind to be sitting outside
when he might be dry and warm in the carriage. But there
was only so much temptation Trevillion could take. He'd
spent weeks, maybe even months, in hopeless, unrequited
yearning, and now to have Phoebe offer herself to him
like a luscious ripe apple to a man starving...

Except Phoebe didn't even know *what* she was offering. She'd led a sheltered life, one circumscribed by her
brother and her blindness. What did she know of men and
their baser desires? She should be with someone younger.
Someone unscarred, unscathed, and able still to look at
the world with uncynical eyes.

MacLeish was such a man—and Phoebe had rejected him. Trevillion wasn't sure what to think about that. He knew what he *wanted* to think—that she might prefer a man like himself—but that way lay madness. He wasn't right for her.

He had to keep that firmly in mind.

"I see a light, up ahead," Reed shouted.

Trevillion peered through the darkness, streams running off the corners of his tricorne. "If it be an inn, we stop for the night."

"Aye, sir."

The horses labored, their hides gleaming in the carriage's lantern light. The road was naught but a muddy stream and the carriage rocked from side to side as they neared the lights.

It was an inn—if an ancient stone edifice with a meager yard and a lean-to stable nearby could be called such. The carriage pulled to a stop in the yard and Reed jumped down to run inside. He returned a moment later with two men and the news that they did indeed have rooms for the night.

Trevillion climbed down from the box, nearly falling to his knees when his feet hit the muddy ground. His leg had locked, the muscles spasming in the cold. He cursed under his breath and made his way to the carriage door.

"We're stopping for the night," he announced when he wrenched the thing open.

Lady Phoebe raised her head from the seat cushions. Somehow she'd been sleeping. She looked flushed and warm. Clean. Good.

He wished he could carry her to the inn's door, but his leg wouldn't bear her. He wasn't sure it would bear him.

"Come." He took her arm, gently pulling her forward. "It's not far, thank God."

"Oh!" she exclaimed at the first blast of wind and rain. "Oh, it's so cold."

"And wet." He helped her to the inn's door, trying to shield her from the gusts of water, but even so they were both drenched by the time they made the door.

"My wife needs a warm fire," he said to the innkeeper, a stout little man with a fringe of graying hair about the back of his head.

"Right away, sir," the innkeeper said. "This way, please."

He led them up a narrow staircase and to a bedchamber, which, though tiny, looked perfectly clean. The draped bed was piled high with blankets.

"Sit here." Trevillion guided Phoebe, already trembling, to the lone chair by the cold fireplace. He needed to get her warm.

"I'll make that, sir," said the innkeeper, indicating the hearth.

"No, I can do it," Trevillion replied. "Better you bring my wife a basin of hot water and whatever hot victuals you might have."

"And beer," Phoebe said, through chattering teeth.

"My best!" the little man said. "I brew it myself. A bitter such as you've never tasted before."

"Very well." Trevillion lowered himself awkwardly before the cold hearth as the innkeeper rushed out.

"Your leg is hurting you," Phoebe said, wrapping her arms about herself.

"Aye, it is," Trevillion replied matter-of-factly as he laid the fire with coals and a bit of shredded bark for tinder. He applied the flame of the candle left behind by the innkeeper and was pleased when a flame flared up.

"Oh, that's better." She held out her hands to the fire,

but he could see that she was still shivering. She was such a little thing. What if she caught a fever?

He turned and began working on the buckle of her shoe.

"What are you doing?" she asked.

"Making sure you don't freeze."

He'd just gotten off both shoes when the innkeeper came back in the room with a basin of hot water and several cloths over his arm.

"Set it here." Trevillion indicated the floor near Phoebe's feet.

"There you are, sir," the innkeeper said, putting the basin down on the floor and draping the cloths on the bed. "The food and drink won't be but a moment."

Trevillion nodded and the man left.

"We'd better have your stockings off before he comes back," Trevillion said, his voice rough.

He reached for one foot again, dainty and small, and set it on his knee. He trailed his hands up her calf, hidden by her skirts, feeling the slide of the silk, the warm skin beneath, up over her knee to the ribbon tied around her thigh. He could feel the bare skin above it, soft, inviting.

Warm.

He glanced up just as he pulled the ribbon free.

Phoebe had her head tipped back, a smile flirting with her lips, her cheeks a sweet pink, and Trevillion caught his breath.

What was he doing? This was madness. He ought to take his hands out from under her *skirts*. Ought to leave her to take off her own stockings.

Instead he felt his hands shake as he began unrolling the stocking over knee and calf and slim ankle. He set it on the chair by her hip.

He inhaled and reached up for the second stocking, aware suddenly what lay just above that ribbon, hidden in the recess between her thighs.

Sweat broke out on his back.

Slick silk, warm flesh. He found the ribbon, the flimsy little thing caught in his large, rough hand.

Phoebe inhaled as he watched her, her tongue peeping out to lick her lips.

He swallowed and pulled the ribbon, letting it fall as he took the stocking's edge between his fingers and slowly rolled it down her leg.

Something clattered outside the door, waking him from his forbidden reverie. He ought to have been grateful.

Yet Trevillion cursed under his breath as he hastily stood. He pushed the basin of hot water in front of Phoebe. "Put your feet in the water—it'll warm you."

The door opened, heralding the innkeeper's return. He bore a tray with the food and drink. Behind him was a woman—presumably his wife—with another basin of hot water, and following her were two boys, one with a small table, the other with a chair.

Trevillion stepped back as the innkeeper handily directed the placing of everything. When he was done, their dinner was nicely set up on the table before the fireplace.

He beamed at Trevillion. "Will there be anything else for you or your wife, sir?"

"No, thank you. I believe we're very good for the night." Trevillion pressed some coins in the man's hand and the innkeeper bowed himself out the door.

Trevillion limped to the table and sat.

"It looks like a chicken stew with dumplings," he said, trying to regain some normalcy.

His voice sounded too loud to his own ears.

"Lovely." Phoebe was taking off her soaked cap. "Will you tell me sometime, do you think?"

Had she no idea what had just occurred? What a man felt when he put his hands under a woman's skirts? "Tell you what?"

"How you were lamed."

He looked up sharply at her.

She sat with her fingertips on the edge of the table, feeling what was before her, and it struck him how brave she was. She lived with her blindness day in and day out, had followed him trustingly, and had met each challenge of their journey with good spirits and curiosity.

He felt his mouth curve gently. "There's a tankard of bitters just to the right of your right hand."

"Is there?" She looked excited, pulling the tankard toward herself. The sip she took was more careful than the one the night before, but she still came up with her nose wrinkled.

He found himself chuckling, despite the cold and his leg. "Too strong?"

"It *is* strong," she agreed. "But I think I might like it?"

"You don't sound entirely sure," he said as he served her her dinner.

"I told you that I like to try a thing more than once before I give it up."

"Tenacious," he murmured, his voice far too fond. He pushed her plate toward her. "Spoon at three, bread at nine."

"Thank you," she said. "It does smell good."

He took a bite, chewing thoughtfully as he watched her negotiate her plate and food, delicately using the bread to push just enough chicken onto her spoon before eating.

He made a decision and swallowed. "It was my horse."

She looked up—or rather she raised her face to him—but didn't say anything to his vague words.

"Her name was Cowslip—a silly name for a dragoon's mare, but then I didn't name her. She was a lovely beast. Quick and strong and with a heart...such a big heart." He frowned thinking about the mare. She'd been a good horse.

"What happened?" Phoebe was tracing the rim of the tankard, listening intently.

"I was on patrol with two of my men," Trevillion said, remembering that dark night nearly a year ago now. "In St Giles. We were chasing a rather notorious highwayman. I cornered him and he shot Cowslip."

"Oh." Her brows knit over her hazel eyes. "How terrible."

"It was." The sound of a horse screaming in pain was something one never forgot—she didn't need to know that, though. "She fell atop me."

The weight of that great, marvelous beast. Her shrieks. The visceral snap of his bone. Wakefield's white face, staring down at him.

He looked up on that last thought. "Your brother was there. He pulled me out from under her. And then..."

"What?" Her face was so young and innocent in the firelight, the flames limning the side of her face, making a nimbus of her hair.

"Wakefield—your brother—had to put Cowslip down." He picked up his own tankard and took a deep swallow, but the acid of that night still stayed on his tongue.

She shuddered. "That must've been horrible for both you and Maximus."

He stared at her. How was it possible that one so young

should possess such empathy? Such compassion, given so freely?

A woman such as she should never become weary of life, cynical about both pain and love.

He wasn't good for her.

"Your brother saved my life that night, you know," he said to her. Had she ever been told? A lot seemed to be kept from her and she was right: she was no longer a child to be wrapped in cotton. She was a woman grown. Deserving of information. "He bore me to your home and sent for a doctor. My leg had been broken previously and the second break was compounded by the earlier injury. Had he not acted when he did I probably would've lost it."

"I never knew the injury was so dire," she said quietly. "You must've been in so much pain."

"The doctor kept me dosed." Not that the various medicines the doctor had left by his sickbed had made that much difference to the pain he'd felt. She was right: it'd been excruciating.

"I knew you were in the house and injured, but beyond that, not much more." She frowned. "*Why* was Maximus in St Giles that night? It seems a very strange place for him to be."

"Your parents were killed in St Giles, did you know?" he replied slowly.

"Yes?" She cocked her head.

"It affected your brother greatly. He sometimes used to help me capture criminals in St Giles."

"Truly? How very odd." She pursed her lips and nodded. "But very like Maximus. He used to be very angry before Artemis came. Does he do it still? Go into St Giles?"

"No." He sighed and began to butter his bread. "That

part of his life is over, I think. As is mine. I no longer chase thieves and illegal gin brewers in St Giles, either."

"I'm glad," she said. "Not how your career ended, of course. But it sounds very dangerous, chasing men with pistols. Men who shoot horses. I'm glad you no longer do it."

And for the first time since his injury he was glad as well.

WAKING WHEN ONE is blind is something of a guessing game, Phoebe mused the next morning. After all, there's no bright light to let one know if it's morning or still night.

There's never any light, bright or otherwise, really. Only eternal darkness.

She lay, her cheek against James's warm chest, in a position almost identical to that of the morning before, and listened. He was breathing evenly and deeply and so was still asleep. Was that because it wasn't yet morning? Or just because he'd been exhausted the night before, the wet causing his leg considerable pain?

Once, a year or so ago, she'd risen, gotten dressed, and gone to the stables to visit the horses—only to find them all asleep.

It'd been one of the morning.

She could hear what sounded like a clattering downstairs in the inn. Perhaps voices. That boded well for its being morning. She supposed she really ought to get a rooster. One would always know it was morning if there was a rooster crowing. Unless the rooster was one of those odd birds that decided to crow at any time of day. That would be confusing.

She inhaled happily, smelling James. His scent was rather strong this morning after his exertions in the rain, and despite that second basin of water the innkeeper's wife had brought. He smelled of the perfume she'd given him and, she supposed, male sweat. A lady really oughtn't to like the smell of male sweat, but there it was, she was an odd female by anyone's standards.

Of course, she doubted she would've liked any *other* male's sweat.

It'd been rather a surprise to find that Maximus hadn't rehired James. That James was protecting her for reasons of his own. It made her wonder *why* he was doing this. Was he simply that dedicated to his former duty?

Or had she become something more than duty to him?

Her hand was on his chest, where his shirt was just parted. It was a plain shirt, not rough, but certainly not as finely woven as her brother's. Cautiously she stroked her fingers over his bare skin and felt again those tickling hairs. She really oughtn't do this, she knew, but it seemed a bit bad that he could *see* her—yet she knew only what she'd been told by others about his appearance. His skin was warm beneath the hairs. They seemed to want to curl about her fingers. She moved her hand and discovered a differently textured bit of skin. She explored it lazily for a moment before she realized what it must be—his nipple.

Naturally men had nipples. Not as large as hers, of course. It rose beneath her fingers and she wondered idly if being touched felt to him anything like the way it felt to her, for she knew that hers were quite sensitive.

She began to move her fingers away, but his hand came down over hers, holding her palm to his chest.

"Phoebe," he said, his voice deep. "Phoebe."

And then he took the back of her head in his other hand and his mouth was suddenly on hers.

It was...it was wonderful.

His mouth was hot, his lips moving on hers, opening urgently, pressing hers to do so, too. They did and his tongue thrust into her mouth, very sure. Very frank. Her heart beat fast as he licked at her, exploring her mouth like a conquering Viking.

James rolled and threw his leg over hers, pinning her to the bed. He was big and heavy and on her, his head angling to deepen the kiss. To claim her and teach her what a man's passion was. This wasn't a gentleman's polite greeting to a lady, this was a lover's embrace, base and animal. His fingers were fisted in her hair, holding her as he plundered her mouth.

She could feel him, his hard thighs and that male part of him, shoving at her, pushing into the softness of her thigh. For some reason it made her want to open her legs, to thrust up into him, to let him do whatever he wanted with her.

She made a sound she'd never made before in her life—a sort of low moan.

He lifted his head. "Phoebe." His voice was grating, but he began to pull away.

"No," she said at once, twisting her hand out from under his, placing her palms on either side of his face. "No, don't stop. Please."

She lifted her head, kissing him frantically all over his mouth until he groaned and took charge of the kiss.

"Spread your legs," he whispered into her mouth and it sounded unbearably erotic.

She gasped even as she did as he instructed, unable to catch her breath.

He settled there on her, his...his *penis* hard and on her mound, quite clear even through his breeches and her chemise. She tried to arch up against him, but his weight prevented her and she whimpered as she slumped back on the bed.

"Sh-sh," he whispered. "Don't fret. I'll make it better."

He touched her chin, tilting her face up. He kissed her again, slowly, his mouth wide over hers, and he was right. It was better.

So much better.

He kissed her lushly, teaching her to take his tongue. To suck and nip—and all the while his hips pressed down into hers, harder and harder, moving in small, measured circles, and she wondered if he had any idea what he was doing to her.

She could feel the lips of her mound parting, her chemise, dampened by her own liquid, being pressed against that nub by his flesh. It was…it was…

He was all around her, big and comforting, and at the same time driving her out of her wits with his control and his hips and his mouth, so very talented. How many women had he kissed in his lifetime to become so skilled? She felt vaguely jealous until he moved to the side just a bit and cupped her breast in his hot palm.

Oh! How strange that her hand against her breast should engender no particular reaction at all, but *his* hand on her made her arch and moan.

He licked her lower lip as he slid his thumb slowly over her nipple.

Something twisted low in her belly. This was wanton. This was something forbidden and she wanted it so much with him.

With James.

She slid her hands into his thick hair, feeling his scalp

under her fingers, the nape of his neck so strong. She opened her mouth as he bore down on her, riding her, thrusting against her hard now, driving them both.

He pinched her nipple and her legs stiffened as if in palsy, trembling, as a wonderful heat blew through her, flooding her limbs in warmth.

He thrust his tongue into her mouth and as she drowsily sucked it, he shoved hard against her once more and stilled unnaturally for a long moment.

Slowly he rolled off her and she murmured her discontent at the loss. Then his hands were on her, turning her. The last thing she heard as she drifted off into sleep again was her name on his lips as he gathered her into his arms.

TREVILLION WATCHED LADY Phoebe in the dim light of the carriage late that night. She had a little smile about her lush mouth as she swayed with the carriage's roll. They'd traveled all day again—a long, wearying day. He'd read to her for part of the way, while it'd still been light outside, from the only book he had with him—an account of an Englishman seized and sold into slavery as a boy by the Ottomans. Phoebe had seemed to enjoy the narrative, though it wasn't a book meant for a lady. There had been plenty of opportunities to speak with her about the events of this morning.

And yet he had not.

He fingered the bookmark stuck into the pages of the book, tracing the lopsided cross-stitches. What could he say, after all? That he'd let himself be seduced by her innocent touching? That he'd waked with his guard down and already aroused? That he'd let himself perpetuate a quite crude act on her without thought for her well-being?

God, he was a cad.

Even now, filled with loathing for his own actions, he wanted to touch her again, hear her soft gasps, the surprisingly loud moan she'd made when he covered her. Wanted to fill his hands with her breasts and feel again the softness of her hips cradling him. Wanted to drink up all that sweet joy. She was spring water to the parched desert of his soul.

A better man would leave her alone. Until this morning he'd thought he *was* a better man.

Trevillion glanced away just as the carriage made an abrupt right turn.

Phoebe looked up. "Where are we?"

"The edges of the world," he replied tensely, peering out the window.

He never thought he'd return to this place. He wasn't entirely sure whether he was glad he was making the journey back...

Or dreading the memories of his own failure.

"What?" asked Phoebe, looking intrigued instead of apprehensive.

He let the carriage curtain drop. "We're in Cornwall—have been since early this afternoon. If I don't miss my mark, we're nearing the end of our journey."

"And where is that?" she asked, just as the carriage lurched hard and jolted to a stop at an angle.

"Damn," Trevillion muttered. He knew an ill omen when he saw one.

The door was wrenched open and Reed stuck his face in, his hair coming down from its usual neat tail. "Can't go no further, Cap'n. The carriage is stuck axle-deep in mud and the road's nothing more than shit and muck, beggin' yer pardon, m'lady."

"That's quite all right, given the circumstances," Phoebe replied.

"We'll have to walk from here," Trevillion said, taking her hand.

Reed's forehead creased with concern. "'Ow will you know the way? Black as pitch out 'ere and I see no light."

"I'm afraid I know the way well," Trevillion said. "Give me one of the lanterns, keep one for yourself, and I'll send someone back to assist with the horses."

He helped Phoebe from the carriage as Reed went to fetch one of the lanterns from the box.

"If we stick to the side of the lane, it shouldn't be too muddy," Trevillion said as Reed came back with the lantern. "Thank you, Reed."

Trevillion took the lantern in his left hand. Phoebe had her fingers on his upper arm, out of the way of the lantern.

"Be careful, sir." Reed shivered, looking nervously around. "It's a right lonely spot, this."

"I will," Trevillion assured him, though he had no such fears of this place. It hadn't been the *land* that had proven so dangerous.

Phoebe had her head tilted up, sniffing the wind. "The air smells different here."

"It's not the tainted air of the city, my lady," Trevillion said, watching their way. If he fell, she'd come down with him.

"I've been in the country before," she said. "It's something more than that."

"We're near the ocean," he said as they came around a curve. A large house loomed up in front of them. Brick, stoic and solid-looking, no lights on inside. "You must smell the salt."

A low shadow came hurtling out of the darkness, belatedly barking as it neared.

Trevillion stopped, eyeing the animal.

"Oh, a dog!" Phoebe said.

"Yes," Trevillion muttered. "That wasn't here before."

The dog had stopped short of them and was now growling between barks. Despite the fact that it came only to his knees, Trevillion wasn't particularly keen on challenging the animal.

The door to the house opened, a wedge of light spilling out into the yard, and a tall silhouetted figure emerged with a long gun at his shoulder. "Who goes there? Name yourself or I blow you to kingdom come!"

"Hello, Father," Trevillion said drily.

Chapter Twelve

Corineus found a pool of water and washed the giant's blood from his own body and that of the sea horse, but though her head drooped he did not remove the iron chain. When darkness fell, the wind whispered the sorrow of the sea maidens, and the faery horse turned her beautiful green eyes toward the distant waves....
—From *The Kelpie*

Phoebe was woken the next morning by the click of canine toenails on a wood floor, followed by a girl's voice whispering, "Shh, Toby!"

She lay quietly, listening to the approach of her morning visitor, and thought about their odd arrival the night before. Apparently James had not bothered sending word to his father that he was coming to visit—and bringing a guest and footman-cum-carriage-driver as well. This had made for an awkward welcome to say the least—although judging by the curt language between father and son, prior knowledge of their visit might not have made a difference.

In any case, the pleasantries hadn't lasted long before a maidservant had shown Phoebe to a room. She'd only pulled off her dress and washed her face and neck before falling into the bed and succumbing to sleep.

"Are you awake?" asked the child in a whisper, the dog panting heavily next to her. "Lady?"

"Good morning," Phoebe said, causing the dog to bark. She sat up in the bed and waited, but there was no more from the girl. She might even have been holding her breath. "Who are you?" The girl hadn't been at the door last night—not unless she'd been very quiet and no one had bothered to introduce her to Phoebe.

"I'm Agnes," the girl replied, as if that were all the introduction she needed. "Granfer says there's breakfast."

"Oh, how lovely," Phoebe said. "Do you know if there might be fresh water for me to wash in?"

"I brought some up. It's over there," Agnes said.

Phoebe tilted her head, wondering how old Agnes might be. Old enough to carry a heavy pitcher of water, certainly. She held out her hand to the girl. "Can you lead me to it? I'm blind."

"Oh! Can't you see at all?"

"No." Phoebe smiled to take any edge from the simple word.

"I'll help you, then." A small hand was slipped into hers, the fingers thin but strong.

Phoebe pulled back the covers and swiveled her legs out of the bed. Immediately a wet nose snuffled against her toes.

"Back, Toby," Agnes said sternly, and then in a lower, confiding tone, "Don't mind him—he sticks his nose in *everything*, he does. And he barks so loudly it fair hurts my ears. I've told him over and over again not to, but he never listens. Granfer says you can't teach a dog not to bark, for 'tis God's will that they do, and I guess he's right enough."

"I think I met Toby last night," Phoebe said, lowering her hand cautiously. The nose thoroughly sniffed her fingers and then she was rewarded with a sloppy lick from Toby's tongue. She stroked back over the dog's head. He had a long nose—she got another lick as she felt it—big upright ears, and a thick, short coat, which her fingers sank into. Though he had a medium-size dog's body, his legs were quite stubby.

"Aye, he was barking at you then," Agnes said, her hand still in Phoebe's. "He woke us all up, but Granfer said we weren't to go down. But I spied through the stair rails and saw you and *him* come in."

That emphatic *him* must be Trevillion. Who was he to the little girl? Had Agnes ever met him before?

"I'm sorry we woke you so late at night." Phoebe stood and let Agnes lead her.

"Mind the chair here," Agnes said as they skirted it. "Here's the washstand." She placed Phoebe's hand on a wide china basin. "Shall I pour the water in?"

"Yes, please," Phoebe said. "Agnes, you said 'us.' Who else lives here?"

"Well"—there was a splash and Phoebe felt the water pour over her fingers—"There's Granfer and me and Mother. Then we have Betty who sleeps by the kitchen—she keeps the house for Granfer. And over the stables there's Old Owen and Young Tom—they help with the horses."

"*Horses?* You have more than one?" Phoebe found a washcloth and scrubbed her neck and face. She really wanted a full bath, but it would have to wait. With so few servants, filling a bath with hot water would be onerous. Perhaps she might ask Agnes to help her wash her hair later.

"We have *lots* of horses," Agnes said, earnest pride in

her voice. "Trevillion horses are the finest in Cornwall. Granfer says the Londoners would gnaw their hearts out with envy if he ever brought them to be sold in London."

Phoebe paused, startled. "Really? Then your grandfather breeds the horses?" Whyever hadn't Trevillion told her this?

"*Everyone* knows Granfer's horses," Agnes said with just a hint of condescension.

"Then I shall have to visit them," Phoebe said. "After breakfast, of course. Would you mind? I have to use the chamber pot and then maybe you can help me with my hair?"

Agnes and Toby obligingly left the room while Phoebe did just that, and then came in to help with the rest of her toilet.

"You're very good at dressing hair," Phoebe remarked.

"I do Mother's," Agnes replied, and it occurred to Phoebe that Agnes had mentioned her grandfather and mother, but not her father. Perhaps her mother was widowed or her father was away on business? "There. Done."

Phoebe stood and turned. "Am I presentable?"

"Oh yes," Agnes said softly. "You look a princess, my lady."

Phoebe smiled and held out her hand. "You may call me Phoebe. Would you like to show me where breakfast is served?"

"Yes."

The slender, strong fingers were once again in hers. Phoebe inhaled discreetly and found that Agnes bore the same scent as the wind the night before—salt and sea—mixed faintly with horses and dogs. Perhaps she spent a great deal of time outdoors?

As they left her bedroom with Toby trotting after, Phoebe could hear male voices raised in anger.

"*He* shouts just like Granfer," Agnes said.

"You mean Trevillion?" They walked down a hallway that Phoebe remembered from the night before.

"Yes," Agnes said. "He said to call him Uncle James this morning when I saw him, but he's different than I thought he would be."

"How so?" Phoebe asked.

"I never expected him to be so loud or so frowning. He wrote such *nice* letters."

"Letters..." Phoebe's brows drew together. "Hadn't you met your uncle prior to this morning?"

"He left before I was born, so says Granfer," Agnes replied, and before Phoebe could ask the *myriad* questions *that* statement brought up, said, "Here's the room where we take breakfast."

"Damn you, Jamie, haven't I told you before that you're still wanted for—" Mr. Trevillion's shout was cut off, presumably by their entrance.

Wanted for what? Phoebe thought, bewildered.

A chair scraped back. "Good morning, my lady," James said, his voice at its most expressionless.

Oh, dear. Phoebe repressed a wince. It seemed a shame to start the day in a rage. She put a cheerful smile on. "Agnes says there's breakfast."

"There's porridge," came a gruff voice. She hadn't actually been formally introduced to Mr. Trevillion the night before. "And that dog belongs outside, Agnes. You know that, girl."

"Yes, sir," Agnes muttered. Phoebe heard the snap of fingers and the retreating footsteps of the girl and dog.

"Toby." The voice was a woman's but somehow thick, as if the speaker couldn't form the word quite properly.

"Come." Trevillion was by her side, the comforting scent of sandalwood and bergamot in her nostrils. "Sit here and let me introduce you. My father, Arthur Trevillion, you met last night. He sits at the head of the table to your left. I'm sitting immediately to your right. Across from you is my sister, Dorothy, though we fondly call her Dolly."

Phoebe sank into the chair and felt the table before her with her fingers. A wide-lipped bowl of porridge was there. "I'm so pleased to meet you, Mr. Trevillion, Dolly."

"Dolly," Mr. Trevillion said gruffly. "Say your how-d'you-do's to Lady Phoebe."

"How do you do?" Dolly's thick voice said slowly.

Phoebe knit her brows, opening her mouth just as footsteps sounded at the door.

"Ah," said Trevillion, sitting down next to her. "Here's Agnes back from banishing Toby. She's with our Betty, who cooks and cleans and keeps the house running for all."

Phoebe inclined her head. "Betty."

"Pleased t' meet 'ee, m'lady." Betty's low voice was wonderfully accented. "Now sit 'ee, Agnes, girl. Thy porridge grows cold."

"What's become of Reed?" Phoebe asked.

"He had a bed over the stables last night," Trevillion said. "I've no doubt he'll find work to do with the horses today."

A harrumph came from Mr. Trevillion's end of the table.

"Shall I pour you some tea?" Trevillion asked, his voice low and intimate.

"Please." Phoebe felt heat climbing her neck. She'd missed sleeping beside him last night. Strange, since they'd only lain together two nights, but there it was. She missed the other things they'd done as well. For a moment she remembered his weight on hers, the strange, wonderful motion of his hips, the feeling it had given her. Did he think of it as well? Would he do it again if she asked him?

Phoebe shivered at the thought, hoping she wasn't blushing for all to see.

The strange thing was, though, that she wanted more from Trevillion than those moments in the bed, wonderful though they'd been. She wanted to talk to him alone, wanted to ask so much of him: why he hadn't returned to his family home since before Agnes's birth, if he'd always been called Jamie here, why he fought with his father, and above all, why he'd been so secretive about his family.

She wanted to know all about him, really, inside and out. But her questions would have to wait for a less public time.

Though it nearly stifled her to keep them all inside.

Phoebe turned in the direction of Mr. Trevillion and smiled. "Agnes says you breed horses?"

"Aye."

Phoebe waited, but apparently that was all the answer she would get. Trevillion had obviously learned his conversational skills from his father.

There was a crash from the end of the table and then Dolly sobbed and said in her thick voice. "Oh! Spilled porridge. I'm sorry. I'm sorry. I'm sorry."

And all at once Phoebe realized what was different about Dolly's voice.

Agnes's mother was weak in the head.

*   *   *

IT'D BEEN ALMOST twelve years since he'd last stepped into the old Trevillion stables, but oddly they still looked—and smelled—like home.

"Mm, I love the smell of horses," Phoebe murmured, tilting up her face in bliss. "Why did you never tell me your family bred them?"

"I didn't know you'd be interested," he muttered. Horse-breeding was a trade, after all, and weren't the aristocracy supposed to look down upon dirtying one's hands with trade?

She turned to him, looking skeptical. "You know I love horses!"

He couldn't help softening at that. "Then you'll like our stables."

The stables were an ancient building, built of gray stone. The cobblestones that lined the main corridor were worn smooth underfoot. Beside them trotted the odd little dog that seemed to belong to his father, but was obviously more loyal to his niece.

The dog had also obviously become enamored with Phoebe. Toby glanced up at her as they walked, his tongue lolling from the side of his mouth, his ridiculously too large ears flicking away a fly.

"I can hear the horses stamping their hooves," Phoebe murmured. "Won't Maximus find out we're here?"

He shook his head. "I've never told His Grace where I came from—and no one in London knows."

She thought about that a moment, then said, "Why didn't you tell me about your family—that we were traveling to your childhood home?"

He shrugged uneasily. "Why would you be interested in your guard's family?"

She was silent as he took her deeper into the cool building. Most of the horses were outside in the pasture, but one stall was occupied farther down.

"I grant that at one time I might not've listened if you'd told me of your family," she said slowly. "When you were first made my guard I was not overjoyed—"

He snorted under his breath.

"But," she continued a little louder, "I've come to know you since and we've agreed we are friends, have we not?"

She was much more than a friend to him.

But her face was expectant, so he answered gently, "Aye, we're friends, my lady."

She smiled up at him, her entire face lit like the sun.

"Jamie!" Old Owen called from down the stables. "Is that 'ee, lad? Could've knocked me down wi' a feather, 'ee could, when Hisself told me 'ee'd come home."

"Yes, it's me, Owen." Trevillion transferred his cane to his left hand to shake the old man's hand. "What's become of my man, Reed?"

An evil smile lit Old Owen's face. "Sent him out to yonder pasture to see if he could catch Wild Kate. That'll test his mettle, it will. She's not called wild for naught."

Trevillion couldn't help but laugh.

Old Owen had been in his father's employ since Trevillion was a young boy. The man was bent now with lumbago and ancient injuries received from his work. Few good horsemen made it to old age without a broken bone or two from a horse's kick. But his blue eyes under his wispy gray hair were as shrewd as ever.

"An' who be this fair maid?" Owen asked.

"My lady, may I present Owen Pawley, the finest horseman in Cornwall and the man who first put me in a saddle. Owen, this is Lady Phoebe Batten, the woman I've been hired to guard."

"I'm very pleased to meet you, Mr. Pawley," Phoebe said.

"Call me Owen, do, m'lady," Owen said. "Everyone hereabouts does. Why, I hear me own last name so little I scarcely recognize it."

"Owen it is, then," Phoebe replied, smiling.

"An' this here is Young Tom Pawley," Owen said, pointing to the other man. "Me great-nephew he is an' a fine horseman he'll be...in ten more years or so." Owen guffawed, but not in an overly mean way.

The younger man blushed. He was as wiry as his great-uncle, but a good deal straighter. He pulled a forelock and said loudly, "M'lady."

"Now, Young Tom, th' lady's blind, not deaf, lad," Owen chided.

Tom scuffed his feet and muttered an apology.

"Have 'ee come to see our new queen, then?" Owen nodded to the occupied stall behind him. In it was a white mare, heavily pregnant, her head over the stall door and looking at them curiously. "This 'ere's Guinevere. Himself bought her last autumn and she's a dainty piece, she is. She's due to drop any day, or so I figure."

Guinevere nickered as if she knew she was being discussed.

"She sounds lovely," Phoebe said, her face wistful.

Trevillion glanced quickly at Old Owen, meeting his gaze.

The old man's eyes flashed with sadness. "Why, would 'ee like to pet her, m'lady? She's gentle as a lamb, I promise."

"Please."

"She's just here," Trevillion said, taking her hand from his sleeve. He guided her small fingers to the horse's head, then let go.

Phoebe ran her fingers over the delicate head and down to the soft nose. Guinevere snuffled at her palm inquisitively.

She laughed, turning in his direction. "She's a beauty, I can tell."

"Oh, that she is, m'lady," Old Owen said, grinning proudly.

"Bit o' carrot," Tom said shyly, giving Phoebe a carrot. "She's right fond o' them."

Trevillion stepped back, watching as Phoebe petted and talked to the mare.

"She's a rare one," Owen whispered conspiratorially. "Sweet an' lovely."

Trevillion stiffened. "She's a duke's sister. I'm not of her league."

"Ah." Owen rocked back on his heels. "Might want to ask the lady about that, I'm thinking."

Phoebe turned her head toward them and Trevillion silently cursed Owen's carrying voice.

But she didn't remark on that. "Will you show me the other horses, Captain Trevillion?"

"Certainly." He limped forward to offer her his arm.

She placed her soft fingers on his sleeve, then turned to the two horsemen. "Thank you for showing me your queen, Owen. And thank you for the carrot, Tom."

"Anytime, m'lady," Owen called cheerfully.

Tom just blushed beet red.

Trevillion led her to the opposite end of the stables. It let out into a small paddock. Beyond that was one of his father's fields. The paddock itself was empty, but at the far side four horses had gathered at the pasture's fence. Toby had trotted on ahead, and was busy barking at the unimpressed horses.

"We're in luck," Trevillion told Phoebe. "There are four horses waiting for us at the pasture fence. They look a little like village wives gathered for a gossip."

She laughed. "Has your family always bred horses?" she asked as they strolled toward the fence.

"As far back as anyone can remember in these parts," he answered easily. "And that's a fair ways back."

She turned her face toward him, her cheeks pinkened by the light wind, and he had an urge to kiss her, to taste again that joy of life. "But you decided to become an army officer instead. Why?"

He looked away. "At the time I had little choice in the matter."

"I don't understand—?"

"Here's Bess," he said, holding out his hand to the older mare. "She must be nearly fifteen years old now. And I think she remembers me."

Indeed the mare was lipping his coat sleeve affectionately. He'd used to bring her apples and carrots when Bess was young—when he was young. For a moment he was nearly overcome by the memories. He'd lost so much when he'd made that one devastating mistake.

When he'd failed everyone so utterly.

"Which one is she?" Phoebe asked, bringing him out of his dark thoughts.

He took her hand in his and drew it forward slowly, letting the mare see their approach. "This is Bess. She's mostly white with dark stockings." He waited as Phoebe felt over the soft gray muzzle. "Now next to her is a pretty lass, a bit shorter, and all white. I don't know her name, but if I'm not mistaken, she's pregnant." He moved her hand just as slowly to the second horse, but the mare snorted, backing away. "And, I'm afraid, a bit skittish."

"Well, that's only to be expected," Phoebe said softly. "We're strangers to her, after all."

"True." He moved their hands to the third mare, who immediately stretched her neck to snuffle.

Phoebe giggled. "She's not so shy."

"No, indeed." Trevillion watched with a slight smile as Phoebe ran her palm over the horse's nose. "That's Prissy. She was a two-year-old when I last saw her and now she's about to be a mother. She's got a nice straight back and strong legs."

"And the last?" Phoebe asked.

"I don't know her by name, but she has the arched neck and fine little head of a princess." He laughed softly. "And she must be friends with Prissy, for Prissy has her neck over hers."

"Like sisters whispering together," Phoebe said.

"Mm," he murmured. "She's a bit shy—she's standing back from the fence. Perhaps if we're still…"

He stood behind her and took her left hand in his. He held out her hand, tangling his fingers with hers, and slowly turned it, so that her palm was uppermost, cradled within his, an offering to the beautiful mare.

They were silent. Each inhalation brushed his chest and belly against her back. The top of her head came only to his chin. He leaned his right hand on the fence, near her hip, and as they waited, she placed her own right hand over his. It was warm and soft, reminding him that she did no physical labor, this lady. She was an aristocrat—

a world apart from his yeoman upbringing. But here, in this quiet paddock, the only sound the soft thump of the horses' hooves on grass, they were just a man and a woman. That simple.

And that complex.

At last the mare moved, stretching out her neck curiously, whuffling over Phoebe's palm, and then letting herself be petted.

"Thank you," Phoebe breathed, and at first Trevillion thought she was speaking to the little white mare.

But then she turned her head up to his.

"For what?" he asked, his voice deep.

"For taking me here. For showing me your horses."

"They're my father's horses," he said, the reply rote. "Not mine."

She merely shook her head and smiled. "This is such a lovely place. Might we walk up on the moor? I've never been so far west and I've never been on the moor."

He sighed and took her arm, turning to lead her back toward the house. "It's beautiful on the moor, but rough as well—the ground is quite uneven."

"The horses graze there." Her plump mouth was creased with stubbornness.

"And they have four legs and are used to it," he retorted. "It isn't safe, my lady."

He felt her fingers squeeze his arm. "Perhaps I'm tired of being safe."

"It's my job to—"

She stopped, jerking him to a halt.

He looked down at her, watching her brows draw together over unseeing eyes, her mouth turning down in a definite frown. "I don't *want* to be your job anymore. I hereby sever your commitment to protect me. And before you tell me that my brother is the one who employs you, let me remind you that you *left* his employment. You aren't my guard anymore and you haven't been since before I was kidnapped. You're doing this for reasons beyond dashed employment and I'm tired of—"

He stopped her tirade by the simple expedient of covering her mouth with his own.

His cane fell to the ground as he yanked her body against his, forcing her head back with the pressure of his lips. Her pretty mouth parted under his, and something animal surged in his chest as he thrust his tongue into her. He licked his way inside, tasting her, grinding her body against his, wanting to bear her to the ground and put his cock in her. He wanted so much *more* than what she could give him here.

Only when she sighed into his mouth, a small submission, did he whisper against her lips, "*I'm* tired of you tempting me."

"I'm not tempting you anymore," she murmured back, her wet lips brushing his.

He nipped her bottom lip in punishment. "Aren't you?"

"No," she whispered. "You've given in."

He groaned and bent once more to her, losing himself in her softness, her hope.

It wasn't until he heard someone clear his throat that Trevillion lifted his head again.

And saw his father glaring at him.

PHOEBE WAS QUITE pleased with herself when she started off to dinner with Agnes that night. She'd managed to spend the afternoon taking a quite decadent bath with the help of Agnes and Betty. The bath had performed the double service of cleansing her and giving her a reason to hide in her room from Mr. Trevillion. It'd been rather embarrassing to be discovered shamelessly kissing his son in the middle of the stable yard.

And while she'd been hiding in her lovely steaming bath, turning into a veritable prune and languidly scrubbing her knees, Betty had sponged and brushed her one dress. That, together with a clean chemise borrowed from Dolly, meant that she felt quite presentable.

So she was rather looking forward to seeing Trevillion again until she, Agnes, and Toby neared the dining room to hear shouting. *Again.*

"Does your grandfather argue at *every* meal?" she inquired of Agnes, who, it turned out, was quite a font of information.

"He didn't *used* to," sighed the child. "Does Uncle James?"

"I've never noticed it before." Phoebe cocked her head. They seemed to be shouting about…a neighbor? How intriguing. "They sound a lot alike, don't they?"

"*Yes*," Agnes said emphatically. "I hope they stop. Mother doesn't like it."

Phoebe hadn't even thought about Dolly and how all this was affecting Agnes's mother—which made her feel quite guilty. But of course discord in her house would be confusing for Agnes's mother. And on that thought came another: who was Agnes's father? No one had made any mention of him.

A crash brought her back to the present problem.

"We really need to stop them," Phoebe said, making up her mind.

She marched into the dining room with Agnes by her side.

The men immediately stopped yelling, though to judge by the heavy breathing they were by no means calmed.

"Where is your mother, Agnes?" Phoebe asked.

"She's already at the table," Agnes said, and a distressed muttering from one end of the room confirmed her pronouncement.

Phoebe lifted her chin. The men ought to be ashamed of themselves, upsetting Dolly, really they should! "Well, let's sit by her, shall we?"

She followed the tug on her hand and found James already waiting with a chair.

"You're seated between Dolly and me," he said.

"How nice," Phoebe murmured acidly, and sat.

She felt a brush against her legs and realized that Toby had sneaked under the table and was now leaning against them.

"What are we having?" she asked with forced cheer.

She began making her usual exploration of the table edge only to find Dolly's hand at her right. It was large and soft and trembling slightly. Phoebe gave Dolly's fingers a reassuring pat.

"Roast beef," rumbled Mr. Trevillion from the head of the table, "boiled vegetables, and bread made by Dolly."

"I make bread," Dolly said softly from Phoebe's side.

Phoebe realized now that the woman had the faint scent of yeast about her. "Do you? How lovely. I've never made bread."

"Mother makes all the bread for us," Agnes chimed in. "She's very good."

"Sometimes I make small cakes," Dolly said slowly. "But mostly I make bread."

"You'll have to show me how," Phoebe decided.

"There's beer as well," James said in her ear. "A bitter ale."

"Why are you giving the lass beer, boy?" his father said irritably. "Wine's a lady's drink."

"I like beer," Phoebe said.

"Do you?" James asked just for her ears.

"I'm almost certain I do," she murmured back.

"Stubborn." In a louder voice, James said, "If she doesn't like the beer, she can have the wine later, Father."

Mr. Trevillion muttered something that sounded like "Daft."

"James showed me your horses today," Phoebe said as she felt the plate before her. "I quite enjoyed them. They were so beautiful."

"How do you know that, might I ask?" snapped Mr. Trevillion.

Phoebe heard a clatter from James's plate and knew if she didn't say something fast none of them would be able to eat the meal.

"Because I could feel it, that's how. Lack of sight hasn't stolen either my wits or my perception." She reached out and found James's hand to her left on the table. It was in a fist. Gently she covered it. "I was wondering who named your horses, Mr. Trevillion? Guinevere seems a fanciful name."

"I did," Agnes said. Her voice was very small.

"Did you?" Phoebe fought to keep a pleasant expression on her face, despite Mr. Trevillion's ill humor. Antagonizing the old man would get her nowhere. "How many horses have you named?"

"Almost all of them," Agnes said, her voice relaxing with what was obviously a favorite subject. "I name the new foals when they're born and sometimes a new mare when she's bought. Not the stallion, though. His name is Octavian, which I suppose is good enough."

Phoebe didn't have trouble with her smile anymore. "And what are some of the names you've chosen?"

"We-ell," Agnes said. "There's Guinevere, you already know. Her name was Chalk when Granfer bought her, which was an ugly name. Then there's Seagull, Mermaid, Pearl, Sky, and Merlin—he was sold just last month to the younger son of the Earl of Markham."

"Paid well for him, too," Mr. Trevillion said, sounding pleased for the first time since Phoebe had entered the room. "Merlin's a bonny lad."

"And I named Uncle James's mare," Agnes said, sounding shy again, "the one he had in London."

Cowslip, Phoebe remembered. Had Trevillion told his niece what had happened to poor Cowslip?

She cleared her throat. "Will you name the new foals as well when they're born?"

"Yes, if Granfer lets me."

"Oh, aye, you'll do the naming, lass." Mr. Trevillion's voice was gruff, but Phoebe rather had the idea he doted on his granddaughter. "Might as well since all this will be yours when I'm gone."

Phoebe felt the fist clench under her fingers. "But surely James—"

"Jamie left us of his own accord when we needed him most," his father said, his voice hard.

"You know damned well why I had to leave, old man," Trevillion said, his voice low and lethal. "I had a price on my head. You yourself told me—"

"I never told ye to stay away over a decade!"

"You kept writing that it was too dangerous. That Faire was still looking." While his father's voice had risen, James's voice had lowered, grown more controlled. "I sent you what money I made. I—"

"You came back a cripple!" Despite the harshness of the older man's words, there was an undercurrent of anguish. "What good to me is a cripple? Tell me that, boy!"

"*Oh.*" Phoebe couldn't help the exclamation. She knew how much Trevillion hated the weakness in his leg. For his father to—

James's chair scraped against the floor as it was shoved back. "Stop calling me that. I haven't been a *boy* for over a decade." His fist slipped away from her hand as he rose.

She heard his boot steps leave the room.

Next to her, Dolly whimpered, and underneath the table Toby had his warm little body pressed against her knees, shivering.

Phoebe wanted to follow him. He'd followed her once when she'd argued with Maximus and stormed out of the room. But that had been in her own house, which she knew inside and out.

Here she was still a stranger, learning the paths and distances between objects. She couldn't follow James. Couldn't ask *why*, for God's sake, he'd had a price on his head. Couldn't comfort him or argue with him or possibly make love to him, because she was blind.

Now and forever.

Chapter Thirteen

*Agog, the last of the giants, lived in the cliffs that led
to the beach along the sea. He was three times as ugly
as his brothers and ten times as mean. Two heads
lay upon his broad shoulders, each with one eye and
one long fang. His hair brushed the clouds and with
one stride he could cover ten leagues. He carried
a club made from an oak tree and he could kill a
hundred men with only one blow....*
—From *The Kelpie*

It was just before dawn when Trevillion pushed open the
door to Phoebe's bedroom. He held the candle high as he
walked to the bed and for a moment he simply looked at her.

Her brown hair was spread upon her pillow like skeins
of unraveled silk. Her plump lips were slightly parted and
her hand was tucked under her chin.

She looked all of twelve.

He was a lecherous bastard, plain and simple, but he could
no longer deny the pull she exerted on him just by breathing.

He was well and truly damned. What was worse, he
knew that inevitably their time in Cornwall would end.
The kidnapper would be found, Wakefield would want his
sister back, and they would have to return to London.

Would he be able to walk away from her when that happened?

He shook his head, bringing himself back to his present mission.

"Phoebe," he said out loud, and gently stroked that pink cheek. "Wake up."

She stirred, murmuring sleepily. Those sightless hazel eyes opened and stared directly into the candle. "James?"

"Come," he said. "Guinevere is foaling. I thought you might like to witness the event."

"Oh!" She sat up, affording him a gorgeous view of her round breasts. "Do I have time to dress?"

He cleared his throat, tearing his gaze from her bodice. "Yes. I'll wait in the hall."

Trevillion went out and leaned against the wall near the door, listening to the small sounds she made as she dressed: rustling, a murmur or soft exclamation now and again. This was the house he'd been born in, had grown up in. He'd always thought he'd never leave—until almost a dozen years ago when it had all fallen apart. Strange. What would his life have been like had he not made that one terrible mistake? He probably never would've left Cornwall, never would've joined the dragoons and learned to lead men.

Never would've met Phoebe...*that* he could never regret.

A moment later her door opened and Phoebe peeked out. "James?"

"I'm here." He straightened, touching her arm so she knew where he stood. "Place your hand on my arm. I'm holding the candle in my left hand."

Slowly he led her down the dark-wood-paneled hallway and to the stairs. They were without ornament, but the wood was kept polished to a gleam by Betty. Downstairs they left by the kitchen door, which led out into the stable yard.

"I can hear a bird," Phoebe murmured as they made their way across the yard.

"Dawn's just breaking," he answered, glancing toward the east. "There's a sort of pink glow on the horizon."

"Mm." She tilted her head back, sniffing the air. "I can smell the sea and the heath on the moor. Will it be a beautiful day, do you think?"

He looked at her. "Oh yes."

She smiled at him and then they were at the stables. Guinevere was in the largest stall at the end, five people watching her over the door. He led Phoebe toward the stall quietly.

As they neared, Agnes turned and hurried to them. She gave him her usual shy glance and then whispered to Phoebe. "Granfer says we must be quiet for 'tis best for Guinevere. I had to lock poor Toby in my room so he wouldn't bark."

Phoebe held out her hand to the girl. "We'll give Toby a special treat later, shall we?"

Agnes nodded and tugged Phoebe's hand. "Come and see— Oh!"

Phoebe smiled. "That's all right—you can see for me."

Trevillion watched as his niece led Phoebe to the stall. Somehow she'd won Agnes's trust when the girl was still wary of him, though he'd sent her letters since she'd learned to read. He sighed and followed. His father and Owen were at the rail, Reed hanging back a bit with Young Tom. Owen and his father were of an age, but his father towered over Owen. Usually his father wore a white wig, but this early in the morning he was bareheaded and Trevillion noticed that his short hair had turned white.

It'd been merely gray when he'd left for London.

Owen looked up and made room for him at the railing. The mare was lying in fresh straw, laboring, her sides glossy with sweat.

"How goes it?" Trevillion asked.

"Won't be long now," Owen said sagely. He'd midwived dozens of mares in his time. "It's her first, but she's a strong un. She'll do well, I reckon."

Agnes was whispering a commentary to Phoebe, who had her face pressed to the rail so she could listen. Trevillion noticed that his father was watching the two out of the corner of his eye.

Trevillion glanced at Owen with a question. The old man looked from him to Phoebe and nodded.

Trevillion moved over to the females. "Would you like to touch her?" he asked Phoebe.

She turned her face to his. "Can I?"

He smiled. "I don't think it'll bother her. She's quite close to the stall door."

He took her hand and, opening the stall door slowly, crouched in the doorway. Guinevere rolled her eyes toward them, but she was obviously caught in her own body's task.

"Here." He laid her palm against the mare's distended belly.

Phoebe's eyes widened. "I can feel the foal...and her labor. Oh, she's so strong. So beautiful."

Guinevere suddenly heaved and Trevillion drew Phoebe back.

He wrapped his arms around her and whispered in her ear. "She's pushing now with all her might. There's a—"

A gush and a slither and the foal was all at once there, wet and trembling.

"Oh!" Phoebe whispered, her hands clutching his. "Is it here? Is it alive?"

"Yes and yes," he said, smiling at her eagerness. "Owen's gone to tend to it."

"A lass," Owen called. "Bonny and fine! Now what'll 'ee call her, Miss Agnes?"

"I think..." The girl's brow crumpled as she thought. "Lark! Is that a good name, Granfer?"

"A pretty name for a pretty filly," the old man pronounced.

"What does she look like?" Phoebe asked.

"She's very delicate," Trevillion said, observing the foal. "Her knees look much too big for her legs, and she's a dark gray at the moment, but she'll turn white as her dam as she grows."

Phoebe sighed contentedly. "How wonderful."

"It is," he murmured close to her. The foal lurched to its feet and wobbled to its mother. "And she's already found her mother's teat. Which reminds me, we ought to go in for our breakfast as well."

"I'm starving," Agnes said. "And Toby must be so sad."

"Best we go in, then, lassie," his father rumbled.

Agnes took Phoebe's arm, chattering to her as they started back to the house.

Trevillion found himself a few paces behind with his father by his side. The old man was matching his stride to Trevillion's own limp.

"She's a fine woman," his father said.

Trevillion glanced at him, surprised. Up until now he'd seen only indifference or a slight contempt from the old man toward Phoebe.

His father lifted his chin as if sensing Trevillion's surprise. "Well? I'd have to be daft not to see that. Despite her blindness. She's a good woman. Good with Agnes and Dolly. Good with the horses."

"Yes, she is," Trevillion said.

"Is that why she's wearing your mother's ring?"

Trevillion cursed himself for forgetting to ask Phoebe for the ring back. "It was easier to travel as man and wife. She needed a marriage ring."

"And you had to use your *mother's* ring for that?"

"It was the only one I had," Trevillion muttered, knowing as he said it how weak the explanation sounded. The truth was, he'd liked putting his mother's ring on Phoebe's finger, and he liked the ring even more each time he saw her wearing it.

"Your mother was a good woman, too," his father said.

Trevillion stiffened at the words.

"Your mother was gay and young—*too* young—but she was a good woman. Just not for me." His father stopped and looked at him. His eyes were the same color as Trevillion's—bright blue—set in a face lined by wind and age. "Lady Phoebe is a good woman too, but not for you."

Trevillion watched his father for a long minute and knew the older man believed what he said from the depths of his heart.

As did he.

"I know."

PHOEBE SAT AND listened as Dolly kneaded the dough for bread later that morning. They were in the kitchen, which smelled wonderfully of flour, yeast, and tea—Betty had made a pot for her—and every now and again Dolly picked up the dough and threw it back down on the table with a great *whack*.

"Why do you throw the dough, Dolly?" Phoebe asked.

Wakefield House had three cooks—one who did nothing but the baking—but she'd never actually been to the kitchens. She had no idea, really, how bread was made.

"It's to knead it," Dolly said.

Betty, who was busy cutting vegetables, said, "Makes the bread rise better, it does, when it's thumped around a bit."

"How very interesting," Phoebe said. "Dolly, is James your older brother or your younger?"

"I'm older than Jamie," Dolly said proudly. "He's my brother. He reads me books. But not anymore."

"Perhaps he will again now that he's back from London," Phoebe said.

"And letters," Dolly added. "I saved his letters."

"Letters?"

"Wrote regular like," Betty put in. "From London. And he sends little presents to Miss Dolly and Miss Agnes."

How odd—all this time Trevillion had been living a secret life and she'd never known it. Never even thought to ask about it. But then most people had secrets in their lives—especially when it came to those closest to them.

"Phoebe!" Agnes burst into the kitchen with a clatter and Toby panting on her heels. "Uncle James said to fetch you."

"Fetch me?" Phoebe repeated, amused. "I sound like a forgotten glove."

Agnes giggled. "Come on."

"Well, if you insist." Phoebe swallowed the last of her tea, bid farewell to Dolly and Betty, and let Agnes lead her from the kitchen.

"Where are we going?" she asked the girl.

"It's to be a surprise," Agnes said with excitement in her voice. Toby barked once alongside them, apparently caught up in the mood.

Outside, Phoebe could feel the sun on her face. They were walking in the direction of the stables and she wondered if Trevillion meant to show her Lark again.

And then she heard a whinny.

Agnes giggled.

"What's this?" Phoebe asked.

"I thought we might go riding," James said from nearby. "Riding when we aren't being chased, that is. You'll have to be on the horse with me. Is that amenable to you?"

"Oh yes," she said, thrilled at the prospect—both of a horse ride and of being close to Trevillion again.

He took her hand, his warm and large. "This is Regan. Owen's holding the bridle for us while we mount."

"She's got a nice even gait, does Regan," Owen called.

"And she's one of our largest horses," Trevillion said. "She should carry us both without a problem. Now here is the step."

She felt for the step with her hand and then mounted it, fitting her shoe into the stirrup before swinging herself up. Regan shook her head and stepped back a pace. Phoebe patted her neck.

She felt Trevillion swing on behind. "I've got her, Owen. My thanks."

"Aye," Owen called.

Then they were away. Trevillion started at a walk, his arms around her, and it was lovely to be out in the open, to feel the horse beneath her and him behind her.

"Where will we go?" she asked.

"Wherever you want," he answered. "Though I have a place I think you'd like."

"Then I leave it up to you," she said, laying her head back against his neck, inhaling horse and sandalwood, bergamot and Trevillion—pure Trevillion.

For a moment more she simply enjoyed the ride, but then she remembered all the questions she wanted to ask him.

She sighed. "James?"

"Yes?" He sounded relaxed and happy for once and she wondered if she should really bring up all the things that troubled her.

But if not now, then when?

"Why did you say that you had a price on your head last night?" she asked quietly. "Why is it dangerous for you to be in Cornwall?"

Immediately she felt the stiffening of his arms. "Do you really want to—"

"Yes." She twisted a bit in his arms to face him, so that she could talk directly to him. "All this mystery, all this anger and *hurt* between you and your father. Don't you think I want to know you and your past and what affected your life?"

"God, Phoebe, it doesn't reflect well on me—not at all."

She inhaled slowly, bracing herself. "Even so."

He sighed. "Very well. I beat a man once, nearly to death. His name was Jeffrey Faire and his father is the local magistrate. As a result Lord Faire called for my arrest. I fled the town, Cornwall itself, at the urging of my father. That was when I joined the dragoons."

She knit her brow, thinking. "Why? What happened between you and this man?"

"I got angry," he drawled.

That made her mad. "I don't believe that. You wouldn't have resorted to violence without reason, not even as a young man."

"Perhaps you ought not to have such faith in me, my lady."

She was beginning to dislike it when he called her "my lady" instead of plain Phoebe. "But I do."

He didn't reply, but his arms tightened around her.

Another thought suddenly struck her. "Is Lord Faire still after you?"

"No doubt."

"But we should leave at once," she said. "James, we ought never to've come here if you're in danger."

"I'm not in danger," he replied, sounding irritated. "Lord Faire has no idea I'm here."

"And if he finds out?"

"He won't. This was the safest place I could think of for you. We're almost to the ends of the earth—or at least the ends of England."

She wanted to shake him, she really did. What did he think would happen if he was arrested? How would Agnes and Mr. Trevillion feel? She couldn't bear the thought of his making such a sacrifice for her.

But moving Trevillion once he'd made a decision was nearly impossible. Perhaps if she enlisted the aid of Mr. Trevillion or even Agnes, she might make him see reason.

Phoebe shook her head.

"Come. Don't let's argue," he said finally. "Would you like to gallop?"

Her heart caught. "Can we?"

In answer he pulled her tight against his chest, leaned a little forward, and gave Regan her head.

Phoebe shrieked as they galloped into the wind, Trevillion's body surging behind hers, the horse's muscles bunching and releasing beneath them. This felt like true freedom, like life itself.

When he pulled Regan to a canter and then a trot again, Phoebe realized that she could hear the ocean's roar.

"Where are we?" she asked, her heart still beating fast from the gallop.

"There's a beach," he answered in her ear. "I thought you'd like to walk it."

"Did you used to come here often?" she asked as the mare began going downhill. "It must be beautiful."

"It is," he said simply. "And I did used to come here as a boy. 'Tis said that mermaids can be seen swimming the waves in the evening."

"Did you ever see any?"

"No, but you can be sure I looked hard. The only sort of thing I saw in the waves was more like to be smugglers bringing in French brandy."

"*Smugglers?*"

He chuckled. "There are quite a few in these parts. Had my dragoon regiment been assigned to Cornwall, I would've spent my nights chasing them down in the surf."

Regan was now walking on level ground and Phoebe could hear and smell the surf coming in. She hadn't been near the ocean since she was a little girl.

Since she'd become blind.

Phoebe caught her breath. "Can we get down?"

"Of course." He brought Regan to a standstill and dismounted. She felt his hands on her waist. "Come here."

She slid into his arms. He held her a moment, his chest warm and strong. The wind was blowing gently off the ocean and she could smell it: brine and fish and the wildness of the water.

"There's sand here," he said in her ear. "Would you like to take off your shoes and feel it?"

"Yes," she whispered, not knowing why she kept her voice low. She was trembling a bit.

He guided her to a boulder and she sat as she drew off her shoes and stockings.

Lifting her skirts up, she tentatively patted the sand with her toes. It was cool and dry here—they must be sitting in the shade.

She stood, holding her skirts. "Can I walk in the water?"

"Yes, the waves are low today." His voice was warm and close. He hesitated. "Do you want to take my arm?"

"No." She turned her head in his direction, hoping he understood. "Just tell me which way to go. Maybe walk with me?"

"Of course. I'll be right by your side."

"Have you taken your shoes and stockings off as well?" she asked, curious. He was usually so stiff. So formal.

Especially with her.

"Naturally," he replied, a laugh in his voice. He sounded nearly boyish. "It's de rigueur at the beach. Come, walk this way."

And she did, feeling the sand beneath her feet, the wind flattening her dress against her legs. As they neared the shore, she could hear the waves crashing louder, a roaring thunder. The sand was damp now, warm and squishy, an odd feeling but enjoyable nonetheless.

And then a wave lapped at her feet, cold and sudden.

"Oh!" she exclaimed.

For a moment she stood stock-still, feeling the cool water coming over her instep and then retreating, sucking the sand out from between her toes.

She took another step in. The water covered her instep as her toes sank into the suddenly softer sand, and then the wave retreated again, leaving her feet wet and cold.

She laughed aloud, breathlessly, the sun on her back, Trevillion at her side, and tilted her face up as she stood, her toes dug into the sand beneath her feet. The waves caressed her like a sister's touch, warm, alive, and familiar.

Eternal.

She must have looked like a madwoman but she didn't care at all.

Not at all.

And all the while Trevillion didn't say a word, simply stood by her, there in case she needed him.

She felt as if she could soar. She hadn't been so free in years.

TREVILLION WATCHED PHOEBE in the sea, the waves lapping about her ankles. She was laughing, her skirts lifted to her knees, her face shining in the sun, and he wished he could paint the scene. Keep it in his memory always.

Somewhere, at some indefinable point, he'd crossed a bridge and the bridge had crumbled behind him. There was no going back. He cared for Lady Phoebe Batten more than anything else in life. More than his family. More than his honor.

More than his freedom, should it come to that.

Bringing her joy was worth more than any amount of

money. He knew—without doubt, without fear—that he would kill for her.

That he would die for her.

It was almost a relief, this realization. He might fight intellectually against it, using all those well-worn arguments: he was too old, she was too young, they were too far apart in class, but it simply didn't matter. His heart had performed a coup d'état over his mind and there was nothing more to be done about it.

He loved Phoebe Batten, now and forevermore.

Phoebe turned almost as if she'd heard him speak aloud. "Are there shells upon the beach?"

"A few." He bent and collected several small shells, then walked to her. "Hold out your hand."

She did, staring sightlessly at nothing, a soft smile still playing at her mouth. The wind had made her cheeks pink, had blown loose a few strands of her hair.

He thought he'd never seen anything so lovely in his life.

Trevillion took her hand and placed the shells in her palm like an offering to a goddess.

She dropped her skirts and felt the shells with the fingers of her other hand. "What do they look like?"

He cupped one palm under the hand holding the shells, and tangled the fingers of his other hand with hers. "This one"—he touched a smooth little shell with their index fingers—"is a dark blue on the outside, paler gray-blue on the inside. This one"—he directed their fingers to a ridged open clamshell—"is a delicate pink."

The exact shade of her cheeks, in fact, though he did not say that.

She looked up, so close, the wind throwing a lock

of hair across her plump mouth, and she smiled just for him.

He wanted to hold that smile, to keep it in his chest forever.

Instead he cleared his throat. "We have a picnic basket Betty made."

Her face lit up. "Oh, how wonderful!"

"Come." He took the hand not holding the shells and led her up the beach to where Regan was lipping at the sparse grass. He unbuckled the basket and an old blanket from the back of the mare's saddle and brought them to a patch of dry sand. "Here's a place we can sit."

He spread the blanket and she lowered herself.

"Oh, I've got my skirts wet," she murmured.

He glanced over. Her damp hem was over her bare feet. "Flip them up. There's no one here to see but Regan and I doubt she'll care."

"But what if someone comes?"

He shrugged. "There's not much cause for people to come here—unless they want a picnic."

She smiled and pulled up her skirts, baring her lovely legs to the knee.

He tore his gaze away and opened the basket. "Betty's given us some bread, cheese, and apples, and a bottle of wine." He looked up at her. "That's a disappointment, I know, after days of beer."

"Silly." She held out her shells. "Can you place these somewhere safe?

Trevillion found himself stowing the common sea-shells as carefully as if they were pearls.

He poured her some wine into an earthenware cup and wondered if she'd ever drunk from such a plain vessel in all her life. She didn't seem to mind, though, sipping the wine while taking delicate bites from the slice of cheese he'd given her.

She turned to him suddenly, her face unusually grave. "Tell me, has Dolly always been the way she is?"

"Simpleminded, you mean?" His words were harsh, but his tone was not. He'd lived with Dolly most of his life. "Yes, or so I'm told. She was a difficult birth for my mother and at first they all thought the baby would die. But she didn't. She was sickly as a child, but she lived." He broke off a piece of the bread, but then just stared at it. "She's very affectionate, you know. She used to follow me about when I was a boy, even though I was four years younger. She's been my duty for as long as I can remember."

"What do you mean?"

"Well…" He took a bite of the bread and ate it before answering. "My mother died when I was four, as you know, so there was only Father. He had the horses to tend to. We did have servants—Betty came when I was ten or so—but Father made it clear it was my job to watch Dolly. Make sure she didn't harm herself with the fire or wander onto the moor. That sort of thing."

Phoebe's brows knit. "It sounds like an awful responsibility for a little boy."

He shrugged, though she couldn't see it. "Father knew what he was doing. Someone had to watch Dolly while he worked and he trusted me." He grimaced bitterly at the thought. "And then we both grew up and I was supposed to keep her from other harm."

Phoebe knit her brows. "Other harm?"

He looked up at her, realizing. "Ah. You don't know.

Dolly's quite pretty, despite...well, everything. She's got dark hair, graying now, of course, and our father's blue eyes. When she was younger..." He inhaled sharply, remembering that day. His fearful worry for Dolly. Finding her at last with her dress and hair all undone. The confusion on her sweet childlike face. His rage—and the shame when he'd had to tell his father. "Well, suffice it to say I failed in my duty. Failed completely."

"James," she said, sounding distressed, "Is that...is that how Agnes was conceived?"

"Yes. I'm sorry," he said abruptly. "I shouldn't have brought up such awful things."

She cocked her head. "I rather think it's I who should apologize for making you relive these memories."

He couldn't say anything to that.

She sighed. "Tell me what Agnes looks like?"

"Pretty. Dark like her mother, like all the Trevillions, except for her eyes. They're green." He threw the bit of bread rather viciously at one of the wheeling seagulls.

"Your eyes aren't green, are they?" She'd scooted closer to him. "Your eyes are blue."

He stilled, watching her venturing closer. "Yes. How did you know?"

"Hero and Artemis told me what you looked like," she said, a little smile playing about her mouth. "I was curious, so I asked."

He blinked, wondering how the duchess and Lady Hero had described him. Wondering when Phoebe had become curious about him.

She knelt in front of him now, reaching out one hand. It connected with his cheek.

"Blue eyes," she murmured. Her fingers spread and

trailed down his cheek, a butterfly's touch. "High cheek-bones." Her forefinger found the bridge of his nose and followed it down. "A straight nose." She found his lips and ran her finger across his mouth.

Both their breaths caught.

"A wide mouth," she whispered, tilting her head and leaning forward. "With soft, beautiful lips."

She wasn't for him. His father had told him so and he'd acknowledged that truth.

But at the moment Trevillion knew only one thing: he no longer cared that he couldn't have her forever as his. He had her right now, and when, inevitably, she turned from him, he'd cherish this memory.

Forever.

He leaned forward and kissed her.

Chapter Fourteen

*Corineus drew his sword, kicked the sea horse into
a gallop, and charged Agog. The giant swung his
club, but the faery horse leaped the blow, her cloven
hooves flashing. Then such a fearsome battle ensued
I can scarcely tell you! Agog swung again and again,
each blow gouging great holes in the cliffs, while the
sparks flew from the sea horse's cloven hooves and
Corineus rent the air with his battle cry....*
—From *The Kelpie*

Phoebe shivered at the touch of James's mouth. He was so
hot, so sure. There was no hesitation as he drew her closer
into his arms and it occurred to her that something had
changed.

That this time he wouldn't stop.

She trembled uncontrollably at the thought.

Above the seagulls called. The waves still crashed
to the shore, and she tasted salt on his lips and hers.
She spread her fingers on his face, touching, wanting to
absorb this man into her very bones. She could feel his
hair drawn back from his face, the curve of his ears, the
velvet of his tongue in her mouth, and she clutched him
closer.

Until she pulled away, gasping. "Untie your hair. Let me feel it."

His arms moved, muscles bunching, clothing rustling, as he took off his coat and then his waistcoat before reaching up to untie his hair. She followed his hands, feeling as the strands came undone. He'd had his hair in a tight braid and the hair was wavy beneath her fingers. She drew it forward, stroking, even as he bent and kissed her temple, trailing his lips down her cheek, nosing up her chin to kiss her jawline.

Another shiver racked her body.

"Are you cold?" he asked, his voice rasping.

"No," she gasped. "Not at all."

How could she tell him that his touch was almost overwhelming, when he'd not even gotten below her neck?

But he seemed to know. He chuckled darkly, pulling her fichu from where it was tucked into the edge of her bodice. The fabric slowly slid over the tops of her breasts, whispering a caress.

He bent suddenly and opened his mouth on her collarbone, hot and wet.

She gasped and grasped his head for balance, to keep the world from spinning.

He raised his head, his lips at the corner of her mouth. "Tell me right now if you wish me to stop."

She licked her lips and he nipped at her tongue, making her gasp again.

"I don't..." She swallowed. "I don't want you to stop."

"Then I won't," he said, low and intimate.

His fingers were at the laces at the front of her bodice, deft fingers pulling free the strings.

Undoing her.

"Lift," he murmured, and she obeyed, raising her arms so that he could draw off her bodice. Her stays followed.

And then he stopped.

She waited, her breath shuddering in and out. "What is it?"

He groaned, the sound almost inaudible. "Do you know what you did to me each night when you wore only this chemise?"

His fingers trailed over the top edge. It was a simple garment, far less fine than the ones she usually wore. The neckline merely had a line of decorative stitching. No lace, no fancywork.

Yet she felt as if she wore silk and gold thread as his fingertip traced the chemise. Her skin felt sensitized, her breasts swelling.

"I can see your nipples, did you know that?" he asked, and his voice sounded almost angry.

She knew what he felt wasn't anger.

"Yes," she said, bold as any Covent Garden soiled dove. "I know."

He grunted what might've been a laugh. "They're a deep pink, so sweet, so round, and every time I saw them, they were pointed, as if they wanted my attention. Wanted my mouth. As they are now."

She swallowed a moan.

He slowly cupped her breast, his palm cradling her without touching her nipple. "Is that what you want? My mouth on your nipple, Phoebe, sucking until you scream?"

Oh God.

"Y-yes," she said, and though the word came out more a squeak than anything else, she simply couldn't care because he did just that.

James bent his head to her breast and drew her nipple into his searingly hot mouth right through the thin lawn of her chemise.

She arched her back at the sensation—like nothing she'd ever felt before. A yearning sweetness so intense it was nearly pain. She gasped, and he steadied her, his hands at her back, holding her even as he drove her nearly mindless.

He suckled tenderly, using his lips and tongue, and then he drew back and before she could speak he was on the other breast, mouthing it as well. The lawn of her chemise was sodden from his mouth and the wind blew across it, tightening her nipple, making her swallow and push up against him.

"Shh," he murmured, and she realized she'd been moaning without even knowing it. "I'll take care of you."

He plucked at the ribbon holding her chemise up and untied the bow. He spread the chemise, drawing it down over her breasts, exposing her fully to the sea air until she was bare to the waist.

"So sweet," he murmured, kissing between her breasts, nowhere near where she really wanted his lips. "So very lovely." And he licked up to her collarbone.

Was he attempting to drive her mad?

"Please," she said, sounding less ladylike and more demanding. "James!"

"Yes, my lady?" he asked, innocent, nearly disinterested. "What would you like?"

"You know."

He trailed teasing fingers around the sides of her breasts, not quite touching her nipples. "This?"

"N-no," she stuttered. "My ..."

"Yes?" he whispered in her ear, his hot breath making

her shiver. "Tell me, Phoebe. Tell me what you want me to do to you."

"Oh, please," she moaned. "Oh, please touch me."

"How?" The one word was stern. Commanding.

"With your mouth," she whispered. "Suck my nipple."

He moved immediately, drawing her nipple into the heat of his mouth. Oh, and it was so much better without the chemise in between. His tongue was on her bare flesh, teasing her, arousing her, making her shift restlessly.

"You're so beautiful," he murmured. "Your breasts wet and red from my mouth. I could do just this all afternoon. Hold you here and feast on your nipples."

She arched her back at his words, offering herself, and though he seemed the one teasing, tempting her, she heard him swear beneath his breath.

He wasn't as in control as he wanted her to believe.

She smiled then, secret and feminine, and let her own hands drift over his head, his hair, as he turned his attention once more to her oversensitive nipples. He still wore his shirt and she yanked at it, wordlessly asking.

He pulled away from her for a second and when he came back, his chest was bare. Oh, how she delighted in all that warm skin! She ran her palms, flat, fingers spread to feel as much as she could, over him. His strong neck, his hair brushing the backs of her hands as she trailed them down to his shoulders, bunched with wiry muscle. His arms, with those intriguing muscular bulges in the upper parts. His chest with that hair that she so loved. She ran her fingers through it, touching his nipples, running her thumbs over them.

He tongued her nipples, flicking them back and forth, and she wondered if she could do that to him as well.

Would he like it as much as she did? For she couldn't help it, her head was falling back, exposing her neck, her vulnerability to him. He was wrapping her in sorcery, beguiling her with his lovemaking.

"James," she moaned, her hands at his waist, pulling him toward her. "I want... I want..."

"What do you wish? Tell me and I'll do it."

"Take these off," she said boldly, tugging at his breeches. "Let me feel all of you."

Oh, she should be embarrassed to be so wanton! To ask a man to strip naked so that she might enjoy his body. But she couldn't find it in herself to be ashamed. If he would let her, she'd discover all of her James. Find out what a man was really like, at base.

He drew away from her and she wished—oh, how she wished!—that she could see what he did. How he unbuttoned the placket of his breeches and slid them down his thighs. What he looked like in only smallclothes.

What he looked like after he'd taken his smallclothes off.

She might give the use of her right hand to see James Trevillion naked in the sun. Just once. Just one small glimpse to hold forever within her.

But that wasn't a bargain she could make.

So when he came back to her, all warm, smooth skin, smelling of the ocean and the sky and her sandalwood and bergamot scent, she had to restrain herself from grabbing with needy hands.

"Can I..." She swallowed, for her mouth was dry. "Can I touch you?"

"Anywhere," he murmured into her mouth.

She clutched him. At lean hips, over muscled buttocks,

feeling that patch of hair just above his cleft, hard thighs tightening and flexing as he pushed her legs apart. The hair on his legs.

She laughed aloud. She'd never felt a man. A man with his hips between hers. A man intent on making love to her.

"Take off my skirts," she said, suddenly pushing against his broad chest. "Let me be nude with you."

And he was gone a moment. Just gone. For that was what blindness was: a great void. One could hear sounds, sense things nearby, but without sight, without touch, nothing was truly there, was it?

Blindness could be a great loneliness.

But then his big hands were on her again, anchoring her, and she knew she wasn't alone anymore. Wasn't *lonely*. Not with James here with her.

He helped her as she wriggled and gasped and even cursed, taking off her skirts. Then she was as nude as he, lying on a scratchy blanket in the sun on a beach in Cornwall.

His body covered hers, hard and male and foreign and *here* with her. Just them and the seagulls and Regan, munching on grass somewhere.

"Put it in me," she said, impatient. She wanted him to make it real. "Now. Put yourself in me."

He gasped a laugh, his hand sliding between them. She could feel him—his penis. His *cock*. That was what it was. The thing that made him male. A cock. Thick and hard and rather bigger than she'd thought it would be. She was surprised that he had to take it in hand, to guide himself as he put it into her wet folds. Somehow she'd thought he could do it without his hands, for horses did, didn't they?

But then he was pushing, pushing in and she wasn't wide enough, she could tell. It burned a bit and she froze and thought he might stop. Might call it off as an impossible thing.

Instead he shoved hard, breaching her entirely, and the burn intensified.

And then . . . and then he was inside her.

She gasped, catching her breath. How strange! He'd impaled her almost violently. This wasn't a gentle act—a reverential act. This was animal. This was mating.

He pulled out slightly, grunting, and she smelled sweat and sex, just before he shoved back in, joining with her, moving in her. She gripped his thrusting buttocks, feeling him as he labored on her and she wanted something . . . longed for something . . . just out of reach, a shining, exquisite thing.

He turned his head and caught her mouth, thrusting his tongue in. She could taste the wine they'd drunk, taste his basic *want* for her. She arched up, not knowing if she should try to move or if she should shove back. She widened her legs, pulling them up, giving him room to move in her. He thrust, slow and steady, the very inevitability of his rhythm driving her higher.

"Please," she sobbed. "Please." Not even knowing what she pleaded for.

He grunted, his body slick with sweat now, and let his head fall beside hers, his cheek rubbing next to hers, and she felt a quaking within him, a seizure of the soul.

He stilled, his cock still in her, and she gasped for breath, tracing the indentation in the middle of his back.

Suddenly he withdrew from her, rolling to the side, and she thought, *Is it over?*

Wetness seeped between her legs.

But then he did something odd.

He placed his palm on her belly, simply let it lay there,

warm and still, and kissed her. His mouth was tender moving over hers, nipping, licking.

She stirred restlessly, her legs moving. She wanted that thing she'd felt in their bed at the inn. That wonderful bursting.

As if understanding her desire his hand slipped downward. Into her damp curls. Farther. Into that place where he'd just plundered her.

Somehow it seemed more obscene for him to put his fingers there than his cock.

"What?" she asked, her voice cracking.

"Don't think," he said against her lips. "Just feel."

His thick fingers dipped and found a small part of her—so very tiny—and yet, apparently, the center of her body. The place where her blood rushed to, the heart of her pulse. He touched her there on that small nubbin and she trembled, feeling exposed. Feeling hot with want.

He held her in his hand.

He took her mouth then, thrusting in his tongue as he delicately played with her below, plucking and tapping and flicking his fingers on her flesh until she thought she would burst.

Until she did burst.

It rushed up, crashing over her like one of the waves on the beach, washing up everything she'd ever kept hidden inside.

In that moment she was his, completely and utterly. But she knew something more:

He was hers as well.

EVE DINWOODY SAT staring at the white dove Val had given her. The dove stared back. Of all the useless and usually quite eccentric gifts he'd presented to her, the dove was perhaps the most useless. It didn't even sing.

"You ought to name it," Jean-Marie offered from the door.

"If I name it, I can't let Tess cook it for supper," Eve replied dourly.

"You're not going to have Tess cook it for supper anyway," Jean-Marie said.

He was probably right.

Eve frowned at the dove as it let out an adorable cooing sound and pecked at the grain on the bottom of its cage.

"I *should*," she muttered. "I really should, just to teach him."

"He'd care not at all if you ate that dove," Jean-Marie said gently, "and you know it well."

Which was the problem with Val right in a nutshell. He didn't care for other people's opinions or, for that matter, for other people. Eve wasn't even sure he cared for *her*. How else to explain his involving her in what she suspected was a very nefarious plan—and then lying to her face when she went to confront him about it? He'd looked so innocent in the firelight, offering her Turkish delights and proclaiming his ignorance.

Eve snorted to herself. What else had she expected from Val?

Someone knocked at the door.

Jean-Marie lifted his eyebrows at her.

Eve shrugged.

He left to answer the door, returning a short while later, his expression all that could be correct in a butler. "Mr. Malcolm MacLeish wishes to call upon you, ma'am."

This was unexpected. "Show him in."

Mr. MacLeish looked strained as he came into her

sitting room, though he was trying his best to keep a cheerful smile upon his face. He wore a light-brown suit and carried a black tricorne. "Miss Dinwoody, thank you for consenting to see me."

She nodded. "Not at all, Mr. MacLeish. It's nice to have company of an afternoon. Would you like to sit?" She gestured to one of her rose silk chairs.

He perched on the very edge and shot a wary glance at Jean-Marie, who had taken up his post next to the sitting room door. "I was wondering...er...well, I'd like to speak to you."

She smiled.

Mr. MacLeish cleared his throat. "In private."

Eve considered this. Usually she didn't like being alone with men—Val and Jean-Marie being the only exceptions—but her curiosity had been aroused.

She nodded to Jean-Marie and he left the room without a word, closing the door behind him. She knew, though, that he'd be right outside it, listening for her call.

Eve looked at Mr. MacLeish and spread her hands. "Yes?"

"It's about the Duke of Montgomery," he said abruptly. "You have a special relationship with him, I think."

Eve merely watched him, neither confirming nor denying his statement.

Her lack of response seemed to make him more nervous. "That is, I *hope* you are a confidant of his, because he's blackmailing me."

At that Eve did stir. "Val blackmails a great many people, I'm afraid. It's rather a hobby of his."

Mr. MacLeish barked a laugh. "You say it as if blackmail were like breeding hunting dogs or collecting snuffboxes."

"I assure you I do not mean to be flippant," she said gently. "I don't particularly approve of his hobby. It hurts people."

"Yes, it does," he muttered. "Can you speak to him for me? See if he'll let me go?"

"I don't hold sway over the duke. He does as he wishes—he always has." She spared a glance for the dove, asleep in her cage.

Mr. MacLeish closed his eyes. "Then I'm lost."

Eve pressed her lips together. "Can you not simply ignore him? Whatever information he has about you, surely 'tis better to be free than to let him control you?"

The young man shook his head, the sunlight from the windows glinting off his red hair. The light also revealed the lines beside his eyes. "I can't. There are others involved."

She waited, watching him sympathetically.

At last he said, "I was...indiscreet with a married person and there are letters—letters the duke has in his possession."

"Ah. Well, that is unfortunate, but perhaps if you warn the lady, she can—"

He shook his head once. "It isn't a woman."

"Oh." Eve wrinkled her forehead. An affair between two men wasn't merely scandalous—it could be punishable by death. "I am quite sorry, then."

"Yes." His lips twisted rather tragically. "And Montgomery is asking me—forcing me—to do something I just...it's not right, don't you see?"

She didn't, really, not knowing exactly what Val intended for Mr. MacLeish, but she could see he was distraught.

Not for the first time, she silently damned Valentine Napier, the Duke of Montgomery.

She leaned forward impetuously. "Go abroad then, to

the Colonies or somewhere else. He's a duke, but his reach isn't infinite. If you leave he can no longer touch you."

"And my...friend?" Mr. MacLeish smiled bitterly. "He can't leave, you understand. He has family here. A wife. If Montgomery publishes those letters..." He shook his head.

"Are you willing to put your soul to let for your friend?"

"Yes." He laughed quietly. "I thought it a matter of honor to make sure the letters were never published, but the thing that Montgomery wants me to do is horribly despicable. Perhaps I'd lose more honor if I agree to do it."

"I *am* sorry," Eve said truthfully. "And I'll speak to him, you have my word. I just don't want you to be disappointed. He's likely to take no notice of me at all."

Mr. MacLeish nodded, rising from his chair. "I thank you, Miss Dinwoody, for your kind ear and your honesty." He hesitated, twisting his hat. "I'm impertinent, I know, but do you mind if I ask what Montgomery has to blackmail *you* with?"

"Oh, he has no need for blackmail, Mr. MacLeish. He has a hold far worse over me." Eve smiled a little sadly. "Love."

TREVILLION CLOSED HIS eyes against the sun as he lay on the blanket, Phoebe's head pillowed on his bare shoulder. Soon he would have to rise, to face what he'd done and make decisions, but just for a little while he wanted simply to rest and enjoy.

Phoebe was playing with his chest hair, which seemed to fascinate her. "How many times have you done that?" she asked.

He opened one eye, a little alarmed. "'Tisn't a thing a gentleman tells tales of."

"I don't mean *specifics*." She wrinkled her nose. "I just wanted to know...was it a lot?"

"Do you imagine me some Lothario?" he asked, amused.

"Nooo. It's just..." She sighed. "You do it very well."

"Thank you," he said cautiously. Did she wish he'd been a virgin? Some dewy youth, innocent and without cynicism?

"Do you wish I were more experienced?" she asked, as if reading his mind.

He turned so that they lay on their sides facing each other. "I want to make love to *you*, Phoebe, not a particular type of lady or one who has more or less experience." He hesitated, watching her brow wrinkle as she listened to him. "When I was young and first came to London, it might've mattered if a lady were buxom or had red hair or some other attribute. I bought most of my sex back then and *what* those women were was probably more important than *who* they were. But I'm older now and making love to an attribute holds no thrill for me anymore. What I want is you, Phoebe, no one else. What we do here is between you and me. What came before, what may come after—that doesn't matter. Right now only we two and what we want matter."

A corner of her mouth lifted. "Do you know, I never would've guessed how wise you were, back when you used to give me such terse answers. 'Yes, my lady. As you wish, my lady.' You were so very sober."

He leaned forward and kissed her. "And now you've made me into a frivolity."

"Well, not quite *that*, but I have heard you laugh now." She smiled. "I like the sound of your laughter."

"You'll cover me in blushes," he said, kissing her again. It was intoxicating, kissing Phoebe. But the sun was moving across the sky. "Come, we must bathe and dress or they'll send out a search party after us."

She squeaked at that and sat up.

He walked to the water's edge and wet his handkerchief to wipe her thighs. There was a little blood there—just a smear showing pink on the white of his linen—and he knew he should feel shame for despoiling her, his charge.

All he felt was pride. He'd meant what he'd told her. Right now, here on this lonely beach, she was no longer the sister of the most powerful man in England. And perhaps he was no longer a man scarred by faulty decisions.

They were simply Phoebe and James, lovers.

Would that they could always be thus.

But the day was advancing and with it the intruding world.

So they dressed and packed the picnic basket back up and he helped her to mount Regan, using a rock as a stepping stone.

The ride back to his father's house was slow and peaceful. They didn't talk much and Phoebe almost dozed against his shoulder.

As the house came into view, Trevillion saw his father outside, talking to Old Owen. He raised his hand to the two, but his father merely said something to Owen and turned to wait for their approach as the old horseman disappeared into the stables.

His father's face was set. The lines incised even deeper in his weathered cheeks.

"What is it?" Trevillion asked as he drew Regan to a halt.

His father caught the bridle and stared up at him, his jaw clenching. "Jeffrey Faire has returned—and Agnes has gone missing."

Chapter Fifteen

*For four and twenty hours Agog and Corineus and
the sea horse fought with no stop until at last the sea
horse struck the killing blow, driving her hooves in both
the giant's eyes at once. Agog fell like an avalanche,
flattening everything he landed on.
"We have won this new land!" cried Corineus,
joyous in his victory.
But as he did so, the sea maidens' song rose,
dire and compelling....*
—From *The Kelpie*

"Agnes has taken one of the mares," Mr. Trevillion said,
sounding every one of his years. "She must've overheard
Young Tom and Old Owen talking about Faire's return. If
she went to see that bastard..."

Phoebe felt a thrill of fear go down her spine—both
for Agnes's safety and at the thought of what Trevillion
might do.

He had a *price* on his head.

"You both need to stay here," Trevillion said, his voice
suddenly expressionless. All the lightness, the laughter,
the part of him that had made love to her so sweetly, had
disappeared. "Come."

He dismounted Regan and before Phoebe could say anything he had his hands around her waist, lifting her from the saddle.

"James—" she began, trying to think of the words that would stay him. But what could she say? Someone must bring Agnes back if she'd gone to meet the man who'd fathered her.

"You can't go, Jamie!" Mr. Trevillion said, his voice cracking. "They'll clap you in irons!"

"I have to," Trevillion bit out. "Watch her for me."

And then she heard Regan canter off.

"Has he left?" Phoebe reached out a hand, feeling suddenly frightened. "Has he left me?"

"Yes, but he'll be back." Mr. Trevillion didn't sound as if he believed his own words.

Dear God, what if James was arrested?

"We have to go after him," she pleaded with the older man.

"No point," he replied. "No one can catch my Jamie when he's on horseback."

"But…" She felt a hand take one of hers. A man's hand, wrinkled, with calluses on the palms. She didn't particularly want to be "watched" by anyone, let alone by dour old Mr. Trevillion.

"Come, lass," the older man said, and he sounded so weary that she hadn't the heart to protest.

Phoebe took his arm and Mr. Trevillion led her across the courtyard and inside the house.

"We can sit awhile in here," he said, and took her down a hallway to the end of the house.

She hadn't been in this part of the house before. "Where are we?"

"The library," Mr. Trevillion said curtly.

She raised her eyebrows. "You have a library?"

"I do."

She ran into something quite hard with her right hip.

"There's a chair here."

"Thank you," she said drily as she sat. "Do you know what James will do if he finds Agnes and Jeffrey Faire is there?"

The library smelled rather comfortingly of leather and dust.

Of course her companion was less comforting.

"That's none of your business, my lady," Mr. Trevillion snapped. From the sound of it, he'd gone to the far end of the room to pace.

Phoebe shifted in the not-very-comfortable stuffed chair. After this afternoon's activities she was actually just a little sore. Add to that the fact that she'd just been unceremoniously abandoned by her new lover—who might be riding to his imprisonment or worse—and really, she was just not patient enough for Mr. Trevillion's usual grumpiness.

"It is, actually," she said. "My business, that is. I'm living in your house and I have a deep affection both for Agnes and your son. What concerns him concerns me."

"As to that, missy," Mr. Trevillion growled, "I don't approve of my son—"

"Mr. Trevillion," Phoebe said in her Daughter of a Duke voice—rarely employed, but the more effective for all that—"please don't change the subject."

There was a rather fraught silence.

And then Mr. Trevillion laughed. It was a startling sound and not an entirely cheerful one. His laugh was rusty and it was obvious he'd not tried it out in quite some time.

Still. It was a laugh.

"You're a feisty one, I'll give you that," he said, and it almost sounded admiring.

"Thank you," she said. "Now tell me what you know, please, or I shall be forced to go ask Old Owen and I think that would make him most uncomfortable."

"Yes, it would." He sighed and walked closer. "Would you like a taste of French brandy? I know I need one."

Phoebe thought about James's tales of smugglers and decided she shouldn't ask how the brandy had been acquired. "Yes, please."

She heard a decanter being unstoppered. The gurgle of poured liquid, and then a glass was pressed into her hands.

"Best drink it slow like," Mr. Trevillion said. "It's not like beer nor wine."

Cautiously she sniffed her glass. The aroma was powerful. She took a tiny sip and felt as if she'd swallowed fire. "Oh!"

He chuckled, not unkindly. "Well?"

"I never judge a thing on one taste alone," she said loftily.

"Wise," he murmured.

She took another sip, waiting. This time she let the liquid sit in her mouth a moment, tasting. Really, it was like nothing she'd ever had before.

"You know how Dolly is," Mr. Trevillion began.

She turned her face toward him at once, sitting straighter. "Yes. James said she's been this way since birth. He told me"—she hesitated, wondering how she should phrase this—"James told me how Agnes was conceived."

There was a short silence.

"Did he now?" He stopped for a moment and she heard an inhalation. When he began again, his voice was level. "Dolly's mother had a hard time birthing her. The midwife thought the babe wouldn't live the night. But she did. You might think that was a bad thing."

She raised her eyebrows a little. She didn't think Dolly's having lived was bad, but then she wasn't the one whose opinion was important. "Do *you*?"

"No." The word was emphatic. "When she was older, when it became obvious that she'd never be like other little girls, the neighbors, the vicar would say that 'twould have been better had she died. I packed them right off. Should've seen that vicar's face. So outraged that I showed him the door for telling me my daughter was better off dead. Fool."

She could hear him swallow and she took another tiny sip of her brandy as well. She was getting used to the burn as the liquid slid down her throat. Somehow, knowing that Mr. Trevillion loved Dolly no matter what made her feel more sympathy for the man, gruff though he was.

"She was the light of my wife's life," he said, his voice low. "Martha was ill after Dolly's birth, but she loved the babe. Doted on her, like. And then four years later we had James. We kept Dolly close to home. Martha and Betty taught her a few things like how to bake bread. She was—is—happy, I think."

He paused as if uncertain.

"She seems happy to me," Phoebe said gently. "I sat with her this morning and she was very confident while making bread."

"Aye." He sighed. "Well, she grew up a pretty thing, though her brain didn't work as others' did. By that time I'd lost my Martha." He paused. "She was younger than me, you know."

She cocked her head. "No, I hadn't realized."

"A dozen years," he said, some sort of warning in his voice. "And after the first couple of years, none too happy about it, either. I was too old for her, too set in my ways. She said I took the life from her. Made her old before her time."

"I'm sorry," she said quietly. She'd had no idea that James's parents' marriage had been so unhappy.

"Anyway, after she passed on I was doubly busy. The horses took my attention and sometimes Dolly wished to go into town to buy things for baking. To shop as other young girls did. I'd send her with James, for she wasn't safe alone. I told him..." He swallowed heavily. "I told him that his sister's life was in his hands. That he could never turn his back, never let his attention wander."

Phoebe felt a chill up her spine. She didn't like where this story was going. "How old was he?"

"When she first started going to town? Maybe fourteen. Remember, she's four years the elder, but much younger in how she thinks."

"And when it happened?"

"When it happened he would've been two and twenty. A man."

Oh, and that would've made it worse in James's mind. To be old enough to be responsible and yet to have failed... "And the man who did this to Dolly—this Mr. Faire?"

"Jeffrey Faire." Mr. Trevillion spit the name as if it were foul in his mouth. "The second son of Baron Faire. Lord Faire owns all the mines hereabouts, owns the land and the people. He's rich and titled and his son never lacked for anything in his entire life. He could've had any lady in the area. Anyone and yet he cast his eye on my Dolly."

Phoebe swallowed, feeling ill, and whispered, "I'm so sorry."

"He told Dolly he would be her beau if she...well. At least he didn't beat her or hurt her...physically, and I thank God for that," Mr. Trevillion said, his voice shaking. "That's the only thing he didn't do. James found her and brought her home. We questioned Dolly. She said he was kind to her. He gave her a sugar stick."

Something slammed against a table and Phoebe jumped at the noise.

"Bought my daughter, my Dolly, with a sugar stick!" The words were roared out of grief and rage and broken pride. "Damn the man! I wanted to kill him, I did, but Dolly needed me. Lord Faire's a powerful man. There was nothing I could do, but James..."

"James told me he beat that man nearly to death." James must've been anguished, he who took his responsibilities so very seriously, especially when he felt he'd failed in them.

"Aye, Jamie found Jeffrey Faire that night and nearly beat the life from him," Mr. Trevillion said, and though his voice was grim, there was a note of satisfaction in it as well. "Jamie told Jeffrey to leave Cornwall—and so Jeffrey Faire did. Left the very next day, though he had broken ribs, or so I'm told."

Phoebe frowned. "But Lord Faire..."

"Lord Faire is the local magistrate. He called for Jamie's arrest. Jamie fled to London...and never returned."

Phoebe sat thinking furiously. "But they're *both* back now, James and this awful Jeffrey. Do you really think Jeffrey would hurt Agnes?"

"Hard to tell. I didn't think the man a rapist afore he attacked my Dolly," Mr. Trevillion said heavily.

Phoebe swallowed. "What will happen between James and Jeffrey?"

Mr. Trevillion sighed heavily. "I don't know, lassie, but the last time Jamie saw Jeffrey he told him if he ever stepped foot in Cornwall again, he'd kill him."

FAIRE MANOR WAS ancient and ugly, dominating the surrounding landscape with its cold gray walls and crumbling battlements. The Faire lords had lived on this land since time immemorial with no one to contest their right.

Except him, Trevillion thought as he rode up the gravel drive. Twelve years ago he'd beaten Jeffrey Faire's soft face into a bloody mess—a scandal that would be talked about in these parts long after he was dead. He'd told the man who'd seduced Dolly never to show his face here again—on pain of death.

Yet Mr. Faire apparently didn't think Trevillion a man of his word.

More fool he.

Trevillion glanced around, but saw no sign of either Agnes or one of the Trevillion horses. He dismounted by the front steps, looped the mare's reins over an ornamental stone vase, and limped up them. He might be a cripple now, but he was quite capable of shooting a man if that man didn't see reason. Trevillion didn't want to actually kill Jeffrey, but then again, he wasn't going to let him live anywhere near Dolly or Agnes.

A man came around the corner as he climbed the front steps. Lord Faire was in his seventh decade, tall and lean with graying hair. He wore boots and a wide-brimmed hat and looked as if he'd come back from a walk on the moors. Everyone in the area knew the lord liked to take daily rambles. Two spaniels milled about his feet and when the dogs saw Trevillion, they immediately started barking.

Trevillion turned. "Where is your son?"

Faire drew himself up, hushing his dogs. "James Trevillion. How dare you show your face here? Don't think because twelve years have passed that I won't have you arrested for what you did to my son."

Trevillion lifted his lip. "You might want to wait until you see what I'm *about* to do to him."

"What do you mean?" Lord Faire's exclamation came at the same time that the door to the manor opened behind Trevillion.

"Father!"

Trevillion turned.

Jeffrey Faire hadn't aged well in the last dozen years. Though only in his early thirties, he had a paunch and his face was jowled. He stared a moment at Trevillion, startled, before his green eyes narrowed. "You!"

"Yes, me," Trevillion said, drawing both his pistols. "If you remember me, then I trust you remember why I am here."

"Lay a hand on my son and I'll arrest you!" Lord Faire shouted behind him.

Several footmen crowded the doorway behind Jeffrey, and Trevillion could hear men coming from the nearby stables.

He raised one of his pistols, aiming it straight between Jeffrey's wide eyes. "Well? Where is she?"

Jeffrey did a very good impression of a man confused. "Who?"

The sound of horses' hooves came from behind him.

"I'll see you hanged for this, Trevillion!" Lord Faire roared.

"Stop!" The voice was Agnes's.

Trevillion turned with relief. *Thank God.* Agnes was pulling a horse to a halt behind him, Toby running beside.

Out of the corner of his eye, Trevillion saw Jeffrey leap for him.

Just as a small, furry shape darted past Trevillion and hurtled straight up the steps at Jeffrey Faire.

Jeffrey swore and kicked at Toby, catching the dog in the belly. Toby yelped shrilly and tumbled backward down the stone stairs.

"Oh!" Agnes cried. "Oh, Toby, no!"

She rushed to the little dog lying still at the foot of the stairs to Faire Manor, and knelt by his side.

For a moment all the men simply stared.

Then Lord Faire said, sounding bewildered, *"Agnes?"*

Trevillion shot a sharp glance at him.

"Agnes?" Jeffrey said. "You know the little bitch's name? Who is this girl?"

"Your *daughter,*" Trevillion growled.

Jeffrey's mouth twisted in distaste. "Father, stop delaying. Have Trevillion arrested and this wench thrown off the estate."

"You!" Agnes stood. Her face was wet with tears, but it was also red with rage, her hands fisted by her side. Her dark hair was half undone as she glared her hatred at the man who'd fathered her. "You *kicked* Toby! You're an evil, fat, *stupid* man!"

Jeffrey's mouth dropped open. "Why you little—"

"Go inside." The clipped order came from Lord Faire.

Jeffrey turned toward him, outrage plain on his face.

His father jerked his chin at the manor's doors. "You heard me. *Inside.* Or I'll order the footmen to take you bodily."

Jeffrey looked stunned. He turned and went without saying anything more.

Trevillion holstered his guns and hurried over to where Agnes had knelt again by Toby's side.

She lifted her face to his, tears streaming down her small cheeks. "Uncle James, can you help him? Don't let Toby die!"

He crouched by the little dog just as Lord Faire knelt on the other side.

Trevillion spared him a narrow-eyed glance before looking at the dog. Toby was making pathetic whining noises under his breath. Gently Trevillion felt his side.

The dog rolled his eyes to look at him as Trevillion slid his hand over his bones. "I can't find anything broken."

A chuckle from Lord Faire surprised him. "Likely Toby here is feeling very sorry for himself."

"Do you really think so, Grandfather?"

Trevillion blinked. "You *know* Lord Faire, Agnes?"

At that the girl looked torn between guilt and defiance. "Yes. He's not nearly as bad as he looks."

"Thank you, my dear," Lord Faire said drily. He looked at Trevillion, his expression wary. "I met Agnes two years ago on one of my walks on the moors. I understand that she's not allowed to go walking by herself, but apparently she . . . er, has learned how to sneak away."

"Agnes." Trevillion looked sternly at his niece. "You know what happened to your mother and why your granfer has told you you're not to go beyond our land on your own."

"Yes, Uncle James." She hung her head.

Toby made a sudden, miraculous recovery and got to his feet to lick his mistress's face.

"There, you see," Lord Faire said, "as right as rain is our Toby."

Trevillion cleared his throat. "Agnes, please take Toby to your horse and wait there for me."

His niece lifted her chin. "Only if you promise not to fight with Grandfather."

Trevillion narrowed his eyes at her, but nodded.

Both he and Lord Faire watched her walk with Toby to the mare.

"She has her grandmother's spirit," Lord Faire said softly.

Trevillion looked at him, brows raised.

"My late wife." Lord Faire coughed. "She had green eyes as well. I hope you'll not punish her for meeting with me on the moors. I knew at once who she must be the first time I saw her—those eyes, as I say. I couldn't help asking her to meet me again."

"Your son raped my sister—Agnes's mother," Trevillion said bluntly.

The older man's nostrils flared and for a moment Trevillion thought he'd have to perjure himself to his niece.

Then Faire sighed. "Jeffrey has always been . . . a disappointment to me. He does not have the sense of honor he should for one of his rank."

Trevillion thinned his lips but said nothing.

Lord Faire sighed again. "I never approved of what he did to your sister, Trevillion. I was quite appalled, in fact, when I found out the truth."

"And yet you ordered me arrested."

Lord Faire glanced up, his eyes shrewd. "You *did* thrash my son, Trevillion. No matter what he'd done, he was my son."

"And Dolly is my sister," Trevillion said, his voice level.

"She is," Lord Faire said. "Which makes Agnes of both our blood." He glanced over to where the little girl was bent over, petting Toby. "I shan't have you arrested, if only for her."

Trevillion watched him warily. He'd spent over a decade exiled from his home. Redemption never came as easily as this.

But Faire shook his head. "Look here, Trevillion. I've all but lost Jeffrey already. He only returned home to collect a few items of sentimental value. He's recently married and bought a plantation in the West Indies with his wife's dowry. He intends to sail there at the end of the week. I doubt he'll ever set foot in England again. The West Indies are half a world away. Should he have a family there I may never see them. But he has a daughter here still."

Trevillion stiffened. "Your son has no right to Agnes. He's never even acknowledged her as his."

Faire bowed his head. "He has no right and I have no right. I know that. There's no reason at all you and your father should let me see her, but I'm asking anyway."

"Why?"

Faire looked up at that. "She's my blood...and I love her."

PHOEBE LISTENED TO the noises that old houses make that night as she lay in bed. The wind blew outside, rattling the shutters on her window. Somewhere a clock chimed the hour, and the walls and floorboards creaked rhythmically, almost as if someone were walking down the corridor outside her room.

She clenched her hands on top of the coverlet and then consciously relaxed her fingers and smoothed the covers.

Trevillion had still not returned, though Agnes had, with Toby limping behind. She'd seemed cheerful and reported that her uncle James was talking to Lord Faire in a friendly manner.

Phoebe privately thought that it was only Mr. Trevillion's relief at her safety that kept him from punishing the girl for running off. As it was, they'd had a quiet dinner and gone to bed early, exhausted by the day's events.

Except she couldn't sleep. Mr. Trevillion said that there was no need to worry. That even aside from Agnes's report, had James been arrested or...or had any other horrible thing happened, the news would've traveled almost at once to them.

But Phoebe couldn't help thinking of the very worst. Maybe Lord Faire and Trevillion had started arguing again—or maybe Lord Faire had simply waited for Agnes to be gone to arrest her uncle. For all Phoebe knew, Trevillion was even now languishing in a dank prison or fighting for his life with—

The door to her room opened, which meant, she supposed, that the noises in the hallway really *had* been footsteps.

"Phoebe," Trevillion whispered, and relief rushed through her.

"Where have you been?" she asked, sitting up. "What happened? Did—?"

"Hush," he hissed, drawing nearer. "You'll wake the house and I hardly think you'll be pleased if I'm found in your room."

She wanted to retort that it wouldn't bother her all that much at the moment, but he was at her side now and she felt his mouth on hers, warm and demanding.

She reached up, winding her arms around his neck. His face was chilled from the night.

"What happened?" she whispered. "I was so very worried."

"There was no need to be," he said, and she heard a rustling as if he was doffing his coat. "Jeffrey Faire is leaving for the West Indies and I suspect we'll not hear from him again."

"I'm glad." She heard a shoe drop to the floor and raised her eyebrows.

"Old Lord Faire wants to acknowledge Agnes as his granddaughter, however."

"What?"

"It seems," he said ruefully, "that Agnes forgot to mention that she met Lord Faire on the moors over two years ago—and has been seeing him once or twice a month ever since."

"Oh, dear. Does your father know?"

"I don't think so." She felt the bed depress as he sat down on the edge. She moved over to give him more room. "But I'll let Agnes herself explain to Father in the morning."

She winced, thinking of Mr. Trevillion's pride. "He may not take it well."

"He may be quite angry at her at first," Trevillion agreed, "but she put herself in this position and I think she's old enough to face my father with what she's done behind his back. Besides, I doubt he'll stay mad for long."

"And do you think your father will let her see Lord Faire?"

"I don't know. He's never much liked Lord Faire."

Phoebe frowned. "Do you think Lord Faire means Agnes harm in any way?"

"No. Quite the opposite. He appears to simply want to know his son's get."

"His granddaughter," Phoebe said.

"Yes, his granddaughter." Trevillion sighed and lifted the coverlet, sliding in beside her. The bed suddenly became much smaller. "Funny after all this time that he asks."

She reached out and felt his arm, braced on the bed beside her. He was still wearing his shirt. "Perhaps he hasn't known how to approach your father until now."

"Perhaps, but I think Faire realized today that he might lose Agnes if I stopped her seeing him—and he doesn't want that." His voice hardened. "None of this would have happened had I been doing my duty toward Dolly that day. I was such a fool."

"You were young," she said.

"Twenty-two. Old enough. Older than you," he pointed out, an edge to his voice.

She found his hand and squeezed it, hoping she might give him some comfort.

"I was bored," he said softly, his voice wrecked. "Dolly was looking at a sweetshop. I left her there for just a moment to go look at a new book on horse husbandry that the bookseller had got in especial. When I got back she wasn't there. It took me nearly two hours to find her—in back of the churchyard."

She stroked his arm, warm and intimate, trying to think what to say for such an old hurt. "And so you ran from the law to become the law. Didn't you worry about that risk?"

She felt his movement as he shrugged. "I had no choice after I'd beaten Jeffrey and seen him on a ship away from Cornwall. I had to leave that night and horses are one of the few things I know. The dragoons are a mounted regiment. It seemed a good fit."

"You must have been lonely, though. Homesick." To be exiled from one's home.

"I used to write long letters, though my father hardly answered," he said quietly. She wondered if he'd put out the candle, if he was staring in the dark. "Dolly can't read or write so there was nothing from her. It wasn't until Agnes learned that I started getting regular letters from home."

She sat up, her hand still on his arm. "What did they say?"

"All sorts of things. She wrote nearly every week." His voice had warmed. "They weren't very well spelled at first, but she'd tell me about the horses and her mother and my father. Funny, he was much more doting in those letters than I ever remembered."

"A grandfather has a right to dote on a grandchild," she reminded him. Stroked up his arm, over his broad shoulder, until her fingers found the top of his shirt. She began unlacing it. He'd already removed his cravat. "You know she's shy around you."

"I don't understand it," he said. "She seemed to tell me everything in those letters. She even sent me a scrap of her needlework. I use it as a bookmark."

"I'd wager you're more intimidating in person than you are in a letter," she said drily. "You should spend some time with her."

She urged his arms up to draw off the shirt.

"What would I say to her?"

She would've rolled her eyes had she been certain he could see them. "Talk to her about horses and Toby and her grandfather. Tell her what her mother was like when she was a little girl and what you remember of your own mother. It isn't much different than writing a letter, really, and according to Agnes you know how to do *that*."

"Naturally." He sounded affronted.

"Well then."

"Well then, indeed. I think you're mocking me, my lady."

"Only a very little," she replied, and bent her head to taste his nipple.

She felt the ripple of his aborted start at her touch, and his chest expanded with his inhalation. She hoped this was correct. Perhaps ladies didn't taste their lovers, but she'd wanted to do this since the afternoon.

His skin was crinkled under her tongue and tasted faintly of salt and not much else. She circled the little nub, painting it with her tongue, and he inhaled again. She'd been so fearful when he was gone, for his safety and, more selfishly, for *herself*. She didn't want to lose him. He'd become companion, friend, lover. The most important person in her circumscribed life, and she wasn't even entirely certain what he felt for her. Affection, she knew, duty—that horrible word—but was there anything else?

Was she more to him now than simply a duty?

Because she wanted to be. She wanted, really, now that she thought of it, *everything* from James Trevillion.

She wanted to spend the rest of her life with him.

On that thought she sat up and ran her hands across his chest, feeling the rasp of his hair, the rounded muscles underneath. An urgency was rushing through her veins, a need to know *all* of him while she could. Her hands trailed downward. She hadn't had a chance to explore this part of him earlier.

"What—?" he began, his voice gruff.

She paused. "I want to touch you. Touch you all over. May I?"

He stroked her cheek, his hand large but infinitely gentle. "Of course, Phoebe."

That gentleness calmed some of her wildness. She smiled and bent to her explorations again. Over his ribs—bump, bump, bump—the hair disappeared, but in the middle of his torso there was a thin line, trailing down over his belly. How soft his skin was here!

"What color is it?" she asked. "Your skin?"

She circled his navel with her fingertips.

His belly tightened beneath her touch. "Pale?"

She shook her head. "No, I mean are you naturally fair? Or is your skin a bit darker even under your clothes?"

"I suppose darker, given that choice," he replied, his voice sounding amused. "Though since that part of me never sees the sun, 'dark' is relative."

She hummed noncommittally and reached the waistband of his breeches.

His hands tangled with hers, but she stilled them. "I'd like to. May I, please?"

"Since you ask so politely." His voice was rough as his hands fell away.

Her fingers fumbled, seeking the buttons she knew must be there. She could feel him under the material—his hard thighs, the crease on each side, his cock in between. She brushed against it now and again as she moved. At last she found the buttons and quickly undid them.

"Take it off," she urged, plucking at the breeches.

He arched his hips off the bed and took off both breeches and smallclothes.

She laid her hand on his thigh. There was curling hair

here—sparser than that on his chest, but quite thick nonetheless. She moved her hand up, encountering a slanting muscle on top of his hip. She traced it down, hearing his breathing growing rougher, until she encountered his pubic hair. It was springy to the touch and she was tempted to pet it.

But she was more tempted by what was below.

He was smooth and hot and fit into her palm. She traced her fingers over him, feeling the swelling of the flesh, the astonishing hardness underneath, the elastic skin. At the top it widened and she could feel a cuff of skin. She traced around it, wonderingly. It was so delicate a thing to have shoved inside her, and yet much more blunt than her own flesh. The tip was wet. She smoothed her fingertip over it, finding the tiny hole.

She retraced her journey, discovering that he'd grown in the meantime, lying hard against his belly. She inhaled, and smelled his musk, heady in the quiet of the room.

She stroked him again, unable to stop touching.

"Does it hurt?" she asked. "To be this way, I mean?"

"Hard?" His voice was a gentle rumble. "No, not hurt, but there's a yearning, certainly."

She paused. "What do you yearn for?"

"You," he said simply. "You."

And he drew her down to him, capturing her lips with his. She lay half over him, her breasts flattened to his chest, and she kept one hand on his cock, stroking as he kissed her, his mouth hot and relentless. If this was yearning, she felt it, too—in the ache of her nipples, in the swelling of her sex.

He broke away suddenly. "Take off your chemise, Phoebe."

He helped her draw it off so that she was as naked as he.

"Come here," he said, grasping her leg. "Like this." He pulled her over him so that she straddled him, her sex spread wide. "You can ride me like this if you want."

"Ride you?" She felt a smile stretch her lips. "Like a horse?"

"Your own stallion." Amusement was in his voice again.

Strange that at one time she'd thought he had no sense of humor.

Wonderful that he showed it only to her, in their most intimate moments.

"How—?" she asked, her voice catching. There was an emotion welling at the back of her throat, behind her eyes.

"Lift up a little," he said, helping her to kneel. "Now, carefully, seat yourself on me."

"On..." She lowered herself and felt his cock at her entrance. She explored with her hands and found that he was holding himself, holding his flesh up for her. She tangled her hand with his and pushed against him.

He began to widen her.

This seemed obscene somehow, on her knees, his cock partially in her, shoving herself on him while he lay there like some indolent pasha.

The thought made her wetter.

She shifted, angling herself, and pushed down again. He slid in, wide and hard, a welcome invader.

"Oh," she whispered, tears springing to her eyes.

"All right?" he asked her, his voice low. He had one hand on her hip and he traced soothing circles on her skin.

"Yes?" she said. "What do I—?"

"Brace your hands here," he said, drawing her hands to his warm chest, showing her how to lean a little forward. "Now use me."

"Use you?" It seemed a scandalous idea.

"Use me," he repeated. "Ride me until you come."

Well, when put so bluntly . . . she lifted her bottom, feeling him slide a little out, then sat back down. She shifted a little, finding her balance, feeling him move within her, tightened her thighs . . .

And began galloping.

Oh, it was a wonderful feeling! His hard flesh in her, thrusting back and forth as she rode him. His panting breath—though he did no work—the sensation of being in control, of being able to make this man shatter beneath her.

She felt whole. She felt invincible.

"Come here, my little Amazon," he growled, and pulled her down enough to catch a nipple in his mouth.

That—that single small point of pleasure/pain sent her over the edge, shuddering, grinding against him, completely and utterly out of control. Heat surged through her veins and she cried out at the sensation, feeling as if she'd become a fiery star.

He pulled her down, fully into his arms, as she curled around him, her face pressed to the pillow, gasping in the aftermath of her release. He placed both hands on her buttocks, thrusting heavily up into her.

He grunted, and she remembered, vaguely, his leg, but before she could ask, he stiffened beneath her, still thrusting, and she tightened herself all around him so that she might feel with him. His release.

His joy.

All that Trevillion was.

Chapter Sixteen

The sea horse turned to look at Corineus and he saw
that she was ragged and worn. Her sides were streaked
with sweat and foam, her delicate legs bloodied and
torn, and her once-proud head hung low, her white
mane grayed and stringy.
"Very well," said Corineus. "You have served me faithfully
and I shall set you free, my brave faery horse. But I ask a
boon of you: will you tell me your name?"…
—From *The Kelpie*

Late the next morning Trevillion stood in the sunny courtyard and groomed one of his father's mares. Reed had offered to do the chore for him, but Trevillion enjoyed working with the horses. Old Owen had given him a knowing smile and left him to it. Now the old man was talking to Phoebe, sitting on one of the mounting blocks a little distance away.

A bark sounded and then Toby was galloping up to Phoebe from the house.

Trevillion watched as Toby did his best to climb into Phoebe's lap despite the fact that he was too big to be a lapdog. She was laughing as the dog licked her face and muddied her skirts.

How strange it was to be in love. To spend some three-and-thirty years not even *aware* of the existence of a small, pretty, kind, funny, ferociously stubborn woman; to spend day after day with her, arguing, debating, sitting silently sometimes; all to finally come to this day and the knowledge that she was everything to him. That if he lost her from his world, the sun might as well disappear from the sky.

He wondered if she had any idea at all the power she wielded over him with her tiny palm.

"Toby'll never learn if Phoebe lets him climb all over her," Agnes said, walking to his side. She sounded frighteningly like her grandfather.

Trevillion glanced at his niece. She came only to his shoulder, but if she continued to grow at the same rate, she'd top Phoebe soon. He felt a sudden pang. He'd like to be here to see Agnes grow to womanhood.

But Agnes was staring up at him now. "Uncle James?"

She probably thought him soft in the head. "Yes, well, Lady Phoebe for some reason seems to like dogs jumping on her."

Agnes gave him a doubtful glance. "Are you *sure* she's the daughter of a duke?"

His lips twitched. "Quite positive."

"Hmm." Agnes hummed doubtfully. "Granfer says you can't marry the daughter of a duke."

He looked away, his lips thinning. It was a subject he'd been avoiding thinking about. "I expect he's right."

"He isn't always, though," she assured him. "He thought for sure Guinevere would foal a colt but instead she had Lark." She hesitated and then squared her shoulders, as if playing her trump card. "And she likes you, you know, Phoebe does. She likes you a lot."

He didn't tell her that "liking" often had nothing at all to do with an aristocratic marriage.

Some illusions shouldn't be shattered.

Phoebe stood precariously as Toby tumbled off her lap. Trevillion strode over to catch her arm so that she wouldn't fall.

"Is Agnes here to show us more?" she asked.

Agnes had been giving them the grand tour of the estate—all of which Trevillion already knew like the back of his hand, but Phoebe had elbowed him sharply in the ribs when he'd started to say that this morning.

He looked at Agnes now. "What's left?"

"There's a stone up on the moor," Agnes said eagerly. "You can see for miles and miles and the wind blows ever so strong."

"I'll see to th' mare," Old Owen said cheerfully, turning to do just that.

Trevillion watched him go, frowning. He didn't want to disappoint Agnes, but the ground on the moors was uneven, with clumps of gorse and grass. Not exactly an easy place to walk.

"Lady Phoebe might fall," he said. "Let's find another place to walk."

Agnes's lower lip drooped. "Oh, but—"

"James," Phoebe said, placing her hand on his arm. It was the first time she'd called him by his Christian name in front of another. "Let me. I want to experience the moors."

"I don't want you hurt," he said gruffly.

"I know." Her smile was winsome. "But falling isn't the end of the world. I may fall, it's true—in fact, I probably *will* fall—but really, one can't live without falling now and again."

"Phoebe…" he said helplessly. The thought of her being injured was unspeakable. He'd rather be hurt himself.

"Please."

That one word and the pleading look on her face were like an arrow to his heart. "Very well."

"Huzzah!" cried Agnes, and Toby began barking wildly. "It's this way."

Trevillion followed his niece, leaning heavily on his cane with one hand, holding out his arm for Phoebe to grasp with the other. He wasn't much good on uneven ground either, he thought ruefully. He was just as likely to take a fall as she.

Agnes led them through one gate into the pasture and then through another gate, and then they were out onto the moor. The gorse was knee-high, some of it blooming with tiny yellow flowers.

"Oh, this is wonderful," Phoebe said, bending to trail her hand in the leaves.

The wind brought the smell of salt and the ocean and Agnes was right—they could see for miles up here. The sky was an endless blue expanse, a dome encompassing the world. Trevillion sucked in a deep breath and smiled when Phoebe tipped back her face to feel the sun. They continued climbing until they came to a wide, flat area, dotted with gray stones cropping up out of the earth.

Phoebe lifted her face to him. "Can I walk by myself? Just for a bit? I know you haven't always liked the things I've wanted to do and the places I've wanted to go." She took a deep breath. "I don't want to *deliberately* endanger myself, but I also want the freedom to make the choice of what is too dangerous for me. This isn't, James. I just want to live."

He started to protest—there were so many obstacles should she wander off the footpath—but he swallowed the words. She wanted her freedom, he knew that—he'd always known that, and as her brother's man it'd been his job to keep her caged.

But Wakefield wasn't here. More importantly, Trevillion no longer agreed that the only way to keep her safe was to limit all her movement.

Perhaps Phoebe was right. Perhaps in order to live one had to stumble and fall once in a while.

He wanted Phoebe to live.

He took a deep breath. "Yes."

She stepped away from him gingerly. Both Toby and Agnes had stopped farther along the footpath to watch. Phoebe inhaled, tipping her face to the sun, and spread wide her arms like a seagull floating on the wind. She took another step and another.

And then she stumbled and fell.

Trevillion stared in horror. She was on her hands and knees and she must've at least scraped her palms. And she was shaking.

"Oh, let me help you," Agnes cried.

But Trevillion shot out his arm, halting her. He took a moment to steady his voice. "Phoebe, do you want help?"

"No," she said cheerfully, and when she lifted her face he saw she was laughing. "No, I can make it."

And she did. She stood and felt with the tip of her toe until she found which way the path went and set off again.

He hovered not far behind, of course, constantly checking the urge to go to her. To take her arm and guide her. Keep her safe. But he knew that as much as it mattered to him to keep Phoebe out of harm's way, it mattered more to her to be free.

Free from help. Free from constraints.

So he followed and watched like a hawk and let her fall. Once. Twice. Thrice. And each time he had to bite down on a gasp, had to stop himself from catching her or pulling her up.

But each time she rose again, laughing. Strong.

By the time they reached the outcropping of rocks he couldn't stand it any longer.

He caught her arm gently, pulling her laughing face toward him.

"I love you," he whispered in her hair. "I love you, Lady Phoebe Batten."

And when she caught her breath, her eyebrows winging up in surprise, he bent and kissed her on those sweet rose lips. Not in a show of passion, but as an offering and a promise.

Which was when Tom Pawley found them, bearing the note from the Duke of Wakefield.

PHOEBE STOOD AT Guinevere and Lark's stall and listened to the horses. The quiet munching of Guinevere eating her mash, the suckling of Lark taking her own dinner. The stables were quiet and warm, the smell of the horses comforting.

She heard a sharp bark and then Toby was trotting toward her, panting, footsteps following his.

She let a hand fall and was rewarded with a wet tongue over her fingers.

"Do you have to go back?" Agnes asked softly.

Phoebe felt the girl's little body pressing up against hers. Toby flopped down, leaning on her other side.

For a moment the only sound was that of Lark having a baby gallop around the stall.

"I live in London," Phoebe said at last. She tried, she really did, but her voice emerged dull and dispirited. It had been so wonderful on the moor. She'd felt so free. And then Trevillion had kissed her and said he loved her and she'd thought her bliss would know no bounds.

It had been the happiest moment of her life.

She'd actually considered pleading with Trevillion to just stay here when they'd gotten the letter. Though it was from her brother, he'd sent it through Alf, Trevillion's mysterious St Giles informant. Alf had kept their secret, it seemed, and Maximus still didn't know her whereabouts. Phoebe couldn't help thinking how frustrated it must've made Maximus to have to rely upon a St Giles urchin to communicate with his sister.

If they stayed Maximus might never find her.

Except she knew that was cowardliness. She loved her brother—truly she did—and she'd miss him and the rest of her family if she never saw them again. Besides, she'd hate for her family to worry over her.

It was just…going back to London. Going back to her old life.

Could one voluntarily return to a cage once the door had been opened?

"You could live here," Agnes said. "We've lots of room."

Phoebe let her head rest on her arms, which were crossed on the top of the stall door. "I truly wish I could."

"Then *stay*. The house is *huge*—why we don't use even *half* the bedrooms! Granfer says you can't marry Uncle James, but if you *did*, you'd be his wife and you could *both* live here. It's better with you here. It's better with Uncle James here, too."

Phoebe's mouth quirked at her hopeful tone. "There'd

be quite a lot of shouting if your uncle and your grandfather lived together permanently. I'm sure you wouldn't like that."

"It was awful quiet before you both came," Agnes said thoughtfully. "We could put cotton wool in our ears at supper."

Phoebe laughed wearily at that. "I'd like to stay, but you see it's not my decision. My brother has summoned me back to London and it's the way of the world that gentlemen are the ones who make these decisions."

"That," Agnes pronounced, "is very silly."

"It is rather," Phoebe murmured. "But even if he didn't have the power to force my return, I suppose I'd have to anyway. I've friends there, you see, and family, too."

"You do?" Agnes sounded astounded that Phoebe apparently had a life outside Cornwall.

"Yes. I've two baby nephews and I shouldn't like to never see them again."

"Could they…could they *visit* here, do you think?" Agnes asked hopefully. "I like babies and we could show them the horses."

Phoebe smiled sadly. "It's a rather long trip for babies, love."

"Will you be visiting again?" Agnes asked in a very small voice.

"I don't know," Phoebe said with something like despair, just as she heard a snuffling quite close by.

"Oh," Agnes whispered. "Lark's come to the door."

Very slowly Phoebe held out her hand and in another moment a tiny soft nose nuzzled her fingers, blowing warm air gently.

She stood still, not wanting to frighten the little foal—

and she wished with all her heart that she could stay here in Cornwall forever.

"His Grace writes that the kidnapper has confessed and is safely locked away in Newgate awaiting trial," Trevillion said, leaning on his cane. "He asks that I return with Lady Phoebe as soon as is possible to London. We'll leave at once."

His father stood with his back to the room, ostensibly looking out at the view from the library window. "And you intend to take her back."

"It's her home," he said without inflection. For the ax to fall so suddenly had been a terrible shock—one that he should've been better prepared for. After all, he'd known that Wakefield would eventually capture the kidnapper.

That he would have to deliver Phoebe back to her family someday.

He wished, though, that it weren't today.

"And you?" His father didn't turn, but his back seemed to straighten even more. "Is London your home now, too?"

"Are you asking if I'll return?" he asked cautiously. His father's question caught him off guard. He hadn't been thinking of anything beyond Phoebe and London.

But of course there would be something beyond that. He'd have to go on living without her if it came to that. He'd be in need of a job in any case.

"You could," his father said slowly, "now that Faire no longer seeks to have you imprisoned."

Trevillion waited a beat, but his father said nothing more. "That isn't exactly an invitation from you."

Finally the old man swiveled to look at him. "Is that what you need, Jamie? An invitation to come home?"

Trevillion looked him in the eye. "Perhaps."

His father blinked, his lips tightening fiercely in his lined face. "I never blamed you, Jamie, not ever. Oh, I know I might've yelled and said things when it first happened, but that was anger. It wasn't your fault, I know that."

Trevillion looked down. Hadn't it been?

His father groaned quietly and sank into a chair. "A man makes many a mistake in his life, some small and inconsequential, some that change the course of everything. The trick is leaving it behind you and going on anyway. Because if you become stuck in the past, in things that can't ever be changed, well then, you're done for."

A corner of Trevillion's mouth twitched up. "Grown wise in your old age, have you, Da?"

His father mirrored his expression. "I have indeed."

Trevillion nodded slowly. "Then maybe I'll be back."

His father looked down at his hands. "It's for the best you take her back to her family, Jamie. Your mother"—he grimaced to himself—"ah, but she was a beauty when she was young. I couldn't help myself, though she was much too young for me. But after we were married, she pined. Pined for a husband not so dour and old. Don't make my mistakes, Jamie. An unhappy wife makes for an unhappy marriage."

"Never fear, Da. The mistakes I make will all be my own. Besides"—Trevillion looked the old man in the eye, gentle but firm—"I'm not you and Phoebe isn't Mother."

Half an hour later Trevillion pulled back the carriage curtain to wave to Agnes and a sobbing Dolly, to Da and Old Owen, to Betty and Young Tom. Toby barked and ran after the carriage wheels until his stubby legs could no longer keep up.

And when the house disappeared around a corner, he let fall the curtain.

Trevillion looked across the carriage at Lady Phoebe, her eyes red-rimmed from weeping, and knew for a fact in his heart that all his future mistakes, good, bad, insignificant, or ground-shaking, would involve her.

Chapter Seventeen

*Corineus pulled the iron chain from the sea horse's
neck. Before his eyes she turned into a faery maiden
with long white hair and uptilted green eyes, once
again whole and beautiful.
"My name is Morveren," she said.
Corineus caught her hand. "Stay with me this
night, Morveren."
To this she consented and they made love there on the
beach to the sound of the crashing waves....*
—From *The Kelpie*

Phoebe couldn't tell night from day, but she knew they'd
been traveling for hours and hours when they finally
stopped at an inn.

She stepped down wearily from the carriage, her hand
on Trevillion's arm. They were no longer in hiding, running from possible kidnappers, so James said there was no
reason for them to continue to pretend to be man and wife.

But still he hadn't taken back his mother's ring.

She touched it now with her thumb, rubbing it surreptitiously like a talisman. She'd grown used to its being on
her finger. A better-mannered lady than she would offer to
give it back.

She didn't.

The inn was larger than the ones they'd spent their nights in on the way to Cornwall. She could hear men calling to each other as they changed horses on a carriage, the bark of dogs, the bickering of weary travelers.

"I'm sorry, sir," Reed said close by as they made their way to the inn. "The private dining rooms are all taken."

"We'll dine in the common room, then," Trevillion said. "Unless you'd rather our dinner be brought to our rooms, my lady?"

Rooms? He meant for them to sleep separately tonight? And another thing: he was back to calling her by her title. Truth be told she rather resented it. "No, let's eat in the common room, please."

They went in to the smell of cooking beef and the low chatter of guests. Trevillion steered her to a table and she sat, pressing her fingers against the worn wood in front of her.

"What'll ye have?" asked a woman's coarse voice.

"Beer for both of us and two plates of the beef," Trevillion ordered.

"Right you are, luv." And footsteps clattered away.

Phoebe turned her head, sniffing. She could smell the smoke of the fire, but there was also tobacco smoke from the gentlemen enjoying their pipes. Someone nearby had apparently never washed in their life.

A tankard was banged down in front of her.

"There ye are," the same woman said. "Say . . . is she blind?"

Phoebe smiled. "Yes, I—"

"That's a burden," the maidservant said, her voice sorrowful. "A wife what's blind. God bless ye, sir."

Phoebe found herself with her mouth still half open in the silence as the woman left again. She suddenly wondered if everyone was staring at her, thinking the same thing as the maidservant: *poor man*.

"Damn it," Trevillion hissed under his breath. "Don't pay attention to her. You know damned well you're not a burden, Phoebe. Any man—*any* man—would be honored to have you as wife."

She smiled then, though it might've come out a bit wobbly. "Would you?"

"Yes."

She felt a thrill go through her at his word, firm and without hesitation.

She leaned a little forward. "Then why do you want us to sleep in separate rooms?"

"Try your beer," he said. "It's the color of oakwood and I think you'll like it."

She wasn't such a fool that she didn't notice he hadn't answered her. "James—"

"Here ye are, luv." The same maidservant set down plates on their table.

Phoebe felt with her fingers, touching a pewter plate and warm meat covered in gravy.

The woman *tch*ed. "Like a little child, isn't she, sticking her fingers in her food."

Phoebe froze.

Trevillion growled and she heard the clink of coins. "We'll not need any more of your help tonight. Begone."

The woman huffed and stomped away.

Phoebe licked her finger and picked up her fork. She knew her cheeks were flaming, but she sat straight as she carefully pushed some food on the fork.

Trevillion huffed a laugh under his breath and she froze.

Then she heard his voice, low and intimate. "You look like a princess, did you know? I'm surprised she had the bravery to say anything at all to you. But then I don't think she actually looked at you. Anyone who did would know what you are: a petite Amazon princess."

Her lips twitched at his hyperbole, sweet though it was. "I think you might be biased."

"No." His reply was sure. "When you walk into a room, every man looks at you and it's not because you're blind. They see sweetness. They see a laughing face and a figure that a man just wants to touch."

Oh, she was blushing now!

"But the few who look closer see something else as well. They see a woman who meets adversity every day and walks right through it with a smiling face. They see strength and perseverance and endurance and they are in awe, my lady. They are in awe. Now"—he took her hand in his big warm one—"drink your beer."

She did, licking her lips of the foam.

"Well?" he asked, his voice huskier than before.

"I like it," she pronounced. "In fact I love it. I think I shall make Maximus serve beer at every meal in Wakefield House."

He choked. "I'd like to see Wakefield's face when you propose that."

She tilted her chin in the air. "Can I help it if my brother isn't such a person of the world as I?"

He laughed aloud at that and she was uncommonly pleased with herself.

The meal wasn't particularly wonderful, but the company

was, and when they were finished she was disappointed. Trevillion rose to talk to the innkeeper and Phoebe sat by herself for a moment, pensively tracing the edge of her plate.

"Come," Trevillion said softly when he returned. He helped her to rise. "Let me show you your room."

She didn't reply, merely nodded. They would be back in London in another day or so. It seemed a terrible waste to sleep apart tonight.

They climbed a flight of stairs, the wooden steps creaking beneath their feet. The voices from the common room faded as they made their way to the back of the inn.

"It isn't much," Trevillion said as he opened a door, "but the innkeeper assured me it was his best room."

He ushered her in, his hand still warm on her arm.

And closed the door.

She turned toward him. "I thought you had your own room?"

His cane fell to the floor with a clatter as he took her other arm, pulling her close. "I told the innkeeper that there'd been a mistake. That we didn't need it."

"Oh," she said. "Oh, I am glad."

And then she reached up and caught his face with her hands and pulled him down to kiss him. She licked over his lips, widening her mouth, nearly sobbing. She wanted him so much—tonight and always.

"Phoebe," he groaned into her mouth, and she'd never heard his voice so deep.

The earth whirled as he picked her up suddenly. She clutched at his shoulders, but never broke from their kiss, and he carried her easily as he walked. He set her down on a soft surface and she realized it must be the bed. Except she was sitting on the very edge, her legs hanging off.

"James?" she asked, not really caring what he had in mind.

He started to unlace her bodice, but then, seemingly impatient, abandoned it to push up her skirts.

He ran both hands up her legs, over the silk of her stockings to her bare thighs.

"Do you know what it did to me, when I took off your shoes and stockings that night?" he asked, his voice a growl.

"N...no." She'd started working on the hooks to her bodice, but she stilled at the sound of his voice.

His hands reached the tops of her thighs, his fingers spread, framing her mons. "I was so *close* to this and yet I couldn't see. Couldn't *touch*."

"Oh!" She was aware suddenly that he could see now—all of her, laid before him like some pagan offering.

"Open your bodice and stays," he said, nearly absently. "I want to look at your titties as well."

She gasped and obeyed him, oddly aroused at being a display for him. She pushed aside the edges of her bodice and stays, loosened her chemise just enough to pull it down under her nipples.

Cool air brushed her breasts.

And he pushed with his hands, forcing her legs apart widely as she lay back.

"So so pretty," he murmured. One of his hands left her leg and she felt a finger, delicately stroking her. "Do you like this? Is it good?"

She arched her neck, pressing the back of her head into the mattress. "Yes."

He stroked through her open folds to circle her entrance. "You're wet."

His hands left her and she waited, breathless, open and wanting, the night air cooling her flesh.

There was a rustle of clothing and then he was over her, around her.

Thrusting into her.

She gasped at the sudden intrusion. He thrust once, twice, seating himself fully in her.

And then he stopped.

"I thought about this all day in that damned carriage," he whispered in her ear.

She felt his mouth, hot and wet, close over one nipple, sucking strongly. She whimpered at the pleasure, clutching at his head, feeling his hair, pulled back and braided.

He still wore his coat and waistcoat, she realized.

Then the thought scattered as he found her other breast, cupping it for his mouth, drawing on her nipple.

She bit her lip, not wanting to cry out. It was so lovely, what he made her feel. And she was aware, all the time that he made love to her breasts, that he was still sheathed within her. Hard and waiting. Heavy and wide.

He drew back to flick both nipples with his thumbs and she gasped. "Please."

He chuckled to himself, a dark sound. "You have the most beautiful breasts, did you know? Plump and round, with big rosy nipples. I used to dream about your nipples, before I saw them. I once put my hands on myself while thinking of your breasts."

She clenched as she thought of his doing such a wicked thing while thinking of *her*. "Oh God!"

She couldn't wait any longer. Her sex was wet and swollen, open and throbbing, and she needed him to move. To give her that exquisite feeling again.

She wrapped her legs around his waist, shifting.

And now he was the one to gasp.

He abruptly took his hands away from her breasts and by the shift of the mattress, braced them by her shoulders. He withdrew and shoved himself back into her.

Hard.

She groaned. So close. So very beautiful. She scrabbled to clutch at his shoulders, but they were still covered by his shirt.

She wanted his bare skin.

He thrust into her again, swift and powerful, and now the bed was shaking.

She put her fingers on his face, feeling the prickling of his stubble, the dampness of sweat on his forehead and temples, his lips parted, the breath huffing out hard.

He worked himself in her, on her, faster and faster, and she pulled him down to her, chanting, "Now, now, now."

As his mouth touched hers, wet and open and feasting, she felt him shudder. Felt that one last powerful thrust and the spill of his hot seed.

And she arched into his kiss, into his arms, filled and filling, and quaked anew with delight.

TREVILLION WATCHED PHOEBE sleeping from across the carriage the next day and knew he couldn't leave her.

Couldn't live without her.

If she'd have him, he'd make her his wife.

The decision brought a certain calmness—but it also brought innumerable problems, the biggest being the Duke of Wakefield. He knew that Wakefield in no way thought of him as good enough to be a husband to his sister.

Nevertheless, he wasn't going to keep Phoebe from her family. If he simply eloped with her she'd be an outcast. He couldn't do that to her, not after watching her laugh and chat with her sister and friends.

Somehow he was going to have to court the sister of the Duke of Wakefield.

Trevillion frowned and looked out the window. They were making good time now that they no longer had to take the less traveled routes. Too, they could change horses at the posting inns along the way, so Reed could drive faster.

Wakefield had written a frustratingly cryptic letter, omitting the kidnapper's name and motive and even how he'd been captured.

Trevillion frowned, shaking his head. The whole thing seemed unfinished to him, but perhaps after he'd heard from the duke himself he'd be satisfied that everything was over.

By tomorrow they would be back in London, and then...

And then he would deliver Lady Phoebe to her brother and withstand the man's justifiable wrath.

Good *God*, he'd set himself up with an impossible task.

Phoebe murmured and yawned before sitting up. "James?"

"I'm right here," he assured her.

"Oh, good," she said, slumping back on the seat. "How close are we to stopping for the night?"

He judged the sun. "Several hours away."

She nodded, not saying anything.

He cleared his throat, feeling unaccountably ill at ease. "I wondered..."

"Yes?" She cocked her head to the side.

"Ah. Well. I'd hoped to call upon you once we're in London again. That is, if it's amenable to you?"

A dazzling smile spread across her face. "It would delight me above all things."

He couldn't help an answering smile, though she couldn't see it. "Would it?"

"Indeed, Captain Trevillion," she said, teasing. "But don't you have to ask my brother as well?"

"I thought I'd best make sure of you before I bearded your brother in his den."

"Very wise of you." She nodded and then yawned again. "Oh, dear, I'm so sleepy, but the cushions of this carriage aren't very cushiony at all."

"Then let me help." He crossed to her seat and drew her against him. "Lean on me."

"Hmm," she murmured sleepily against his shoulder. "You aren't very cushiony either, but you *are* very comfortable."

And Trevillion thought he might be very content with that.

PHOEBE STEPPED FROM the carriage and discreetly stretched. One wouldn't think it would be so tiring to sit all day, but in fact it was.

The inn seemed much the same as the one the night before: crowded, the smell of horses and manure in the yard, warm cooking inside. She sat across from Trevillion at yet another worn wooden table and thought, *This might be our last night*. Even if Trevillion succeeded in convincing Maximus to let him court her, it would be a very, very long time before they were allowed to be alone together again.

So after they ate, after she'd tried another beer, after he'd seen that Reed was comfortable for the night, after he'd shown her to a room and told her where the bed sat and where the fire, she took his hand.

"Make love to me," she said. And it wasn't in any way a seductive whisper or a plea.

It was a command.

She reached up on tiptoe and pulled his head to hers, crushing her mouth against his. She'd had some practice in the last week in kissing, but this wasn't a graceful kiss. This was a desperate crashing of mouths.

This might be our last night. This might be our last night. This might be our last night.

It was a terrible chant, repeating itself in her brain. They were out of time all of a sudden and she wasn't ready for it. She couldn't stand the thought of parting from him. Of all the uncertainty London and Maximus brought.

Tomorrow was coming much, much too soon.

She scrabbled, losing all delicacy, all finesse, plucking open the placket of his breeches even as his hands tried to stop her.

But he wasn't prepared for her to drop to her knees. For her to rip open his breeches and reach in—

"Phoebe. God damn it, Phoebe."

His words ended on a groan as she found him, already half erect, and here she paused and slowed. Oh, he was so warm, so hot. She pushed her face against him, inhaling, and smelled him, Trevillion. Her man.

Hers.

He throbbed against her cheek and she turned her face to kiss him, that thick shaft, pulsing, growing. She opened her mouth wide and tasted salt and man.

Somewhere above her he groaned again.

The funny thing about being blind was that sometimes people thought you were deaf as well. It made no sense, but there it was. She'd had occasion once, a year or two ago, to overhear two maids talking—and the discussion had been most enlightening.

She tasted him, holding his cock so that she might lick up the underside, and he actually staggered, his hand coming down on her hair, not heavily, but there. Whether to hold her or to hold himself steady, she wasn't sure, but it hardly mattered.

Her mouth reached his crown and she opened it wide, fitting her lips around him, swallowing him whole.

"Phoebe, God, Phoebe," he whispered above her, his voice a rough rasp.

This was in some ways more intimate than the other. This taking his most male part into her mouth. A mouth was for words, for eating, for more civilized pursuits.

And this was completely uncivilized.

She tongued him, tasting the bitter liquid seeping from the tip, feeling the slickness of his head.

She sucked.

When he cried aloud she knew she'd broken him with her uncivilized act and she rejoiced. This strong man. This brave man. Making incoherent sounds because she held him so sweetly in her mouth and nursed at his cock.

He moved suddenly, grabbing her arms and jerking her upright, and for one horrible moment she thought he would toss her across the room for her temerity and storm out the door.

Instead he staggered to the bed with her, muttering all the way, until he threw her down.

"Phoebe, dear God, Phoebe, what you do to me." He crawled atop her, pulling apart her legs. "Where in hell did you learn that? No, don't tell me. I still want to be able to sleep of a night." He bunched up her skirts, pulling and yanking, baring her to the waist. "I don't know why I thought I could ever withstand you. Ever think I could come out of this unscathed and whole again."

She opened her mouth to say something, but he slithered down her and thumbed apart her vulva, and then he placed his mouth right there, right at the center of her, and licked.

Oh! She'd never felt the like before in her life. It was an exquisite torture on flesh almost too sensitive to the touch. She arched beneath him, her hips moving involuntarily, but he placed his palms flat on her stomach and held her down.

Held her down as he flicked his tongue against her, driving her quite out of her mind.

He lavished worship on her, with tongue and lips, licking her trembling flesh. A week ago she would've died from mortification at the mere thought.

Now she reveled in his attention.

Her breath came in short pants, her lungs never quite filling, and she fisted her hands in her own hair, wanting him to stop, wanting him to continue until she went up in flames.

He lapped at her clitty, tender little licks, and at the same time thrust his thumb into her.

And for a moment she saw stars. Bright lights flickering behind her blind eyes, sparking and igniting as she burst into flames.

She was still gasping, still trembling and shaking, when he rose and mounted her, driving his flesh into her softness, grasping her legs and urging her to wrap them high over his waist.

"Phoebe," he growled into her ear as he thrust hard.

"Phoebe. You haunt me. You drive me. You possess me. I cannot—"

He arched, his penis deep within her, his big body shuddering on hers.

She gripped his shoulders, pulling him down to her, opening her mouth and swallowing his moan as he spilled inside her, pumping and thrusting against her.

When he at last stilled, he laid his head next to hers on the bed and whispered hoarsely, "You've ruined me. I don't know if I can breathe without you. I don't know how I can ever live without you."

"Then don't," she murmured into the eternal darkness. "Then don't."

And knew that if he was ensnared, then so was she.

She loved James Trevillion, body and soul.

Chapter Eighteen

In the morning Morveren rose. She looked between the sea
where her sisters called and Corineus and then held out
her hand to him. "Will you come with me, mortal?"
"How can I?" Corineus laughed. "I've a
newly won kingdom."
Her eyes grew sad before she turned to
wade into the blue sea.
As the water rose about her waist she said, "Should you
change your mind, simply call my name."
And then she dove beneath the waves....
—From *The Kelpie*

Late the next day Trevillion stood as he often had in the last several months: at attention before the Duke of Wakefield in his study. Strange. His sojourn with Phoebe in Cornwall might've never happened.

Save for the fact that he'd made love to Phoebe. That he loved Phoebe. That he was going to do his very damnedest to fight for Phoebe.

"What," the duke said, his hands steepled on the desk in front of him, his voice deadly quiet, "did you think you were doing, spiriting my sister away, hiding her—*from me*—and leaving that ragged urchin as the only one who knew of your location?"

"I thought I was protecting her," Trevillion said, his gaze steady on the other man.

"Protecting her from her family? From *me*?" Wakefield's glare could have turned boiling water to ice. "You have a goddamned cheek, sirrah."

"Her *maid* told the kidnapper of her movements," Trevillion said, fighting to keep his voice level. "There could've been any number of spies within Wakefield House."

Behind the duke and to the side, Craven cleared his throat loudly.

An irritated grimace crossed Wakefield's face. "In that at least you were right: we did have another spy in the house. One of the stableboys confessed to being paid by Mr. Frederick Winston—I don't suppose you've heard of him?"

Trevillion shook his head.

Wakefield shrugged. "The younger son of the Earl of Spoke and quite deeply in debt. He confessed at once when we confronted him. He meant to force Phoebe into marriage for her dowry, apparently." The duke's upper lip curled. "He's cooling his heels in Newgate even now while his father roars and threatens. I've given Winston the choice of leaving the country or hanging. I think we'll soon see the back of him."

He placed both hands palms-down on his desk. "But that doesn't excuse you."

"Doesn't it?" Trevillion arched a brow. "Had she stayed in London, Lady Phoebe could well have been kidnapped again. I protected her—"

"By ruining her reputation!" Wakefield roared, slamming his hand down on his desk. "What were you thinking, man? Half the town is gossiping about my sister."

"I was *thinking* that Phoebe's *life* was more important

than her reputation," Trevillion bit out, and as soon as he said it, he knew his mistake.

"*Phoebe?*" Wakefield's eyes narrowed. "How dare you—"

"I dare because *I'm* the one who took her to safety," Trevillion said, his voice rising. "I'm the one who *kept* her safe until—"

Wakefield stood, this time ignoring Craven's throat-clearing. "You are dismissed."

"No, I'm not," Trevillion said through gritted teeth. "Phoebe and I have an understanding. I'll be calling upon her tomorrow and—"

"You're a goddamned gold digger," Wakefield bellowed. "And I want you out of my sight."

To hell with it.

"Don't you ever," Trevillion ground out, "*ever* so malign your sister again. I love Phoebe for the woman she is, not her money. And if you should decide to disown her, be assured I can take care of her."

"Get out. I won't be disowning my sister and *you* won't be seeing her ever again."

"Tell me, Wakefield," Trevillion said quietly. "Do you truly fear for your sister—or your own reputation? Phoebe is safe because of me. What is that against a bunch of petty tattle-tongues?"

Wakefield stared at him.

Trevillion nodded. "She once told me that she didn't want to be thought of as a precious *thing*. You might want to think on that."

He turned and limped to the hall.

Phoebe had already been sent to her room—supposedly to rest and recover, but Trevillion now wondered if Wakefield intended to keep her under lock and key. He'd never thought the duke that much of a despot, but he'd heard of worse in the aristocracy.

He turned to the front door and found the duchess standing at the door to one of the lower sitting rooms. "Your Grace."

"Mr. Trevillion." Her gray eyes looked distressed. "I heard shouting."

"Indeed, Your Grace, your husband did not approve of my methods of keeping Lady Phoebe safe."

Her lips tightened. "He's been very worried about her."

He inclined his head. "Your husband has already dismissed me and told me not to come back."

"More fool he," she said, making Panders, the butler, hiss an indrawn breath. She glanced briefly at the butler. "Don't tell me you aren't thinking it as well."

The butler blinked. "I couldn't say, Your Grace."

She snorted. "No, of course you can't. None of you can, but I certainly will. Phoebe comes alive in your presence, Mr. Trevillion. I see it and so does everyone else, even my stubborn husband. Keep that in mind, Captain. Please."

Trevillion bowed. "Thank you, Your Grace."

And, turning, he made his way to the front door.

So he had the duchess's good word. That was something, though hardly everything, for without Wakefield's approval, he might well have lost Phoebe forever.

PHOEBE SAT IN her bedroom that night, her hands folded together on her lap, and thought.

About her life.

About Trevillion.

About what her life would be without Trevillion.

She'd heard the shouting below, heard the whispered words of the maids as they'd brought her water for the bath she'd taken earlier. Sadly, she hadn't been surprised. Trevillion was stubborn and brave, but she'd known Maximus all her life, and while she loved him deeply, she had no illusions about him.

He wouldn't take *anyone* courting her well, let alone an older former dragoon not of the aristocracy.

Maximus had probably never stopped to understand her situation. On many levels questions of station and age didn't pertain to her. She couldn't see a person's looks. She couldn't tell at first glance what a person wore or how they carried themselves. Yes, she wore silks and jewels, but when wool and linen were just as comfortable—in some cases *more* comfortable—did it really matter? She was, on a fundamental level, apart from her peers.

Why then couldn't she choose a man different from those her peers were wed to?

A knock came at the door.

"Yes?" she called.

The door opened and she listened as Maximus's distinctively sure tread interrupted her solitude. "Phoebe, I have the names of several gentlemen I can hire to guard you. It's been...erm, *suggested* to me that it might be wise to let you help pick one."

Her eyebrows drew together. "A guard? But didn't you say the danger is past?"

"The danger of that particular kidnapper," he replied, a hint of impatience in his voice. "But there is always the possibility of another. And of course there are the every-day dangers—footpads, crowds, that sort of thing."

Phoebe lowered her head and the thought came to her—if her brother had his way—of years and years and *years* with her hands shackled, followed everywhere by different faceless men, for her own good.

Her protection.

And at that moment something snapped inside her. Maximus had decided—entirely on his own—what was best for her and really, truly, she was tired of it.

"No."

"Now the first one—" Maximus interrupted himself at her word. "I beg your pardon?"

"I said, *no*," she repeated, quite politely.

"Phoebe," Maximus began in his stern ducal voice—a voice she'd heard and obeyed all her life.

Not tonight.

"No," she said, less politely now. "No, I will not help you pick out my own prison guard, Maximus. No, I will not have a guard at all, in fact. No, I will not consent to be followed around and told where I may go and where I may not. No, I'll not let you tell me what I must and must not do."

She gasped, slightly out of breath, but feeling quite giddy with the freedom of telling her brother her mind.

"Phoebe!"

"And," she said, "I might very well fall—I'm warning you now—I might fall, but I'll get up again because I *can*. I'll dance and trip, I'll talk to men and *women* I shouldn't, I'll attend salons where we discuss theater and scandals, I'll shop on the most crowded of streets and be jostled, I'll drink beer if I've a mind to, and I'll *like* it."

She stood, a little unsteadily, true, but on her own two feet. "It's not my blindness that cripples me, it's everyone else deciding I can't live because of my blindness. If I stumble, if I run into things and fall and hurt myself it's because I *can* and I'm free to do so, Maximus. Because without that freedom I'm just a dull, chained thing and I won't be that woman anymore. I simply won't, Maximus."

She made her way to the door, her fingers trailing over the backs of familiar chairs and tables, and there was absolute silence. Perhaps she'd struck her brother dumb.

When she got to the door she opened it pointedly. "And one more thing: I intend to marry Captain James Trevillion, with or *without* your permission. I love him and he loves me. I only tell you my plans as a kindness so that you might get used to the idea."

And for the very first time in his life the Duke of Wakefield was forced to leave a room without the last word.

THAT SAME NIGHT Trevillion sat eating a rather dispiriting supper of cod soup in his rented room and missing Phoebe when there came a knock on the door.

He looked up warily, his eyes narrowed. He didn't know all that many people in London, despite his twelve years there. Phoebe should be safely tucked in her bed. No doubt Wakefield would be making more threats soon, but it seemed a bit early yet for that. He'd only left the man a few hours before.

Trevillion rose with a pistol gripped in his hand.

When he cracked the door he was surprised to see the Duke of Wakefield on his doorstep.

For a moment he merely stared.

"Might I come in?" The duke lifted his eyebrows at him.

Trevillion silently waved him in.

Wakefield glanced about curiously and then took a seat on the bed without asking.

Trevillion thought about offering him something, but besides the cooling cod soup and a rather dismal wine he had nothing.

"I've come," the duke began in his usual proud tones . . . and then oddly he stopped.

It was Trevillion's turn to raise his eyebrows. "Your Grace?"

"Maximus."

Trevillion cocked his head. "I'm sorry?"

"My name is Maximus," the duke said wearily. He took off his tricorne and set it on the bed. "Yours is James, is it not?"

Trevillion blinked. "No one calls me that." Lie. His family and Phoebe called him that.

A corner of Maximus's mouth kicked up. "Trevillion, then." He sighed. "She lectured me tonight, did you know that?"

The question seemed rhetorical, so instead of answering Trevillion took his own seat.

"Without ever raising her voice," Maximus said thoughtfully. "And gave me a rather long speech about her rights." His gaze flicked to Trevillion. "She said she was going to marry you."

Trevillion nodded. "Yes, she will, Your Grace, with your blessing, I hope."

"Maximus," said the duke absently. "I'm not entirely sure she wants my blessing, actually, but I'm here to give it."

Trevillion's eyebrows shot up. What exactly had Phoebe said to her brother? He had opened his mouth to inquire when the door burst open.

Trevillion stood, recognizing two footmen from Wakefield House.

"Your Grace," Hathaway burst out. "Lady Phoebe has been taken!"

Chapter Nineteen

*Now Corineus was crowned king of that new land and
he ruled it wisely and well so that the people prospered
there. But though many other rulers sought to give
him their daughters' hands in marriage, he never
took a wife. Years passed and King Corineus's
beard turned from blackest pitch to
bone white.
And sometimes in the midnight hours he dreamed of
waves crashing and uptilted green eyes....*
—From *The Kelpie*

Really, she ought to be used to this by now, Phoebe pon-
dered as she sat in yet another carriage surrounded by
men of highly dubious reputation. All she'd wanted to do
was visit Hero and pour out her difficulties with Maximus
to a sisterly ear, and somehow she'd been snatched right in
front of Wakefield House.

And now once again she was being trundled into some
awful part of London. Two things were different this
time at least. One, they hadn't bothered with the hood,
for which she was very grateful. And two, Mr. Malcolm
MacLeish sat in the carriage with her.

The latter she was less grateful for, particularly since

Mr. MacLeish seemed to be under the impression that he would be marrying her.

"Please, Lady Phoebe," he said. "It's for the best, really. I'll spend the rest of my life making this up to you. It's just that we cannot go against *him*. He's powerful in ways you'll never understand."

Phoebe yanked her fingers out of Mr. MacLeish's hand. "Well, I'll certainly not understand if you won't explain in plain language. Who is the man you're afraid of? Are these men holding a gun on you as well, Mr. MacLeish?"

One of the kidnappers guffawed.

"In a way, yes," Mr. MacLeish said rather stiffly. "I'm as much a victim as you."

"You'll pardon me if I don't believe you, sir," Phoebe shot back. "Who, exactly, is making you marry me—and for goodness' sake, *why*?"

"I'll take care of you," Mr. MacLeish replied, conveniently not answering her questions. "I'll be sure you don't ever want for anything."

"I think I might want for making my own decisions," Phoebe muttered as the carriage jerked to a halt.

She thought briefly of trying to run, but besides the obvious difficulty, she was a bit afraid of the men who held her. They'd fired their pistols when she'd been grabbed in the street directly outside Wakefield House. It had been impossible to tell, but she dearly hoped they hadn't shot Hathaway or Panders.

"Time t' get out, m'lady," one of the kidnappers said. "An' don't you think about makin' any noise."

She noticed that he made no such admonishment to Mr. MacLeish.

They seemed to be in a different place from the last

one she'd been taken to. Phoebe lifted her head, sniffing the air. She smelled rotting vegetables and the stink of gin, very nearby, before she was hustled inside what seemed to be a cellar.

"Ah, you've arrived," a cultured voice drawled. She didn't recognize it, but she *did* recognize the scent that went with it: amber and jasmine, exotic and rare.

The last time she'd smelled the exact same scent was outside Eve Dinwoody's house.

"IT ISN'T YOUR fault," Jean-Marie said soothingly as he and Eve rode in a carriage through London. "You have no control over him."

"He *used* me, Jean-Marie," Eve said, watching the streets anxiously. "Again and again. He *lied* to me, telling me he'd given up his insane scheme—and I fell for his tricks. I'm a fool, and if I don't do anything about it, it *will* be my fault. Here! Here it is."

The carriage halted even as she said the words and Eve scrambled from it in unseemly haste.

Jean-Marie strode ahead of her and raised his fist to knock upon the boardinghouse door, but then he paused, glanced over his shoulder at her, and pushed the door. It swung open, unlocked.

Eve hurried forward past him, hearing raised male voices as she found the stairs inside. Jean-Marie was close behind as she ran up them.

"Damn it, I thought you said she was safe, that the kidnapper was in Newgate!"

Eve made the first floor and found that the voice belonged to Lady Phoebe's guard. He was facing the Duke of Wakefield, and she halted at the sight. She'd come for the guard, for she knew he'd found and rescued Lady Phoebe the last time. She hadn't counted on the duke as well.

Wakefield turned, a tall commanding presence. "Who are you?"

"Miss Dinwoody." Captain Trevillion stepped around the duke. "Why are you here?"

"Because," she said firmly. "I can't let him do this, not again. He's kidnapped Lady Phoebe and I won't stand for it. Please believe me, if I'd known what he intended I would've warned you from the start."

"Who?" both men said as one.

"Valentine Napier, the Duke of Montgomery." She raised her chin, her gaze steady, though her lips trembled as she betrayed him. "My brother."

TREVILLION RODE THROUGH the darkened streets at full gallop, leaning forward over the back of the horse, urging the valiant beast to go faster. Maximus was behind him somewhere. Trevillion had taken one of the horses the footmen had ridden to tell them the news of Phoebe.

Now they both rode hell-for-leather through London in a desperate attempt to get to Phoebe before it was too late.

All Trevillion could think about was what Miss Dinwoody had told them—that the Duke of Montgomery was behind all the kidnapping attempts, every one. That he wanted to marry Phoebe—not to himself, but to Malcolm MacLeish, whom he had some kind of hold over. That Montgomery had black-mailed the man Wakefield had had arrested to confess to the kidnappings, though he'd not been involved at all.

That Eve Dinwoody had no idea why her brother would make such a convoluted plot or why he'd targeted Phoebe.

Damn Montgomery's insanity and damn MacLeish's

cowardliness. That they thought they could use Phoebe like some crown jewel to fight over made his chest tighten with rage.

He leaned forward, clenching the mare's sides with his thighs as he urged it to jump several barrels in the lane. Behind him Maximus shouted, but Trevillion didn't turn. Phoebe was being held in St Giles of all places—the very seat of vice in this foul city.

When he found Montgomery, he'd wring his duplicitous neck, duke or no duke.

Trevillion leaned to the side, guiding his mount down one of the narrow alleys that ran toward the rabbit warren that was St Giles. After years patrolling these streets as a dragoon he knew them as he knew his own hand.

Miss Dinwoody had given them an address—a place where Montgomery had once done business. She'd thought her brother might bring Phoebe there, but she hadn't been sure.

If she was wrong...

He rounded a corner and saw a carriage—one much too grand for St Giles. As he came abreast of it, a man emerged from a brick house next to the carriage. The man glanced up at the sound of the horse's hooves and froze when he saw Trevillion aiming a pistol at his head.

"Where is Lady Phoebe?" Trevillion growled.

The man ducked back inside.

Damn it, to attack a guarded door was suicide.

Trevillion slid from the saddle, a pistol in each hand.

He took two steps to the brick house and stood to the side. "Open the door!"

A blast blew apart the wood of the door, sending splinters everywhere.

Trevillion charged through the door, kicking aside debris, ignoring the pain that shot up his damned right leg. The interior was dark, but he saw a man turn, a pistol in his hand. Trevillion shot him in the chest, making the man fall back.

"Don't shoot!" someone called from the dark inside.

And then Maximus rushed in, punching with his great fists, knocking men aside like bowling pins.

Trevillion saw MacLeish cowering by a table and swung his pistol hard across his face.

Blood splattered from the architect's nose. "Where's Lady Phoebe?"

MacLeish didn't say anything, but his eyes rolled, glancing toward the far corner. Trevillion looked and saw an inner door.

He went to it and shoved his shoulder against it.

It burst open, revealing an empty room.

Someone tried to rush past him.

Trevillion caught him by his hair, his bright-yellow hair, and pulled, putting the remaining loaded pistol to the Duke of Montgomery's temple. "Where is she?"

"Yield!" cried Montgomery, his hands in front of him, a smile playing about his mouth. "I yield."

"I said, *where is Lady Phoebe?*"

"I don't know!"

"Liar," Maximus said, his eyes blazing. "You took my sister."

Montgomery's eyes narrowed and he suddenly looked quite deadly. "Yes, I took your sister. I consider it fair trade for the wrong you did me."

Maximus blinked. "*What* wrong? I've never done anything to you."

"You shut down the gin stills in St Giles. This"—Montgomery waved his hands to indicate the building—"used to be a very profitable enterprise. Now it's merely a pile of bricks. You took it away from me and so I took something—*someone*—away from you." He smiled like a blond cherub with too many teeth. "I make it a point to never forget a slight and I certainly never let one go unavenged."

"You're insane," Maximus said, his lip curling.

Montgomery cocked his head, his blue eyes glinting coldly in the lantern light. "One man's raison d'être is another man's madness."

Trevillion pressed the barrel of his pistol into Montgomery's temple. "I don't give a damn if you bark at the moon. Tell me where Phoebe is or I'll blow your brains out."

Montgomery opened his mouth, but MacLeish coughed wetly in the corner. "That Irishman."

Everyone turned to him.

"What?" asked Montgomery.

"One of your henchmen," MacLeish said. He was attempting, not very successfully, to stanch the blood from his nose with his cravat. "He's missing. I saw him go into the room we were keeping Lady Phoebe in right before they came charging in."

Maximus swore and caught up a candle, holding it high to illuminate the inner room.

A hole in the back wall was clearly revealed by the light. A decrepit cabinet that must've been covering the hole had been pulled away from the wall.

Montgomery chuckled quietly, and for a ghastly moment Trevillion thought he'd truly lost his mind.

But what he said next was worse.

"She was taken by one of my men, d'you believe it?"

For a moment Trevillion only stared, his heart frozen. Phoebe in the sewers of St Giles with some criminal. Dear, sweet God. "*What?*"

"Comes of hiring cut-rate help," said Montgomery, which was when Maximus punched him in the mouth, laying him out flat on the floor.

But Trevillion didn't care.

Phoebe was in St Giles, blind, and in the company of a criminal.

And night had fallen.

Chapter Twenty

*At last the day came when King Corineus knew he
would soon breathe his last. He called for a chair and
four strong men to bear him to the sea and then he bid
them leave him there on the beach.
And when he was alone once more he faced the waves
and called in a quavering voice, "Morveren!"*…
—From *The Kelpie*

"Pick up yer feet or I'll pull you by your hair," growled the
nasty man who had Phoebe.

Phoebe struggled desperately against him, despite his
threats. He'd dragged her out of the kidnappers' den, but
this was certainly no rescue.

In fact she very much feared what he had in mind to
do with her. The nasty man wasn't very big, but he was
strong, as she had cause to know. He kept a hand clamped
painfully around her wrist, pulling her bodily along a
lane or street or some such. She didn't even know exactly
where she was. There were uneven cobblestones beneath
her feet—she'd fallen twice already—and a stinking
channel in the middle of the lane. She could hear laughter
nearby and now and again voices raised in argument, even
a yell that sounded like her name. So far she'd refrained

from calling for help, fearful of who or what might come to her aid.

The nasty man was muttering now, either to himself or to her, she couldn't tell. "A nice piece like you, I ought to be able to get a pretty penny. Might even ransom you after a bit. 'Eard you was from some fancy family."

"I'm the Duke of Wakefield's sister," she said clearly. "If you let me go, he'll pay you a fat purse."

The nasty man stopped so suddenly she ran into him and for a moment she thought he'd take her up on the offer.

Instead he drew her against his malodorous body. "Nah. I ain't never porked an aristo."

Which was when Phoebe decided it was past time to scream.

TREVILLION LIMPED OUT of the cellar into St Giles, Wakefield behind him. Phoebe was nowhere to be seen. It was dark and since this was St Giles the usual lanterns that householders and shopkeepers put by their doorways were sparse and dim.

He'd left his cane in his rented rooms, he had only one loaded pistol, and he had no idea in which direction she'd been taken.

"He could've taken her in any direction," Wakefield said, echoing his thoughts.

Trevillion fought down panic. He was a soldier. He'd been in any number of hopeless situations and prevailed.

Every one of them were but dress rehearsals for this. "You check that lane"—Trevillion gestured to the right—"I'll go this way."

Wakefield didn't even balk at taking the order from him, just turned and strode into the darkness.

Trevillion turned to the left. "Phoebe!"

Dear God, the man who'd taken her could already be streets away by now.

"Phoebe!"

She might be lying in an alley, unable to hear or respond to him, hidden by the labyrinth of lanes and the darkness.

"Phoebe!"

She might be dead.

His boot caught on a loose cobblestone and he staggered and fell to his knees, cursing his leg, cursing Montgomery, cursing his own pride in leaving her at Wakefield House. He should've damned Maximus and taken Phoebe with him. Made her his wife at once.

She'd be lying in his bed now, safe and warm and in his arms, if he had.

Trevillion set his hand flat on the cobblestones and heaved himself upright. His leg felt broken anew.

A scream tore through the night, high, shrill, and terrified.

Phoebe's scream.

Trevillion ran. Ignoring pain, ignoring his leg altogether. Fear and horror for Phoebe raced through his veins, pushing him on. He crossed a street, peering into the darkness.

Another scream.

He turned a corner.

There she was, struggling wildly in some brute's grasp. The man reared back, his hand raised to strike—

And Trevillion caught it in his fist, twisting it up and behind the man's back until something *popped*.

The brute screamed.

"Let her go, you piece of *shit*," Trevillion snarled into his ear.

The man staggered against Trevillion as Phoebe pulled free.

Trevillion struck him across the back of the head anyway, letting the brute drop to the ground unconscious.

"James?" Phoebe called, her face pale and frightened, her hands outstretched. "James, are you there?"

"I'm here," he said, and she rushed to him.

He wrapped his arms around her, holding her to his heart where she was meant to be. "Are you all right? Are you hurt?"

"No." She pulled away enough to put her palms on his face. "He meant to hurt me, but you came in time."

"Thank God," he said, kissing her, running his hand over her cheeks, her hair, her nape. "Thank God." He pulled her close again, burying his face in her neck. "I thought I'd lost you forever, Phoebe."

"Well you haven't," she whispered to him. "I'm right here. You saved me, James. You saved me."

"I'm not letting you go after this." He raised his head. "Marry me, Phoebe, please. Damn the courtship. Damn your brother. Damn the *waiting*. I can't...I can't *breathe* when you're not with me. I love you with all my cynical heart. Be my wife and teach me to laugh and let me buy you beer and ride with me on the beaches of Cornwall. Be my love and my wife forevermore."

"I will," she whispered to him. "Oh, James, I will."

Epilogue

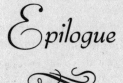

At once the waves began to churn and up from the depths rose the sea maiden Morveren. But how strange! Though many years had passed and King Corineus himself was now a bent old man, the sea maiden was just the same. Her skin was smooth and clear, her eyes sparkled green, and her hair still flowed white and otherworldly beautiful.

At the sight of her, King Corineus became aware of how foolish he must look—an old man calling to a young girl. But as he started to retreat, Morveren called to him.

"How now, my lover? Will you turn from me yet again?"

At that King Corineus straightened proudly. "You mock me. How can you want anything to do with me, bent and withered as I am?"

She smiled then, sweet and gentle. "I think you know little of a woman's mind, King. Will you come with me?"

"Will you take me as I am now?" he retorted bitterly. "I am no longer a handsome young man."

She simply held out her hand in reply.

And though once he'd laughed at her offer, now he took her hand gratefully.

"Come," she whispered. "The sea is truly a wondrous place. Time passes very differently there."

Morveren held his hand as King Corineus stepped into the foaming waves, and as the water began to rise a change came over the king. His bent limbs straightened, the wrinkles smoothed from his face, his withered flesh filled

*with strong muscles, and his white beard darkened until it
was black as pitch once more.*

*King Corineus looked down at his body made youthful
again and exclaimed in astonishment, "How is this
possible?"*

*Morveren merely shrugged. "A gift from the sea and me.
Even if you return to land now you'll retain your youth. Do
you still want to come with me to my sea home?"*

*Corineus looked at her and grinned. "I had everything I
had ever wished for in my life. A kingdom, wealth, respect,
and power. And yet I feel that I missed many things when I
refused your offer. If you'll let me, I will be your husband
and stay with you always."*

*"Then come with me," Morveren said, "and I'll show you
all the things that you've missed—including this one." And
she pointed to a small boy frolicking in the waves. He had
hair as black as pitch and eyes of deepest green.*

*Corineus took the little boy's hand and together all three
dove into the waves.*

*And what became of Corineus then? Well, that I cannot
tell you, for no mortal returns from the sea. And yet there
are tales told by sailors of a glittering kingdom lying far,
far beneath the sea, made of seashells, whale bones, and
pearls. 'Tis said that Corineus ruled there for many, many
years with his wife the sea maiden Morveren and their son.
And who knows? Perhaps he rules there still....*
—From *The Kelpie*

TWO WEEKS LATER ...

Eve Dinwoody sat in bed reading a book about beetles.
She wasn't particularly interested in beetles, but Val had
given her the book several years ago and she was feeling

a little nostalgic. The hand-tinted drawings of the insects were very beautiful.

She sighed as she turned another page. The book was probably worth an outrageous fortune.

The candles beside her bed flickered and when Eve looked up, Val was standing at the foot of her bed.

Slowly she closed the book.

"I have to leave England," Val said, his petulant look heightened by his bottom lip, which was two times its normal size.

Eve winced. Val also had fading bruises on both cheeks and one eye was spectacularly blackened. The Duke of Wakefield really had not been pleased by his sister's kidnapping. "You kidnapped a peer's sister, Val. He could've had you thrown in prison or even hanged. I think you got off rather well with an informal banishment from Wakefield."

Val threw himself moodily onto the foot of her bed, making the whole thing shake. "He couldn't have hanged me—I'm a peer myself. 'Tisn't done."

"Neither is kidnapping." She sighed. "Whyever did you do it, Val? Lady Phoebe is one of the nicest ladies I've ever met. You would've ruined her life."

"It wasn't *her* I was after," Val said, fingering his lip. "It was her brother. It's not my fault he's so fond of his sister." He tilted his face back, hanging his head upside down to look at her—a particularly disconcerting sight, considering the present state of his face. "And *you* know why I did it. I don't allow anyone to cross me and not feel my ire. It's a simple rule. People ought to stick to it."

"But he didn't even know he had crossed you!" she said in exasperation.

"As I said, not my fault." Val sounded bored now. "Anyway, the whole thing's over now."

She looked at him cautiously. "You're done with the Duke of Wakefield and his sister?"

"Certainly his sister," Val allowed. "She went off to marry that dragoon fellow in Cornwall." He flipped his hand in the air. "I won't go to Cornwall for anything."

"And the duke?"

"Oh, him as well—at least for the present." Val sighed and got nimbly off the bed. He wasn't moving as if he'd been beaten not a fortnight ago. "But that's not why I'm here, dearest sister. I have a favor to ask of you."

Eve immediately grew wary. The last favor her brother had asked for had resulted in the kidnapping of Lady Phoebe. "What is it?"

"Now don't look so frightened, Evie darling. This is something quite simple. Something you might even enjoy." The fact that Val was smiling charmingly didn't add at all to his argument.

Val was at his most dangerous when he was charming.

"Just tell me, Val," Eve said.

"I made an investment about a year ago in Harte's Folly," he said. "I want you to oversee it."

Eve blinked. "Oversee it? How? And why me?"

"You'll just be checking on the money, making sure Harte is spending it correctly. You know you like accounting books and all those tidy rows of numbers."

Sadly, this was true. Eve had loved numbers and their strict adherence to rules from the time she'd been a child. "But—"

"As to why I asked you, it's because you're my sister and the only one I trust in the world," Val said simply and rather disarmingly. "That and I'd rather my men of business not know about this particular venture."

"Why? Is it illegal?"

"So very suspicious!" he replied. "I'd wonder where you'd got it from, if I didn't know perfectly well."

"Val—"

He was suddenly in front of her, taking her hands, which for Val meant this was quite important.

He hardly ever touched other people.

"I need you, Eve," he said, looking into her eyes. "Can you do this for me? Please?"

Really, it had been inevitable since he'd appeared in her room.

"Yes."

MEANWHILE IN CORNWALL...

"I don't know," Phoebe said as she flopped onto the bed in a most unladylike manner, her arms spread-eagled, "if it was such a good idea to introduce my brother to your father."

"Why do you say that, my darling wife?" Trevillion asked.

Oh, she did like it when he called her his *wife* in his deep, rasping voice! And as they'd only been married that morning, it still had a thrillingly new ring to it.

Thank goodness, though, that it was *finally* evening. The day had been full of excitement and celebration with all her family and all Trevillion's family in attendance, but it had also been exhausting. They'd decided to marry in Cornwall, in the town near the Trevillion family house, which boasted a tiny damp Norman church. The entire town had turned out for their nuptials. It seemed a wedding was exciting enough for the locals, but the appearance of a duke and duchess made it a once-in-a-century event.

Which brought her back to the topic at hand.

"I found Maximus in a corner with your father talking horses after the wedding breakfast, and Maximus had that tone in his voice which means he's making *plans*," Phoebe said disapprovingly.

"What sort of plans?" Trevillion asked. Somehow he'd taken off most of his clothes, for his chest was bare as he began kissing her neck.

She tilted up her head to give him better access. "Plans to buy horses from your father or invest in horse-breeding or something else meddlesome. Maximus is always *plotting*, you know."

"I do know," her new husband replied as he began to unlace her wedding dress. "But I think I may be tired of talking about Maximus now. There must be something we can do on our wedding night."

"Do you think so?" she asked innocently. "I suppose we could go walk on the moors—"

"Phoebe—"

"Or ride on the beach—or groom one of the horses—"

His mouth covered hers, cutting off her silly suggestions, which, technically, was cheating, but Phoebe didn't care at all at the moment.

She loved Trevillion's kisses.

He licked into her mouth, gently, softly exploring, catching her chin in his hand to hold her as he angled his head over hers.

She gasped and opened her mouth wider, tracing his lower lip with her tongue.

He drew back and she noticed his breathing had quickened. He settled his big body on hers and asked, "Are you happy, Mrs. Trevillion?"

"I am," she whispered back.

"Even though I haven't a gilded castle nor scores of servants?"

"You," she said, cradling his face between her hands, "have a loving father and sister, a niece I adore, and just the right amount of servants. As for gilt... well, it's rather wasted on me, don't you think? I'd rather have moors and the wind off the ocean, and horses to ride. And you, Mr. Trevillion. I'd trade gilded castles any day to spend my life with *you*."

She could hear him swallow, and then his face was against hers, his own damp. "I'm so lucky you would have me, my Phoebe, as my wife and my love. You've brought the sun into my lonely, gray life."

"Lonely no more," she whispered back.

And then she kissed him.

SEE THE FOLLOWING PAGE
FOR A PREVIEW OF
THE NEXT
MAIDEN LANE NOVEL,

Sweetest Scoundrel!

It took an extreme provocation to rouse Eve Dinwoody.

For five years her life had been quiet. She had a nice house in an unfashionable but respectable part of town. She had her three servants—Jean-Marie Pépin, her bodyguard; his pretty, plump wife, Tess, her cook; and Ruth, her rather scatterbrained maid. She had a hobby—painting miniatures—which also served to bring in extra pin money. She even had a pet of sorts—a white dove she had yet to name.

Eve *liked* her quiet life. On most days she quite enjoyed staying inside, puttering around with her miniatures and feeding the unnamed dove oat kernels. Truth be told, Eve was rather shy.

But Eve could, in fact, rouse herself from her quiet life, given enough provocation. And Lord knew Mr. Harte, the owner and manager of Harte's Folly, was *very* provoking indeed. Harte's Folly was the preeminent pleasure garden in London—or at least it had been before it'd burned to the ground more than a year ago. Now Mr. Harte was rebuilding his pleasure garden and in the process spending quite scandalous amounts of money.

Which was why she stood on the third floor of a disreputable boardinghouse very early on a Monday morning, glaring at a stubbornly shut door.

A drop of rainwater dripped from the brim of her hat onto the worn floorboards beneath her feet. Really, it was an absolutely disgusting day outside.

"Do you want me to break the door down?" Jean-Marie asked cheerfully. He stood well over six feet tall and his ebony face beneath a snowy wig gleamed in the low light. He still had a faint Creole accent from his youth in the French West Indies.

Eve squared her shoulders. "No, thank you. I shall handle Mr. Harte myself."

Jean-Marie raised an eyebrow.

She glared. "I *shall*." She rapped at the door again. "Mr. Harte, I know you're within. Please answer your door at *once*."

Eve had performed this maneuver twice already without result, save for a sudden crash from inside the room after the second knock.

She raised her fist for a fourth time, determined to make Mr. Harte acknowledge her, when the door suddenly swung open.

Eve blinked and involuntarily stepped back, bumping into Jean-Marie's broad chest. The man standing in the doorway was rather . . . intimidating.

He wasn't tall exactly—Jean-Marie had several inches on him and he was only half a head or so taller than Eve herself—but what he might have lacked in height he more than made up in breadth of shoulder. The man's arms nearly touched the doorway on either side. He wore a white shirt, unlaced at the throat and revealing a V of tangled chest hair. Wild tawny hair fell to his shoulders. His face wasn't pretty. The exact opposite, in fact. It was strong, lined, and fierce, and everything that was masculine.

Everything that Eve most dreaded.

The man glanced at Jean-Marie, narrowed his eyes, leaned one arm against the doorjamb, and turned his attention to Eve. "What."

Eve straightened. "Mr. Harte?"

Instead of replying he yawned widely and ran a hand over his face, pulling down the skin around his eyes and cheeks. "I'm sorry, luv, but I haven't any more parts available for the theater. Per'aps if you come again in another two months when we stage *As You Like It*. You might make a passable"—here he paused, eyes fixed *quite* rudely on Eve's nose—"maid, I suppose."

He turned his head and shouted over his shoulder, "*Are* there maids in *As You Like It*?"

"A shepherdess," came the reply. The speaker was feminine and had a beautifully accented voice.

Mr. Harte—*if* it was he—glanced back at Eve without any real apology in his face. "There. Sorry. Although I have to say, at your age and with"—he actually *flapped* his hand at Eve's nose this time—"I'd look into something *behind* the stage, luv."

And he shut the door in her face.

Or at least he tried to, for Eve had had enough, thank you very much. She stuck her foot in the gap, pressed her shoulder against the door, and walked into Mr. Harte.

Who, unfortunately, didn't move as he ought to have done.

He blinked, scowling at Eve.

This close she could see the little red veins in his bloodshot eyes and smell some sort of stale spirits on his person. Also, he seemed not to have made use of a razor in several days.

She could feel the old panic rising in her chest, but she fought it. This man posed no threat to her—not in *that* way, in any case—and Jean-Marie was right behind her. She was a woman grown and ought to have been over these terrors by now.

Eve tilted up her chin. "Move, please."

"Now look here," he growled. "I don't even know your name and if you think this is how an actress gets a part at *my* pleasure garden, you're—"

"I'm not an actress," she enunciated clearly in case he was hard of hearing as well as a drunken oaf. "And my name is Miss Eve Dinwoody."

"Dinwoody…" Instead of clearing his brow, her name made him scowl harder.

She took the opportunity of his distraction to slip triumphantly past him.

And then she stopped dead.

The room was an absolute shambles, crowded to overflowing with mismatched furniture and dusty *things*. Stacks of papers and books slid off chairs and tables, falling to alluvial mounds on the floor. In one corner a huge heap of colorful fabric was piled, surmounted by a gilded crown; in another a life-size portrait of a bearded man was propped next to a four-foot-tall model of a ship, complete with sails and rigging. A stuffed raven eyed her beadily from the mantelpiece, and on the hearth itself a kettle steamed next to an enormous chipped pink teapot and a teetering tower of dirty dishes and cups. Indeed, so filled was the room that it took Eve a moment to notice the nude woman in the bed.

The bed itself sat square in the middle of the room, an overgrown, unwieldy thing, hung with gold and scarlet curtains like something from a Turk's harem, and in the middle reclined an odalisque, the golden coverlet barely concealing her curves. She was dark and sensual, her ebony hair spilling to olive-tinged shoulders, lips a deep natural carmine.

The woman sat up, the coverlet falling perilously to the very tips of her breasts. "Asa, who are dees peoples?"

Mr. Harte clutched both hands in his hair. "I don't know, Violetta!"

"I do apologize," Eve said stiffly to the woman, presumably Violetta. "Had I known you were in dishabille, I assure you—"

Mr. Harte laughed sarcastically. "You came bursting in. When, exactly, would you have stopped to—"

"I *assure* you," Eve began, glaring at the awful man.

"Is no problem," the odalisque said at the same time, grinning and revealing an incongruous gap between her two front teeth. She shrugged again and the coverlet gave up the fight, falling to her waist.

Mr. Harte glanced at the woman, paused, his eyes fixated on her now-revealed bosom, and then visibly shook himself before turning back to Eve. "And who are you anyway?"

"I already told you," Eve said through gritted teeth. "I am Eve Dinwoody and—"

"Dinwoody!" Harte exclaimed, pointing at her. "That's the name of the Duke of Montgomery's man of business. Signs his letters 'E. Dinwoody' in the most affected hand I've ever seen..."

He frowned suddenly.

Jean-Marie and the odalisque looked at him.

Eve raised her eyebrows, waiting.

Mr. Harte's moss-green eyes widened. "Oh, the devil damn me."

"Yes, no doubt," Eve said with a completely false smile. "But before that happens I've come to cut off your credit."

Fall in Love with Forever Romance

PASSIONATELY YOURS
by Cara Elliott

*Secret passions are wont to lead
a lady into trouble...* The third
rebellious Sloane sister gets her
chance at true love in the next
Hellions of High Street
Regency romance from bestselling author Cara Elliott.

THIEF OF SHADOWS
by Elizabeth Hoyt

Only $5.00 for a limited time!
A masked avenger dressed in a
harlequin's motley protects the
innocents of St. Giles at night.
When a rescue mission leaves
him wounded, the kind soul
who comes to his rescue is the
one woman he'd never have
expected...

Fall in Love with Forever Romance

RESCUING THE BAD BOY
by Jessica Lemmon

Donovan Pate is coming back to Evergreen Cove a changed man...well, except for the fact that he still can't seem to keep his eyes—or hands—off the mind-blowingly gorgeous Sofie Martin. Sofie swore she was over bad boy Donovan Pate. But when he rolls back into town as gorgeous as ever and still making her traitorous heart skip a beat, she knows history is seriously in danger of repeating itself.

NO BETTER MAN
by Sara Richardson

In the *New York Times* bestselling tradition of Kristan Higgins and Jill Shalvis comes the first book in Sara Richardson's contemporary romance Heart of the Rockies series set in breathtaking Aspen, Colorado.

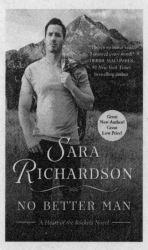

Fall in Love with Forever Romance

WEDDING BELLS IN CHRISTMAS
by Debbie Mason

Former lovers Vivian and Chance are back in Christmas, Colorado, for a wedding. To survive the week and the town's meddling matchmakers, they decide to play the part of an adoring couple—an irresistible charade that may give them a second chance at the real thing...

CHERRY LANE
by Rochelle Alers

When attorney Devon Gilmore finds herself with a surprise baby on the way, she knows she needs to begin a new life. Devon needs a place to settle down—a place like Cavanaugh Island, where the pace is slow, the weather is fine, and the men are even finer. But will David Sullivan, the most eligible bachelor in town, be ready for an instant family?

Fall in Love with Forever Romance

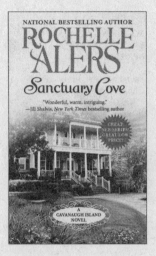

SANCTUARY COVE
by Rochelle Alers

Only $5.00 for a limited time! Still reeling from her husband's untimely death, Deborah Robinson returns to her grandmother's ancestral home on Cavanaugh Island. As friendship with gorgeous Dr. Asa Monroe blossoms into romance, Deborah and Asa discover they may have a second chance at love.

ANGELS LANDING
by Rochelle Alers

Only $5.00 for a limited time! When Kara Newell shockingly inherits a large estate on an island off the South Carolina coast, the charming town of Angels Landing awaits her... along with ex-marine Jeffrey Hamilton. As Kara and Jeffrey confront the town gossips together, they'll learn to forgive their pasts in order to find a future filled with happiness.